Twice Upon A
Time

AYA LING

CONTENTS

I don't remember that I had ever met him, much less falling in love.
But why do I feel like I've already heard of this story?
He mentioned a book.
A book that started it all.
The Ugly Stepsister

PROLOGUE

"And they lived happily ever after."

A happy sigh rose from the baby goblin girl. She was sprawled on the floor, face upturned, her large, yellow, cat-like eyes shining with joy. Next to her sat a middle-aged goblin wearing spectacles with a book propped on his legs, the binding creased and the pages worn. Except for the sparkling golden crown sitting askew on his head, he looked rather ordinary.

"How many children did they have, Daddy?"

"The book doesn't tell us, sweetie. It just ends with their wedding."

"But what about Kat's family in her human world? Did she ever see them again?"

"Of course she did. She returned to the human world once she completed her mission."

The child gave a horrified gasp. "So, she just *left* Edward standing at the altar like that?"

"He wasn't left alone, pumpkin. The original Katriona returned to her body, so he still has a bride. Edward arranged it so that no one would suspect Kat had switched places with the storybook Katriona. And Kat remembers nothing about her life in the fairy tale, so she is spared the pain of losing her true love. Don't worry your pretty little head about it."

Said pretty little head was now shaking in pure outrage. "That's not a happy ending, Daddy! You lied to me! You lied!"

"Pippi!" The goblin king exclaimed. "Do stop bawling, angel."

"You're such a meanie! I'm never trusting you again!"

Barthelius tried to calm her down by ruffling her hair, but his fingers grew tangled in her mountain of extraordinarily curly hair—hair that reminded him of that corkscrew-shaped pasta humans called fusilli. "Really, there's no need to be so distressed about the ending. Let's read another story together, shall we? Or do you want to see the new doll Daddy got for you?"

He looked around at his court, silently pleading for one of them to offer a helping hand. Unfortunately for him, it was the goblins' nature to take pleasure in another's misfortune. Most of them only shrugged innocently or tried to mask their grins behind knobby hands.

Barthelius had no choice but to exert his absolute power as king.

"Krev!" he barked. A long-suffering goblin slunk slowly to his side. He had a face that looked as though he were squashed and ironed as a baby. "Take the princess down to the nursery. Give her another book or toy or candy—it doesn't matter. When I come back, I want to see her pacified."

Krev looked alarmed at the prospect of calming the little princess. "But Your Majesty . . ."

"It's all your fault," Barthelius muttered. "You should have united the real Cinderella together with the prince, instead of letting Katherine Wilson continue to interact with him."

"Who, me?" Krev raised one thick, worm-like eyebrow. "Your Majesty was the one most amused when the plot went awry. We were taking bets every time I had a new report to make. Why, the queen even won a purse of gold!"

"That was before I could anticipate *this*—" Barthelius jerked his thumb at the spectacle on the floor beside him. His daughter was now rolling across the floor, her wails filling the air. "I had no idea she would be so fixated on that damn book. It's been how many—six years?"

"Seven."

"Hmph. It seems like only yesterday that we witnessed the completion of that book."

"Can't we rip up *The Ugly Stepsister* instead?"

Barthelius raised his eyebrows and jabbed a finger at Krev's chest. "To borrow a human phrase: You. Are. Nuts. First, how are you going to track down Katherine Wilson after so many years? Second, how is she going to tear up the book when it's only seven years old? You can't compel a human to act unless through forbidden magic. You know the rules. Third, let's assume she re-entered the book. The prince is already married to the real Katriona Bradshaw—are you asking him to divorce his wife and marry the human? Even if he risks the wrath of the entire kingdom by leaving a wife who did him no wrong, Katherine Wilson will *still* have to return to the human world once she has completed the happy ending! You're going to break the prince's heart twice."

Krev heaved a sigh. His ears and shoulders drooped. "Come along, Your Highness," he called to the little goblin princess. "Want to hear a secret story of Kat and Edward—one that didn't appear in the book?"

Pippi asked so many questions that Krev suspected that were she living in the human world, she'd be one of those diehard fans who created book trailers and wrote fanfiction and dressed up as characters in the story. He pictured her wearing a ball gown and acting out a court presentation to the queen . . . no. The dumpy figure of a typical goblin was simply unsuited for huge frilly dresses. They usually wore plain, sack-like clothes. Goblins weren't known for their fashion sense.

"Why is your face all scrunched up, Krev?" Pippi asked, her eyes alight with curiosity. "You look like you've swallowed a lemon."

Like a child being caught stealing from a jar of cookies, Krev tried to look innocent instead. Most goblins would have declared him a poor actor, but fortunately, the little princess wasn't that perceptive. Yet. "Nothing, Your Highness."

Pippi hugged the book close to her chest. Of all the books Barthelius had created, it was this messed-up version of *Cinderella* that she enjoyed most. She belonged to the post-office—or wait, was it post-modern?—category of readers who preferred their heroines strong and feisty. The damsel-in-distress was a thing of the past.

"Did you actually see Kat return to her family?"

Krev scratched his head. A couple of long, mottled-green hairs fell off. Dang, his premature baldness was speeding to the finish line.

"Did you?"

"Well . . . yes. There wasn't anything we could do about it. The spell works automatically. Once she fulfilled the happily-ever-after requirement, she was compelled to leave. She had no choice but to return to her mother and sister in the human world."

"But why couldn't she go back for a while to say goodbye, and then come back? Oh, the poor prince! You can't leave him stuck with a girl he doesn't love!"

Krev heaved yet another sigh. He lost count of how many times he'd sighed when talking to Pippi. Really, it was entirely Barthelius and Morag's fault for spoiling her and giving her whatever she wanted when she wanted it. Every toy she demanded had to be given to her, and every candy she coveted had to be procured. "Once the book is completed, it stays that way forever. It's permanent."

Pippi banged on the table with a fist. A crack appeared on the surface. Krev made a private note to mention to the king that the princess's strength was showing early. "You've got to get them back together! It's so UNFAIR to keep them apart!"

"Your Highness, unfortunately, the spell doesn't work that way—"

"I don't care! I want a happy ending for Kat and Edward! I want it NOOOOOOOW!"

***

Pippi stalked to her room, sniffling. Everyone was useless. Why were they all okay about Edward and Kat being apart? How could they be so heartless? Didn't they all tell her that fairy tales end with happily-ever-after?

"Liars," she muttered, scuffing her small foot on the ground. "Why didn't Daddy stop Kat from returning to America? I don't want Edward to marry another girl—he and Kat were perfect for each other! And how could Kat agree to leave him? Why couldn't she remember him anymore? Did somebody put a spell on her?"

"Your mother did."

Pippi whirled around so fast that her short legs got tangled into each other and she landed on the floor with an undignified bump. "Who—who are you?"

6

Another goblin, who seemed around her father's age, hovered above her, his wings flapping. He looked friendly, but Pippi wasn't sure that she liked his crooked grin.

"Morag put a strong memory charm on the human being because she knew the girl could become seriously depressed if she went home with the prince on her mind. It was hard enough that she had to choose between her family and him."

"But what about Edward? Did Mommy also make him forget Kat?"

The goblin wagged a finger at her. "Morag offered, but he refused. The real Katriona would return to her body once the human girl's soul left, and he needed his memory intact to deal with her. Besides, he didn't want to forget Katherine Wilson."

Pippi promptly burst into tears. "That's so cruel!" she wailed. "Kat should be the one with him, not the other girl!"

"That can be accomplished."

The wailing stopped. Pippi stared at the goblin with huge, suspicious eyes.

"What did you say?"

The goblin tilted his chin upward. "I am Borg the Invincible, elder brother of Barthelius. Your father was afraid of my powers, and he feared that I'd overpower him and take his throne one day, so he devised a plan and stole most of my magic away."

Pippi gasped. "Daddy wouldn't do that! He always said it's wrong to steal."

"He told you that you shouldn't steal, but did he say it's wrong for him? Parents." Borg sneered. "Always nagging at the kids while failing to set a good example themselves. Anyway, do you or do you not want to see the human girl reunited with the Athelian prince?"

"Of course!" Pippi jumped up. "Can you really do that, Uncle Borg?"

Borg's eyes gleamed. "With enough magic, it shall be no problem. However, Barthelius would never agree to perform the spell, so it will depend on you."

Pippi didn't understand. What did this have to do with her? She was only five. She didn't know how to cast any spells. Barthelius and Morag refused to teach her until she was at least a few years older and had a better grasp on her magic.

"Barthelius doesn't want to see me," Borg said. "He knows I've been trying to get my magic back, so he will try to banish me from court as soon as he lays eyes on me. But you, the daughter of the king, can get it."

"You want me to steal?"

"It isn't called stealing, sweetie, just returning an object to its rightful owner."

Pippi frowned. "If there was a spell that could send Kat back to Edward, why didn't Daddy tell me about it?"

"Because it's forbi—because your father isn't confident in his abilities to wield so much magic. It takes a truly powerful spell to send a human girl from one realm to another. And if you want Katherine

Wilson to return before the prince is married, you will need to perform a time reversal spell as well. All this together will cost big magic—enormous magic, I tell you."

Pippi chewed on her lip. The book, still tightly grasped in her arms, seemed to grow warmer. What would Daddy say if he found out? He'd be mad, for sure, but if he did steal from Uncle Borg in the first place . . .

"How am I going to get the magic?"

"Easy. It's sealed in that emerald green ring your father has on his forefinger. Get it and bring it to me. I'll regain my magic in an instant."

"How do I know you are telling the truth?"

"Suspicious little thing, aren't you?" Borg held up his hands. He had short, stubby fingers—quite a contrast to Barthelius's long, slender ones. "Suppose we do a simple pact that won't need much magic? Repeat after me: I, Princess Pippi, daughter of King Barthelius, will retrieve the emerald ring for Borg the Invincible. In return for your efforts, I, Borg the Invincible, swear to transport Katherine Wilson to Athelia, and also to revert Athelia to the exact moment when Prince Edward's wedding takes place, in order for Katherine Wilson to resume her relationship with him without further complications. There, are you satisfied?"

Pippi hesitated. Yellow-green light glowed from Borg's hands. Then, with a determined nod, she held out her chubby little hands, and the light twisted and wove around their hands like a pair of serpents.

9

1

Life sucks.

Of course, it is rare that anyone can go through a day without any frustrations, but today, everything seemed to go wrong in epic proportions.

It started early in the morning. I was walking down the street, clutching my scarf around my neck, balancing my umbrella in one hand and making sure to keep my bag clamped tightly under my arm, when a car whizzed past and sent a wave of muddy water into the air, most of it landing on my jeans.

It wasn't just any pair of jeans. They fit me perfectly, snug but not too tight, hugging my thighs in a way that made me feel sexy. For me, they were the equivalent of the jeans in *The Sisterhood of the Traveling Pants*. The first day I wore them, I was asked out by Jason. And now, they were drenched. On a cold, windy day in downtown Portland.

"Damn!" I pulled out a tissue and tried to clean up the best I could, but some nasty brown stains remained no matter how hard I scrubbed.

I glanced at my watch: 7: 45. I was running late for my morning shift.

When I rushed into the café, it was already packed. Typical Monday morning.

"Kat, over here. Right now." My colleague, Paul, didn't even bother to ask why I was late. There wasn't time to yell at me. Right then, the most important thing was to take care of the customers. Most of them were glancing at the clock, their watches, or their cell phones, their expressions full of frustration mingled with impatience.

"I'm sorry." I hung up my coat, washed my hands, and started my first order—all in five seconds. And because I was trying to keep up with the orders, I bumped into Paul right when he'd finished pouring a full cup of coffee.

As expected, the hot liquid splashed on my blouse. My new lilac blouse that Paige got me for my birthday. Great.

"Jesus, Kat, are you okay? Did you get burned?"

"I'm fine." Grabbing a cloth from the table, I dabbed on my blouse, wondering why I had been such an idiot. No matter how busy I was, I should have donned that ugly brown apron we're given. In less than three hours, I'd managed to get muddy water *and* coffee on me. And it wasn't even lunch break yet.

By the time my shift was over, I was so ready to collapse. I sank into a chair and took out my phone, glad that I had bought a waterproof case for it.

I swiped on the screen and discovered a blinking text message from Jason, my boyfriend of two years.

Although I had long cured my tendency to stutter and stare in front of hot guys, my relationships with boys hadn't been completely smooth-sailing. Gabriel was my first real boyfriend, who also happened to be a super sexy exchange student from Australia. We dated for a while, and he was surprisingly decent for a guy who looked like a magazine model, but when he went back to Australia, things cooled off pretty fast. He went to college a year earlier than me, and he soon found another girl. Later, I went out with a couple of guys, including a real jerk who had the nerve to cheat on me with my roommate. It burned me out on relationships for a while. Until I met Jason.

Jason is everything I could ask for. Tall, but not so tall that I had to crane my neck to look at him. He's good-looking, but not so gorgeous that I'd feel like I was going out with a movie star. He's loving, but he didn't try to get laid too soon, taking our relationship slow and steady. He's fond of animals and volunteers at a pet shelter. And he's studying for his PhD in physics, which especially made Mom (who dropped out of college when she got pregnant) approve of him in the beginning.

Hey, baby. How's it going over there?

I flipped my phone sideways to landscape mode so the on-screen keyboard was bigger and easier to type on. *Just great. Really great.*

His reply was almost instantaneous. *Lousy day, huh?*

I poured out my woes to him, though in the end, I

12

was feeling kind of stupid for complaining. What I had endured was about the same as any overworked person in a coffee shop.

Maybe I was just feeling exhausted. I was fired from my old job in publishing due to the company's profits going in a downward spiral, and for two months, I had been working at the coffee shop. I get tired easily, especially when I used to sit in my cubicle for hours, but now I have to be on my feet eight hours a day. I had been trying to look for a new job, but so far, no luck.

After a while, my phone buzzed again. *When's your shift off tomorrow? Todd's going to Boston this weekend, so why don't you come and stay over?*

I hesitated for a second. I have an extra shift during the weekends, and Jason's place is way farther from the coffee shop. He lives near the university, which is in the outskirts of the city. Still, it had been a while since we had seen each other, and I miss him. Messaging and calling aren't the same as having his arms around me. And besides, I bought a super sexy Victoria's Secret babydoll slip last month—the price tag is still attached. What better chance to wear it?

"Sure."

***

Before I arrive at Jason's apartment, I decide to make a detour to the supermarket. While I am picking through tomatoes, trying to find the best ones for making salsa, my phone rings.

"Hey, Kat!" Paige's voice, excited and bubbly, transmits from the speaker. "Guess what happened?"

I wonder what it can be that is making her so excited. Generally speaking, Paige rarely has to worry about anything. Having inherited Mom's beauty and Dad's brains, she's popular, pretty, and smart. If she went to a prestigious school in a big city, it might be more difficult to stand out, but in our small rural high school, she easily gets all the attention.

"Jennifer Lawrence is filming in Oakleigh, and you got to be an extra on the set?"

"Ooh, nice guess." She giggles. "You'll never believe it—I got that freaking grant for Australia!"

I almost crush the tomato in my palm into pulp. "The one you were talking about that includes a round-trip ticket, tuition fees, and a monthly stipend?"

"Yup. It's for one year only but renewable for three years!"

"Wow." I knew my sister was smart, but I didn't imagine that she would be so freaking awesome. "Congratulations, little sis. I'm so proud of you."

"I was mad when that exchange program terminated last year. I so wanted to visit Australia after Gabriel told me all those stories when you were still dating. But this is even better! You've got to visit me once I'm settled."

"You bet I will." I imagine myself petting a koala or a kangaroo. "Have you told Mom yet?"

"I would have, but she's probably still on the plane."

14

"Don't tell me she's going to see Ryan."

Ryan is this middle-aged widower who has a son around my age. He and Mom met during my graduation ceremony, and it was love at first sight. At first, we didn't take it seriously because the guy is from Canada and they only met for like a day, but it turned out that Ryan is pretty serious about Mom. He flies to Chicago and then drives up to our house every quarter. A few months ago, he took Mom on a luxury cruise tour in Alaska.

"Yeah, I know. Mom is crazy about him, but he's even crazier about her. Most of the time it's Ryan flying down to see Mom, though you can say it's because he can afford to. If this continues, we'll be getting a stepdad soon."

We've met Ryan. He seems nice, but still . . . I guess I still need a little time to get used to the prospect of having a stepfather. It has always been the three of us in our family for about fifteen years. But maybe it's because I don't know Ryan well enough. Ever since I moved to Portland, I only see my family like twice a year.

"And speaking of Ryan, he'll be coming to my graduation in June. They've chosen me as valedictorian. Oh, and bring Jason. I owe him one for helping me with my applications!"

I have to smile. "I need to check with Jason—I think he might have his qualifications coming up, but I wouldn't miss your graduation for anything."

***

When I get to Jason's house, lugging multiple shopping bags full of groceries, he opens the door even before I raise my hand to knock.

"When I heard footsteps on the front porch, I knew it would be you."

"It had to be me." I flash him a cheeky grin. "Because you'd be in big trouble if you were expecting someone else."

"Nah, because I have no life." He chuckles, pulls me close for a kiss, and relieves me of my bags. "Geez, Kat, there must be enough tomatoes to feed an army in here. Let me guess—homemade marinara sauce?"

"Sure, if you can wait several hours for it to get done."

"I'll wait," he says, but I know he's joking, of course. "Honestly, I swear you can quit your job and open an online business with canned jars of sauce."

"You'd have better luck asking my grandmother. It's fun to do it once in a while, but I'd be bored stiff if I had to make sauce all day. Anyway, I thought I'd make salsa. I don't think you'd be bothered to make it by yourself, even if it's super easy."

"You betcha. Frozen pizza is my best friend."

I step inside his apartment. It's tidy—no beer cans littering the carpet or sweatshirts cushioning the sofa—though I'm certain it's because I'm coming over that Jason took the trouble to clean up. Bubbles, a stray kitten Jason adopted from the shelter, ambles over the floor, pauses and stares at me for a second, and pads toward the kitchen before I can say hi.

16

"Why did Todd take off to Boston?"

"He has to present a paper at a panel conference." Jason starts toward the kitchen, and I follow him. "I expect he won't be back until next week, actually. His girlfriend is in New York, so it's much easier for him to take a coach down there than to fly cross-country from here."

"Ah, the long-distance thing." I should know. The long-distance thing is really difficult to work with. After Gabriel went back to Australia, we kept up communication for a few months, then it died out when he found another girl. I was sad to break up with him, but I guess when it takes thirty hours by plane, it's super hard. That's why I decided to stay in Portland, even though I didn't really want to be so far away from home.

As I look for the cutting board, Jason's arms go around me. "I'm so glad you're here," he murmurs, nibbling my ear. "You know, even though those tomatoes look really amazing, I'd rather have you for dinner."

I turn my head and we share a long, passionate kiss. I want him, I do. Ever since I got my job at the coffee shop and Jason started preparing for his qualifying exams, it has been weeks since we've been together.

A pitiful meow interrupts us and we break apart. Bubbles stares at us with huge, reproachful eyes. His tail gives an indignant thump on the floor.

Both of us laugh. "Someone is hungry," I say. "Honest to say, so am I. Let's have dinner first."

Jason shrugs and sighs in an exaggerated manner

17

of a stage actor. "Grilled ham-and-cheese sandwiches?"

"Ooh, yes, please." I love ham and cheese sandwiches, especially when the cheese is hot and bubbly and melting.

Moments later, we're stretched out in front of the TV, munching away on sandwiches and salsa. The sandwiches are heavenly, and the tanginess from the salsa balances out the richness of the cheese. Even Jason admits that it was a better idea to have some food first.

The TV channels, though, leave more to be desired. We flip through the channels, going through tons of shows that make me yawn, until a hot red-haired guy holding a dark-haired woman, both astride on a horse, shows up on the screen.

"*Outlander!*" I stab my tortilla chip in the direction of the guy who's playing Jamie, the heart-melting Scottish highlander from the eighteenth century who falls in love with a twentieth-century nurse. "Isn't it awesome they adapted the book for TV?"

"Hey, don't tell me you're still obsessed over that book." Jason's voice is affable, but I think there's just a small amount of derisiveness in it. Oh well. I suppose it's too much to ask for a guy to appreciate— I mean truly appreciate, not out of politeness—the fantastic escapism that a romance novel offers.

"It's a *classic*," I say, pretending to look offended. "And strictly speaking, it's not a romance. There are too many elements in it to be labeled your typical romance novel."

"Okay, whatever you'd like to call it, but I just don't get it. The girl gets thrown into centuries back in time, where they don't have electricity or running water. When you're used to modern appliances, how are you going to tolerate going without them? Can you give up those comforts for the dashing hero who probably has outdated, sexist views?"

Realistically speaking, of course not. But . . .

"We're talking about a novel here, not realistic non-fiction. It's the story that counts."

"Yeah, but if you can have a gorgeous, caring guy in the twenty-first century" —he points at himself with a smirk— "why would you choose an anachronistic man, even if he looks good with his shirt off?"

"I get it." I throw up my hands in a *you win* gesture. "You just can't stand the sight of me drooling at another guy in front of you."

"Come on, baby, you know me better than that. Hypothetically speaking, you'll never choose a guy from the past over me. Anyway, there's no point arguing over a TV show. Let's move on to something more important."

He puts a hand on my thigh, right where the remnant of the mud splatter is.

"Just a second." I stand up. "I'm freaking stinking—let me take a shower."

"What stink?" He leans in and kisses me. "Seriously, I don't smell anything. Except you."

I hesitate, but then I remember that I brought my brand new, hot pink Victoria's Secret lingerie, which

I've been saving to wear for an occasion like this.

"I really need a shower." I push him away and head to the bathroom. There's a slightly annoyed look on his face, so I manage what I hope is a seductive grin. "But I promise it'll be worth the wait."

***

The shower did a world of good, washing away the stiffness in my joints and the discomfort I've had wearing mud-splattered, coffee-stained clothes all day. Excitement races through me as I slip into the smooth, silken babydoll slip. The front is a deep, sexy V that shows plenty of cleavage, and the back is almost bare except for two crisscrossing straps.

I hope Jason didn't drink too much or he might rip the slip apart. But then if he does . . . I find myself not too averse to the idea. He can always pay for a new one.

Just when I'm ready to call him, there's a strange humming noise in the air. I shake my head and tuck my hair behind my ears, but the noise grows louder. Then there's a popping noise, rather like a bottle uncorked, and a ball of light appears in the air, several feet above the bed.

"What the . . ."

I stare at the light, and I gradually discern that in the center is a book. It revolves gently in the yellow-green glow, and when the front cover is shown to me, I gasp.

The Ugly Stepsister.

One of the few paperbacks that I still own. How did it get here? It's supposed to be at our home in Oakleigh. I am absolutely certain that Jason doesn't have a copy, and even if he did, the book can't be revolving in the air, defying gravity.

Then, if things can't get more bizarre, the pages start flipping, right to the very last page.

This can't be happening.

I stare in horror, wondering if my eyes are playing tricks on me. I blink once, twice, pinch my cheeks, and rub my eyes.

The book is still there.

A black vortex appears in the middle of the book. The air around me starts to swirl, as though I'm in the center of a tornado, making my hair whip about my face.

What is happening?

I back away, trying to put more distance between myself and the book, but suddenly, my body is lifted in the air and I plunge straight into that black hole. A thick mist surrounds me, and I can't see anything— I'm in complete darkness. Terrified, I start to scream, but no sound escapes my throat.

Then a strange dizziness overcomes me and I lose consciousness.

2

This isn't Jason's room.

I'm lying on a cot that resembles the kind you see in a hospital, only much smaller and harder. A flimsy white blanket covers my body. Apart from a wooden stool next to the cot, there isn't any furniture in the room.

I sit up. There's a nauseous feeling in my stomach, and my head feels dizzy, like I've just gotten off a ride on a drop tower. I put both hands on my temples and try to concentrate, thinking frantically, *how the heck did I end up in this room?* Before I woke up, I'm sure I was still in Jason's bedroom. Maybe I passed out somehow and was brought to the hospital?

The door opens. Instead of a white-uniformed nurse, an incredibly good-looking young man dressed in some medieval prince outfit enters, carrying a tin cup and a paper bag, from which the tip of a baguette pokes out.

"Katriona, here is some . . ." his voice dies away. He stares at me, his mouth slightly open, like I'm an alien with several arms and legs.

I realize that I'm half-naked in my Victoria's Secret babydoll slip. Blushing furiously, I pull the blanket up to my chin. "Excuse me, but you must have come to the wrong ward."

He doesn't move. He just continues to stare at me in disbelief. "But . . ." he starts, then shakes his head. "It doesn't make sense."

I could have said the same thing. Am I really in a hospital? The clothes or costume the man is wearing simply aren't normal, unless it's Halloween, which is still several months off. Or maybe I'm in a children's ward? Maybe the guy is hired to do a Shakespearean play for child patients here?

"Can I . . ." I look around wildly, but there's nothing, not even a cellphone lying around. "Can you tell me where I am?"

The blush remains on his cheeks. You'd think he is a teenage boy barely entering puberty, but I'd put him around twenty. Well over six feet, a body built like an athlete, and a face to die for. This is getting really weird. I pinch my arm until my fingernails leave marks, but nope, I am not dreaming.

He stares at me for a long moment, like I just spoke to him in a foreign language.

"One question," he finally says. "What is your sister's name?"

"Huh?"

"Your sister's name. I need to ascertain your identity."

"I don't understand what you—"

"Answer me." His tone is firm, commanding, like he's used to giving orders and expects to be obeyed. And there's a desperate look in his eyes, like if I don't give him the correct reply, he'll be forced to do something drastic.

"Paige. But why do you—" I don't get any further, because he takes a huge stride forward and envelopes me in his arms.

For a second, pure shock turns me into a statue.

"Thank heavens it's still you," he whispers.

I have no idea what he's talking about. But I do know that he shouldn't be embracing me. I have a boyfriend, for Gods' sake! I try to shove him away, but the movement causes my blanket to slip off my shoulders.

"Get off!" I hiss, frantically trying to accomplish the impossible task of pushing him away *and* keeping the blanket wrapped around me.

He drops his arms and backs away, but still, he remains annoyingly close to the cot. Close enough that if Jason suddenly enters, I doubt he'll believe that I have nothing to do with this guy.

"I thought the old Katriona came back," he says slowly, "but instead, you showed up in your world's . . . is that what you normally wear?"

His gaze flickers to my chest, and even though I'm fully covered under the blanket now, my cheeks still heat up.

24

"Look, I don't know if I have an unknown twin out there, but you've got the wrong person. You'd better go to some other place to find her—Katriona? That's her name, isn't it? My boyfriend is going to show up any minute, and your being here" —I scoot farther away from him— "is definitely going to give him the wrong impression."

"I have no idea what you are talking of." He studies my face with the wariness of a cat eying a bird about to take off. "You do look a little different from what I know. Your face seems rounder, your hair is shorter, and most of your freckles have disappeared. You *are* Katherine Wilson, are you not?"

He knows me. He knows my name. Then why was he talking about some girl called Katriona in the beginning? And what does he mean by my looking different—the version he described of me is more similar to what I looked like several years ago. Can I have met this guy such a long time ago? I'm pretty sure I'd remember if I had met someone like him. He's so impossibly handsome that he could be a rising star in Hollywood.

I dart another frantic glance at my surroundings. The more I try to ascertain where I am, the more suspicious this place seems. It's too small, too threadbare, too stuffy—there aren't any windows— for a hospital room. The tin cup the guy brought looks worn and has floral patterns embossed along the rim. It doesn't look like something a hospital would use. Ha. Maybe I *am* in Hollywood.

"Who are you?" I find myself saying. "I don't know why—how—I ended up here, and everything you say is so confusing! *What on earth happened?*"

His answer is so shocking that I don't think even Darth Vader can top it.

"We are married."

My jaw drops so low it could have hit my collarbone. "MARRIED? I've never seen you in my life! Listen, buster, if you think . . ."

There's a knock on the door. Someone is asking if everything's all right.

"Just a moment," the man calls. Then, to me, he lowers his voice. "Until we find the cause of your extraordinary return, you must know my name is Edward. I am the prince of Athelia, and as my bride, you are now the princess of Athelia."

3

This is freaking insane.

PRINCESS? Me? I suddenly wake up and find myself accidentally married, and a princess on top of that?

Ridiculous. Outrageous. Impossible. I'd sooner believe I won the lottery.

The term *Athelia* sounds familiar, though. Just when I am struggling to figure out what I should do, the door opens again. This time, a young woman enters, carrying a bulky sack.

"Your Highness." She dips a brief curtsy, then sets the sack on the cot. A flash of amazement appears in her eyes, but it's gone in a second. "Would you please step out of that . . . that atrocious apparel and get properly dressed?"

I gape at her. "Me?" I point at myself. "You're addressing me as 'Highness'?"

She raises her eyebrows. "Or would you prefer

'Her Royal Highness of Athelia'?"

I roll my eyes. "Royal Highness, my ass. And I have no idea what Athelia . . ."

Athelia. A name that is familiar—the name of a country, I think. But where did I hear about it?

While I'm musing, the girl steps forward and yanks off my slip. Before I can yell sexual harassment, she has slipped a creamy white top over my head. Actually, it's more like a smock that artists use. It goes way past my thighs, barely covering my knees. But it's more high-class than a smock—the material is pure silk, smooth and cool, sliding over my body like a waterfall.

"Hey! What do you think you're doing?"

She ignores my protest. "Raise your arms. Now."

From the sack, the girl draws out an item that looks suspiciously similar to a corset and wraps it around me. It feels like a giant's hand squeezing my ribs to the point of bruising.

"Oy!" I tug the ribbons on my back, trying to rip them off. "You're suffocating me."

A second later, I can feel my lungs inflate. Immediately, I take a deep breath and exhale. Thank God. The air has never felt sweeter.

And before I can stop to wonder why I'm wearing a corset instead of a bra, something heavy is slipped over my head. There's a light thud of fabric hitting the floor. I look down.

Oh, my God. I'm wearing a gorgeous white gown embroidered with golden threads and rose-pink pearls. The girl weaves a wide silken scarf around my waist, twice, which makes me look slenderer than I really am, ties a knot at my hips, and lets the rest cascade down my side like a shimmering mist.

Wow, this is super elegant. I don't dare to move, lest I trip or something. I've gotten over my stupid clumsiness, but sometimes, on occasions like this, the awkwardness resurfaces.

But it isn't over yet. The girl brings out a glittering object that looks like a diamond tiara, the kind you only see in movies, and places it firmly on my head.

"Wait . . . what?"

Another knock on the door. The girl opens a crack and says something in a low voice. Then she stashes my slip in the sack she brought and slips out the door.

Hollywood Guy steps in, a serious, urgent look on his face.

"We shall depart for our honeymoon in a few minutes. There will be a carriage ride through the city, which will last approximately an hour, until we reach the railway station. I shall need you to wave and smile at the crowds that are already gathered along the streets."

Honeymoon! And a carriage ride? Have I suddenly switched places with some actress by a random mistake?

"But I . . ."

He seems to have anticipated my confusion, for he holds up a hand, motioning that I should listen to him first.

"No doubt, you have many questions, as do I, but save them until we are alone. For now, it is imperative that you act like nothing has happened. Pretend that your memory is intact, or there will be great trouble."

I stare at him, mouth agape. "Why? What's going on?"

Hollywood Guy holds out his hand. I hesitate for a second, but I take it. I don't know what's come over me. Those gorgeous golden-brown eyes are hypnotizing.

"Trust me."

***

The bright light streaming in from the tall, arched windows blinds me when we re-enter the cathedral. Guests, attired in period costumes that look straight out of a movie set, gawk at us. Hollywood Guy leads me to a raised dais, where there are two people wearing long, fancy robes embroidered in gold and silver.

My eyes bulge. The crowns they are wearing look so real—intricate designs of gold inlaid with rubies and pearls, with bits of purple velvet peaking between the arches. This film set sure has some serious financial backing.

The woman playing the queen comes forward, her gaze filled with concern. "Katriona, are you all right?"

It looks like she is referring to me.

"Excuse me, but I think you have it wron—ow!" Hollywood Guy squeezes my arm so hard that tears spring in my eyes.

"It seemed that nervousness, combined with the suffocation of the layers of clothing, have contributed to her unfortunate loss of consciousness." Hollywood Guy keeps an iron grip on my arm no matter how many daggers I glare at him. "However, with a change of clothes and a drink of water, she has fully recovered. There is nothing to worry about."

Like hell there isn't! But with so many people staring at us, I'm reluctant to make a scene.

"I suggest that the sooner you leave for Enrilth, the better," says the man who's acting as king. He really is an impressive actor. The way he carries himself—chin raised, gaze firm, and a voice that resounds with authority—probably, few people dare to defy him even in real life. "Edward, see that your wife has an early rest. You still have a long journey ahead."

Wife? They must be crazy—they all are. "I'm not—"

"My thoughts exactly." Hollywood Guy—I mean, Edward—strokes the underside of my arm in a loving caress. "Besides, it will not do to keep the train waiting. Come, Kat."

Kat. He says my name with such ease and comfort that it's difficult to believe that we're mere acquaintances. To call me with such familiarity, to touch me with such audacity—it's more like he is an ex-boyfriend that somehow, I've completely no recollection of. Or maybe he is simply an extremely accomplished actor. Even though he told me to trust him, I'm not convinced.

There isn't any time to dwell upon my doubts, for he is striding toward the exit. An arched doorway

31

opens to a glorious cornflower-blue sky, dotted with fluffy clouds. Since I'm as good as handcuffed to him, I've no choice but to follow him. Plus, once we leave this amazingly big-budget film set, I'll have a better chance to slip away and find someone who might be able to help me.

It's dreadfully difficult to walk briskly in this magnificent gown, however. I do my best not to trip up, but once I make it to the exit and get a good look at what's outside, I completely forget about my step. I tread on the gown and pitch forward.

"Kat!"

Strong arms wrap around my waist, preventing my fall, and a clean, masculine scent of freshly washed linen and soap surrounds me. Another time, I might be elated that a super-hot guy has his arms around me. But my mind is too overwhelmed to think of anything romantic.

What is this place?

Stretching ahead is a flight of steps carpeted in red velvet. On the foot of the stairs stands the most magnificent carriage I have ever seen, with ornate golden trappings and tall white stallions, complete with footmen, coachmen and the driver, making me feel like I'm in a Cinderella movie. But what really shocks me is the wide road stretching ahead and packed with people on either side. From where I'm standing, I figure there have to be hundreds at least, and that is only what I can see so far. I thought that the guests in the cathedral were pretty impressive, but all these people outside who seem to be waiting for us . . . there are too many of them to be plausible for a film set. They look . . . *real*. Too real to be filming for a Hollywood movie.

When the first few people in the crowds see us, a shout rings out in the air: "Long live Prince Edward! Long live Princess Katriona!" The others take up the chant, followed by a smattering of applause.

I look up at the prince, who is smiling and waving at the crowd.

"I don't believe this. This can't be real."

He raises one perfect eyebrow. "Of course it is. Look, there is a camera."

I don't see any around, but suddenly, a flash goes off. "Did someone just take our picture?"

This is insane. But he just smiles and pats my arm. "Don't worry, Kat. It is typical for the press to snap a few pictures for the morning paper."

And then he takes my hand and starts down the stairs. Numbly, I stumble along with him, numerous questions swimming in my mind. I look around wildly, but nothing, absolutely nothing, seems to resemble anything I've experienced before.

The buildings are too old-fashioned—yellow or brown, with arched windows and turrets—something that looks straight from a historic European town. There isn't a single car, nor any traffic lights in sight. And the crowds that are lined up along the main road ahead, held behind wooden barriers and waving flags and banners, are all dressed in historic costumes. The men wear either top hats or caps, while the women are in large skirts and shawls. Some women also wear hats wreathed in flowers or decorated with feathers. None of the women wear pants or shorts. Even though it's warm enough that I don't feel chilly in my short-sleeved dress, not a single woman is showing any skin below the waist. It's like shorts and mini-skirts don't exist.

Oh, my God. That episode of *Outlander* must have come true for me. I've tumbled through time and ended up in some historical period in Scotland. Only it looks more fancy and royal.

"Kat." Edward squeezes my hand. "Our carriage is waiting."

The carriage is in fact an open-air vehicle that lacks a roof, with luxurious crimson velvet seats, a gold-rimmed door, and stallions that pull the carriage with matching crimson puffs on their heads. Surrounded by a legion of liveried soldiers and several coachmen, it's just like the procession seen in Prince William and Kate's wedding.

"Oh, my." I bite down on my lip and feel pain. "I can't get on that thing."

An urgent look flashes in his eyes. "We must. The people are waiting. It's part of the tradition."

"To sit and be gawked at, like an exhibit in a museum?"

He makes a choked noise, like he's suppressing a laugh. "Worry not, for there are two of us. Now, if you will not walk on your own, I shall forcefully carry you to the carriage and throw you in, whether you like it or not."

Annoyed at his imperious tone, I glare at him.

34

"This playacting had better end soon, because no way am I marrying you for real."

"When you recover your memory, I doubt you shall maintain the same resolve." He lowers his voice to a whisper, and a wicked gleam flares in his eyes. "More than once, you told me that there was nowhere you'd rather be than in my arms."

"I don't know what kind of lovesick fool you're talking about, but that is not me." Still, my traitorous mind conjures up an image of me snuggled against that broad chest of his, and I'm sure a blush has crept into my cheeks.

When we approach the carriage, a man dressed in a splendid crimson tunic and golden brocade takes off a plumed hat and bows to me.

"Your Highness." He offers a large, meaty hand. I glance at the carriage seat, which has an alarmingly high foothold situated at the height of my waist. Considering the awfully fancy and binding gown I'm wearing, I am forced to admit that I need the help.

I put my hand on his palm, take a deep breath, lift my skirts out of the way, and step on the foothold. The next second, the prince takes my other hand and eases me into the seat.

"Allow me," he says in an amused tone, and promptly straightens the tiara on my head. Before he pulls away, he whispers, "Relax, Kat. Just smile and wave at our people, and soon, we'll be on the train."

Our people? Since when did I acquire . . .

"It's the princess!" A little girl cries out, pointing a chubby finger in my direction. She's sitting on her father's shoulders. "I can see her, Papa! It's Princess Katriona!"

Without thinking, I wave to her, which elicits a surprised gurgle of laughter. "She saw me, Papa! The princess saw me!"

A whistle blows shrilly, and then we're off. Jolted by the sudden start of the carriage, I unceremoniously fall back against the seat with an "oomph!"

Fortunately, only the takeoff is so jarring. The road we're traveling on is well-paved and smooth, even though it isn't asphalt. Plus, the carriage is sturdy and heavy, and the thick padded seats are a balm to the bum. Because of this, I'm able to follow Edward's example, convince myself that I'm a huge royal celebrity, and keep smiling and waving like a mannequin, even when my lips become dry and chapped and my arm feels like it's going to fall off.

"Here they come!"

"Look, there's the prince and his new bride!"

Not all reactions from the onlookers are positive, though. One middle-aged guy, a cigar in his mouth, stares at me with a mixture of scorn and disappointment.

"That is the princess? I thought she'd be more . . ."

A loud hushing sound drowns out the rest of his sentence. I sneak a surreptitious glance at the prince. It's a bit deflating to the ego, but yeah, I have to admit that if looks were the only thing considered, he could do better. I can be pretty when I have the right makeup and hairstyle, but I know that I'm a far cry from beauty queen material.

Why did they pick me? As if hearing my thoughts, Edward reaches out and squeezes my hand for a quick second, like he's reassuring me that nothing is wrong and everyone else other than him is blind.

The carriage goes on for some time. I wish I had my watch on, but unfortunately, I left it at Jason's apartment. I couldn't be bothered to wear the watch after a shower.

"How much longer is this going to take?" I whisper. He barely hears me, though I can't blame him. The noise from the crowds, plus the trumpets blaring from the procession that follows our carriage, make it difficult to communicate without shouting.

I sit back, resigned, and resume the nodding and smiling and waving. Finally, when I think that my arms can't take it anymore, the carriage makes a turn toward a large building about three stories high, with a tower-like structure in the middle and an old-fashioned clock hanging on it.

"Are we there? The train station, I mean."

He nods, and a cloud of apprehension seems to fall over his face. "Remember, Kat. Act like everything is normal." He surprises me by taking hold of my chin and lifting it. "There. You are now the princess of Athelia. You bow to no one."

The carriage stops. Edward helps me get down and, like he's escorting me to the prom, he holds out his arm. After a moment's hesitation, I place my fingers on his sleeve. After all, I have no idea which direction to go. Better wait till I can find a cellphone or something.

The train station looks rather similar to Grand Central Terminal in New York, all golden and grand. But there isn't much time to admire its beauty. Edward leads me directly to the platform, where a huge retro-looking train is waiting. It's navy blue with a white roof, and silver letters and flowers are painted on the carriage. Plumes of smoke rise from its top.

It is then that a sinking feeling enters my stomach—from the moment I woke up in that hospital-like room, I have yet to detect a trace of modern technology. I got decent grades in geography in high school, but even I can't figure out which country I could be in. So far, it looks like some European country, but I'm sure that even the most underdeveloped areas would have a car.

Edward leads me to the train. A conductor is shouting, "All aboard!" I look back once, wondering how many people are getting on the train, but it seems that apart from us, there are only about a dozen more passengers, who actually look more like attendants. There's the huge guy who helped me into the carriage, following a pretty young woman who happens to be the same person who helped me dress. She's walking in the brisk, firm steps of a businesswoman. Were she in modern attire, I'd expect her to wear oblong spectacles and black heels.

"Where are we going?" I ask faintly. At this point, I'll believe anything.

"Wait until we get there." As he pats my hand, a look of alarm crosses his features. "Where is your ring?"

"What ring?"

"Why, your wedding ring, of course." He raises his hand, where an expensive-looking diamond ring glitters on his finger.

"I never saw any ring. I swear."

He stares at me, looking deeply into my eyes, like he's trying to ascertain if I'm telling the truth.

"Amelie."

The young businesslike woman appears. "Is everything all right, Your Highness?"

"I need a pen and paper," Edward says. "Normally, I'd have some on me, but I can't carry much in these wedding garments."

The young woman whips out a fountain pen and a small notebook from a handbag, her movements so nimble it almost seems she made the stationary appear out of thin air.

Edward writes on the notebook, tears off a page, and hands it to the woman. "Have it sent to the jeweler's straight away. Kat lost her ring. I want it replaced immediately upon our return."

She doesn't even blink or look surprised. "Certainly, Your Highness."

"Is she your secretary?" I ask.

"Amelie is your personal maid." He pauses for a second. "While she is not fully cognizant of your memory loss, if you fail to remember a person or event and I am not with you, you may confide in her. Her family has served us for generations, and from my experience, she has never been anything but loyal and trustworthy. Now, let us embark on our honeymoon."

There doesn't seem to be anything else to do but follow him. Edward pulls open a door, and I gape.

It's like traveling on a first-class train, vintage-style. The cabin is the last word in elegance, with polished oak paneling, banquette seating by curtained windows, lacy white coverings on the seats, rose-patterned lamps, and a vase filled with orchids on a table. On another table near the wall lies a fully-laden tray, a tea set complete with a three-tier dessert stand.

"Pinch me," I say faintly. "I must be dreaming."

Beside me, Edward chuckles. He brings my hand to his lips and kisses my knuckles. "Does this feel like dreaming?"

The young giant shows up. He has to stoop in the doorway before entering, but he does it pretty smoothly, like he's used to ducking wherever he goes.

"Your Highness. Princess Kat." He bows and grins. I snatch my hand back from Edward's grasp, feeling totally embarrassed. "If there's nothing else you'll be needing, I'll tell the driver to get ready for departure."

Edward's gaze sweeps over the compartment. "We're ready."

"Very good, Your Highness."

"One thing—guard the doors. I wish no interruptions until we arrive."

The giant's grin grows even wider. From how he caught the prince kissing my hand, I can imagine what he's thinking—the prince doesn't want to be disturbed because he can't wait to be alone with his blushing new bride. Probably looking forward to a steamy make out session.

As if I'd let him kiss me again. As soon as I figure out what bizarre accident I was in, I'll find a way to return to my sane, non-luxurious, boring home. Well, maybe I don't have to figure it out immediately . . .

4

Edward settles on one of the plush covered chairs. "Tell me what you remember."

"Do you always talk like this?"

"Pardon me?"

I imitate his imperious tone, cross my legs, and look at him like he is beneath my nose.

To my surprise, he laughs. There really should be a law that forbids a guy this good-looking to laugh like that. It easily melts my defenses.

"If I needed the last bit of proof that you are the Kat I know, this is it. My Kat wouldn't tolerate any arrogance."

"*My Kat*? Since when did I become your property?"

"I apologize," he says, though he doesn't really sound sincere. In fact, he looks kind of pleased, even relieved. I wonder for the hundredth time what is going on, and who is this other Kat he is referring to?

"Let us start again, shall we? Please tell me what you can remember thus far."

I glance outside. The townhouses have become increasingly sparse, replaced by cottages dotted in farmlands. It confirms my suspicions. I really am in a different world. There is no way a movie set could be this big. With a sinking heart, I wonder how I am ever going to get home. I wonder if I'm dreaming. I wonder if I've lost my mind.

A sweet, rich aroma tantalizes my nose. Surprised, I find a cup of hot tea pressed into my hands, the steam still rising from the caramel-colored liquid.

"Here," Edward says in a soothing tone. There's no trace of the haughty manner as might behoove a prince. All I can sense is a compassionate, concerned look in his eyes. "Perhaps some tea will be more conducive to conversation."

He pours himself a cup as well. I raise the cup to my lips and take a sip. Strong, bold, without any bitter aftertaste. It contains the precise amount of sugar to make the taste sweet but not cloying. The addition of cream enhances the flavor, warming my insides. It's almost as if he knew what I preferred.

Edward catches me staring at him, and he smiles. "When we were engaged, I taught you to appreciate a good cup of tea. Before that, you told me you preferred coffee."

I do remember developing a taste for tea several years earlier, when Gabriel and I started dating. But this guy—prince—doesn't look like Gabriel. Well, they're both tall and gorgeous and friendly, but the

43

similarities stop there. Gabriel is your ordinary, down-to-earth guy, whereas Edward gives off a polished, refined, debonair air that speaks of a man whose upbringing is anything but ordinary. I could imagine going to the movies and getting popcorn with Gabriel, but never with Edward. A candlelit dinner in a Michelin restaurant with flowers and champagne seems more like the latter's style.

"You said you are a prince," I say slowly. "And you said I'm a princess. How the heck did I become princess of a country I don't even know exists?"

He pulls out a pocket watch and consults it. "It is a long story, but we have a few hours' journey." He gives me a twisted smile, but there is a sad, lonely look in his eyes. "Is there truly nothing you can remember about me, Kat?"

For some reason, I feel sorry for him. I must look exactly like that girl he confuses me with. I wonder what kind of amazing girl she is to catch the attention of this prince, who seems totally devoted to her. "Tell me your story. Perhaps after hearing it, I can give you a better answer?"

He looks around, like he's trying to make sure that he's not overheard, and then leans back in his chair. "Shall we start with the day we first met?"

And he tells me the most ridiculous story I have ever heard. Apparently, I was transported to his old-fashioned country when I ripped apart an old Cinderella book. The only way I could get back to America was to complete the story, which basically means that Cinderella has to get married to the prince.

44

But in the end, he fell in love with me instead.

I don't remember that I had ever met him, much less falling in love. But why do I feel like I've already heard of this story?

He mentioned a book.

A book that started it all.

The Ugly Stepsister.

Most of the stuff he told me had happened in the book, I realize with startling clarity. Except that there was no background on the ugly stepsister being from another world. But everything that happened between her and the prince is exactly the same as the story he told me. And the prince . . . and the prince . . .

Both are named Edward.

It can't be true. According to what he said, I am now Katriona Bradshaw, the other stepsister in the Cinderella retelling. The same retelling that I owned. But I don't remember anything of ripping up the book. It might be a bit worn after numerous re-readings, but all the pages are intact. Speaking of the book, an image of the book spinning in the air, right above Jason's bed, flashes in my mind.

Impossible. There is no way that the book could be at Jason's. As much as I loved the book, I couldn't take it along with all my luggage to Oregon. Yet . . . I reach into my mind, desperately trying to remember what the book looked like, but somehow, the more I try, the hazier it becomes. One moment, I recall the book rotating slowly, and the next moment it's gone . . . gone where?

Pain explodes in my head.

I let out a cry and put both hands on my head. The dizziness returns in full force and I massage my temples, trying to compose myself. In a second, the prince is by my side.

"Kat? Kat, where are you hurting?"

"I'll be . . . I'm fine." I try to wave him away. "Just let me lie down for a second."

He suddenly gets up and leaves, but soon, he is back with a middle-aged man in a black suit. "Dr. Jensen, it seems that my wife has a severe headache."

The doctor checks my pulse and asks a few questions, which I'm able to answer clearly. The pain has subsided, but my head is still throbbing.

"Her Highness seems to be all right, apart from the sudden attack that I cannot find the reason for. I would suggest that she have some nourishment and take a good rest. She seems healthy enough, so hopefully it was simply over-exertion."

Edward says a few things to him in a low voice. The doctor looks at me, shakes his head, and tells him in an equally low voice that I can't discern. "Memory . . . temporary loss . . ." seems to be what they are talking about.

But I am in no mood to listen. My conversation with Edward was so shocking, so ridiculous that I refuse to believe it. I *can't* have traveled to a storybook and later returned home. I can't have met him, gotten engaged, and not remember anything about him. The most plausible explanation is that I happen to look like the princess, who has somehow disappeared. When the train stops, I must try to find where the real

46

princess is and try to get home.

I pretty much sleep through the rest of the journey. Edward converts one of the chairs into a makeshift bed so I can lie down, using one of the cushions as a pillow. Once or twice in my sleep, I am dimly aware of the brush of his fingers on my forehead, smoothing back the hair from my face, but I'm too exhausted to care. My last conscious thought is to get away from this strange but fascinating world. I am not, and cannot be, this princess of Athelia.

***

"Kat. Kat, wake up. We have arrived." I crack one eye open. Edward is leaning over me, that damned gorgeous face of his too close for comfort. I feel a fierce blush rising in my cheeks. I scramble up and try to put some distance between us.

"Where are we now?"

He smiles. "Enrilth, my childhood home. I've always longed to show it to you." Then he takes a deep breath. "I am well aware that you do not remember anything about me, or us, but until we can figure out what has caused your memory loss and how we can deal with it, I fear that we must act as a couple in front of others. As the notorious royal family, I guarantee there are plenty who will take advantage, or even bring harm to you, should your condition be widely known."

I bite my lower lip. I admit that his suggestion makes sense, but it makes me uneasy. In every

47

romance I've read, couples that pretend to be in love *always* end up together. But in my case, this is a risk I can't afford unless I absolutely cannot help it. I already have Jason, and besides, I've got to get home.

"Only in front of others." I manage to keep my voice frosty. "When we are alone, you had better behave like a friend. Like a casual acquaintance."

He doesn't even blink. "Certainly. As long as it is necessary."

I consider arguing with him about what constitutes as necessary, but my thoughts are interrupted by a rap on the door.

"Your Highness." The curt, no-nonsense voice of the young woman rings out from the other side of the door.

Edward holds out his hand. I take it, and my heart beats faster when he wraps his fingers firmly over mine like he doesn't want to ever let go.

"Remember, her name is Amelie," he whispers. "And Bertram is the man who looks like he has giant blood."

"Got it," I whisper back, trying to ignore our joined hands. He held my hand earlier, but now that I'm aware that we must playact as a married couple, somehow, it's more distracting.

Amelie is waiting for us, a folded cloak in her arms.

"It's turning dark outside." She hands me the cloak. "I heard it can get pretty chilly up here in the north."

No way do I want to catch a cold, which seems easy with my short-sleeved gown, so I thank her and draw the cloak around my shoulders. I fumble for a moment with the clasp—it's fashioned in an intricate twist of brass and bronze, which proves to be difficult compared to the simple modern ones that I'm used to.

"Allow me." Edward reaches over and deftly fastens the clasp. Then he tucks a lock of my hair behind my ear and holds out his arm expectantly. "Ready?"

All of this happens so fast that I've barely time to reflect on how he touches me so naturally, so easily, like he's used to taking care of me. Amelie doesn't even blink or offer any help, even though she's supposed to be my maid.

But since we've agreed to act like newlyweds, I can't show any discomfort over the fact that a stranger is treating me like a cherished jewel. And the way he looks at me when he smooths back my hair—intense, affectionate, devoted, like I'm the only girl in his universe—I'm not even sure Jason has ever looked at me that way.

Jason. What is he doing now? It's been hours since I've disappeared from his bedroom. He must be worried sick about me. He probably even reported to the police. My heart twists with anxiety and fear. It won't be long until Mom and Paige know I'm missing.

I look away and focus on the place we've stopped at. I had expected a huge, magnificent station after all the grandeur I've experienced, but the station is actually quite small and quaint. It's built almost entirely from logs, the fences are painted buttercup yellow, and the signs are hand-drawn, not printed. Ivy and honeysuckle hang from the roofs, the ends only a

49

hand's breadth from the fences.

"There they are!" Someone shouts.

Gathered behind one side of the fence are around a dozen people, including old and young, male and female. All of them are gawking at us in the same manner as the crowds during the carriage ride.

"I thought I specifically requested not to have anyone line up for our arrival," Edward says in a low voice.

"No matter how you try to conceal your schedule, there's bound to be gossip around the village," Amelie says in a matter-of-fact tone. "Not to mention that the papers have widely reported where you chose to stay for your honeymoon."

"Three cheers for Prince Edward and his bride!" A man calls.

The cheers echo through the air, followed by a smattering of applause and whistling.

There's nothing to do but to respond with more nodding and waving and smiling, but what I really want to do is run away. Whoever is supposed to be the real princess had better return, because this royal thing is getting on my nerves. I feel like an impostor, no matter what Edward says.

Fortunately, because the station is so small, it takes little time to leave the platform and head outside, where a new carriage awaits. Bertram, the young man who looks like the Hulk with normal tanned skin, is holding the door open.

"It's all right, Kat," Edward says. "The ride to our house is much shorter compared to the one around the city."

I don't answer. All I want to do is look for any way I can escape. But the sun has gone down, the sky is a dreary gray, and I can already see several stars. Outside the station, there is just one lone cottage, and the rest is undeveloped plains. And with Bertram looking on, I doubt I'd have any chance of success. Edward himself, with his broad shoulders and six-feet stature, is impossible to get away from.

I have no choice but to get on the carriage. The only comfort is that it is a normal one with a roof and curtains, so we're instantly invisible to the eager villagers.

Once we're in the carriage, I let go of Edward's hand and scoot as far away from him as possible. I've wounded his feelings, but I'm already in a relationship. Briefly, I wonder if I should mention Jason so he'd stop treating me like I'm his wife, but will it work? He doesn't seem the type who would back down. Besides, I don't feel like imagining his expression if he learns that I'm already taken.

"How long is this honeymoon thing?" I ask quickly before he can speak.

"One week." His tone is clipped and he doesn't look at me. Can't blame the guy.

"And for the whole time, we'll be here? In this Enrilth place?"

"Correct."

My chances don't look good. Enrilth seems pretty deserted, from what I can see out of the window. Cottages appear few and far between. On the road, there is nothing but carts and carriages. No traffic lights. It's a bit puzzling that they have railways, but cars aren't available yet. And apart from the train, I have yet to see anything that resembles modern civilization.

I let out a frustrated sigh. I have to get back. I have an extra shift tomorrow! Our boss is going to be furious if I don't show up, especially since we're understaffed.

But without any tangible help, what hope do I have of getting away?

5

It's completely dark by the time we arrive at Enrilth House. The windows are bathed in a warm yellow glow—lamps? candles? I doubt electricity exists— allowing me to perceive a large, but not gigantic, building. Wreaths of flowers decorate the walls and there's ivy crawling over at least half of the entrance gates.

Edward helps me out of the carriage, though with considerably less warmth. No brush of his fingertips against my skin, no solicitous voice asking if I'm all right, no affectionate look into my eyes. Which is how it should be. *He's a stranger.* We haven't even known each other for one day.

A gust of wind cuts over my face, and I can't help but nestle closer to Edward. Amelie wasn't kidding about the colder weather here, and I have no doubt the temperature will drop further at night. Chicago has pretty harsh winters, but the chilly air here still makes me shiver. Edward says nothing, but he puts a hand against the small of my back, urging me to get inside quickly.

Enrilth House isn't exactly the kind of place that I'd expect a royal couple to be staying for their honeymoon. The cozy interior is more like a bed-and-breakfast place. No glittering chandeliers, marble floors, or gilt-edged furniture. After the splendid procession we had when touring the city and the luxurious car on the train that oozes wealth, this is somewhat of a surprise.

"Is this where you spent your childhood?"

"Disappointed?"

"Oh no, it's much better this way. I don't think I'd be able to relax if everything were marble and gold. I'm just surprised that given you are a prince, you didn't grow up in some place fancier."

"It was my parents' wish to focus on simplicity and comfort over an overt display of wealth, so when my father was still the prince, he chose to build this house and settle here during the summers." Edward steers me toward the living room and indicates that I settle on a dark green couch before taking a chair across from me. The large brick fireplace in the sitting room has a homey, country feel to it. A few paintings adorn the top of the fireplace. One, in particular, catches my eye—an extremely handsome man, whom I suspect is where Edward gets his looks from.

"My grandparents were known for their reckless extravagance and decadent lifestyle, which was not well-received by the people. It did not help that my grandfather went mad in his later years. Therefore, when my parents ascended the throne, they attempted to repair the royal family's image. They made a conscious effort to live a healthy and productive life, such as adherence to industriousness, morality, punctuality . . ." his voice drifts off when Amelic approaches us, carrying a jug and two cups.

"Dinner will be ready in a quarter-hour," she announces. "Your Highness, I hope you'll forgive that Bertram has already raided the kitchen. It seems that he couldn't wait a second longer to sate his hunger." She sounds exasperated.

Edward grins. "Leave him be. The lad's worn out. As a matter of fact . . ." his gaze strays to my face, "I believe it is not necessary to prepare a normal dinner with cutlery and napkins. It has been a long journey, and we have already partaken of refreshments whilst on the train. A simpler fare should suffice. Kat, what do you say to a grilled ham and cheese sandwich?"

"That sounds wonderful. But how . . ." He squeezes my hand and gives me a warning look. I gulp down the rest of my sentence, but I can't ignore the question. How does he know that I have a weakness for grilled ham and cheese sandwiches?

The tea, along with the fire blazing merrily in the grate, proves to be the balm to soothe my soul. The sandwiches are also heavenly—I have to restrain myself from licking my fingers clean of melted cheese. I attempt harmless small talk, like asking who the guy in the painting is—his great-great-grandfather, who reminds me of the infamous English poet, Lord

Byron—or how long it snows in the winter. Edward answers me readily, but I sense there's something weighing on his mind, which I can totally relate to. I'm desperately worried about how to go home, but with servants dropping in now and then, we can't discuss the mystery of my being here.

After dinner, Edward calls for Amelie. "See to the princess's needs before we retire. Have Mabel or more servants assist you when necessary. There are a few matters I need to take care of."

Amelie orders for a hot bath to be prepared. This is kind of alarming. A large brass tub is carried into the bedroom, a silken screen set up, and then the maids start carrying buckets of hot water into the room. Uh-oh. Looks like they haven't installed modern plumbing.

Uncomfortable with all those servants going up and down the stairs, I cross over to the threshold and try to take the pail from a middle-aged woman with graying hair. I have to do something rather than lounging in a chair and watching the maids pour water into the tub.

"Let me have the pail, please."

The woman jerks back in surprise. "But Your Highness—"

"If it's going to be my bath, then I'm going to lend a hand."

Despite her protests, I grab the pail and haul it toward the tub. I had expected Amelie to stop me, but maybe since I don't splash any water or teeter dangerously, she lets me take over without further comment.

Getting out of that heavy brocaded gown is a pain, so I let Amelie undress me, but I refuse her offer to wash my hair. The soaps are handmade and smell natural, a nice change from the chemical smell from our modern manufactured brands. Once I'm done bathing, Amelie enters the room—it seems she has the sense of a trained hound—carrying a snowy nightgown, and insists on drying and brushing my hair.

"By the way, the queen asked me to give you this." She fishes a small ruby pendant from her pocket. "Wear it when His Highness . . . when you go to bed."

"I'd rather not, thank you." I place the pendant on the table. "I don't like having any ornaments on while I sleep."

"But you should." She flushes—the first time I've seen her look discomfited. "Her Majesty specifically requested you wear it. It's a charm for, ahem, procreation."

It's my turn to get embarrassed. At dinner and during the bath, I had briefly wondered how we're going to deal with sleeping in the same room, but I didn't dare to ask Edward. As I've made it clear that I have no memory of him, it's unlikely he'll demand his husband rights tonight. On the other hand, the prince does seem quite besotted with me. If his gaze is intense enough to kindle a fire, then what can happen when we're alone and expected to . . . um . . . *procreate*?

A wave of heat washes over me when I imagine

him taking his clothes off, his lips hot on my skin, his hands moving over my body . . .

Stop. I will not succumb to mindless lust. I wouldn't even be having these ridiculous thoughts if he weren't the hottest guy I've ever met.

"Your Highness." Amelie steps aside, and I'm confronted with the object of my insta-lust. Said object has taken off his dark jacket and is currently wearing only a pure white shirt and black pants.

My heartbeat starts racing and my throat goes dry. I don't have heaps of experience with men, but I swear a muscle moves in his throat when he looks at me. The nightgown is long-sleeved and reaches right to my ankles, but I feel naked under his heated gaze.

"Amelie, wait . . ." My voice comes out as squeaky as a mouse. Amelie probably didn't even hear me, for she curtsies briefly and walks away. The door closes behind her with a soft thud.

I'm now completely alone with the prince.

6

My heart is pounding in my ears. To make things worse, I hear the sound of a key turning.

"Did you lock the door?"

A chuckle escapes him.

"Relax, Kat," he says, his voice deep, warm, and startlingly sensual. "I wasn't planning on taking you to bed, however appealing the idea is. Locking the door is merely a precaution. Suppose Amelie enters our room in the morning and discovers that we aren't sharing a bed? Remember, we have to keep up appearances."

"Oh." I didn't consider that servants might enter without knocking. Amelie seems capable of being discreet. "Right. Okay. Then I'll take the lounge over there and—"

"Absolutely not. I will not have my wife freezing." He strides across the room, and for a second, I think he's going to touch me, but he sinks into an armchair a few feet away.

"We should talk."

Suddenly, the locked door sounds like a good idea.

"Right." I push back a chunk of hair that fell over my eyes, and the movement causes my nightgown to slip a bit lower, baring my collarbone. Edward looks away, but a telltale blush starts spreading from his ear. As I snatch up a wrap and pull it around my shoulders, I wonder how old he is. He definitely isn't the kind of playboy prince you read in romances.

"Has anyone unusual—for example, has a goblin, or some other supernatural being shown up?"

Bemused, I shake my head.

He purses his lips, apparently deep in thought for a moment.

"Do you remember anything before you woke up in that scanty dress?"

It takes a moment until I realize he is referring to my Victoria's Secret slip.

"Well, before I passed out, I was at . . . at home." Better not tell him that I was at Jason's house. How he can blush just from seeing my collarbone gives me the idea that Athelia must be pretty strict with morals and propriety. At least Edward's education is. "I took a shower, it was late, and I was ready to go to sleep, when the book appeared out of nowhere. I got sucked into it, and the next thing I can remember is that I woke up in that tiny room. Then you came in."

"What is the book you speak of? Is it the old picture book, titled *Cinderella*, that you accidentally ripped up and came to Athelia in the first place?"

"No, it's a plain text paperback, a retelling of *Cinderella*. It certainly isn't new. I've had it for several years since high school, but it's one of my favorites, and I know I took special care with it." Wait, when we were on the train, didn't he tell me that I had ripped apart *The Ugly Stepsister*? Why is he talking about some old picture book called *Cinderella*?

And then I realize another thing that has confused me for ages: I DID have an old Cinderella book, but it seems to have vanished, even though I remember I had stashed it away in a box in the attic. But when Mom asked me to clean out the attic for a yard sale, I could never find it.

Edward frowns. "Did you mention that it has been several years since you were in high school?"

I nod, wondering why he asks. "Seven years, I think. I got the book when Gabriel . . . in my last year of high school."

"I thought you looked slightly different from what I remember," he says slowly. "Apparently, the explanation is that you have aged seven years since I met you. Which means that you must be twenty-four now. However, by some reason I have yet to fathom, time has remained the same here."

Part of me gets annoyed when he uses the word "aged," even though twenty-four is by no means old . . . or is it by Athelia's standards? "If I did meet you when I was in high school, then I guess I'm too old for you now."

His gaze slides over my body, slowly and deliberately. A wolfish gleam lights in his eyes. "I see no problem."

I cross my arms over my chest. "How old are you?"

He ignores my question. "We are bound by marriage, and nothing will change that. Certainly not an inconsequential matter of age. But . . ." Suddenly, he looks as though thunder has struck his face. "Since you're past twenty, then it's highly possible that . . . are you married?"

There's such a dejected look on his face that I shake my head without thinking.

"Then are you engaged?"

"Not . . . no."

"Truly?" There's a shrewdness in his expression as he searches my face. "It seems highly unlikely that an attractive young lady like you would not have at least a suitor or an admirer."

I have to suppress a smile. His speech, along with the surroundings, make me feel like I've traveled back in time. I have an image of Jason dressed in a black tux and holding a bunch of roses and kneeling before me. Or him trying to climb up to my balcony, Romeo-style.

Should I deny him Jason's existence? I'm sure that he'll be mad, but if he thinks I have no attachments at home, then he will probably make me stay in Athelia. Which is not what I want.

"There is a man in your life," he says, and it's not a question. "You are not engaged to him, but there is at least enough of an attraction that it causes you to hesitate before answering me."

I decide there's no point in lying. "I'm sorry, but it's true that I am in a relationship now. I can't . . ."

"Don't." He holds up a hand. "Don't tell me that because of this other suitor in your world, you cannot consider becoming my wife. Well do I understand that for you, today must have been a strange, harrowing experience. But for me, I had expected that I would be married to a woman who doesn't know me any more than I know her. Yet with an astonishing stroke of luck, *you* were sent back to me."

Again, I remember *The Ugly Stepsister* rotating slowly in the air, bathed in the yellow-greenish glow. For some inexplicable reason, the image gives off a sinister vibe. There's something decidedly wrong about being pulled to the book by force, as though it were a swirling black hole in the universe.

"I do not know the reason—perhaps the goblins took pity on us and reversed the spell. In fact, if you did not show up in that revealing piece and with your appearance slightly altered, I might even believe that you'd never left Athelia. Whatever may have occurred, all I know is that you are now here with me. If you were married and with child, I may have reservations, but since you are not officially attached to another, I shall endeavor to make you stay."

The passion in his voice startles me. In a novel, perhaps, as a heroine, I'd be flattered and thrilled at the alpha-ness of him. But experiencing it firsthand, while I am definitely flattered, there's a part of me that rebels. He may be the prince of his country, and he may be used to having others defer to anything he wants, but in a relationship, we are equals. He has no right to keep me shackled to Athelia simply because he doesn't want me to go.

I open my mouth, but drowsiness happens to overtake me at the moment, and all that comes out is, "I d–don't . . ." followed by a huge yawn. Weird. I already had a nap on the train. Maybe I have something similar to jet lag. I've definitely come a long way from home.

Edward smiles indulgently. "I suppose it is rather late, and you have been through a lot today. We shall talk more tomorrow." He rises and casts a glance at the bed—the large, comfy-looking four-poster bed with fat white pillows and an apple-green spread. For a moment, I wonder if he's going to claim his wedding night, regardless of my memory loss, but he abruptly turns and heads to a narrow door in a corner. When he opens the door, I glimpse rows of suits and dresses in another small room. A changing room, I guess.

"Good night." The door clicks shut.

I breathe a sigh of relief, even though I know perfectly well that he could return if he changes his mind. At the same time, there's a tiny part of me that's disappointed. Given how he professed his love to me on the train, he might have struggled a bit more.

Stop it, Kat. This is no time to be worrying about whether a stranger finds you sexually attractive.

Despite feeling sleepy, I force myself to stand up. I need to make sure there really isn't any chance of escaping. I go to the window, but not before flinging on a heavy cloak and discovering a balcony beyond the window. Tentatively, doing my best not to make a sound, I step outside. As I expected, it's completely dark except for the moon shining luminously above. There is nothing outside except for some grass, bushes, and trees. There's a distant light within a cottage, but it's so distant that it provides a mere pinprick of light. Everything is completely silent, save for the soft whinny of the horses in the stable, which I suppose must be located somewhere near the house.

I am trapped in the middle of nowhere.

A shiver runs down my spine.

How am I going to get home?

When it starts to get too cold to bear, I trudge back to bed and try to gather my thoughts. If I had somehow met this guy and fallen in love with him, it would have taken a big chunk of time out of my life. I never had the chance to go abroad. The longest trip I've ever taken was to Florida. I cannot imagine having weeks—no, months—of my life completely wiped out. I went straight from high school to college, and I'm positive I didn't miss a single semester. Can Athelia be some tiny European country I have never heard of? But there is no way that it can be so nineteenth-century, like a fancy, aristocratic version of the Amish with a monarchy, which doesn't make any sense.

The only explanation is what Edward told me—I was sucked into the *Cinderella* book, met him, fell in love, and returned to America. But that's impossible. This isn't a novel or a movie, and it's even more incredible than time travel.

Besides, everyone calls me Princess Katriona. I am most definitely not Katriona. It can't be that I changed my name. The best explanation I can come up with is that this Katriona has disappeared and somehow, I have taken her place at the same time, and as it happens that we look alike, Edward has mistaken me for his bride.

Then how does the prince know that I have an old picture book of Cinderella? How does he know that I have a sister named Paige? How does he know that I have a penchant for strong milk tea and a weakness for ham and cheese sandwiches?

I yawn again, despite fighting to keep my eyelids open. In the end, I surrender and climb into bed.

7

I wake up in the morning to the sun streaming through the window. I sit up abruptly, my mind blank. How did I end up in some bed-and-breakfast place? And then it all comes rushing back to me. Yesterday, somehow, I was dropped into this old-fashioned country called Athelia, and what's more ridiculous is that I'm the princess of this country.

I jump out of bed and look around. It's so bright outside that I am positive that it's no longer early morning. I guess the prince must be up already. He doesn't seem the type to sleep in.

Sure enough, when I peek into the changing room, it's empty. Whew. It's much better this way. If we wake up at the same time, it's going to be dreadfully embarrassing, especially if he walks around half-naked, searching for a shirt or belt.

I look for a dress to wear. Fortunately, the gowns here seem okay. Probably because it's summer, they look pretty and well made, but not yards of fabric that one might drown in. But how am I going to get dressed? I don't think it's a good idea to go without the corset. It doesn't have zippers, making it impossible to put on by myself. Not to mention that I can't do my hair either, unless they can accept a sloppy ponytail, hah! I'll have to find Amelie.

With a sigh, I open the door. A tall man in a dark blue uniform happens to walk by, and he freezes when he sees me. "Highness . . . you shouldn't . . ."

In a few seconds, Amelie appears—so fast that I suspect she was hiding close by.

"Get inside." She shuts the door with a bang. "Don't you let anyone, other than His Highness and me, see you in your nightgown. His Highness will be very displeased if another man sees you half-dressed."

"I'm not his property," I grumble. "Where is he, by the way?"

"His Highness went riding in the morning, and he told us to let you sleep as long as you like." Amelie appears a little uneasy as she looks at me. "Is everything all right with you, Princess Kat? Do you feel up to a bit of breakfast?"

It takes me a second to guess that she's wondering if I might be pregnant. "Of course. I'd love some breakfast," I quickly assure her. "I'm so hungry that I could eat a horse."

"Oh." She seems disappointed, then she nods. "Would you like to have a breakfast tray served here, or would you rather go downstairs to the dining room?"

I look around the bedroom. There's only a small, round table in front of the fireplace. And I'm not really keen on the idea of having breakfast in bed.

"Downstairs, please."

"Let's get you dressed."

As Amelie laces me into a new corset and gown with amazing efficiency, an uneasy thought enters my mind. If Amelie is concerned about my getting pregnant, then what'll the king and queen say when we return to the palace? Am I going to be pressured to produce a son so that the royal family will have an heir?

I really should get back as soon as possible.

***

Breakfast is like a full banquet, with strips of crispy bacon, flaky croissants, fluffy pancakes with a pat of butter and a pitcher of syrup, a hard-boiled egg sitting in a patterned egg cup, yogurt topped with freshly sliced strawberries, and steaming hot coffee served in expensive-looking silverware. Grudgingly, I admit there are perks of being a princess.

I've just finished a pancake when the door opens and Edward comes in. His sleeves are rolled up to the elbows, and beads of water glisten on his neck, like he just washed his face.

"Good morning," he says, coming over to me. "Enjoying breakfast? I confess that seeing you makes me hungry again." He swipes a piece of strawberry from my yogurt.

"You're just hungry from riding," I say, but remembering that we have to pretend to be in love, I fork a piece of bacon and hold it out to him. "Here you are, darling."

My voice sounds fake, but it seems to be working. A maid dusting the furniture looks away, and one has her hand over her mouth, like she's trying not to giggle.

His eyes shining, Edward pulls out a chair next to me and takes my fork. Together, we finish the monstrous quantity of my breakfast. Doing my best to play the part of a loving wife, I try to act like I've known him a long time. It comes across easier than I expected when he's such a willing participant, and we end up fighting over the last croissant. I'm still trying to grab his arm and make him give up when Bertram appears.

"Pardon me, Your Highness, but the coachman is waiting."

"Where are we going?" I ask.

Edward breaks the croissant and hands me the larger piece while consuming the rest himself. "Would you like to travel back hundreds of years in time?"

***

I'm not really into ancient historic sites, but when I step off the carriage, a gasp of wonder escapes me involuntarily. Enrilth Castle—can't they come up with a different name?—is just like the setting you see in big-budget historical and fantasy films. A vast

70

structure of stone, complete with multiple towers and battlements, is surrounded by a deep, wide moat. It would be complete if the two men in front of the drawbridge were in shining armor and carried a lance or a sword. But no, they look just like the villagers waiting for us at the train station. Both are stout and ruddy-faced, and they wear checkered shirts and dark pants. Upon seeing us, they remove their caps and bow deeply.

"Ah, it's our bonny Prince Edward and the new princess!" The taller one says, grinning. "We have been waiting for you all morning long."

I glance at Edward. There's a frown on his face. Guess he isn't pleased at being called "bonny." Ha.

His companion elbows him. "Hold your tongue, Gil. It's not every day that you get the prince and the new princess visiting."

For such an impressive castle, I'm surprised there aren't more tourists, which is kind of puzzling. The train makes the place accessible, and the weather is lovely.

"What are you looking for?" Edward asks.

"Nothing…I thought this was supposed to be a popular tourist attraction, but there aren't any people here."

"The castle is yours today, Princess Katriona." Gil winks. "Everyone else must make way for you."

"Oh." I feel a bit embarrassed. "But honestly, there is no need—"

"Let me show you the castle, Kat. It will take a long time for the entire tour." Edward puts a hand on

71

my back and steers me forward. Leaning over to my ear, he whispers, "Trust me, you'd prefer touring the castle without a number of villagers following and staring at you."

Makes sense. But still, I'm not certain I like this privilege. If I were one of the tourists, I'd be annoyed that I have to avoid this particular day just because the monarch is visiting.

Anyway, I'll be going home as soon as I get the chance, so I focus on crossing the drawbridge. Wooden planks creak under our feet as we make our way to the entrance. I dart a glance at the moat. It is a deep sea-green with ducks floating on the water.

"The castle was built nearly five hundred years ago." Edward steadies me with his firm grip on my arm. "Our ancestors came from another country, Moryn, which lies to the west of Athelia. Enrilth happens to be near the port where they first landed."

I don't remember *The Ugly Stepsister* mentioning anything about Moryn. Looks like this is another piece of info I must remember in order to play my part of the princess.

"Were you different countries in the beginning, or did Athelia separate from Moryn later?

"Originally, we were colonies under the great Moryn empire," Edward says, leading me into what seems like a courtyard. Interestingly, there are a few knights astride horses made of stuffed sacks. This is certainly a tourist attraction. "We had our own leaders to run local affairs, but the Moryn king overruled us. For several decades, we lived in peace until the demands from them became more and more ridiculous. There was a tax law that allowed them to impose heavy taxes on everything, including both imported Moryn goods and Athelian local goods."

"And so you retaliated by dumping chests of tea into the harbor, and later went to war?" The words are out of my mouth before I can help it.

Edward stares at me. "Tea?"

"Never mind. Just pretend I didn't say anything."

"Tea did not exist then, but the taxes did escalate tension between the two countries. Eventually, we declared war on Moryn, which sent troops across the sea. The most famous battle occurred here, right at this castle."

He leads me to a flight of steps, unevenly cut from stone, up to the castle wall.

"The Moryns tried to enter the castle by climbing up the wall, but we shot them down using arrows that had explosives attached to the ends. Still, casualties amounting to thousands were recorded on both sides. Irrevocable damage was done to the city despite our eventual victory, so my ancestors decided to relocate to the second largest city, which is now the capital where we live."

I gaze at the great expanse of grass that stretches in front of me, ending in a thick forest. Hundreds of years ago, there must have been bloodied bodies lying all over the battlefield or floating on the moat. I shudder and turn away.

"The war sounds awful, but it seems you did a good job patching up the damage. If you didn't tell me about Moryn, I wouldn't have known there was a war here."

"My grandfather decided to turn the castle into a sightseeing attraction, and he commanded to restore it to its original state. It took many years, but eventually, we succeeded. He was highly unpopular with the people, but there were a few things that he did right during his reign. This is one of them. Castle Enrilth has brought in much revenue from both Athelian and foreign visitors, and it has helped many people learn more about our history."

A while later, we start down the steps. Edward wants to show me the great mead hall where the ancient Athelians used to celebrate festivities—or in other words, occasions that gave them the excuse to get drunk.

"So, what's your relationship with Moryn now?"

"Currently, we maintain pretty good relations with them. Our forefathers worked hard, establishing schools and offering handsome rewards to professionals. It was not long before steam technology was discovered, and that made a huge difference in our industries. In fact, we are arguably much stronger and more developed now. The Moryn Empire is still splendid, but no longer is it the most powerful nation in our world. They would never dare to initiate a war if the same tensions occurred again."

"I guess that Moryn still has a monarchy?"

"They certainly do. In fact, their monarchy retains a lot more executive authority than us. I suppose you know that for Athelia, it is the parliament, not the royal family, that wields political power?"

I nod. *The Ugly Stepsister* had mentioned Katriona and Edward working together to pass a child labor law in the parliament.

"Won't your parents prefer that you marry a Moryn princess?"

Edward laughs. "Their princess is currently five years old. Were she eligible, I will not deny that my parents would encourage the idea of a marriage alliance." He regards me gravely. "However, it makes no difference. I would have chosen you, even if Moryn has a hundred princesses."

I have an urge to laugh and chide him at the same time. "Don't be ridiculous, Edward. I'm just an ordinary girl, not one in a thousand."

"Ordinary?" He taps my temple lightly. "You've always fascinated me with your otherworldly ideas. But it wasn't the same with you. I could not attract you the same way you attracted me. My position as the crown prince, I frankly admit, makes it unlikely for any unattached woman to reject me. But you are different. You see Athelia as undeveloped, oppressive, and even brutal. You didn't care that I was royal. No matter how I tried to get your attention, your priority remained with your family." He stares at a large tapestry hanging on the wall, which depicts a group of people hunting a stag. No wonder there's a stag's head hanging on top of the mead hall. "How is your family now, by the way?"

"Are you asking me about my family?" I ask, surprised.

He nods. "Tell me." I sense there is something that he isn't saying, but I don't know how to ask.

"Well, we're doing fine. Better than several years ago, actually. Mom got a new job, and she is going out with this guy called Ryan. And Paige is going to Australia after she graduates."

"Australia? Is that the place that your school has an exchange program with?"

"Yeah, but they discontinued it. Paige is going to study there as a full-time college student." I lift my chin. "She wants to become a doctor."

"A doctor?" He gives me an incredulous stare, then shakes his head. "Ah, I should know that it is not uncommon for a woman to practice medicine in your world. How long will it take?"

"Five to six years at school, two years of pre-vocational training, and then she gets to register as a medical practitioner. But she could need further training, depending on what she'll specialize in. Why do you ask?"

He seems to be turning over my information in his mind, and although his expression is not an open book, nevertheless, I can sense that my answer has relieved him. Maybe I should have lied. I'm sure he'd be more willing to let me go if Mom was still working herself crazy, or if Paige was still a kid. Or if I had already married Jason. But then, what if I'm stuck here forever? What if I have no chance of seeing the ones I love?

I slip my hand out of Edward's and sit down on one of the long benches. Suddenly, the fun of touring

76

the castle has faded away. What if I never see my family again? What if Jason is still searching frantically for me, after I disappeared from his house?

Someone makes an oomph sound, and Bertram enters the hall, rubbing his forehead. I guess he entered through the servant's door, which is unfortunately smaller. I wonder if the size was constructed on purpose, or if the servants that lived in the past were, on average, shorter.

"Your Highness! Forgive me for barging in, but the mayor of Enrilth is waiting. They have a welcome party   for   you."

8

An alarmingly large group of villagers is waiting outside when we emerge from the castle. Cheers, whistling, and clapping echo in the air, and bunches of flowers are tossed over our carriage. It's kind of sweet, honestly, and it shows that Edward is beloved by his people. He may be a tad domineering and possessive, at least for my standards, but I have to admit he seems a good ruler.

When we arrive at the mayor's house, Edward tells me what I should do when greeting them. "Don't shake hands with anyone. Steeple your fingers together, place your hands on your stomach, and incline your head gracefully."

"Princesses are not supposed to do that?"

"A lady does not shake hands. She curtsies when introduced, but since you are higher ranked than any of them, all you have to do is bow your head."

"Okay." I practice what he tells me, but the head-inclining feels horribly pretentious. I don't have years of royal training like him. "This is so hard to get right."

"Don't worry. It is well known that you behave awkwardly when it comes to propriety and manners. Also, do not say 'okay.' That word does not exist in our vocabulary."

"Okay," I say automatically, which causes both of us laugh. "Sorry."

This is going to be fun.

***

The mayor is an old man with white tufts of hair and a friendly smile. I nearly put out my hand, but I remember I'm a princess. "What an honor it is to have the prince and princess here for dinner. Come right in. You must be exhausted and hungry from touring the castle."

The mayor's wife is a plump, rosy-cheeked woman who looks much younger than her husband. She appears rather nervous when we enter, wiping her hands on a big green apron now and then, and she keeps apologizing for her cooking.

"Afraid that our country meals are too simple after what you're used to at the palace," she says, flustered.

I had a full breakfast, but surprisingly, the homemade pasta topped with cheese and smoked bacon is so good that I finish my dish in mere minutes.

"Simple is good," I say earnestly. "I wouldn't

know what to do if I had more than one fork and one knife. Besides, this tastes like . . ." I clamp my mouth shut. I was going to say that the food tastes just like Jason's homemade mac & cheese. "This tastes really good. May I have a second helping?"

The mayor and mayor's wife are both pleased and embarrassed.

"You're such a nice lady," the mayor says. "We knew His Highness since he was a boy, and we couldn't be happier when he found himself a bride."

Edward smiles, but it seems a bit strained. "I'm fortunate, indeed, to have found Kat."

I blush. Just at that moment, there comes a knock at the door, and a tall young man enters. He is about Edward's age, I think, dressed simply in a white shirt and black pants.

"Liam, m' boy!" the mayor exclaims. "Was there too much traffic on the road? Anyhow, you're just in time to meet our new princess."

The mayor's wife hastens to ladle a dish while the mayor pulls out a chair.

"This is indeed a wonderful surprise." Edward gets up, and he and the young man clap each other on the shoulder. It looks like they are good friends, though *The Ugly Stepsister* never mentioned any of Edward's friends other than Henry. "Let me introduce you to my bride. Kat, this is Liam, the mayor's grandson."

The young man called Liam greets me with a spark of interest in his leaf green eyes. He's about the same height as Edward, but he is much leaner, like a walking pole. He wouldn't look out of place with the guys in my computer science class. "An honor to meet you, Your Highness."

"Liam and I both grew up together. When we were twelve, however, I moved to the capital while he went to secondary school. He is now a university student, studying biology and sciences. Henry once took classes with him."

"Call me Kat," I say, offering him a warm smile. "A friend of Edward's is a friend of mine. And it's so nice to meet someone who also went to college."

Confusion appears in Liam's face. Immediately, I realize the error of my words.

"What Kat meant is that she wishes to study in the university," Edward quickly says. "She is very fond of books, you see. I had to install several bookshelves in our rooms, or she wouldn't have accepted my proposal."

"Indeed," Liam says, though he gives me a curious glance. "I assure you, Princess . . . Kat, that you are not missing much."

Everyone laughs, and Edward explains to me, "For many, the university is more of a place to cultivate connections rather than to acquire serious knowledge."

"Well then, I doubt the princess shall have time for extra education, even if they let her in," the mayor's wife says, slicing more bread and placing the pieces on a plate. "Especially when she gives birth to an heir. She won't have much time for anything."

I try very hard to keep a straight face. It's going to be really troublesome if people keep expecting me to get pregnant.

"Excuse me, Susan, but I believe the princess is one of a kind," Liam says. "Not every noble lady can write articles on social issues, not to mention interviewing factory children and writing about them."

I remember that in *The Ugly Stepsister*, Katriona had published an article called The Curse of the Factory System. Or, should I say, *I* had published it. Come to think of it, it seems impossible that I could have done the task. Breaking into a factory and knocking out an adult male and interviewing child workers? I sound amazing, even to myself.

"His Highness chose her from thousands of girls." The mayor pokes Liam with a walking stick. "I only hope that you have the good fortune to meet someone half as remarkable as our princess."

"I doubt I would be so fortunate," Liam says with a smile that doesn't reach his eyes. "Edward always has the best."

Am I imagining it, or is there a drop of jealousy or resentment in his tone?

***

Whenever I imagined what my honeymoon would be like, I had pictured somewhere sunny and relaxing. Possibly a Caribbean cruise. I fancy a glorious day reclining in a chair, sipping a margarita, and enjoying the hot, salty sea air. Jason would be next to me, spouting some obscure physics knowledge, and when

I get bored, I'd shut him up with my lips. I didn't expect that in reality, my honeymoon would consist of a crash course in royal knowledge.

Since Liam asked me about the articles I wrote, Edward insisted that in order for me to play my role more convincingly, I must be filled in on the knowledge gap, which includes everything an Athelian princess must know. While I know some events that transpired earlier, thanks to countless re-reads of *The Ugly Stepsister*, I've no idea about many other details, such as the history of Athelia or the customs of receiving guests.

"When is my father's birthday?" Edward asks one evening. After dinner, he summoned Amelie and told her to relay to all servants that he wished to retire early with me and would have no need for any services. I wonder what the servants would say if they could see me now.

"Um . . ." I think frantically about what he had told me earlier. "Some date in December—the 7th? Or is it the 17th?"

"The 27th," he says, rubbing a hand on his forehead. "And it's in January, not December. When did the historic battle with Moryn occur? The one over the dispute of the string of islands along our western coast?"

"Um . . ."

"Where is the soup spoon's position during a five-course meal?"

"Next to the soup bowl?"

"Next to the salad fork."

I groan and hold up my hands. "I surrender. I'll never learn how to be a princess."

"Nonsense. It is only a matter of time before you can memorize the details. Besides, if you have trouble remembering, you can always give me a hint. It is not like you are taking an exam."

"But I can't behave like a princess." I plop on a couch and blow out my cheeks. "I can't act all regal and aristocratic—something *you* can pull off without trying."

"That is less of a problem than you may expect. It is well known at court that you have difficulty carrying yourself as a conventional princess. Very few nobles have not heard of your performance during your presentation."

It takes a few seconds before I realize what he is talking about. "Did I really fall on my butt in front of your mother?"

"There is no need to be alarmed, Kat. Although you may make mistakes, she genuinely loves you. As do I."

"I thought you promised no flirting when we're alone." I keep my eyes focused on my hands.

"I wasn't. I was merely stating a fact."

I wonder how he manages to keep a straight face while saying that. "I don't know what I ever saw in you," I grumble. Which only causes him to look amused.

"A great deal, love. Otherwise, you wouldn't have married me."

I roll my eyes. Who would have thought that this

guy, who rarely cracks a smile when the servants talk to him, would turn out to be a huge flirt? "Next question."

Edward continues to drill me with royal princess stuff until I start to yawn. My "jet lag" symptoms are much better by now, but I still need at least nine hours of sleep, plus a half-hour nap.

"We'll continue tomorrow," Edward says. He writes something in his pocket book and sets it carefully on the mantelpiece of the fireplace. "I have arranged for us to go picnicking in the forest, so we'll have plenty of time alone."

"Are . . . are you going to sleep there again?" I blurt. Having peeked into the changing room, it seems awfully small and stuffy for Edward. My conscience suffers when I imagine him lying in there, tossing and turning, or even sneezing. After all, this is his house.

He raises an eyebrow, but he doesn't speak, like he's anticipating what I might say.

"Let me switch places with you. I'm shorter than you, so I'll be able to fit in—"

"Absolutely not." His voice is curt, leaving no room for argument. "Either I sleep in the adjoining room or share the bed with you. Your choice."

Yeah, right. If I sleep with him, I doubt it can be just, you know, sleeping. In fact, I doubt any sleeping would be going on.

I stalk to the bed and pull up the blankets until only my hair spills on the pillow. He sighs, so faintly that I wonder if my ears are deceiving me. A moment later, the door of the changing room swings shut.

Guilt assaults me, even though I tell myself I have nothing to be guilty for. At the same time, I find myself wishing that I didn't have to treat him so unfeelingly. Especially if what he said was true—how can I blame him for wanting me to stay? But staying here is simply out of question. By now, Mom and Paige would have known that I've disappeared. They'd definitely be frantic with worry. My picture is probably somewhere in the news, and Jason might be questioned, since it is at his place that I went missing.

I've got to get home.

I roll over to the other side and contemplate my chances. What can I do when there's no cellphone or internet? I guess I can only wait until I get back to the palace, but I'm not optimistic. I remember that array of guards, like a solid wall, marching in our procession. And even now in Enrilth, there are at least a dozen servants—housekeeper, stewards, maids, stable hands—to wait on us. There will only be more people when we return.

"Girlie, open your eyes. It's time to wake up."

9

A peculiar voice that sounds neither male nor female is speaking into my ear.

"Wake up!" Someone pulls my blankets down, and I feel a sharp tug on my ear.

"Ow!" I open my eyes and receive a huge shock. Hovering before my eyes is an unnatural being with an ugly squashed face and pointed ears. His skin is a hideous mottled green, and his eyes, huge and yellow and bulbous, take up nearly half his face. He has his arms crossed, and he looks down at me with annoyance.

What?

"Took me ages to finally find you," the creature grumbles. "Who would have known that Eddie would have taken you this far?"

"Who are you?" I sit up, fully awake. "Actually, what are you?" I pinch my arm, but nothing happens. I am still awake, in the dark room with only moonlight streaming in through the curtains.

The creature peers at me, his large yellow eyes blinking. "You really have lost your memory. Too bad we haven't enough magic to restore it." With a resigned air, he snaps his fingers, and poof! A book appears in midair. On the cover is a red-haired girl in a gorgeous dress.

The Ugly Stepsister.

"How did you get my book?" I rub my eyes, but both book and goblin are still there. You'd think that waking up in a strange world is bizarre enough, but apparently, this craziness knows no end.

"Wrong. This is our book, not yours. It's the property of Barthelius, our king."

I don't understand. He seems to read my thoughts, for he clicks his fingers again and the book flips open. There is a small whirring noise as the book flips itself to the last page, where the prince and the ugly stepsister get married.

"That's you," the goblin says. "Yes, don't look at me like I'm mad. That girl standing on the altar is you. Didn't you find yourself married when you re-entered Athelia?"

What Edward had told me that night comes roaring back to me now. I came into this world because I ripped a book. Can it be . . .? No, it's impossible, but with a goblin bouncing in the air and my book flipping its pages on its own, nothing seems impossible at the moment.

"Katherine Wilson," the goblin says. "We must get you back to the human world. You shouldn't be here."

I can't believe my ears. All this time, I've been waiting to find a chance to get back, and this goblin that can perform magic is offering to help me? "You know my real name," I say slowly. "You know that I don't belong here!" Then something clicks in my head. "You are the goblin that Edward was asking me about. You're the one responsible for bringing me into Athelia when I was in high school! You're . . . you're . . ."

"Krev. The one and only."

There is no mention of a goblin in *The Ugly Stepsister*. Nevertheless, his name sounds familiar.

"Now, girlie, listen up. You've already made a mess of Athelia's history, so in order not to let you wreak any more havoc, we need to get you back."

Not even Beethoven's 9th Symphony Orchestra can sound sweeter to my ears.

"You can help me get home? Right now?"

"Remember how you came into this world?"

The book, still floating in the air, gives me an idea. "Before I came to this world . . . the book appeared in Jason's room, and I was drawn to it." I look up, hope soaring in my chest. "So, you can get me back by traveling through this book?"

"It was powerful magic that brought you here." He blows out his cheeks and shakes his head. "Don't know if the spell Barthelius gave me will work, but let's give it a try."

Krev tells me to leave the bed and stand by the window. My heart pounding with excitement, I do what he tells me. But then I remember Edward, who is still sleeping in the changing room. "Wait," I say, and reach for a pen and paper. No matter what, I owe him an explanation before I go. Quickly, I scribble a message that I will be going home.

"Girlie!" Krev bellows. "Make haste. The spell won't last long!"

He starts to chant some incomprehensible words, and the book begins to glow. A current surrounds me, a magnetic force pulls me toward the book, and my feet leave the ground.

There's a thud in the room, but I don't look back. I'm finally going back to Portland. No more of this bizarre princess roleplaying. A twinge of guilt and sorrow pricks me when I think of Edward.

Goodbye. I'm sorry that I'm leaving you without saying goodbye to you in person, but I'm just an ordinary girl from the States. Whatever past we had will have to remain in the past. Find another bride. There must be plenty of girls eager to replace me.

A sturdy arm encircles my waist, pulling me back to the ground. I struggle and twist as hard as I can, but Edward's grip is like a bar of iron around me.

"Let me go!" I snarl. "Get your hands off me!"

He loosens his hold, but his arms remain around me. Horrified, I watch the book shrivel up into a tiny cloud the size of my palm. I leap up and make a wild grab at it, but it vanishes.

"Wait!" I sob. "Don't abandon me! Krev, where are you? I need you to take me back home!"

The goblin reappears where the book has

disappeared, a flash of regret on his face.

"Sorry, girlie," Krev says, "You'll have to wait till next time."

"What do you mean, *next time*? Can't you cast your spell again?"

"Borg's magic is too strong for my spell to work. I have to go back to the king and figure out how we can bring you back another time. Don't panic, okay? We'll get you out of here soon enough."

"But I have to get home . . ."

He doesn't listen to me. The goblin just gives me a wave and disappears in a puff of smoke.

I can't let him leave like that. I open the window and rush out in my bare feet. There's nothing outside, only the moon and stars against the huge black canopy of night sky.

I can't freaking believe it. I was so close to leaving this place! And Krev didn't even tell me when he'll come back. Frustrated, I feel like throwing myself off the balcony, but there's no energy left in my body. I sink down against the balustrade, unable to keep the tears from flowing.

Edward crouches in front of me.

"Kat?" He tries to wipe my tears away with his thumb. "Kat, calm down. Tell me what happened."

I shove him away and give him the nastiest glare I can manage. "Stay away from me," I hiss. "If you didn't just interfere, I would have been able to go home! You've ruined my chance to get back to my own world!"

His eyes widen for a second and his lips move, but

no sound comes out.

"We'd better go inside," he suddenly says. "You will catch cold in that nightgown, and besides, there are servants sleeping in the house. We cannot let them overhear us."

He grabs my arm and drags me indoors, shutting the door firmly behind us.

"Forgive me," he says, lighting one of the lamps. "When I saw you levitating, I assumed your life was in danger. There was no way to know otherwise."

"Didn't you see the goblin?"

He shakes his head. "Nothing—all I saw was you rising into the air. I had to pull you back. On my life, I can never let any harm come to you. I had no idea that you were trying to leave me and return to your world."

I don't care how hot he is. I don't care that he's in love with me. All I know is that he stepped in and prevented my returning home. "Go away."

But my words fall on deaf ears. Edward simply folds his arms and sits on an armchair. "Not before you explain how you rose from the ground. Seldom have I believed that magic exists, but when it comes to you . . ." he rubs a hand over his forehead. "Was it Krev who came to take you away to America?"

"*Back* to America," I correct him.

Alarm flashes in his face. "Did he offer any explanation why he sent you back to me? And why is he coming to take you away, when you've only been here for a few days? What's going on?"

I simply wrap my arms around my torso and look

away. I'm still frustrated and mad—I was SO CLOSE to getting home.

"Kat." Edward strides toward me. Ignoring my attempt to back away, he clamps both hands on my shoulders, forcing me to look at him. "I understand that you are disappointed, but answer me this—do you believe me now? Can you deny that we have met previously?"

Reluctantly, I meet his gaze. Those eyes—hazelnut flecked with gold—cause a sharp jolt in my mind. As much as I want to say no, I have to admit that his face *is* familiar, though I still have no idea how and when we were acquainted.

I nod.

He sighs, obviously relieved, and releases his hold. "I realize you are anxious to go home. No matter what you feel for me, your attachment to your family remains your first priority. That was why I had to let you leave the first time. But now" —he takes my hands— "circumstances are different. Your mother found another suitor. Your sister will be attending school far away. Couldn't you consider a life with me?"

The intensity in his tone and gaze startles me. "But I already . . ."

"I understand that you also have a suitor in your world." He presses a kiss on the back of my hand before I can stop him. "Promise me that you will do your best to regain your memory. If you do remember our past and still wish to leave, then I shall not stand in your way. But you must promise me—even if the

93

goblin shows up—you won't leave with him until you remember."

I swallow. How could I make such a promise when I've just narrowly missed my chance to go home?

"Say yes." He pins me with his intense gaze. "You owe me a second chance, Kat."

If Krev *does* appear and I still haven't regained my memory, it's going to be tough to refuse leaving with him. And I desperately want to go back. Besides, Krev stated that I shouldn't be in Athelia. Even if I tell Krev I cannot leave, what's to prevent the goblin from forcefully transporting me back to America? *I* was powerless when the book brought me to Athelia.

Reluctantly, I nod.

He closes his arms around me. I'm too tired to struggle, but I am as rigid as a block of wood. "I know you must hate me now," he says, his lips moving over my hair. "But I do not regret what I did. I simply cannot let you go when your impression of me is that of a stranger."

10

It is time to return to the palace. Nervous and tense, I continue practicing on the train. In the capital, there will be a lot more servants and guards, plus his parents, relatives, and members of the aristocracy. Moreover, as it's early summer, we are approaching the height of the Season, which means more parties, outings, balls, etc. Basically, events that I wish I could get myself out of. Katriona was a gauche young lady, but it had to be easier when everyone's attention was on Bianca, the movie-star glamorous sister. Now that I'm princess, it'll be difficult not to draw attention.

Once we get off the train, a camera goes off. Several reporters are gathered around the platform. Geez. This new celebrity status is really annoying. Edward puts his arm around my shoulders and whisks me toward a carriage with the skill of a celebrity's bodyguard.

I grasp the folds of my gown and take a deep

breath. Frankly, I am not sure if I can pull off this princess role—my head is still bursting from all the cramming I had to do. At the same time, I *am* kind of curious. You know, when I was a kid, like many girls, I imagined myself like one of the princesses in those storybooks. Mom dressed me up in a pink tulle skirt for Halloween when I was four. She kept a picture frame on the table until I got embarrassed about seeing it, especially when Paige also had her own princess picture taken. She looks so much better than I do in pink.

I never expected that my childhood playacting could be realized like *The Princess Diaries*, except I'm married to a prince.

The carriage stops at a stupendously huge courtyard. Edward takes my hand and squeezes my fingers. He doesn't say anything, but the warm pressure implies that he will stand by me, no matter what happens. Feeling slightly more reassured, I mimic his posture—straight back, raised chin, steady gaze—and try to walk as steadily as I can in my huge gown.

The palace is a maze of winding stairs, marble corridors, arched galleries, and ornate rooms. I try very hard not to gawk when we enter through the main entrance. The gates are huge, just like a movie's, and require at least four people to pull them open. A grand staircase inlaid with gold and carpeted in crimson takes my breath away. Servants either bow or curtsy to us when we pass. Hopefully, my face doesn't give too much away. It's not easy pretending that I've lived in this palace for months.

Then, for what seems like hours, we stop outside a cream-gold door. Edward signals to Bertram, who produces a set of jingling brass keys.

"Is this our room?" I ask.

"Our rooms, in fact," he says, unlocking the door. "Welcome home, darling."

I put a hand over my mouth to stifle my gasp. In front of me is a beautiful sitting room that wouldn't look out of place at the Ritz. It's a suite, actually, and as Edward guides me through the rooms, I truly feel privileged.

My jaw drops at sight of the bedroom. The ceiling is so high that I feel like a dwarf. The bed is so much grander than the one in Enrilth, with its ivy green headboard, embroidered gold heraldry, and a violet satin canopy complete with golden tassels. Heat engulfs my mind when I imagine the possibility of Edward getting into that bed with me and letting down the canopy and . . .

"We have separate bedrooms," Edward says, as though sensing my concern. "Previously, I thought I would end up with Katriona Bradshaw, and I was glad that we need not share a bed. But now . . ." He stares at me as though I am on the dinner menu. "I wish I had not agreed to this traditional layout."

I flush at the implication of his words. Geez, Kat, you're past twenty. You're not an inexperienced school girl. It's ridiculous to be so easily affected by his words, which aren't even explicit.

"This place is beautiful," I say, glad that my voice

is steady, normal. "But it's too grand. I don't think I can be comfortable here. I'm too awed at so much splendor."

"Perhaps this will make you feel more at home."

He leads me to an adjoining room. It's furnished like an office, with a cherrywood desk and bookshelves that cover an entire wall. To my delight, there's a comfy-looking padded seat installed under the windows. Outside is a magnificent view of the palace gardens. Sunlight streams into the room, illuminating the silken cushions on the window seat and the rosewood floor. I could imagine myself sitting on that seat, knees drawn up, a book propped up in front of me.

"Oh . . ." I breathe, feeling seriously overwhelmed. "Look at that window, and the view down there—it's too freaking awesome. I could stay here all day long."

"You could stay here forever."

Oh, how I wish he wouldn't say those heart-melting things. It makes me feel horribly heartless. Every time he flirts, every time I look up and catch him staring at me with desire in his eyes, it feels like I *have* to love him or the world would come to an end.

I turn away from the window. No matter how breathtaking the view is, it belongs to a royal family, a family that I am still reluctant to associate with.

"Your Highness." Amelie's crisp voice floats into the room. "Pardon me, but it's time to get dressed for dinner."

I glance at my attire. I'm wearing a lovely apple green gown embroidered with white roses, and I have a string of pearls around my neck. My hair isn't as tidy as when Amelie arranged it in the morning, but it's hardly inadequate for a meal.

"We're dining with my parents," Edward says, as though guessing what I'm thinking.

"The Duke of Somerset will be attending as well," Amelie adds. "It's best that you wear something more formal."

In Enrilth, I ate with Edward most of the time, whether it may be breakfast served in the bedroom, dinner in the dining room, or a picnic in daisy-dotted fields. The thought of dining with his parents and other nobles, when my memories of them are non-existent, makes me anxious and nervous.

Edward looks at me with a concerned expression. "Are you feeling all right, Kat?"

I have a sudden urge to plead absence on an upset stomach or a splitting headache. His eyes seem to indicate that if I were less inclined to attend dinner, he'll think up some excuse for me.

No. On the train, Edward had told me we usually have breakfast with his parents in the morning, and occasionally, we must receive foreign guests or high-level dignitaries. Even if I can get out of this dinner, there will be countless other non-private meals. I might as well deal with this sooner than later.

"Perfectly fine." I attempt to appear confident by smiling at him. "I'll see you in a moment. It won't do to keep the king—our parents—waiting."

Edward looks both pleased and relieved, especially when I say 'our parents.'

Amelie leads me to my bedroom and into the changing room, which looks like a salon for trying on wedding apparel. Dozens—no, hundreds—of gowns hang from racks on three sides of the room. Gowns of every color on a palette. Gowns with lace, ribbons, frills, and even puffed sleeves that look as big as balloons. Gowns that range from simple to sophisticated, for every purpose imaginable.

Wow. I could hold my own fashion show, Victorian style.

With her typical efficiency and competence, Amelie dresses me in a gorgeous lavender bodice with a row of diamond buttons running down the front and layered skirts trimmed with exquisite laces and ribbons. My hair is twisted into an elegant chignon, held together by numerous pearl-tipped pins. My collarbone and arms are powdered, and a glittering diamond pendant that matches my buttons is fastened around my neck. It feels like I'm going to attend some old-fashioned beauty pageant. I might even be crowned princess of the—hang on, I'm already a princess.

When I join Edward later, the air seems to be sucked out of my lungs. He's dressed in a black silk suit and white shirt, a pristine white cravat around his neck, and a single red rose peeking from his coat pocket. Basically, everything about him is immaculately done. It's like he's taking me to the prom.

"Um." For a moment, I'm unsure what to say.

He smiles, seemingly amused at my cluelessness,

and holds out his arm. "May I have the honor of escorting you to dinner, my lady?"

I can't help it, I burst out laughing. "The pleasure is all mine, my lord." I try to sound as snobbish as possible, but I have trouble trying not to contain my laughter.

He leans toward me, but not before glancing at Amelie, who promptly leaves the room. Was that a cue to give us some privacy?

I withdraw my hand, but he slips a folded paper between my fingers.

"It's a reminder," he whispers. "Try to memorize as much as you can."

***

When we arrive at the dining room, my nervousness threatens to overwhelm me again. The table only seats about ten, but still, it's the fanciest place I've ever been to. White tablecloths are covered by an extra layer of crimson velvet, candlesticks burn in silver holders, crystal vases overflow with roses and ferns, tableware is polished and glistening, and of course, an entourage of servants stand ready in royal crimson-and-gold uniforms and the most banal expressions I've ever seen, like they're part of the furniture.

Okay, Kat. You can do this. Edward had covered royal protocol on the train.

Who am I kidding? I've already forgotten half of what he said. And given the situation, it's going to be even harder to remember.

Trying hard not to act like a country bumpkin, I move toward the dinner table with the grace of a robot. A servant pulls out my chair, and I sit down gingerly. I shake the napkin—a bit more vigorously than necessary—and spread it across my lap. Using the napkin as a cover, I glance at the cheat sheet that Edward created for me.

The king and queen. I've seen them at the wedding, so even though they've shed the crowns, I can still recognize them. Plus, Edward told me they always occupy the head of the table. The king is well past middle-age, with graying hair and evident crows-feet, but his features are still handsome enough to star in a Bond film. It's obvious where Edward got his looks. The queen, on the other hand, isn't dazzlingly beautiful, but she has a pleasant face that makes her seem likable and approachable. I feel slightly more at ease. My in-laws seem nice enough.

I also have no problem recognizing Henry right away. Even without Edward's note, I know from the book that his cousin has doe-like eyes and curly hair. Henry smiles at me, a sweet, affectionate smile that immediately makes me warm up toward him.

Next to Henry sits a woman with dangling earrings and peacock feathers in her hair. From the bossy way she interacts with Henry, she must be the duchess, also known as Lady Petunia. She's the one who is greatly opposed to Elle's relationship with Henry in *The Ugly Stepsister*. Our gaze meets briefly, and she deals me a stiff nod.

I consult my note again and locate Duke Philip

102

(Edward's oldest cousin) and Constance (Philip's wife), along with a few other dukes and duchesses.

"Welcome home," the king says in an affable tone.

I bite my lip hard, as though gnawing on my lip will calm my nerves. Edward grasps my right hand under the table. He looks at me, his gaze steadfast and calm. "Relax," he mouths.

It's easy for you to say that, I want to retort. The fanciest dinner I've ever been to is this French restaurant that Ryan treated us to in Chicago. Paige and I were a bit overwhelmed, but we eventually loved it and even made fun of the numerous forks and spoons. This meal I'm sitting down to now—let's just say a dinner with the president seems more palatable.

It's hard enough getting through dinner with all those royals sitting around you, trying to fake it like you're one of them. Even harder is that the tableware is mostly made of china and crystal—why can't they use good ol' plastic or stainless steel or wood? Wait, they probably haven't even invented plastic or stainless steel.

I manage to get through the appetizer and soup without any mishap. I copy what everyone does—breaking off bread instead of biting into it, and using the pieces to wipe off soup remains. Since I'm afraid that something stupid will come out of my mouth, I chew my food and pretend that I'm just choosing not to speak, but if I did, I'd say something brilliant.

"Kat," the queen says with a twinkle in her eyes. "How did you find Enrilth?"

103

I have no choice but to answer. Luckily, this is an easy one. "I loved it. It's such a pretty village, and the house is so cozy, it reminds me of a bed-and-breakfast place we stayed in at Itha . . ." Edward nudges my elbow. Dang, I've been babbling about my own world.

"Bed-and-breakfast place?" The king furrows his brow. "Is that some new-fangled term that you young people have coined? What does it signify?"

"Just . . . er . . . just a nice place to stay at, Your Majesty . . . I mean, Father," I stammer, wishing that I could dive under the table.

"I'm glad you found Enrilth House to your liking, Katriona. I hope that it allowed you to rest fully," the queen says. "We were so worried when you fainted away at the wedding."

"She needs to strengthen her constitution," the duchess remarks. "After all, it is her duty to bear the future heir to the throne. I suggest that Katriona halts pursuing her interests in trivial matters . . . such as running that school for girls."

What school? I thought it was Elle who opened a school.

"It is my duty as well," Edward says calmly. His hand moves subtly, re-arranging my salad fork in the correct position. "Besides, if bearing an heir is the only requirement for my wife, then I needn't have held the ball. Any girl would do."

Despite my reluctance to marry a stranger when I already have a boyfriend, my heart thaws upon hearing him say those words. I've only been here for a short time, but from what I remember of *The Ugly Stepsister* and from what I've learned of Athelian culture so far, it takes guts to defy tradition.

The duchess, however, doesn't look impressed. "Naturally, as a member of the royal family, one must be selective when choosing a bride." She glances in the direction of Henry, who colors and focuses on his plate of roast beef and garlic potatoes. In the book, Henry was attracted to Elle. She isn't invited, so they aren't married yet. I wonder if they are still together.

I cannot help but breathe a sigh of relief when dinner is finished. Despite the fact that no one suspected me (I hope so. It's not easy deciphering their well-mannered, etiquette-trained expressions), I don't know how much longer I can keep pretending I am Katriona.

11

Back in our bedroom, after Amelie stripped me of the fancy clothes (whoever invented that bustle thing and the S-shaped corset is sadistic) and I've taken a hot bath, thanking God there's modern plumbing here, I dart a quick glance at the door. After dinner, Edward had told me to go ahead and return to our suite, as he had some business to take care of. I wonder when he's coming back. While I still don't want to go to bed with him (I'm honest. I swear), I don't like the idea of him sneaking around the palace at night. After all, we are newlyweds.

Pulling a shawl over my white silk nightie, I tiptoe into the sitting room. There is a cuckoo clock hanging on the polished oak wall, showing that it's a quarter to ten. A few minutes later, there is the sound of a key turning in the lock, and the main door to our suite swings open.

Edward comes in, his tread firm and assured. An aura of satisfaction seems to surround him. My speculation about him going off to some other place is instantly shot down.

"Kat." The corners of his mouth curve when he sees me pacing on the carpet. "Have you been waiting for me?"

"I . . ." To tell the truth, I *have* wondered where he went instead of coming back to the suite with me. But why should I care? I've been trying to keep him at arm's length, and if he chooses to seek solace with someone more receptive to his attentions, that will certainly make it easier for me to leave Athelia.

Edward steps closer to me, his eyes glowing with a combination of amusement and tenderness. There's a faint smell of alcohol emanating from him. I wonder how much he drank during dinner.

My heart beats faster. There's no mistaking the desire in his eyes. To be honest, my body definitely finds him attractive, though my mind still protests against sleeping with a guy I've only known for a week. Even if he is lawfully my husband in this world.

I retreat a step. The backs of my knees collide with a sofa, and I land on the velvet cushions with a thump. Edward settles next to me, close enough that my nightie rustles against his black trousers.

"Kat, sit still."

"Wha . . . what?"

"I need you to hold out your hand."

I blink at him. Taking advantage of my surprise, he simply draws my arm toward him, and before I can ask him what he's up to, I find myself staring at a glittering ring on my fourth finger.

That's why he disappeared. Before we boarded the train to Enrilth, Edward told Amelie to order a wedding ring for me. He went to see if it arrived— and here it is.

The ring is easily the most dazzling piece of jewelry I've ever seen. It's a rose-gold band, encrusted with three rows of sparkling diamonds of various sizes. My first instinct is that such a magnificent ring doesn't suit me, but before I can take it off, Edward places his hand on top of mine. His ring forms a perfect pair with the one he gave me.

"On no occasion should it leave your finger." He moves closer, and this time, I can no longer ignore the solid warmth of his body. His breath tickles my face, and I can smell the intoxicating scent of the amber-colored wine served at dinner. "That ring is worth a fortune."

"I'll take extra care with it."

"Worry not, love. If you ever lose it again, I shall have you working in the palace. I guarantee that it will take you an entire lifetime." His tone indicates that he very much looks forward to my working off the debt.

"Right. As if your country would allow a princess to—"

He places a hand on my cheek, attempting to turn my face to his. I could bet my newly acquired wedding ring that he wants to kiss me.

Panic races through me—what should I do? He is the most attractive man I've ever met. Everything about him, from his perfectly chiseled features to his immaculate apparel, places him in People's *Sexiest Man Alive* list, if such a thing exists in Athelia. Not to mention he is one of the richest men in the country, judging from the magnificence of the palace. He's the kind of guy who only exists in romance novels.

Come on, Kat. Technically, he is your husband in this world. What's the harm in one kiss?

But we're alone at night. The bedrooms are a few steps away. The prince is half-drunk and infatuated with me. Isn't it likely that one kiss will lead to another, and eventually, it'll end up with the two of us in bed?

Jason. My boyfriend's face appears in my mind—incredulous, disbelieving, outraged. What'll Jason say if he sees me now? Only one week, and I'm having thoughts about doing it with another guy? When I think of our conversation about *Outlander*, and him asking if I could prefer an anachronistic man over him . . . it's so ridiculously close to what's happening now that I could have laughed if the situation wasn't serious.

I push Edward away and try to stand up, but he captures my wrist. The alcohol must have weakened his self-control, and it's so hard not to feel bad when he's looking at me with raw desire, his fingers hot against my skin.

"Don't go."

I swallow hard. I already have a boyfriend. I should pretend I didn't hear him and lock myself in the bedroom. It's too risky staying here with the prince. But when I meet his eyes, filled with love and longing, I can't make myself walk away.

Try to steer him away from his object.

"I just want to get you a glass of water," I lie. "You look like you could use it."

And I rush to the side table before he can drag me back to the sofa. Thank God the maids left a pitcher. I pour him the water and come up with another idea. "I have a question about Henry."

That does the trick. Edward blinks, apparently confused to hear another man's name.

"And Elle. Does the duchess still disapprove of their marriage?"

Much to my relief, he gets up and takes the glass. When he drains it, his eyes seem more focused. Inwardly, I breathe a sigh of relief.

"What do you remember of them now?"

I scan my mind and try to recall the last few chapters of the book. "They're together? No, wait, it's an open ending. Elle isn't sure she wants to marry Henry yet, because she still needs time to think it over."

"You certainly have read the book many times."

I blush. "I told you it's one of my favorite stories. Anyway, you haven't answered my question."

"I am not fully certain about the reasons, but it might boil down to this—Elle is unable, and unwilling, to adapt to the lifestyle of a duchess, and Lady Petunia cannot tolerate it."

"The lifestyle of a duchess . . ." I glance at the sitting room, which is the most magnificent place I've been in. Friezes the color of pine trees decorate the walls, rock-crystal chandeliers hang from the rococo style ceiling, and red velvet armchairs are placed in front of a huge marble fireplace. Roses and heliotropes are everywhere, tastefully arranged in vases made of lapis-lazuli. It feels like I'm in a five-star Renaissance-style hotel. I wonder if I can adapt to the lifestyle of a princess.

"One reason is that Elle, being a former servant herself, is incapable of growing out of her role. She prefers to do tasks herself instead of delegating, supervising, or even giving orders."

I nod. I was also uncomfortable at Enrilth, seeing servants lugging pails of hot water up and down the stairs, all because they were preparing my bath.

"Why is the duchess so against Elle's . . . un-duchess behavior? She's no longer a servant, she's pretty and nice, and she is clearly attracted to Henry."

Edward sighs. "Do you know why there are so many rules for the aristocrats?"

Because they're nuts? "Because it's tradition and they don't want to change?"

"There has been a number of tradesmen striking gold in business. Some of them earn enough to rival a nobleman's fortune," Edward says slowly. "But the aristocracy wish to keep their circle exclusive. And so, they established numerous rules, such as what to observe when paying calls, what to wear for different meals and occasions, and what to write when corresponding. Failure to heed these codes of etiquette is a sign of ill breeding, and so, no matter how much you may make in mining or railroad stock, you will not be regarded as one of their crowd."

"Got it." I feel like I'm in history class.

"Another reason that could have made Lady Petunia uncommonly determined to adhere to tradition is because of Henry himself. His desire to be a doctor is not what a man of his station would do. An aristocrat does not work for a living. The taxes he collects from his lands would be sufficient. Therefore, Lady Petunia hopes that his bride might influence him and steer him in the right direction of a duke."

I have to smile. "Elle certainly is the exact opposite of her ideal daughter-in-law. But your family doesn't seem to have a problem with my behavior."

Edward grins. "They are more inclined to upholding middle-class values. Don't you worry, love. Rest assured that you will always have my family's support, as well as mine."

He's getting that heated look in his eyes again. I fish around for something else to say in case he starts advancing on me again.

"Hey, Edward . . . I mean, Edward. Do you mind telling me more about Athelia? I still can't remember anything, and I'm worried I might blunder again. You stopped me from blabbing at dinner, but what if you're not with me?"

He presses his lips together as realization sinks in. "That certainly is a concern. It would be highly undesirable for people to know you are mentally inflicted, especially when my grandfather is known to have gone mad. Let us proceed to the study, and I shall procure some books for you."

112

12

"Wake up, Your Highness."

I stir and burrow further into the pillow.

"Wake up!"

The curtain is pulled apart, and bright sunlight streams into the bedroom. I throw up a hand to shield my eyes.

Amelie tosses a pile of clothes on the bed. "It's a quarter past seven. His Highness is already up and dressed."

I grumble under my breath. It's the weekend, and I can't even hit snooze on my alarm clock. Here in Athelia, my maid is a human-sized alarm. I don't know how Edward manages it. I didn't get to sleep until two in the morning, as I'm still cramming Athelian culture, doing my best to appear that I have my memories intact.

I roll out of bed. It's a relief that the palace has modern plumbing, complete with running taps and flushing toilets. It's also a relief to get some privacy. I can bathe by myself without a dozen servants hanging around. Yawning, I stumble through the door and run into a solid wall.

"Good morning, dear wife."

I look up to see Edward, looking absolutely tempting in his pristine white shirt and black trousers. Images of the previous night come rushing back to me of how he had lost control and tried to kiss me. If I didn't come up with using Henry's name in time, I'm not sure how far he could have gone. Anyway, I have to keep him at arm's length. No way am I going to leave Jason for a guy I've only known for a week. I hope that Krev will hurry up and come take me home.

"Good morning," I say, ignoring his proffered hand. I open the door and start down the hallway.

Edward grabs my arm. "Do you even know where you're going? The dining room is the other way."

"Oops, my bad. Thanks." Discreetly, I yank my arm back. The problem with having no memory is that I can't even find a room by myself.

Edward takes my hand again. His grip is firm, and I can feel his wedding ring brush against mine. "Remember, we are newlyweds. It is rare that I should walk down the hallway without holding your hand." His breath is warm against my ear. "Act like we are deeply attached to each other."

"I . . ." It's so hard not to blush. "I'm a lousy actor."

"Nor am I good at faking my emotions. I can conceal, but I cannot contrive. Fortunately, I do not need to act."

I feel like holding up a sign saying, *No flirting when we're alone.*

***

Breakfast is scrumptious. The amount can't compare to the dozen-course dinner we had with the nobles last night, but every dish screams high-class, from the delicate salmon rolls topped with cream cheese, the butter shaped like roses, and the flaky croissants, to the freshly brewed coffee with a latte art of a crown on top. I've come a long way from making coffee in a ten-dollar machine at home.

It's a pity that I can't fully enjoy the food, for I'm still sleepy after the tiring day yesterday, starting from the train journey to the Athelian lesson at night.

"Katriona? Are you feeling all right?" The queen asks after I yawn for the third time.

"I'm fine," I answer without thinking. "It's just that Edward kept me up last night . . ."

I shut my mouth like a clam, realizing the implication of my words. The king drops his fork and the queen spills her tea. Edward, on the other hand, is trying to contain his laughter, judging by how his shoulders are shaking.

"Stop it," I whisper and jab my elbow into his arm, but the mirth remains in his eyes. Behind us, a servant's eye twitches. Perhaps I should have pretended nothing happened. After all, I have a royal dignity to maintain.

Needless to say, I'm so glad when breakfast is over, and not just because I feel like catching up on lost sleep.

Sweeping back to the suite, I try to look gracious and walk gracefully as the royal princess I'm supposed to be. Edward has to go to a council meeting with the king—I hope he's bored to death. Servants bow and curtsy when I pass, making me feel uncomfortable. There were house maids at Enrilth house, but they appeared to be more relaxed and carefree, while here in the palace, everyone is disciplined, formal, and well-trained. I feel like I've moved from a comfortable middle-class bed-and-breakfast place to the penthouse suite in an expensive Manhattan apartment building.

"Princess?" Amelie's voice interrupts me from my thoughts. "The suite is this way."

I give myself a mental shake. No matter when Krev may return, I've got to get my memory back. I'd do well to start by learning my way around the palace.

When I step into my room, I gasp. An avalanche of letters sits in our office. Amelie, who follows me into the room, places a mug of hot coffee on the gilt-edged mahogany desk and checks the pens and inkstand.

"There's no need to grimace, Your Highness," she says briskly. "You are now officially the princess. Besides, it isn't as bad as you may think, for this is the accumulation of one week's worth of letters. Two hundred and fifty-one, to be exact."

That's even more than the unread emails in my laptop.

"I need to see your dressmakers, so I had better be off. If you need anything, all you need is to ring up someone else." She points to a polished silver bell lying next to the lamp.

Amelie shuts the door. I scan the multiple stacks of letters, which are skillfully arranged according to their sizes, and consider tossing everything into the wastebasket. A tempting thought that lasts for . . . one second.

With a sigh, I plop on the mahogany chair in front of the desk. Just staring at the envelopes is making me feel tired already. I decide to start by sorting the letters first and then deciding which ones deserve priority. Pity I can't tag or color code them like emails.

My feet are feeling constricted by the leather boots I'm wearing—is it possible that my feet became larger during the seven years I was back in Chicago? Or maybe Katriona had smaller feet. I hope they don't have foot-binding here in Athelia. The corset is already a pain around my ribs.

"You are cordially invited to the costume party hosted by Lady Mansfield . . ."

"Your presence would be greatly appreciated at our grand opening . . ."

"We have reserved a special box in our theatre, and would be deeply honored if you would grace the opening night with your presence . . ."

Wow. I'm well on my way to becoming a social butterfly. Right. Lacking grace or charm, I feel more like a caterpillar that suddenly grew wings.

Is this going to be my future life? Endless parties and balls and openings and operas and plays? Am I really cut out to be a royal figure in this old-fashioned country?

Not all the letters are flattering. Turns out that being princess also means attracting a huge amount of junk mail. A few ask my opinion on current fashions, or does Edward snore when he sleeps—do they have privacy laws here?—or whether court presentations should start earlier in the day. Do I get to choose?

And, perhaps not surprising, hate mail that calls me a witch, a femme fatale, a fraud, and that I must have performed a seduction spell on the prince.

"Poor Edward, tethered to such a plain creature like you. It is a sore to the eyes seeing you sitting next to him on the carriage. I pity the child that takes after you."

Geez, overzealous fans exist in Athelia as well.

"The prince is the one doing the tethering," I mutter, crumpling up the letter and tossing it into the wastebasket.

One letter does catch my attention. It's hastily written, but the tone is warm and friendly, unlike the nauseatingly polite, formal wordiness of non-hate mail.

Dearest Kat, how happy I am that you finally married our prince! You looked lovely at the wedding, like a dream. Was your dress too tight? We were so shocked when you fainted after the ceremony was performed. Hope you're feeling better now. Enrilth is well-known as a relaxing getaway. I'd love to visit some time, but Jonathan insists I stay at home until the baby is born. Yours affectionately, Poppy.

Poppy. I remember her as Katriona's best friend in the book. She eloped with a lawyer, and Katriona even offered to be a witness at the runaway wedding. Now she's already expecting?

I rub my forehead. Edward has also mentioned that Poppy is the only other one whom I've divulged my real identity to. Given that I chose to marry Edward and stayed nine months at the palace till the wedding, I guess Poppy no longer remembers what I told her. She probably thought I was making things up.

I rest my chin on propped hands and sigh. It's nice to know that I have a real friend in Athelia, but I doubt it'll be a good idea to visit her. If she were my best friend, undoubtedly, we had shared a lot of stuff together. Poppy would be concerned or even suspicious if I act like I don't remember our past.

How much longer will it take before I can see Krev again?

I snag a piece of paper—gilt-edged, scented, with a fancy emblem on top—and start jotting down the number of days I've been in Athelia and connecting them to the days in America. I've been in Athelia for ten days. I guess my part-time job is as good as lost to me by now. As for Jason—I don't even want to think about what he's feeling now.

A blot of ink hits the paper, smudging a few of the dates, but I've already worked out that Paige's graduation ceremony is only a week away. I promised I'd be at her graduation.

I don't want to get used to court life. Yes, I know I'm lucky to have all those fancy dresses and having servants wait on me. But I'm too used to a middle-class lifestyle to enjoy those privileges. Honestly speaking, I feel useless that I can't even dress myself or do my own hair. Plus, I have no interest in socializing all day long. Even just sitting in that carriage, waving and smiling to the crowds, feels so awkward and shallow and boring.

More than ever, I want to leave Athelia, leave this overwhelming royal lifestyle. I want to be able to grab a coffee from Intelligentsia rather than ringing a bell for a maid. I want to waltz inside H&M and take my pick among racks of ready-made clothes instead of being taken to the tailors and seamstresses, who scrutinize and measure me like I'm some weird insect under a microscope. I want to go out on dates and get to know a hot guy better before committing myself to a relationship, rather than having one who is continuously reminding me that I belong to him.

A tear runs down my face, and I don't bother to wipe it away.

I want a normal life. I want to go home.

13

The sound of the door of our suite opening and closing disrupts my writing. I quickly crumple up the paper that contains the American dates and toss it into the wastepaper basket.

I wipe away my tears as fast as I can. "Come in."

Edward enters, and his gaze seems to soften when he sees me bent in front of the desk like I belong here.

"Hey." I look up at him and attempt a fake smile. "So, you're finished with your meetings and discussions already?"

"There is never an end unless I relinquish my claim to the throne. It is a luxury I am not allowed, being the only son. However, I'm allowed to have a break while morning tea is served."

Oh yes, Athelians are obsessed with tea time. How they manage to have morning tea *and* afternoon tea plus three meals a day, I will never comprehend.

"How are you faring, dear wife?"

"Great." I gesture toward the stacks of letters. "I don't think I've ever been more popular in my whole life."

He doesn't miss the sarcasm in my tone. "I wish that my position would not bring you this much extra work, Kat. Could you set aside those you have problems with? I have some free time this afternoon and will be able to assist you with them. Once you have regained your memory, you will be better equipped to deal with the letters."

I wonder how long it will take. I still can't remember a thing. Every time I try to think, my head aches. So far, I've managed to fool others, thanks to my knowing the book by heart and Edward stepping in or giving hints. Amelie probably has suspicions that I'm not quite the same, but she gives no sign of being concerned about it. But now that we've returned to the palace, where there are a lot more people who have interacted with me previously . . . I'm not sure how much longer we can keep up the charade if my memory doesn't return.

Edward holds his hand out to me, a gesture that I've become extremely familiar with over the short time I've met him. I'm somewhat surprised, since he usually extends his hand when we're about to enter a carriage or begin a meal.

"May I request the pleasure of your company?"

"Sure." Bemused, I stand up and take his hand. "But what's with the formality? I mean, I'm supposed to be your wife, but—"

"Certainly, love. If you wish less formality between us, I shall be happy to cede to your request." He moves closer, his eyes gleaming, like he's ready to 'cede' to my request right away.

"No, that's not what I meant! It's just your way of speaking. I don't think I can ever get used to your royal style. Like this." I imitate his father, extending my arm and striking up a majestic air that only makes him laugh.

"Oh, Kat," he sighs, his gaze brimming with warmth. "You're simply too precious. I don't know how I ever agreed to let you leave."

"Where are we going?" I quickly say, anxious to change the subject. Guess he decided to ditch the 'no flirting while we're alone' rule.

"To your favorite place in the palace."

"You have a library in here?" I ask, incredulous.

He raises an eyebrow. Looks like I guessed correctly.

"The second largest in the country, after the one in the University. But while the latter holds mostly academic literature, you'll find more books to your liking at the palace. I took the liberty of ordering books from your favorite authors."

Now my curiosity is roused. What kind of books did I read when I was here? I doubt Athelia could match up to the plethora of books I'm exposed to in modern life.

I quicken my pace, eager to see this library. Edward chuckles, and there is warmth in his eyes as he guides me through a corridor.

When Edward opens the door and I step inside, it feels like I'm entering a completely different world. For a second, I feel like I could stay in Athelia, if only for this magnificent library.

Edward touches my arm. "Does this place seem familiar to you?" he whispers.

I glance at the frescoed ceiling, the tall windows, and the ladders against the shelves. It does seem familiar, but maybe it's because the library resembles the one in *Beauty and the Beast*.

"Do you remember visiting this library many, many times and leaving with your arms full of books?"

I blink. This time, I stare with all my might at my surroundings—the winding staircase that leads to the second floor, the ladders that reach up to the ceiling, the tall windows that look out to the bright blue sky, the golden reading lamps with dark green lampshades, and the low sofas installed near the windows.

Something stirs in my mind, as though a pebble is thrown into my mind and ripples spread out in circles.

Edward leads me to a corner near the windows.

"Look, this is your favorite section. I used to order books from the authors you enjoyed most and have them stacked in this section."

I can't hold back my curiosity. I step closer to the shelves and run my fingers over the leather-bound hardbacks. The titles leap out at me—mysteries, Gothic romances, fantasy fiction—I know that I have read those books before and cherished them. Some of them, I have reread many times. I raise my head and meet Edward's eyes. I don't know what happened to me just then, but I know that I have been here. I have been in this library and stood at the spot I'm standing on right now, while he watched me, his gaze filled with tenderness and longing.

The next thing I know, I rush at him and knock him over. Edward lies with his back on the floor, and I am sitting right on his stomach.

Oh, my God. What have I done? What's wrong with me?

For a moment, both of us freeze. Edward stares up at me, and there's no mistaking the astonishment in his eyes.

"I . . . I'm sorry," I stammer, and I attempt to scramble away from him, but my heel digs into his ankle and he lets out a grunt of pain. "I'm so sorry," I repeat, feeling completely mortified. I thought I had gotten over my clumsiness, but when it comes to him, it seems I can no longer maintain a calm and casual attitude. Only a short time, and he's already messing with my mind in a bad way.

Someone coughs. I look up and behold a young man with leaf green eyes and curly chestnut hair. It's Liam, the son of Enrilth's mayor. Also, a few patrons in the library are casting us disgruntled looks. Even in the modern world, lying on the floor with Edward in a tangle of limbs won't be allowed in a public place like this. Not to mention Athelia, which has enough rules to fill an encyclopedia.

I scramble up, my face burning. Edward, however, remains calm. He puts a hand on my back and helps me up, as though it were normal for us to engage in that position in public.

"You wished to see me?"

Liam nods, but he keeps his eyes firmly fixed on a sculpture.

"I could return another time, since obviously, you are busy . . ."

"No, no, we're not busy at all," I say quickly.

It's cowardly, I know, but at the moment, all I want to do is get away as soon as possible.

I smile and turn to leave, only to run smack into the librarian, knocking several books out of arms. Oh, God. Kat-the-klutz is back in full force.

I try to avoid Edward as much as possible for the rest of the day. Perhaps sensing my discomfort, Edward doesn't ask me about my bizarre conduct, but occasionally, I catch him staring at me, a thoughtful, serious look in his eyes. I don't know what possessed me at that moment—knocking Edward over and sitting on his body, as if I were a sex-starved creature. Does it have something to do with the goblins? Did they put some bizarre seduction spell on me? Maybe that's why Krev told me I need to get back to my own world. The last thing I need is to pounce on Edward and rip his shirt with a full audience.

14

I dream of Jason that night.

I'm in the magnificent palace library, browsing through the shelves, looking for the newest volume of a popular manga series. I wish I could read Japanese. I hate waiting so long for the translation to be released in the U.S.

"Kat? Is this what you're looking for?"

Edward stands behind me, and in his hands is a glossy new paperback. I squeal and rush to him so fast that I run him over. I end up on his stomach and clutch the book to my chest.

"How did you get this?"

"I took the liberty to order books from your favorite authors." He grins. "By the way, that is a limited special edition, with the author's autograph on the first page."

"You didn't have to," I protest. "You didn't have to go through the trouble to have the manga shipped from Japan, not to mention getting a special edition!"

"I wanted to." He wraps an arm around my back. "You gave up your family and your own world to be my wife. It's the least I can do for you."

Overcome with emotion, I lower my head. Just before my lips touch his, a cough breaks through the silence.

I look up and see Liam . . . no, it's Jason! My boyfriend is staring at us, utterly shocked.

"Jason?" I scramble away from Edward, my face in flames.

"I'll come back some other time," Jason says, his expression hurt. "Since you're obviously busy."

"No, Jason, wait! I'm so sorry. I was brought to Athelia by force . . ."

He walks away.

I jerk up, cold sweat dampening my forehead. It's still dark in my room. I can barely make out the canopy hung over my bed and the reflection of the glass-encased clock on the mantelpiece. What a nightmare.

Again, Jason appears in my mind. I dig deep in my mind, recalling his arms around me, his lips on mine. I miss him.

Do you, really? A snide voice whispers in my head. *Did Jason occur to you when you were sitting on the prince in the library?*

I let out a frustrated sigh and pound on the pillow. All my life, I've resented Dad for leaving Mom for another woman. There's nothing I detest more than fickleness. Of course, there's nothing wrong with breaking off an old relationship and moving on, but in my case, Jason didn't do anything wrong. He didn't cheat on me or hit me, nor do I love him less. If it weren't for Edward, I wouldn't even think of leaving my boyfriend. And I don't even know Edward that well. I don't know when his birthday is, his favorite food, or any of his hobbies. I'm only attracted to him because he's ridiculously hot and makes my heart flutter with his touch. It's too superficial. I need something more substantial for a serious relationship.

I've got to redouble my efforts to get back to the modern world.

***

There's one advantage to being princess of Athelia that I would normally consider annoying, or even a handicap. On the pretense that I need rest and relaxation in order to prepare myself for child-bearing, Edward sends out a notice that the princess will not be attending any events except for really important ones. I can say no to all those parties and balls, nor do I have to cut ribbons or hand out prizes. This means I have plenty of time to plot how to get out of Athelia.

Edward is in his office in another wing of the palace, no doubt editing some important memorandum or going over a letter to post to a foreign royal. The Athelian monarchy no longer holds any real political power, but it doesn't mean that he can prance around idly, doing nothing but posing as a life-sized cardboard cutout. It's me that doesn't get involved in state affairs. The value of a royal consort is in looking beautiful and bearing children. As Athelia's culture became more sophisticated, the princess-slash-queen is expected to be perfectly groomed in etiquette, but she still isn't supposed to be make her opinion heard. Can't say I'm surprised by that.

Still, I need to be circumspect. Ever since Krev appeared in Enrilth, Edward has been a bit neurotic when it comes to my whereabouts. This morning Amelie took me to the tailor for a refitting— apparently, the seven-year difference had brought extra flesh to my hips and bust, and since my clothes are tailor-made, it was necessary to have them adjusted. When we returned, Edward was pacing in our suite like a tiger in a cage. Relief spread over his face, even though I was only gone for a few hours. If he knew I was still trying to leave . . .

"You could stay here forever." Edward's voice echoes in my mind. It still makes my heart beat faster when I remember him saying those words. Simple words, but more eloquent than any fancy speech. He's deeply in love with me, no question about that.

But I can't reciprocate.

After thinking about various ways to escape, I decide to start with the wedding chapel. It is, after all, the place where I found myself in Athelia, right after I disappeared in Jason's house. Maybe I came through some secret portal in that room which resembles a hospital ward.

But how am I going to get to the chapel? I have no clue where it is, and it may not be a good idea to ask Edward. He might grow suspicious, and I don't even want to think about how he may react if he knows that I am scheming to get away from him.

Pacing in my room, I wring my hands and think hard. Should I ask Edward in an offhanded manner where the chapel is? He might guess I'm trying to head home. I consider summoning a servant and trying my luck when another idea springs into my head.

I give the bell pull a good tug. Only a few seconds pass before a maid enters my room, dressed neatly in the standard uniform of a white apron, a dark dress, and a white cap with streamers. It's Mabel, a young woman who takes over for Amelie whenever the latter is unavailable or has her day off, but while her skill for dressing my hair can rival Amelie's, her character can't be more different. Amelie is serious-minded and bossy, while Mabel is flighty and loves to gossip. "Is there anything you need, Your Highness?"

"Please refill the teapot," I say, just for the sake of playing my role as princess. "By the way, I would like a copy of the paper that came out when Edward and I got married."

"You want to read the paper, Your Highness?" Mabel looks surprised.

"When we left for the honeymoon, I didn't get a chance to read the paper. I would like to see how our picture turned out when the reporters took it at the chapel."

Comprehension dawns on Mabel's face. "Oh, they couldn't have delivered the paper to Enrilth. It's too far." She curtsies and leaves while I settle down to more letter-writing, hoping that soon, I'll be able to get the information I need.

I have finished half a dozen letters when Mabel returns, bearing a steaming pot of tea and the paper tightly furled under her arm.

"Here you are, Your Highness. Hope you don't mind it's a worn copy, but after so many days, it's hard to get a copy that isn't read."

"Oh, no, I don't mind at all. Thank you very much." I feel like giving her a tip, but it's not practiced here in Athelia. Besides, it would appear suspicious if I gave her something, like I'm paying her for her silence.

I scan the headlines of the paper quickly. As expected, the top story is a report of our wedding. *Prince Edward finally ties the knot* is printed above a large black-and-white picture that shows me clutching Edward's arm, right on top of the stairs. The wheels of our carriage are shown on the bottom left-hand side of the photo. I must say, the quality of the picture is better than I expected for a country that doesn't have electricity. Another photo shows a close-up of me, which is actually quite flattering. My skin is smooth and blemish-free, thanks to the lotion I've been using to get rid of my freckles. Were it a picture of my seventeen-year-old self, I honestly think the people wouldn't be happy having a gawky, nerdish girl on the cover.

I scan the page until I find the text that I'm needing. *After the private ceremony was performed in the palace's Red Room, the Prince and Princess journeyed from the palace to St. James Cathedral in a golden carriage pulled by four white horses.*

St. James Cathedral. So, that's where the wedding was held. I wonder how far it is from the palace. If Edward and I needed a carriage to get there, it can't be inside the palace. There's also an article that mentions I fainted right after the ceremony is performed, but luckily, it's only a couple of paragraphs. Maybe the royal family has some influence on the press.

I fold up the paper and tuck it inside a drawer. All I have to do is get to the wedding chapel and find out if there is some route I can use to get back to Portland.

On my way to the courtyard, I run into the chamberlain. According to Edward, the chamberlain is in charge of the royal household—something like the monarchy's equivalent to a butler. He was the same person who poured wine and carved the pot roast during dinner. And he also happens to be the brother of Madame Dubois, the etiquette mistress who once instructed me in court manners and princess behavior when I moved into the palace nine months ago.

"Good morning, Your Highness!" The chamberlain bows, then glances around me, as though expecting somebody else behind me. "How are you settling into your official role?"

Terribly, modern world Kat would say.

"I'm fine. Thank you for your consideration." This is what an Athelian princess would say. At the

133

moment, I'm grateful that Edward took the time to teach me how to 'behave' properly.

"May I inquire why you are unaccompanied at this moment?"

Am I supposed to go everywhere with a servant in tow? "I would like to go out for a short drive. My limbs are stiff from sitting too long."

"If you do not have a particular objective in mind, I highly recommend a stroll in the garden instead, Your Highness. Surely there is no need to go out alone." The way he said 'alone' makes it sound like I'm doing something taboo. "A woman's place is at her husband's side."

I resist the urge to roll my eyes. "Edward is too busy to join me. Please don't look so alarmed, Monsieur Dubois."

I ignore his disapproving glare, find an empty carriage, and tell the coachman to drive me to St. James Cathedral. Geez. If being a princess means that I can't even go out on my own, then I sure don't want to be shackled to this place.

***

St. James Cathedral is only about ten minutes' drive, thank God. Now that I have time to take a good look at it, I'm impressed. Besides being ridiculously large, most of the walls are decorated with ornate carvings. My head could go dizzy from counting the number of roses wrought over the entrance.

But I have no time to admire the stunning architecture around me. I have to look for the small room I woke up in, which is pretty hard to find in a cathedral this large, so I rack my brains trying to figure out where it could be. I'm in the nave with arched ceilings and colorful stained-glass windows, where Edward brought me to see the king and queen. I recognize the rows of seats where the guests were sitting. We didn't go through other rooms or pass any corridor, so I'm guessing it should be one of the doors on either side of the nave.

I have no choice but to find out myself. Trying to act as inconspicuously as possible, I open the doors one by one.

"What do you think you're doing?" Someone says.

Like a child caught red-handed, I whirl around and find myself facing a middle-aged man wearing long, dark robes. One of the priests who work here, I suppose.

"I beg your pardon," I say, managing what I hope is a disarming smile. "I . . . I think I left my wedding ring here. It's kind of costly, and I just thought if I came here. . ."

He squints at me, and recognition dawns on his face. "Princess Katriona?"

I nod. "I'm sorry, I didn't mean to trespass. All I want is to find my ring."

"Prince Edward had ordered to have the place searched thoroughly." The priest shakes his head slowly. "I understand that you are unhappy about losing the ring, but I'm afraid that someone already got it. We clean the chapel quite regularly, I assure you. It would have turned up if someone did not steal it."

"I understand, but I would still like to try."

The priest shrugs but tells me to go ahead. He's thinking that I'm wasting my time. But the ring is the least of my concerns.

I make sure the priest has disappeared around the corner before continuing my search. I search for the small, hospital-like room, and then on the third door to the right, I think I've found it. There's a small cot lying in the corner, the blanket as flimsy as I remember. I take off my white kid gloves because my palms are getting sweaty. Can I really succeed? Is it possible that I can find a way to get home through where I came from? Claire arrived in eighteenth-century Scotland through the ancient stone circle in *Outlander*, and that was how she got back.

I run my hands over the white-washed walls, feeling kind of idiotic but·still praying with all my might that some magic spell would be triggered and that yellow-green glow would engulf me and take me back.

Please, I beg in my mind. *Please, open up the portal and let me go home*.

Nothing happens. I've practically wiped all four walls with my hands—will the priests be surprised that the walls of this room barely need any dusting?— and I'm still staring stupidly at the empty cot.

Maybe this is the wrong room. I try the one next door, and the next, but all I get is a pair of dusty hands.

I should have known. What happened in *Outlander* doesn't apply here. I'm just wasting my time and making myself look a fool. I thought I could find a way out, but apparently, my wish is for naught. I'm an idiot for believing that what happened in *Outlander* could work the same here.

I stumble into the nave and sink on one of the benches, my heart as heavy as the stone pillars lining the sides. Unless Krev appears now, I'm going to miss my sister's graduation. I'm going to miss the chance to introduce Jason to my family. And if Krev never shows up . . .

I sniff and reach for a handkerchief. It's so hard not to burst into tears, but even in my despondent mood, I can't cry in public.

I don't know how long I've sat there until the people who point and stare and whisper get on my nerves.

So, I head back to the palace. As the carriage rolls along, I prop an elbow on the window and try to think of something positive.

There's still hope, I reason in my mind. Krev did say he'd come back for me. He seemed serious about getting me back to America. If only Edward hadn't stopped me . . .

I curl my fingers in my skirts, feeling frustrated. If it weren't for my royal husband, I wouldn't be stuck in this strange world with all these problems, none of which I seem to have any chance of solving.

15

Edward is pacing in our suite when I enter. Once I step into the room, the tenseness in his face immediately melts into relief. He gestures to Amelie with a flick of his fingers, which seems to say *get out*, but it's not enough. When Amelie shuts the door behind her, Edward locks it.

"Kat." Anger seems to simmer within him. There's no trace of his affectionate manner nor his flirtatious tone. "Where have you been?"

Irritation, prickly and uncomfortable, threatens to rear its head. Another time I might have been cooperative, but I'm still annoyed that I failed to return home from the chapel, and since he is the main source of my frustration, I cross my arms and glare at him.

"Stop interrogating me like I'm a convicted murderer, *Your Highness*. I thought I was your wife, not a servant in your employment."

"Do you have any idea how worried I was when I came back from a grueling meeting and found you gone?"

The harshness of his tone both surprises and vexes me even more—he makes it sound like I'm five years old. I was in a carriage with a coachman, and the chapel was only about ten minutes' drive from the palace. I wonder what he'll say if I tell him that back in America, I passed through shady neighborhoods and encountered mentally unstable people on the subway or in the grocery store.

"I . . . I left a note on the desk."

"I didn't see it."

"Maybe it got blown to the floor." I usually have the windows open since the temperature has been going up. It's early summer, and it's getting more and more uncomfortable wearing a chemise, a corset, and a dress every day.

He takes a step toward me and I automatically back away, which seems to annoy him further.

"I asked you a question, Kat. Where have you been?"

"Oh, so am I in a military camp now? Do I have to report to you every time I go out?"

Edward levels an intense stare at me. "If you keep being this stubborn, then I forbid you to leave the palace. In the case of an event requiring your presence, Bertram or I will accompany you. Or both of us."

"What?" I'm completely flabbergasted. Grounding me as though I'm a kid? "You can't be serious!"

"It is not a decision I would like to make, but without mutual trust, I cannot have you disappearing without notice. You are my wife, Kat, and I intend to keep you here with me. Whatever it takes."

His eyes are feverish and flashing, his tone agitated. There's a wildness in his manner. It appears as though he'd go crazy if he doesn't know where I am. For a brief moment, I wonder if the madness in his grandfather's genes was passed down to him—maybe just a little, but it's enough to make me flinch.

Nevertheless, my anger is also stirred up. What kind of man is he to keep me confined within the palace like the animals in the menagerie? I thought his attitude toward me was liberal (for the standards of an Athelian male), but it looks like I was wrong. If Jason dared to make me stay indoors and not go out unless accompanied, I'd dump him in an instant.

"If you treat me like a prisoner, I guarantee once Krev appears, I won't hesitate to leave with him."

I might as well have struck him with the heavy vase on the mantelpiece. Shock, swiftly followed by fury, radiates from him. He takes another step toward me, and I realize he's backed me into a corner. What is he going to do to me?

Tension—thick, stifling, scary tension—stretches between us. I stare at him defiantly, but my palms have grown sweaty. An image of Dad yelling at Mom a few days before they filed their divorce flashes in

141

my mind. My fear must have shown in my face, for Edward suddenly turns away. His shoulders slump and his clenched fists have relaxed.

"It's getting late," he finally says. "Get dressed for dinner."

And he vanishes into the study, leaving me staring at the door of my bedroom. It's the first time we've quarreled. Maybe I should apologize for refusing to be honest with him. But then I'd have to tell him the reason I went to the cathedral, and I don't want to imagine his reaction.

There is a reason why the Grimms' fairy tales rarely tell us what happens after the prince and princess get married. Life after marriage is never fairytale-ish.

***

The king and queen sense that something is wrong. Of course. No matter how much we pretend, the quarrel has soured our minds and made us unnecessarily stiff and formal during mealtimes. Even Edward, who is generally good at faking it, cannot escape his parents' scrutiny this time. At night, when he still instructs me in Athelian culture and customs, his tone is indifferent, his look devoid of affection, and never once does he flirt.

I admit that I miss the way he looks at me like I'm the only girl on the planet, which only makes me frustrated with myself. When Edward was the perfect husband and lover, I felt burdened by his attention.

Now that he's cool and detached, I feel deprived. All I can do is keep up a smiling facade, but I hate to say that I prefer Edward doting on me rather than not.

Although he behaves like a casual friend to me, Edward shows no sign of giving me up. Since we quarreled, he has been guarding me like a hawk. And it's not just Edward. Amelie, Mabel and Bertram also seem to watch me whenever I leave our suite or when I leave the table after a meal. I don't know if Edward told them to keep an extra eye on me, but I do know that it's getting on my nerves.

I try to occupy myself with the letter-writing and books from the library. I did think about going back to the chapel, but I'd rather wait until the storm has passed. I'm not afraid of Edward, but it's best to avoid unpleasantness, especially when the servants also sense the tension between us.

"Not this dress," I say one day when Mabel brings out an off-shoulder pastel blue gown from my wardrobe, which is large enough to accommodate an elephant. "That neckline is way too low. And what's with that decanter on the dresser?"

"I . . . I think His Highness wouldn't mind." Mabel sounds nervous, but she clings to the blue dress like it's worth a million. "Amelie and I thought that he might soften up if you wear this and offer him a glass. Bertram told us His Highness was happier since he met you, but it's been days and he hasn't cracked a smile."

I sigh. "It's not that simple. He won't be appeased just because of a dress."

"But he adores you," Mabel insists, her round face the personification of earnestness. "Surely, he'd prefer to kiss and make up?"

In the end, I give in, but on the condition that I wear a silken wrap as well. Mabel concedes, but she makes me promise I'll take off the wrap once Edward and I are alone.

Amelie arrives a moment after Mabel finishes arranging my hair. As a married woman, I'm supposed to keep my hair up all the time. Only my husband or parents can have the 'privilege' of seeing me with my hair down.

"Miss Elle would like to see you."

Elle. The real Cinderella. Oh, my God. I'm going to meet the character I've read about in *The Ugly Stepsister*, the girl Katriona tried to push toward the prince, but who ended up falling for the prince's cousin. "Show her in."

A lovely girl enters the study. Curly, honey-blonde hair and large, baby blue eyes. Smooth, unblemished skin the color of cream. A face as sweet as a pink rose. She's wearing a simple white dress, and apart from a silver pendant on her throat, she doesn't have any jewelry or accessories. Yet her hands look rough and calloused.

"Hi," I say a bit nervously, wondering how I used to greet her when I was seventeen. "Nice . . . er . . . lovely to see you today."

Elle blossoms into a smile, which makes her look so pretty that I can see why Henry fell for her, even when she was a servant. "Henry was invited to the

144

palace today, so I thought I'd come along and have a chat with you."

"Henry is also here?"

"He's meeting His Highness today about a Food and Drugs Act." Elle glows as she speaks. Her affection for Henry must have grown deeper than depicted in the book. "Henry wants to ensure that our staple foods are safe to consume, so he suggested several bans, such as the use of red lead in coffee and ground glass in sugar. It's a pity that he's so busy that he can't continue teaching at the school."

Since when did Henry become a teacher? I must look blank, for Elle adds, "Didn't you know that Henry resigned his position? We had to place an ad for applications."

"Oh, of course," I lie and slap my hand on my forehead. "I completely forgot."

"We hope to replace him soon, but I'm afraid the girls have grown attached to him." Elle sighs. "Speaking of the school, Miss Cavendish mentioned to me that she wants to hold a meeting, probably next month. I'll see you then, if not sooner."

My heart sinks. I don't even know who this Miss Cavendish is. I'll have to ask Edward to tell me more about this school I'm running, but if it's my job, I'm not sure how much he knows.

"Um, sure."

Elle's forehead puckers, and she gives me a once-over. Unlike Edward's gaze, which is usually filled with warmth and desire, hers is critical and appraising.

"Is everything all right with you, Kat?" She says, looking concerned. "To be honest, you sound similar to that day when you fell down the stairs and couldn't remember anything."

Oh no. She knows, or at least she suspects.

"I'm fine," I say firmly. "It's just a bit . . . overwhelming. Being married."

Elle gives me a sympathetic look. "I suppose there is a difference when everything is official. But I'm sure if you have any difficulties, His Highness will be happy to help. He is one of the kindest men I've met. When he offered me a job in the gardens, he was ever so patient with me. Never once did I have a cross word from him."

For some inexplicable reason, I feel slightly jealous when imagining Edward instructing her in gardening, but I banish the thought. *Stop being an idiot, Kat.* There's nothing between Edward and Elle, and even if there were, I'm planning to go home anyway.

"We're holding the interviews for Henry's replacement next week," Elle continues. "Would you like to come and join us?"

I decline as politely as I can. For one thing, I'm not sure if Edward will let me leave the palace. For another, I still can't remember anything of my past. It'd be risky if I went to this school that I have no recollection of.

Feeling worried, I do my best to curtail Elle's visit, lest she blab to other people that I've lost my memories again. I hate making myself urge her to leave—she's been nothing but kind and friendly—but

I can't risk it. For the umpteenth time, I wish I'd never arrived in this storybook world.

16

"The king and queen request an attendance with you," Amelie informs me one morning, as she laces me into a harebell blue dress with a square neckline and white ruffles on the skirts. Elegant, refined, and respectable. Trust Amelie to pick the most appropriate outfit according to my schedule. "You are to report to the king's receiving chamber after breakfast."

Uh-oh. I have an ominous instinct that I'm not going to like this conversation. So far, from the daily routine of sharing breakfast (and sometimes lunch and dinner) with Edward's parents, they have treated me with kindness and concern. But if this is going to be about my quarrel with Edward...it'd be much easier that they were indifferent. Like, they should have more important things to worry about than their son's married life.

On the other hand, part of me is gratified that my in-laws care about Edward and I. They're willing to accept me, an outspoken girl who defies Athelian rules, just because Edward loves me. They didn't try to force Edward to marry some other aristocratic lady who'd fulfill traditional expectations, like Bianca or Claire.

The king's receiving chamber is located next to his suite that he shares with the queen. It's magnificently furnished in the crimson-gold theme of the palace, with four upholstered chairs sitting on a carpeted dais, and several other smaller chairs forming a semi-circle in front of the dais. When I arrive, King Leon and Queen Isolde are already sitting on the upholstered chairs, conversing in low voices.

"Katriona." The king gestures me to come forward, then snaps his fingers at the servant who brought me, telling him to close the door.

The queen smiles and pats the chair next to her. "Over here, Katriona." When I hesitate, she adds, "You're officially princess now. Your seat is here with us."

I sit down gingerly and fold my hands in my lap, adhering to what Edward had taught me of Athelian customs. "Father. Mother." The words come out more naturally than I expected, and for which I'm glad. I'm supposed to have lived at the palace for a year by now, so it's no longer awkward for me to call the king and queen as family.

"I suppose you're wondering why we summoned you to the receiving chamber...or maybe not." The queen observes my face closely; I make myself meet her eye for a moment before looking away. "Normally Leon and I would rather not pry into your affairs, but it seems that this…lack of harmony between you and Edward, seems to be lasting longer than we presumed."

There's a tightness in the king's face as he speaks. "It is reported that you had an argument yesterday afternoon, and it ended with you slamming the door on him."

I dig my nails into my palm as I remember how it went. I was feeling bad that I missed Paige's graduation. I wanted to go for a stroll in the gardens, when I met Edward in the corridor. After learning where I planned to go, he had signaled to Bertram, indicating that I be followed. Frustrated at being watched every time I leave the suite, I had told him bitingly that I'm not his prisoner and retreated to my room.

"Katriona." The king's voice contains a harsh intonation, but I'm sure it would be even harsher were I not his daughter-in-law. "I do not know what it is that happened between you two, nor do I wish to ask unless necessary, but let me remind you that as part of the royal family, you have a role to play. I would highly recommend that you refrain from having a disagreement in public."

"What he means is that we are supposed to set an example for our people," the queen says, in a gentler tone. "As much as we'd like to maintain a private life that's free from inquisitive eyes, such is not our lot.

150

You must learn to conduct your speech and behavior with the constant reminder that people are watching."

"I'm sorry." I bite my lip. I know it's unseemly for me to shout at Edward in the corridor.

"Of course we cannot expect you to be on amiable terms all the time, but whenever you come close to a conflict, please remember to keep it behind closed doors." The king lets out a sigh. "My father had a bitter relationship with his wife, and took mistress after mistress during his reign. My mother did not take it kindly and they would often have shouting matches in the palace."

"It is only part of the reason why the late king was highly unpopular," the queen says. "Still, the public was much appalled by the nastiness in the royal family, and Leon was careful to ensure that we project a model of conjugal felicity."

If they had tried to instill these principles in Edward since he was a child, no wonder he's so repressed. It's likely that his emotions had been so frequently kept in check that he found my liberal outlook both attractive and appealing.

"You are an intelligent girl." The king directs me an intense look that reminds me of Edward. "I do not doubt that you have understood the meaning of this meeting, and that we may expect that this incident between you and Edward will not occur again."

But we're not machines. I can't flip a switch and suddenly everything is magically repaired. The best I can do is to think before I speak, and make sure that I won't manifest any negative feelings when there are servants around.

"I'll try."

King Leon pats my hand; the sternness in his eyes has disappeared and he looks more like a fatherly figure now. "Remember that you are Athelia's princess, my dear. A royal marriage is different and more difficult to maintain. Which reminds me—Isolde, you were talking of bringing Kat to the court presentation tomorrow?"

The presentation. For me, it brings up one of the most memorable scenes in *The Ugly Stepsister*—the heroine falling on her butt in front of the queen, when she discovers the hot guy she had met is actually the prince.

The queen places a hand on my arm. "Katriona, I would like to ask that you accompany me to the presentation and learn how to receive the debutantes. I may need you to stand in for me sometimes. And besides, this will be your duty when you become queen."

More royal duties. I'm being drawn further and further away from the life I once knew, whether I like it or not, and pulled deeper and deeper into this web of courtly manners and celebrity status. Me, ordinary Katherine Wilson who worked in a coffee shop, becoming Princess Katriona of a large and flourishing country.

This can't be happening. But as I leave the receiving chamber and a pair of liveried servants bow to me, I decide that I need to re-adjust my mindset or

I'd be perpetually miserable. I need to adapt to royal life and prepare myself for the possibility that Krev may never show up. Going back to my own world is no longer a necessity, but an option.

17

Even though I no longer have to work on walking backward with a long train, I am still required to appear in full regalia for the court presentation. The dress is made of ruby velvet and white satin, trimmed with golden lace and bows. It would have been lovely if there wasn't a huge metal hoop—they call it a crinoline—under the dress, making me feel like a walking balloon. I also have to wear this heavy necklace of gold and beads, which causes a strain on my neck, and a glittering crown is jammed on my head. Amelie attaches golden pins around the crown, as I'm afraid that it might fall off.

"I know that it cannot be comfortable," the queen says, watching me walk like a robot. "But the presentation is an ornate ceremony with years of tradition, and it is required that we appear in formal wear."

I want to say that Athelia's casual wear is already too fancy compared to what I'm used to—I wonder how they'd react to jeans and T-shirts—but I just smile and assure the queen that I'm fine, and it's nothing compared with the trial I went through during my presentation. Of course, I don't remember anything about the training, but from what I've read in *The Ugly Stepsister*, I know that it's no easy task.

"Ah." The queen nods sagely. "Well do I remember your presentation. It is the first time that Edward requested to attend the ceremony with me. What a surprise it was when he told me he wished to attend it, since he never took any interest in the presentation before."

Because he knew that Katriona . . . because *I* would be there. I flush and focus on a glittering jewel bracelet slipped over my wrist.

"I had suspected there was a girl he was interested in," the queen continues, waiting for me to catch up with her. "But he wouldn't say anything. I supposed he wished to make sure that the lady returned his affections before he could disclose anything. No doubt you know that Edward has a pride of his own. However, even I couldn't guess that it was you he had his eye on."

"Because there were so many girls he could choose from?"

"Since you'd already met him when you were a child, I thought that if he were interested in you, he would have made it known earlier."

That's because I came to inhabit Katriona's body when she was seventeen. I highly doubt that Edward would have fallen in love with the real Katriona. If I had inhabited Elle's body, he would be attracted to Elle.

"I guess I wasn't much of an attraction when I was a child."

"I cannot fully remember how you looked when you were young, but it was your sister who caught the eye of everyone. All the other mothers were talking about what a beauty Bianca was, and if looks were the deciding factor alone, she might have even become Edward's choice. No one predicted that it would be you." She glances at me, pausing before speaking. "Nor could I have predicted that you were reluctant to accept him until after the ball."

If only you knew the whole story, I want to say.

"But I believe I can understand why you were hesitant to become princess. When Leon asked me to marry him, I wondered if I could shoulder the responsibilities, for it is not simply marrying him, but marrying into Athelia's royal family." She smiles at me. "When I learned about you working with Edward to improve the conditions for child workers, I knew you would be the right woman for him."

I swallow. He's infatuated with me, but him being in love with me does not necessarily mean that I'm the only person 'right' for him. There must be other women in Athelia who are beautiful, compassionate, and willing to take on the responsibilities of being the future queen.

The queen touches my shoulder in a surprisingly mom-like gesture. "Katriona, I assure you that Edward is deeply attached to you. He may be well educated and disciplined, but he does not have much experience being around women. I hope that you can resolve whatever went wrong between you, and if you need any help, Leon and I will always be willing to lend a hand."

I gulp. Really, I can't ask for a better mother-in-law. "Thank you . . . Mother."

***

From the moment I enter the drawing room and am guided to the platform, a strong sense of déjà vu washes over me. I have been in the room before. Two rows of chairs are placed on either side of a grand carpet, which leads to the chairs where we are supposed to sit. Instinctively, I know that the debutantes, after curtsying to us, will walk backward until they reach the seats.

It's the same feeling that gripped my mind when I was in the palace library. It seems that my memory is returning, albeit with the pace of a snail. Hope blossoms in my mind. *Please, don't let this be a one-time occurrence.* Maybe, given sufficient time, I'll be able to remember everything.

The tallest manservant comes up to us and asks if we are ready to begin the court presentation.

"We're ready," the queen says after exchanging a look with me. She leans toward me and whispers, "I hope you ate your fill during lunch, for the presentation will not end till several hours later."

"Several hours?"

"While the presentation itself may be a difficult task, many families wish to have the privilege of being presented, including those who have made their fortune in trade, even though they are not of aristocratic blood. It is unfair to keep the presentation exclusive, but on the other hand, this means that the hours get longer and longer."

One by one, the debutantes enter the room, decorated like Christmas trees, accompanied by their sponsors. Almost all of them are nervous. Some manage a tense smile, while a minority manage to look like they are going to receive a Grammy award. When she reaches the throne, the debutante curtsies so low that it's a wonder her knees don't crack. Then she walks backward with the train trailing behind her and sits in the chairs provided. Since I don't recognize the girls, I keep my mouth shut and just smile. The queen, on the other hand, has something to say to everyone, but even I can see that she finds the task tedious.

There is a girl who seems so nervous that she is literally trembling as she treads on the carpet. She's extremely pretty—in fact, she has a passing resemblance to Paige, but lacking my sister's confidence. This girl looks so young and helpless . . . I wonder if she is older than fifteen. I watch her and wonder if that's what I looked like when I was seventeen. It's not surprising that I tripped up—the atmosphere can heighten the tension.

When the girl takes her first step backward, there is the sound of fabric ripping and the next second, she is on the floor. My heart goes out to her. Before I know what I'm doing, I'm out of my seat. I grab her arm and pull her into an upright position.

"Princess Katriona?" she gasps, her eyes wide and her mouth open.

"There's an empty seat over there," I say in a low voice, also feeling a bit embarrassed. Maybe I acted a bit hastily. She could probably get up by herself.

After the presentation is finished (Finally! Can I rip the crown off now?), the most beautiful woman I've ever seen comes up to me.

"That was quite charming of you to lend a helping hand to Adelaide," the woman says with a smile that doesn't reach her eyes. "Can it be that she reminded you of your notorious fall in your own presentation?"

"Perhaps," I say, rubbing my temples and wishing I could disappear. Can't the future presentations be replaced by a ball or a dinner? Presenting the debutantes one by one certainly takes up a lot of time. "By the way, I'm sorry, but you are . . .?"

The raven-haired beauty stares at me for a long moment, as though she doesn't understand what I'm saying. Her eyebrows almost disappear into her forehead. What did I say that causes her such amazement?

"Bianca! There you are!" An older woman heads in our direction. "I am so sorry that I wasn't available to attend your wedding. Did you receive the gift I sent?"

I feel like someone has punched me in the stomach. This gorgeous woman is Bianca, who is supposed to be my sister in Athelia. And I have just made the fatal mistake of failing to recognize her.

All eyes are on me. Bianca stares at me, a hand on her throat. Even when she is astonished, she still looks like a movie star.

Think, I command myself. I have to say something quickly, or they'll know I've lost my memory. Already, I can imagine the headline story: *The princess is suffering from a terrible disease. It is advisable that she be kept away, locked in a tower until she is fully recovered.*

I give a fake laugh. "You must have heard wrong, Bianca. I didn't even finish my sentence. I was planning to ask you if you were enjoying yourself."

A shoddy explanation, but it seems to satisfy the others. One lady starts to compliment how becoming Bianca's hairstyle is. Another lady starts to talk about how glad she is that it's all over, and how nice it is to finally have something to eat.

Internally, I sigh in relief. Pasting a smile on my face, I pretend that nothing happened. I smile graciously and speak as little as possible, so as not to betray any more ignorance. It isn't difficult; since taking my job at the coffee shop, I'd learned to deal with all kinds of customers with patience.

However, when it's time to leave, Bianca glances at me and I almost recoil. It's a piercing, unfriendly glance, as though she is trying to see into my mind. Just a second, and she turns away. Man, I am so glad that I'm no longer living with her.

Then I meet the queen's gaze. She is frowning, like she isn't completely convinced of my lie.

I gulp. I really should try to get my memory back. But how?

18

When I arrive for our nightly lessons in the sitting room, Edward no longer wears that frosty mask of politeness. He's twisting his wedding ring and shifting on his feet, a troubled expression on his face. He gestures to the sofa, indicating that I take a seat, but he remains standing.

"Mother said you acted out of character at the court presentation today."

I adjust the silken wrap over my nightgown before sitting down. For all the prudish customs in Athelia, my nightgown is rather skimpy—the neckline is so wide that if I shrug, the material easily slips down my shoulder. Then again, recalling how Mabel tried to patch things up between Edward and I by bringing out that off-shoulder gown, maybe the design of this nightgown was made on purpose.

"I failed to recognize Bianca." I look down on the ground. "I didn't remember what she looked like, and when she talked to me, I asked who she is."

Alarm flashes over his face. "Did she suspect anything went wrong with you? Were there many people nearby?"

I tell him how I tried to cover up. "I don't think she guessed that I lost my memory, but I'm sure she's still mad at me for stealing you."

"Cease that thought," he says sharply. "I was never her conquest."

He's using his commanding tone again, but this time, I don't care. "I should have guessed it. I should have pretended I knew her. Anything but asking who she is."

Edward crosses his arms. "We must get your memories back. It cannot be impossible. When you pushed me onto the carpet in the library—was it not a manifestation that you were repeating an action that you did earlier?"

I flush when I remember how shocked Liam looked when he caught us lying on the ground. Edward seems to sense my discomfort as well. He draws away and stares at the windows. The curtains are not fully drawn, which allows for a sliver of moonlight to sift through the glass, illuminating the side of his face. This serious, steadfast expression he wears . . . something stirs in my heart, going deeper than the flutters and jitters when he flirts.

Edward turns and faces me. "Come. I have an idea."

Bemused, I follow him out of the suite, through a series of corridors and staircases, our slippered feet making light thuds on the floor. Lamps glow in brackets on the walls, though there isn't a servant in sight.

"We still have time before the steward makes his rounds and extinguishes the lights."

"Where are we going?"

"You'll see when we get there." He pauses a second. "At least, I hope that you will remember."

We reach a deserted corridor. Edward opens a door, searches for a lamp, and lights it. And then a strong jolt rocks my head. In front of me is a neatly furnished bedroom, with a rose-pink bedspread and apple-green curtains. A handsome bookshelf stands in a corner, with a large reclining chair next to it, laid with plump cushions of multiple colors.

"Oh my God." I settle on the chair and reach for a book, only to find the bookshelf empty. "I . . . I had stayed here. It was . . . it was after the ball!"

Like pages in a book, scenes gradually unfold in my mind. I start to remember everything that I did here. I had eaten, slept, and read in this room, mostly with Amelie and some other maids. Edward never stayed in this room, but I can see him standing in the threshold every morning. Before our marriage, he was expressly forbidden to enter my room.

"My theory is correct." Subtle delight is laced in his deep, rich tones. "I believe I have discovered how to recover your memory. You need to be exposed to the places you are familiar with. Previously, you didn't remember anything since you had never taken that train and you had never been to Enrilth. You never set foot in our new suite. But you had spent an inordinate amount of time in the library and in this room."

An adrenaline rush overtakes me, flooding my senses with excitement. It occurs to me that the same jolt also happened during the presentation—most likely because it's a place I had been in and would likely not forget. On an impulse, I grab his arm and pump it in the air—it's what I usually do with Paige when we're celebrating. Then, sensing that he stiffens, I let go, but a second later, he wraps his hand firmly over my wrist.

"Kat." He looks down at the ground before meeting my eyes. "I wish to apologize for my conduct that day. It was never my intention to confine you in the palace. Every day, I fear that the goblin might appear and take you away. I cannot help but worry when I'm not informed of your whereabouts."

Guilt assails me when he mentions Krev. If I were a normal Athelian girl, he wouldn't be so obsessed about knowing precisely where I am. There's still a mild resentment when I remember his firm, commanding tones, but most of my anger has melted away since I had the time to reflect about it.

"I'm sorry as well." I look at him in the eye. "It's natural that you're worried about me. I won't ask your permission if I can go out, but I'll make it a point to let you know where I'll be going."

"Now that we've made this discovery, I fully intend that you go out more often and explore all the places that you've visited in Athelia. Your old house, for example. Both Lady Bradshaw and Bianca have moved out, so you need not worry about encountering them again." His eyes gleam. "I cannot wait until you remember everything, wife o' mine."

A tiny thrill runs through me at the eagerness in his gaze. Seventeen-year-old me might have melted on spot, but I'm no longer the shy, insecure teenager anymore. Twenty-four-year-old me has a lot more to contemplate, to ponder, to mull over. Especially when we're talking about marriage—a life-long decision here.

"Edward, I know that you're desperate for me to get my memory back, and trust me, that is on top of my priority list as well. I wanted the earth to swallow me up when I didn't recognize Bianca. But don't assume that everything will be magically resolved once I recover my memory. It's not enough."

There's a note of surprise in his tone. "I am not quite certain what you mean by that."

"Did I ever tell you about why my parents separated?"

"I believe I had asked you, but you didn't feel like talking about it."

"My parents met in college. I don't know how long they knew each other . . . maybe a few days? I think my mom's friend introduced them to each other, and they got drunk at a party and went wild. I was the result. My mother's family is pretty religious, and they wouldn't let her have an abortion."

"What's an abortion?"

I explain. Clearly, the concept doesn't exist in Athelia either.

"Anyway, my grandparents on my mother's side practically forced my parents to marry. Mom dropped out of college to have me. Dad's family could afford to support us. His parents were dentists. But after a few years, when Dad made plans to go to medical school, well, they started quarreling more and more."

"I suppose your father no longer cared for your mother."

I gave a hollow laugh. "He never really cared for her in the beginning. He told my uncle that he just thought she was hot . . . it means he thought she was sexually attractive. If she didn't get pregnant, he'd never even dream of marrying her. He blamed her for 'pulling his leg' for the several years he had to stay home and take care of us."

"Forgive me for saying so, but your father hardly seems a gentleman of noble character."

I suppress a giggle at his description of my father. "Don't you see, Edward? My parents didn't really know each other. I don't want that to be the same between us. I don't want to stay here just because you are . . ."

"Hot?" He supplies, a twinkle in his eyes.

I blush and take a deep breath.

"It's been seven years since I left Athelia, and so much has happened—I went to college, I met Jason, I worked for a couple of years . . . I'm not the seventeen-year-old that you knew. And I've only met you for about a month. I'm not ready to commit myself to you for a lifetime when I don't even know you that well. So, what I'm trying to say is" —I clear my throat— "we need to start over. Get to know each other. I want to be sure that I'm staying because I love you and want to spend the rest of my life with you, not because you keep telling me that I'm your wife. Can you accept that?"

"You wish me to court you again?"

"If it's the same as dating in my world, then yes." I smile. I still find the term hilarious in an old-fashioned way. "We need to have a . . . a courtship before commitment."

"I recall that you had mentioned in your world, a man would send gifts of chocolates and flowers to a girl he wants to court."

His expression becomes determined, and I start feeling uneasy. He looks like he's planning to drown me in a sea of bouquets the very first thing tomorrow.

"It doesn't have to be flowers and chocolates in the literal sense," I quickly say. "Just the two of us spending time together will do. I need to know the man I had fallen in love with seven years ago. I want to know *you*, Edward, not the prince of Athelia."

This time, he cracks a smile—a genuine, heartfelt smile that's unlike the ones he puts on with his princely mask. "I suppose I should be disappointed, or even frustrated, that you wish to wait for us to be acquainted again. But Kat." He reaches out and takes both my hands in his. "One of the reasons I love you is because you never cared for the crown I wear. Your request to take your time to know me only reassures me that I won't change my affections. If anything, it makes me want you more than ever."

19

Edward's theory is working. My memory has been returning to me in bits and pieces ever since I started going to the places that I'm familiar with when I was still in Athelia seven years ago. It's great fun, as I get to immerse myself in the settings I've read in *The Ugly Stepsister* firsthand. I visited the greenhouse and had an actual meeting with Galen, I went to Edward's private garden and found it just as beautiful as the book described, and I rode in the carriage with Bertram holding the reins and took tours in the city.

Although I told Edward that flowers and chocolates weren't required for our "courtship," he decided to go ahead and shower me with flowers and chocolates anyway. Probably because flowers happen to be his area of expertise, and he knows that chocolate is one of my favorite foods, right up there with grilled ham and cheese sandwiches and bold, full-flavored milk tea.

One day, when I settle down to the tedious letter-writing and reading the paper, I find an enormous box of chocolates sitting on my desk.

"There must be enough to feed an army," I mutter, making a decision to share them with Amelie and Mabel. No way can I finish them by myself.

Once I open the box, which is gorgeously wrapped in red ribbons and layered with paper tissues, a memory flashes into my mind. I remember Sideburn Sidney, one of Bianca's suitors, and how I had encouraged him to send Bianca gourmet chocolates, which eventually ended up in my own stomach. And when I bite into one delicate truffle shaped like a rose, more memories come up, such as my trying to come up with schemes to annoy Bianca so she'd be swamped with suitors and have no time to go after Edward. It's like Proust dipping a Madeleine cake into his tea and memories of the past springing into his mind, only in my case, it's a lot less romantic.

Giggles and squeals come from the direction of my bedroom. It must be my maids—they come daily to deliver freshly ironed clothes and clean up the room. I gather the half-opened box and head to the bedroom.

"Princess!" Mabel's grin widens and she points at my bedspread. "Do come and see what His Highness got for you!"

Something in her giggling face tells me it can't be a good thing—not by my definition, anyway.

My curiosity piqued, I hand her the box. Luckily, I did so, because I might have dropped the chocolates.

A mass of crimson rose petals are arranged in a heart-shape on the cream-colored bedspread.

"What the..." When did he sneak in my bedroom? Having flowers in the suite is nothing new. Every day, I'd find new vases placed in corners and on tables, overflowing with lavender and violets and starflowers. But *this* . . . I feel like crawling under the bed to hide my embarrassment.

"'Tis so romantic of our prince," Mabel sighs. "Didn't expect that he'd know what a heart shape is. He always looks so serious. Aren't you frightfully pleased, Your Highness? I'd jump over the moon if a man did this for me."

"It's time you take the rugs out for a good shaking," I say, but I'm sure my face is scarlet. Only Amelie manages to keep a straight face, a cotton handkerchief tied around her face. I learn later that she's allergic to flowers. Sometimes, I wonder if a goblin had cast a spell over her that destroyed every romantic bone in her body.

But it's not just the flowers and chocolates that get me. Those gestures are sweet, of course, but nothing is better than spending quality time with Edward. Since my memory has been gradually returning, Edward stops drilling me in Athelian culture and replaces the nightly lessons with nightly conversations. We sit in my study—he takes the sofa while I lounge on the window seat—and talk. I finally learn how old he is (twenty-two, thankfully not much younger than me), and when his birthday is. He tells me about his childhood, his tutors, his friendship with

172

Henry, and even his lack of confidence when he was overshadowed by his older cousin, Philip.

"My grandparents, uncles and aunts have always favored him. His ebullient character, plus his love of sports, are more likely to find support among the people. As you may have sensed already, I have more of an introverted nature. If required, I will perform social duties and attend events, but if given the choice, I would rather not appear in public."

"I so understand," I say, drawing an amused grin from him. He always seems to find my modern phrases 'quirky and charming,' even though I'm not trying to impress him. "That's why I prefer to read. I'd go up to a podium and make a presentation in class, but I'm most at ease with a book."

"As I am with my garden." He smiles—a heart-melting, knee-weakening smile that I realize I had seen frequently, long before the wedding. And even if I don't remember the magnetism of his smile, I can't deny there's a connection between us, and it's occurring more and more frequently.

Edward leans a bit closer and fixes his gaze on my face, his eyes brimming with warmth and attention. "Tell me what kind of presentation you perform in your world."

I brief him on college life—he's hugely curious about how a girl can receive higher education along with boys. In Athelia, there were only boys' schools until Elle and I established one for girls. I describe to him the exhausting schedule of juggling classes, clubs, finances, and a social life.

"A club?" He frowns. "How does a club work in your university? What kind of club did you join?"

I suppress a smile. Tara dragged me to the karate club because she had a crush on the hot mixed-Asian instructor. To my surprise, I found I enjoyed the lessons, and even after I graduated, I continued to practice and take classes whenever I could.

"Self-defense."

"They taught you fighting at school?" Edward lets out a low whistle. "Every time I think I know all the skills you possess, you surprise me with another."

"Intimidated?" I cock an eyebrow.

He laughs. "Not in the least. If anything, I'd feel safer when you are not in the palace. Can you show me how you fight?"

Since I'm in my nightgown, I can't very well kick at him, but I demonstrate a few punches. I can't do a knee smash or a shoulder throw, but I show him how to do a knife-hand to the throat, a back fist, and an elbow smash.

"And this is a crane's beak," I say, curling my fingers to shape my hand into the beak.

"And how do you attack with that?"

"Aim for soft targets like the eye or neck," I say. "Don't underestimate the fingertips. They can be surprisingly effective."

I show him the move, but when my fingers brush over his eyes, I pause. In the dim light, up close, there are distinct dark circles under his eyes. It occurs to me that every morning, no matter how soon I am dressed, he is always waiting in our sitting room, reading the paper, ready to go down to breakfast.

"Edward. How early are you getting up each day?"

"It is of little importance."

"If you don't tell me, I'm going to lie awake all night to find out. Yes, don't look amused—I *will* be able to stay awake, if only to find out when you go to bed."

He sighs. "All right. Five, or six, if you really want to know."

"And when do you go to bed?" I narrow my eyes. Our nightly talks usually don't last past midnight, but I doubt he goes straight to bed after we finish.

Edward looks away. "Recently, we have been handling more issues than usual. It's the height of the Season right now, and Parliament is anxious to deal with as much as possible before it's over."

"The public health acts you've been working on with Henry? Such as that Food and Drugs Act?"

He raises an eyebrow. "You knew already?"

"Elle told me. Anyway, you should be going to bed earlier," I say, doing a good imitation of Mom when she found me staying up the day before my SATs. "Really, there is no need for us to sit up so late every night. It's far more important that you take care of yourself."

"I want to spend more time with you," he insists. "Don't worry about me. The Season will be over soon. It is no hardship to sit here and talk to you. For me, it's an opportunity to relax and be entertained."

I recognize the same desperation in his tone from that day when we quarreled. Like, if he doesn't grasp this chance to make me fall for him, then I'll go home once Krev comes back.

I change the topic, but at the same time, I also make a decision. A highly unconventional, unheard-of move that might get me kicked out of the palace if I weren't the princess.

20

Edward is barely visible behind a mountain of paperwork when I barge into his office on the other side of the palace. As expected, he looks astonished when my flat soles click on the marble floor, the sound fading into dull thuds when I step on a carpet embroidered with intricate patterns and the royal coat of arms.

"What are you doing here?" He darts a glance behind me, and his eyes widen. "Why is he with you?"

I grin and beckon to the person following me. "Over here, Bertram. Right next to His Highness's desk."

Bertram gives Edward a she-made-me-do-it look before setting a handsome desk carved of polished oak, with golden handles for the drawers, on the floor, along with a matching chair. I produce a cloth from a basket I'm carrying and proceed to wipe the desk and chair.

Frantic footsteps pound outside, and the chamberlain bursts into the room, bristling, the ends of his finely curled mustache pointing in the air.

"Princess Katriona! So, the servants weren't lying when they talked of you entering the prince's office with a . . . a table and chair?" He mops his forehead with a large handkerchief. "May I inquire the reason for this extraordinary transgression?"

"I decided my husband could use some assistance." I set the basket on the desk and take out pens, paper, and a few books.

The poor chamberlain almost chokes as he speaks. "A–assistance, Your Highness? But you shouldn't be here!"

I pick up one of the books and flip through the pages. "I've checked the rules of the royal household. There isn't a rule that says the princess can't work in the same office with the prince."

"This isn't child's play!"

"I'm not a child. Anyway, I promise you that the door will remain open. We won't be up to anything depraved in here."

Edward raises an eyebrow, but he doesn't speak.

I finish unpacking my basket. "Excuse me, lord chamberlain." I look him squarely in the eye and raise my voice. "Didn't you tell me that a woman's place is by her husband's side?"

For an entirety of three seconds, the chamberlain is speechless. Then he stomps off, muttering about since when did Athelia get such an unconventional princess. I slide into my seat, unable to stop grinning.

The look on his face was priceless. And oh, how satisfying it is to throw his words in his face.

"Kat." Edward pushes back his chair. "What are you doing?"

"Settling into my new routine."

"Allow me to rephrase that. What are you planning? What is this new routine you speak of?"

"Well." I flash him a cheeky grin. "You've been working yourself to death with all those social problems. I'm bored because there is no Internet—I mean, I have little to do apart from raiding the library. So, I decided I would keep you company instead. Or, should I say, lessen your workload."

Edward stares at me, dumbfounded. "Elaborate."

"I took the liberty of going through some of the papers you've been working on." I spread my hands. "I've got a college education in literature, and I took some classes in economics and social studies. I could help you summarize documents, look up resources, and proofread your writing. Besides, before we married, we had worked together to improve the lives of our citizens. I could be your sounding board. Throw me out if you'd like, but we're not having those nightly talks anymore. You must rest."

He is silent for a long moment. Then he exhales. "I don't mind—of course I don't mind you staying. There's no doubt that traditional duties fail to satisfy you, but you've got it wrong. My sleepless nights have nothing to do with our conversations. It's because—" He stops abruptly.

Another man approaches the office. It's Sir George, who acts as Edward's secretary. He frowns when he sees me and my desk, but after glancing at my husband, George seems to swallow whatever question he has in the back of his mind. He steps forward and holds out a long, flat envelope.

"His Majesty requests that you review the itinerary of the Moryn emperor's State Visit. If there are no objections, His Majesty would like for the preparations to commence."

"Thank you, George. I shall look it over and have it back to you before dinner." The secretary gives me a curt nod and leaves. He is so different from the lord chamberlain. George personifies the stereotypical image of an English butler—stoic, discreet, keeping himself invisible like walking furniture.

"The Moryn emperor is coming?" I say. From the tour of Enrilth Castle, books in the palace library, and personal experience related by Edward, I know enough of Moryn that's required of me. And that's what makes me surprised, and even a bit angry. "Why didn't I know about this?"

He hands me the envelope. "I was going to tell you when the schedule was finalized."

I slide out the contents of the envelope. There is an invitation printed on a high-quality card embellished with the crimson and gold royal emblem. The emperor's name, Augustin, is printed along with his fiancé, Simone.

"Augustin originally planned to come to our wedding," Edward says. "However, a mob uprising occurred at the capital and he couldn't leave until it was taken care of. Hence, my father decided to invite him for a later visit."

I scan over the events that will take place during the State Visit. There will be a military review at the royal park, an Investiture of the Order of the Garter, a diplomatic levee at the Moryn embassy, and a concert followed by a ball.

Since I have no idea what an investiture means, nor of a levee, I ask Edward for an explanation. Luckily, in most cases, the king performs the main duties. All we have to do is stand by and watch. When Edward reaches the last event, he pauses and looks at me.

"Do you remember how to dance?"

Oh no. With a sinking heart, I realize that even if I have fully recovered my memory, I'd still need practice with dancing. After I accepted Edward's proposal at the ball, I didn't get many chances to dance, as the Season had concluded. Balls and dances in fall and winter were infrequent, and besides, I've never been good at dancing.

Edward seems to guess what's going on in my mind. "In that case," he says slowly, "I shall have to teach you."

I gulp. "I . . . I'm sure Madame Dubois can help me." Madame Dubois was my etiquette teacher when I moved into the palace.

He chuckles. "I thought you were fed up with her bossing you around." He leans even closer, so close that his breath fans my cheek. "Besides, she is currently vacationing in the north. I doubt it would be a good idea to summon her solely for extra lessons, when everyone assumes you are already familiar with dancing. Don't worry, Kat. We shall practice in my garden, where no one can bother us."

That means we'll be alone. ALONE. Not that I'm against the idea—indeed, dancing in that beautifully laid out garden is perhaps the most romantic thing ever—but it also means that I'll be getting more and more attached to the prince. To Athelia. It's an idea that I've been trying to resist.

But what else can I do but say yes? As princess, I can't hide away in a corner and be a wallflower, something that used to occur when I was still Katriona Bradshaw, the younger, less attractive sister. I may even be required to dance with the Moryn emperor, and it'll be so embarrassing if I step on his toes.

"Okay," I whisper.

"Good. I cannot wait to have you in my arms." Edward watches me, his smirk still hovering near his lips. "I will arrange with George to block out two hours in the afternoon, thrice a week. Unless in the case of emergency, those two hours shall not be disturbed."

He resumes his drafting of some tedious memorandum for a foreign country. I stare at the invitation, still lying on the table.

Some raw, inexplicable emotion stirs in my heart. Falling for him is not a good thing, considering Athelia's society and culture are definitely not female-

182

friendly, and being with him means that I'll never see my family and friends again. But the truth is that I am falling for him, no matter how reluctant I am or how hard I try to fight it.

21

I descend the stairs leading to the courtyard and wipe sweat from my brow. It has been an uncommonly hot day, and I really wish that I could get into an air-conditioned car and drive away. However, in Athelia, I have to settle for an open-air carriage and a fan, which will not provide me shelter from the dust on the roads. I doubt it'll do much to alleviate the heat, but considering that most citizens are on foot, I can't complain. I duck into the carriage and give Bertram a smile. "Let's go."

It's the day of the school board meeting at Princess College, the girls' school that Elle and I established prior to my wedding. As the head patron, my presence is required. Thank God that I've gained most of my memories by now.

The carriage stops at a handsome stone building. Again, the familiar jolt occurs in my head. It feels like another crack has appeared in the barrier that's keeping my memories from me, and sooner or later, the multiple cracks will break down the barrier and I'll remember everything.

I wander through the corridors as old memories spring in my mind, falling into place like jigsaw puzzle pieces. *The Ugly Stepsister* never mentioned the school, since the book ended at my marriage, but I do remember going down the hallway with Elle, discussing how to design the interior, how to implement the classes, how to advertise, etc. Princess College reminds me of Miss Minchin's Seminary in *A Little Princess*, with an old-fashioned elegance that I find really charming.

Music is drifting from one room. I peek inside and discover it's a room designed like a theater. Rows and rows of chairs are lined in front of a stage with red velvet curtains. A glossy piano sits on the right-hand side. A few students are on stage, singing, while another man sits in one of the chairs, his hands waving as though he is guiding them. For a moment, it seems like I'm attending one of Paige's talent shows. I blink, and I realize that I'm at Princess College of Athelia, not Oakleigh Elementary School.

"Princess Katriona!" One girl shouts, pointing in my direction. All girls promptly drop into curtsies, and there's a chorus of, *Your Highness*.

To be honest, it's kind of cute. I grin and wave at them. "Good morning, everyone. Are you rehearsing for a play?"

A younger girl, about nine or ten, runs toward me, her eyes shining. "We're doing a musical, Aunt Kat."

Aunt Kat? Since when did I get a niece? I blink, trying to remember who the girl can be. She reminds me of a porcelain doll in her white frock and with pink ribbons in her hair.

Click. She's the daughter of Philip, the Duke of Northport, Edward's older cousin. The cousin who, according to Edward, is more suitable to be king.

"Hello, Rosie." I ruffle her hair. "Are you having fun?"

She smiles up at me and nods. "I'm an elf, Aunt Kat."

The man in front gives me a low bow. "We are putting up a fairy story that the headmistress selected, Your Highness. The show will be open to the public in a few weeks. The headmistress has very kindly entrusted me with supervising the children for the play."

"Awesome," I say, and at their slightly bemused expressions, I give them a thumbs-up and say, "Splendid. I look forward to seeing your performance that day."

After talking to the girls for a while, the bell rings, telling me I need to continue on to the conference room.

When I pass one of the classrooms on the ground floor, a familiar voice stops me. "Good morning, dearies. We are going to try a new pattern today. If you would please take out your baskets . . ."

I can't help peering through the back door. Luckily, it's left wide open. There are about twenty girls in class, each of them with a basket on the desk.

In the very front of the class is an old lady with silvery white hair. I squint. There's something familiar about her face. I know that I have seen her before. But considering that most people I know are either around my age or around the king's age, I wonder who the old lady might be. The only person that I know who is above sixty, I think, is Mr. Wellesley. So, who is this elderly lady?

I'll remember soon enough. Although at least half of my memories have returned, there are still details that I cannot fully grasp. Hopefully, with a few more visits to familiar places, I will recover my memories completely. However, I'm still reluctant to think of what I should do after I remember everything. Can I really give up my life in the U.S. and my network of family and friends and live in this country that upholds so many ideas contrary to my beliefs? Can I give up everything I love for Edward?

Before I reach the headmistress's office, which is just around the corner, a voice, shrill and angry, can be heard quite clearly in the hallway.

"I will not have my little girl participating in that vulgar show!"

"Lady Willoughby, if you could just let us explain—"

"I brought my daughter because I believed she would receive an education fit for a princess. And what did she end up doing? Jumping around like a monkey and displaying her bare arms in public! Mingling with girls way below her station! Simply preposterous! Have you heard the way those low-class people talk? Did you know that they taught my girl to cartwheel—exposing her petticoats to the world? Unacceptable. My girl will not associate with . . . any *creature* like that."

There is the sound of the door opening and boots clicking on the floor. I peer around the corner. It's a tall, slender lady in a fancy brocaded dress. How she manages to stand the heat in so many layers is beyond me. Her right hand has a firm grip on a girl in a dainty white frock. As they march down the hall, a few students coming in the opposite direction scuttle out of the way like startled kittens.

"Third student this week." A voice speaks from my other side.

Liam leans against the wall, arms crossed. He's dressed in a smart gray waistcoat that reminds me of Sherlock Holmes.

"What are you doing here?"

He holds out a thick leather-bound book. *An Introduction to Human Anatomy.*

"You're a teacher here?"

He bows. "Since the Duke of Somerset left, there was a vacancy, so I went to Edward to ask him for a recommendation."

I flush. That explains why he suddenly showed up that day, when he found me sprawled on top of Edward in the library. He must be the replacement that Elle eventually found. I cough and look for another topic.

"Did you say something about that girl being the third one this week?"

He shrugs. "It was bound to happen anyway. Lady Willoughby had issues with my teaching biology and science. Girls usually aren't expected to take those subjects."

Oh, yeah. I remember having a discussion on the school board, even before Princess College was established. I had insisted on letting the girls receive the same education as the boys in Athelia.

"However." Liam shifts his weight so he's no longer leaning against the wall. "The Honorable Lady Willoughby did not complain when Henry had the job."

Well, *I'd* also prefer Henry over Liam, though of course I keep silent.

"Do you believe a noble lady enrolled her precious daughter in hope of getting a different education? It's because she's hoping her daughter might catch the fancy of Duke Henry—an eligible young peer who doesn't gamble or fool around with women. There aren't many of them left, especially after you snared the prince."

"But her daughter…" I try to recall how old Lady Willoughby's daughter looked like—thirteen, or fourteen? "Surely she is too young for Henry?"

"An early attraction never hurts, and there's the chance they could be engaged before the daughter is of age." Liam's mouth forms a cynical smirk. "The Willoughbys have been a bit hard up since Lord Willoughby lost his investments in a jewel mine. Were I Lady Willoughby, I'd likely do the same."

A bell rings. I pull out my pocket watch—the school board meeting is in a few minutes.

"Well then, I'd better head to my class," Liam drawls. "Don't look shocked, Your Highness. I'm not against improving the minds of women, but trust me, in the end, you won't be making any difference. Not even for those working-class girls."

I stare at him. "What makes you so sure?"

"Do you know the factory girls still have to work eight hours a day? They have to get up at five, work till two, and come here for three hours of instruction if they aren't falling asleep. Most of them are unable to absorb what we teach. Sooner or later, I'll wager they'll be dropping out as well."

22

Holding the parasol over my head, I make my way through the gardens. Thanks to my recovering memory, I have an idea of where I'm going. Both Edward and I agree that I should try to find it by myself. Right now, I try to look like I'm enjoying a meandering, leisurely walk. Sometimes, I pretend to pause and sniff at some flowers. But in reality, I'm keeping a look out for the direction that leads to Edward's private garden.

Sweat is pouring down my back when I approach a door covered in ivy. My heart pounds. I KNOW this is it. Fingers trembling, I withdraw the big golden key for my pocket and insert it in the keyhole.

Click.

Slowly, as though in a dream, I enter the garden— the place where I spent the most time with Edward. And then, a tsunami of memories hits me like a ton of bricks. My breath catches in my throat. It feels like

I'm in a film, while scenes from the past swirl and converge like a huge montage. I see myself lying on the soft expanse of grass near the flowerbeds with Edward, side-by-side, arguing over insignificant matters like the shape of the clouds in the sky. I see myself sitting in the swing beneath an apple tree while Edward pushes me higher and jokes that I'm getting heavier. I flush when I find the carved stone bench, where Edward used to pull me onto his lap and we'd engage in a passionate make-out session. Nor can I miss the fountain, bright and glistening, sending sprays of clear water into the sky.

Edward appears. He looks tired, but his face lights up when he sees me.

"Amelie dressed you well." His gaze slides over my body in appreciation. This gown fits me snugly in all the right places, flattering my curves. While it is less revealing compared to my usual summer wear in Portland, I feel sexy all the same. I have grown more womanly compared to my teens—considering how Edward could discern the facial difference between me and my teenage self, I'm positive that he has noticed the changes to my body as well.

"Though I wish this image of you were for my eyes alone."

I've got to react better than a speechless blush.

"I can go back and change." I smile. "It won't take long if I can put on a coat."

He closes his hand around my wrist, effectively preventing my escape. "No need." His other hand drifts to my back and stays there, as immovable as a

192

rock. I can't move unless I fall forward, which will bring my body into direct contact with his chest. "Let us start with a basic waltz. Put your left hand on my shoulder and give me your right hand."

Since there is no music, Edward keeps count in his deep baritone voice. To get used to the rhythm, we go through a three-step pattern—step right, bring the left foot next to the right foot, then step in place with the right foot. It should be simple, even for somebody who is not adept at body coordination, but with Edward gazing at me intently, it's so hard to concentrate.

"Relax, darling." Edward sounds amused. "Rest your hand on my forearm instead of grasping the material of my shirt. Unless you want to rip my shirt off? I assure you that I have not the slightest objection to that."

Shaking my head, I try very hard to banish the image of a half-naked Edward from my mind.

"Also, do not worry if your steps are too small. It is the gentleman's duty to match your step and stride."

"Okay . . . I mean, sure." Whenever I'm nervous, modern phrases will slip out. Thank God that we are alone.

Or not. Being alone means that he could take liberties that aren't allowed in public.

Moments later, I feel his hand on my back exerting more pressure, bringing me closer to his body. I'm not sure whether he's conscious of it or not, but my forehead is only scant inches from his collarbone. His clean, masculine scent surrounds me, his chest rising and falling gently. Not that I mind the proximity, honestly, but with my feelings still conflicted and nebulous, I don't want to encourage him until I'm absolutely certain I want to stay.

"I went to the school board meeting the other day," I say, trying to dispel the sexual tension that had inevitably built up. "I met Liam there."

"Liam? How is he getting along?"

"I don't think he enjoys teaching there." I can still remember him with his arms crossed and a languid expression that clearly showed he had no genuine interest in the school. "Why did you agree to write a recommendation for him?"

Edward pauses in his step. "I do not know if your memory includes this, but when you founded the school, you had a difficult time looking for teachers."

"Enlighten me." My tone is such a perfect imitation of his princely one that both of us smile.

"Few female teachers are able to teach subjects other than Languages and Etiquette, and male teachers usually find it effeminate to be teaching girls as young as five. For some, it is the equivalent of being a nanny."

Henry taught for Princess College a while ago, before he became too busy. Was it from a genuine desire to help, or was it under Elle's influence? "Then why did Liam apply?"

"He plans to settle down in the capital when he graduates, and housing can be expensive in respectable areas. The school is not his first choice, but the pay is good and he is undeniably qualified."

194

The waltz comes to an end. He bows, and I curtsy, panting a little as I sink and bend my knees. The dance is by no means strenuous exercise, but combined with conversation, I need to draw breath more frequently.

"Would you like to rest for a while? Or shall we start another dance?"

I wipe a trickle of sweat from my forehead. "Suppose you demonstrate the moves and I rest while I watch you?"

He complies and shows me the basic moves of a quadrille. Another memory surfaces in my mind—when I was still living with the Bradshaws, the dancing master had frequently complained to Lady Bradshaw how clumsy I was at the quadrille, and my 'mother' told me that tripping over my feet was no way to get a husband.

I wonder what Lady Bradshaw thought when I married Edward.

When he finishes demonstrating the dance, Edward holds out his hand. "Will you honor me with your hand for a quadrille, my lady?"

I place my hand into his and warmth flows through us.

"There is more that I learned at the school." In terse words, I tell him about Lady Willoughby.

He frowns. "I have heard something about that from my mother. It seems that those noble families had expected that their daughters would be taught to gain advantage in the marriage market, but finding that the lessons are similar to what is taught at a boys' boarding school, they chose to withdraw. Besides, I suspect that Henry's departure has something to do with it."

Liam's words echo in my mind. *They're just here for Henry.*

"Maybe it will help if you teach a class at the girls' school," I say lightly. "That will definitely bring those girls back."

I'm joking, of course, but he seems to take it seriously. "I'll teach as many classes as you want." Edward tightens his grip on my hand and waist. "If you promise to stay."

I step back, conveniently forgetting that it doesn't match his step, and an alarmed look appears in his eyes.

"Kat, behind you—"

My bum meets something cold, hard and damp. The next second, a spray of water splashes over my head, drenching my hair completely. I've stepped into the fountain. Water trickles down my forehead, running down my cheeks and sliding along my neck, soaking the lovely gown that Amelie selected.

Edward fumbles for a handkerchief. "Did you bruise yourself?"

"I'm bruised, all right. Sore all over."

"Let me fetch our family physician."

"Wait." I grab his arm. "I was referring to my pride."

We look at each other while water continues to drip down my face. Then, I can't help it—I laugh.

"It's so unfair. I can never maintain my dignity before you." I rub my face and neck with his handkerchief. "Lucky for me, the sun is out today. Still, I think I'd better go back and change . . ."

I trail off, as Edward is no longer listening to me. He's staring at me like he wants to gobble me up. I dart a glance at myself. The water has not only soaked through my hair, but it has run down my front, dampening the white material of my gown (what was Amelie thinking? It is so much easier to get dirty in the garden) and revealing my corset. From a straight, red blooded male's perspective, I suppose my look is alluring. And considering what Edward feels for me and that we've been practicing dancing with his arms around me . . .

"Well." I give a nervous laugh. "Maybe we should practice dancing after dinner instead. Your garden is too compact."

"No." His voice is deep, husky. "It is enough trouble trying to keep my hands off you in the evening."

Slowly, he approaches me. My heart pounds. Surely, he isn't going to kiss me—I'm like a bedraggled rat that was caught in the rain. Well, not that soaked, but still . . .

Edward brushes my damp hair from my face and leans in.

23

Someone knocks on the door. Pounding, more like it.

Both of us freeze. Edward halts a few inches from my lips, his expression soon turning from shock to annoyance. I glance at him for a second, my heart still beating fast, and move away from him. Part of me is disappointed, yet another part of me is relieved. I have a feeling that once his passion is ignited, it's going to be really hard to stop him.

The pounding starts again, more urgently this time. Edward strides to the door, muttering something like "wring Bertram's neck."

But it's Amelie who's standing outside, her cheeks flushed and her shoulders heaving. It's so rare that she runs.

"Apologies for the interruption, Your Highness. But Lady Elle sent a message. Miss Poppy went into labor this morning and gave birth. She's asking if you'd like to go down to Miss Poppy's house and see the newborns."

"Newborns? As in plural form?"

"She gave birth to twins."

"That's awesome." I brush past Edward. "Of course I'll go! Please ask Bertram to prepare the carriage."

"Not before you change out of your dress and dry your hair," Edward says firmly. "You'll catch a cold if you run around like this."

"Hey, I'm not a little girl anymore." I wag a finger at him. "Trust me, I can take care of myself."

His response is to pick up his coat and drape it around me. I look up at him, and am touched by the concern in his eyes. "Kat, let's go."

Since I'm only visiting a friend, I have more liberty in choosing what to wear. Amelie and Mabel help me into a light cotton dress of soft, pastel colors, though there's still no way around the corset, and I wish they could invent bras in Athelia.

"There." Mabel twists my hair into a low bun and places a string of real forget-me-nots around the bun. "Isn't it convenient that we have loads of flowers in the room?"

"Thanks, Mabel. You did a great job."

When I emerge from my bedroom, Edward rises from the sofa in the sitting room. "Ready?"

"You're coming as well?" He's supposed to attend a meeting with the king. I know that, because at breakfast the king had mentioned he wanted to talk to Edward about renovating some areas in the capital.

"I already informed George to re-schedule."

"Edward, I know how busy your schedule is."

"Meetings occur daily, but a birth does not. Poppy is your close friend, and I've also become acquainted with her husband. An honest, decent man with whom I'm pleased to be friends." He lays a hand on my shoulder. "When you married me, you had to deal with my many relatives. I would also take part in your circle of friends."

I don't know what comes over me, but I rise on tiptoe and peck his cheek. He freezes, as though I were Elsa in *Frozen*.

"Did you just . . ."

"Is that Bertram over there?" I point at the hulk-like figure in the courtyard. "He already has the horses saddled. Come on, let's not keep him waiting."

"Kat."

Ignoring his request that I 'repeat the action I did to him,' I find our carriage and clamber inside. *I shouldn't have kissed him.* Yet, deep down inside, I know that sooner or later, I won't be able to stop myself from reciprocating his affection. The question is how long I can wait until Krev appears.

***

Poppy lives in a brownstone townhouse that wouldn't look out of place in a colonial-style residential area in Virginia. It's quaint and cozy, a far cry from the overwhelming splendor of the palace. If Edward and

200

I ever get a holiday, I would like to stay at a place like this.

A housemaid opens the door and does a double-take when she sees us. Then she tries to do a deep curtsy, but without constant practice, she wobbles so badly that I reach out and steady her. "Is Poppy upstairs? Can we go and see her now?"

"Certainly, Your Highness. They're all upstairs— the master, Lady Elle, and the parents."

Edward and I mount the narrow staircase. Following where the voices are located, we enter a room specially set up for childbirth. It looks crowded, what with several people surrounding the bed and two cribs against the wall.

Elle is the first to see us. A huge smile lights up her face, and she waves us over. There, Poppy is lying against two pillows, Mr. Davenport stroking her damp hair, and two bundles are placed on her abdomen.

"Hello, new mommy." I hasten to her side, while nodding to the others saying *Your Highness* to me.

Poppy smiles up at me. She looks weary, but she looks just as I remember—straw-colored hair, freckles, and a round face. "I'm so happy you're able to come, Kat. It means a lot to me." She pats the flannel towels wrapped around her babies. "Aren't they the cutest things ever?"

I squeal and coo over the tiny babies, marveling at how perfect they look and how minuscule their hands and feet are. "Oh dear, I can't tell them apart."

"The one on the left is Sebastian Jonathan Montgomery, after his grandfather and father." Elle offers. "And the right one is Katriona Olivia Montgomery. After you and her grandmother."

Seeing my look of surprise, Poppy adds, "It was my idea. Without you, Kat, we couldn't have gotten married."

"Oh." A voice whispers that this isn't my real name, but it isn't the time to protest. "I'm honored. It's the first time that I've had a baby named after me."

"We are the ones who are honored," Sir Montgomery says. He coughs when I glance in his direction, seeming embarrassed. I recall his look of disbelief when Bertram announced I was Edward's future bride in Ruby Red.

"It's mostly Bertram's doings," I say. "Actually, Edward should take the credit, because he sent Bertram to accompany us."

Poppy glances at Edward, and her smile widens.

"Thank you, Your Highness." A playful look appears on her face. "When is your turn, Kat?"

I feel my lip twitch, but all I do is shrug and smile. "Someday."

One of the babies—Sebastian or Olivia—sneezes, and Poppy instinctively adjusts the flannel towel, covering the baby's tiny head like a hood.

"You are going to be a very busy mother."

She smiles. "They are going to be worth it, I know."

Mr. Davenport places a hand on her forearm. "If you cannot handle the babies, I will hire additional help. I want my children to grow up healthy and happy."

"That's why we came to the capital," a man says. Judging from the resemblance, he must be Mr. Davenport's father. "If you have any trouble, all you need to do is to send us word. We should know, after raising eight children."

"We'll come over every day," Sir Montgomery says briskly, as if it's some kind of competition. "We'll see that our grandchildren will not want for anything."

At that moment, Sebastian starts making a queer noise and stretches his tiny legs into the air.

"He's hungry," a dumpy woman says. Judging from her plain clothes and rough accent, she is probably the midwife. "Best that the mother starts breastfeeding. It's a good thing to give the babies something to warm up their tummies."

That's the cue for us to leave. Before I go, I clasp Poppy's hand. "I'll come by some other time. I need to get acquainted with my godchildren."

Poppy brightens and squeezes my fingers. "Promise me it'll be soon, Kat."

We smile at each other. It's then that I realize how I miss having a female friend in Athelia. Amelie and Mabel are my age, and we often laugh and joke with each other, but there's still a subtle difference when they are paid to serve me. Edward is the closest thing to a best friend, but his affection is too mixed up with sexual desire. As much as I enjoy his companionship, I do need other friends like Poppy and Elle.

We chat for a while until the housekeeper comes and asks if we'd like to partake of some tea and refreshments. Sir Montgomery is quick to accept, for he only arrived this morning. Seeing that both Poppy and Mr. Davenport are looking exhausted as well, we wish them good luck and head out of the room.

As the housekeeper offers us tea, I notice Elle sitting in a corner, looking a bit lonely. No wonder—this room is filled with couples—me and Edward, Sir Montgomery and his wife, and Mr. Davenport's parents. When Sir Montgomery approaches us, I whisper to Edward that I need to talk to Elle, and let go of his hand.

"Elle." I hurry over to her. "I haven't seen you for a while. How are you doing?"

"Very well, Kat. Life is busy, but I wouldn't have it any other way. Aren't those babies adorable? I look forward to seeing your own." She attempts a mischievous smile, but there is a sadness in her eyes.

"And how is your family doing?"

Mrs. Thatcher is well and even joined a crochet society. Billy is going to school. After all, Elle can afford his education now. She sent him to one of the best elementary schools in the capital, though he still goes to Mr. Wellesley's on the weekends.

"Billy is doing better than we expected. Maybe it's Mr. Wellesley's influence," Elle says, smiling at the mention of her little brother. "He's fascinated with insects and bugs and small animals, in particular. Mamsie is forever telling him to stop bringing pet mice and lizards into the house, especially after that day . . ." She looks down, seeming to be embarrassed.

"That day?" I say, sensing there's something more to her words.

Elle sips some tea before speaking. "Oh, it shouldn't have happened, but I suppose even if it didn't, her ladyship would still disapprove of me."

My mind goes blank for a moment, then I realize who she must be talking about. "Henry's mother?"

She nods. "When Henry broached the possibility of us marrying, her ladyship paid us a visit. I wasn't at home. Mamsie made sure to clean the flat, but she missed Billy's pet frog that was hiding under a chair."

Oh, dear. I have a suspicion what the disaster is.

Elle meets my gaze and sighs. "When her ladyship prepared to leave, the frog jumped on her new dress. Naturally, it gave her a huge fright, and she tried to get out her parasol to whack the frog, but Billy caught the gold top of the end of the parasol. She called him an impertinent monkey, and she said Mamsie and Billy weren't fit to associate with Henry."

"Oh dear." I really should feel bad for Elle's sake, but the frog incident sounds so comical that I have to suppress a smile. "Did she tell Henry? What did he say?"

"He tried reasoning with her ladyship, but she wouldn't be pacified. Either I disown my family, or I cannot marry Henry. Of course, I can't abandon Mamsie and Billy. Henry suggested that we wait until her ladyship calms down." Elle looks down on her lap. "I'm already fortunate that I've been able to provide for Mamsie and Billy, which is all I ever wanted. More happiness would be a blessing." Elle finishes her tea and exhales. "I should be going. Mr. Galen kindly agreed to lend us a dozen pots of ferns for the girls' musical this week, and I have to oversee the delivery of the plants. Will you be attending the musical? Your niece will be participating. It will also do good if other parents see you present."

I make sure that the date doesn't coincide with my next dancing lesson. "Sure, Elle. I'll be there."

24

Edward has become even busier these days—he barely visits me in the mornings at tea time. The king had asked him to assist with the urban planning of the capital, ever since the mayor wanted to plan more public parks and gardens. Along with his usual duties of drafting memorandums and agreements, working with Henry and other parliament members on various acts, as well as the dancing lessons, I'm glad that I made the decision to cancel our nightly talks and set up a space in his office. If Edward goes on like this, I'll be submitting a royal Eight-Hour-Act on his behalf.

Every day after breakfast, I return to our suite— to my study with the window seat, to be exact—and sift through the never-ending pile of letters. Then I read the papers. I requested a subscription to three publishers, so that I could learn about the same event from different perspectives. I review drafts of

Edward's work and make suggestions or corrections. Then, in the afternoon, I'd head to his office on the other side of the palace.

Today I have to leave the palace, but I want to see my husband before I engage the carriage. Before I enter through the doorway, I hear voices coming from within.

"A woman in this place is a dangerous influence, Your Highness." The lord chamberlain sounds genuinely concerned. "How will you be able to concentrate on your work while she's in here?"

"My wife is not to be labeled dangerous, Dubois," Edward says stiffly.

The lord chamberlain sniffs in disapproval. "I've heard stories of how you're becoming less inhibited ever since she moved in the palace. Do try to remember your father had you carefully brought up. Unbridled passion is a sin, and you know well how some of your ancestors were perceived when they took mistresses and…"

"I have no intentions of taking a mistress." Edward sounds exasperated. "If I were lax in my responsibilities, my father, or the prime minister, would be the first to lecture me. Dubois, I suggest you return to your duties of managing the royal household. I have work to finish."

"But Your Highness, there are people talking, and you must be well aware of how His Majesty is concerned of your image."

I really don't feel like interrupting their conversation, but I have to go soon if I don't want to be late to Rosie's musical.

I rap on the door smartly and sail into the room as though I've just arrived and didn't hear a word of their conversation.

"Master Dubois." I nod at him and smile, before turning to Edward. "Sorry; I didn't mean to barge in like this, but I had to drop by and let you know I'm not joining you today."

Edward nods. "Where are you going?"

"To Princess College. Rosie is taking part in a musical, and she'll appreciate it if her Aunt Kat is there. Because of this, I made certain to finish editing the draft on the tea trade agreement this morning." I lay a sheaf of papers on Edward's desk. "I've flagged several consistency errors, made suggestions to some awkward phrasing, and corrected every grammatical and spelling mistake I could find. If you've any questions, we can go over with them when I come back for dinner."

Edward flashes me a dazzling smile. In my opinion, he is more likely to be a distraction than I. "Thank you, Kat. You've saved me hours of work."

I sweep him a curtsy and grin. "You're most welcome, Your Highness. See you later."

When I walk past the lord chamberlain, who looks as if he's turned into stone, I stop. "I almost forgot—I also compiled a style sheet for you."

"A style sheet? Explain, please."

I raise an eyebrow. Edward knows perfectly well what a style sheet is—he's only asking because the lord chamberlain is listening.

"A list of word usages and punctuation, so you'll be able to keep track of your writing and maintain consistency."

"It sounds like a useful tool," Edward grins. "Do you not agree, Dubois?"

This time the lord chamberlain slinks away in silence. Edward and I exchange a smile, and I realize for the first time that I am actually enjoying my role as princess.

***

As the carriage rattles along on my way to Princess College, I wonder when Krev is going to come back. Although Edward and I have made up, the ghost of our first quarrel hangs over my head. Until I can assure Edward that Krev is not going to take me back to the modern world, he will always be reluctant to let me out of his sight. The only solution is to have Krev appear, but that is something beyond my control.

There are several more carriages than usual lining the street where Princess College is located. I guess they belong to the other parents who have come to see the musical. Elle and I certainly selected a good location for the school. It's off one of the main streets, so the traffic won't cause too much noise, but it's also close enough that transportation wouldn't be difficult.

As I go down the corridor, I almost run into a person who has just emerged from a classroom.

"Sorry, I was walking too fast . . ." The words die away on my lips when I notice the person I nearly ran into.

"Lady Gregory?" Last time she seemed familiar, but by now, my memories have recovered so much that this time, her name springs into my mind without any doubt.

The old lady smiles at me. "Miss Katriona . . . forgive me, it should be Princess Katriona. Congratulations on your marriage to the prince."

"Just call me Kat," I say, feeling uncomfortable about an old lady bowing to me in deference. "We're at school, not the palace. There's no need for so many formalities. By the way, how come you are one of the teachers here?"

"The girls have formed a crochet club, and I was invited to be the teacher, since many of my projects have won prizes."

I remember Lady Gregory's room, so cozy and delightful with all those homemade crocheted objects hanging over the place. "That's great. How are the girls getting along?"

"Most of them are doing fine. It's refreshing for me as well, to be able to teach so many young and eager children."

The bell rings. I'm reminded of my purpose—to see the musical.

"Lady Gregory, would you like to come and see the girls' performance with me?"

Her face lights up. "So, it is today? How forgetful of me. I am sure I wrote it down on my notebook, but I never seem to remember."

Elle had told me that she would save me a seat, but it really is unnecessary. While there are a few parents present, we still have plenty of empty chairs. I guess either most other parents are too busy working, or they don't care enough for their children. I've heard noble ladies at court remarking that that children doing a musical is something trivial or frivolous.

Rosie looks adorable in her elf suit. Their voices are like little angels, and I can tell that most of the girls take genuine pleasure in performing. Once the musical is over, I hand out roses to the girls, who are surprised but excited to receive the flowers.

"From His Highness's garden," I say, and someone squeals. As I expected, Edward is extremely popular among girls.

When I finish handing out the flowers, Elle touches my arm. "Kat, the headmistress would like to have a word with you."

"Are there any problems with the funds?" I asked.

Elle shakes her head. "I don't think so. She merely wants to give you a report."

I say goodbye to Lady Gregory, who smiles just as affably as she usually does.

As we make way to the headmistress's office, there is the sound of a man shouting in one of the classrooms. Elle and I look at each other. There are a few male teachers in the school, and there are men on

212

the school board, but the sound of this man belongs to someone who has never had an education. His pronunciation is rough and uncultured.

The next second, a man in patched, dirty clothes, with a scar running over his right cheek, drags a little girl out of the room. The girl is Molly.

"Excuse me?" I address the man, who looks like he could use a good shaving. "May I ask what you are doing?"

The man bristles at me. "I'm taking my girl home. She has no business coming to a place like this when her family is starving."

"Mr. Ripley," Elle says in a soothing tone. "Surely, there is no need to come to the school and interrupt the lessons. In fact, we are on our way to see the headmistress. If you would be so kind as to come with us and sit down and have a discussion, maybe we can come to a better solution—"

"To hell with your solution," Mr. Ripley growls. "You can afford to say that with your expensive dresses and jewelry, but my girl ain't cut out for a place like this. She's got to come home with me and make herself useful."

Molly tugs on my sleeve. "It doesn't matter, Your Highness," she says in a small voice. "I'd much rather go home. I often fall asleep in class. It ain't much use for me to be here anyway."

Mr. Ripley scowls at me. I guess he didn't hear Molly call me *Your Highness*. With his scar, he looks more grotesque than most people. "What's the use of having children if they can't lessen the burden of the family?"

I feel like punching him in the face, but all I can do is clench my fists and watch him drag Molly away. I've been doing my best to help the children, but so far my efforts aren't producing the results I hoped for.

25

I really want to spend some time thinking about how to help Molly, but unfortunately, royal duties come calling. Soon, the Moryn emperor will be arriving with his fiancée to the capital for the State Visit. Most of my time is filled up with cramming in Moryn customs, business transactions, and even the hobbies and interests of the emperor and his fiancée.

Even though the king and queen will be the ones to perform the main duties, Edward and I are still required to appear at every event. I am so thankful that I've recovered almost all my memories by now. It would be a big deal if I made some stupid mistake in front of the emperor. That's going to be even more disastrous than me blundering in front of Bianca and the queen.

Nevertheless, I am still nervous when the day arrives. I have gotten used to my royal life in the palace now, but this is the first time that I'm receiving a foreign royal. I have to watch myself because my conduct will be reported not only in Athelia, but also in foreign newspapers.

In late afternoon, we line up near the entrance of the palace, where the main road stretching outside is already flanked with crowds waiting to see the emperor arrive. I'm sweating in my multi-layered gown and praying that my crown won't fall off when we're supposed to follow the king and queen into the palace.

Edward stands next to me, attired in full dress uniform, a black frock coat with golden epaulets and a matching black cap with a golden plume. He's breathtaking. I could hardly take my eyes off him when he emerged from his room.

"Thy blush the divinest rosy-red," he whispers, a teasing gleam in his eyes. "Shall I interpret it as an encouraging sign that you are more attracted to me?"

I look away and mutter, "I thought you didn't like it when girls fawned over your looks."

"Not if it concerns you. As long as you fall in love with me, I shall not care whether it is because of my face, my mind, or my character."

Edward-the-Flirt is in full force. I have a feeling that it has to do with my uncertain state of leaving or staying. I don't remember that he was usually this flirtatious.

Before I can think of a witty rejoinder, there is the sound of horses galloping, followed by the sound of trumpets blaring some military-style music.

"They are playing the national anthem of the Moryn Empire," Edward whispers. "It's customary to play it before the monarch arrives."

A long line of carriages appears on the road. Cheers erupt from the crowds, who are shouting and waving and clapping. "It's the emperor!" "Wonder what the future empress looks like?" "Here they come!" It makes me think of the reception on my wedding day.

Not everyone seems to welcome the Moryn emperor. Some people in the crowds are holding up huge signs that read, *Down with the Dictator*. I am reminded of my lessons on Moryn's current state of affairs. The country is still largely controlled by an autocratic ruler—the emperor doesn't allow the people have a say in his decisions. They don't have a parliament to exert a moderating influence on the emperor. The mob uprising in the capital was likely due to disagreement with Augustin's policies.

I'm glad that I was transported to Athelia. While it's frustrating that the parliament is slow to accept our innovations, I'd take a constitutional monarchy over a dictatorship anytime. I dread to imagine how Athelia would fare if Edward were anything like Andrew McVean.

Finally, Emperor Augustin emerges from his carriage. I recognize him from the photos that Edward showed me. Then he escorts a young lady dressed in a huge, frilly pink gown. She has to be Simone, the fiancée of the emperor.

"Let us go welcome our guests," the king says.

Walking beside Edward, I follow the king and queen out of the entrance gates until we reach the Moryn royals, who are also headed in our direction. After exchanging a few courteous words, the king holds out his arm to the future empress of Moryn, while the emperor offers his arm to the queen.

Accompanied by rows of yeomen, we set off to the Reception Room, where introductions are made. It's obvious that Augustin has already met the king, the queen, and Edward, but he doesn't know me. Nor have we met Simone, for she got engaged to the emperor only a few weeks ago.

"Allow me introduce my wife, Katriona Bradshaw," Edward says, and my heart melts at the glow in his face.

Augustin is in his late thirties, with a perfectly curled mustache and a perfectly tailored outfit.

"Princess Katriona." Augustin raises my hand to his lips. "I am at your service."

I curtsy, feeling my knees crack. "Welcome to Athelia, Your Majesty."

I'm next introduced to Simone, who looks much younger than the emperor—Edward had informed me that she is going to be Augustin's second wife. The first wife passed away and left the five-year-old Moryn princess who's too young for Edward.

Anyway, Simone is simply gorgeous, one of the few women who could compete with Bianca in looks. Silky blonde hair falls in glistening coils on sloping porcelain shoulders. Blue-gray eyes are set like priceless jewels, and a delicate chin is so perfectly curved that it could have been molded by a sculptor. She is dressed in a snow-white top lined with pearl buttons, along with a giant, frilly Barbie-pink gown that's puffed out like a balloon. On me, that gown would definitely be too garish and frivolous. However, Simone manages to carry it off, like the gown is custom-made for her. If she were in the U.S., she'd be a perfect model for playing any Disney princess.

"Ah, so you are the famous lady that Prince Edward picked from a thousand girls!" She grabs my hand with evident enthusiasm. "Katriona, is it? May I call you Katriona? So lovely that we finally meet! I've been so curious about you since I read about your engagement in the papers."

Simone continues to chatter until a photographer asks if he can take our picture. A flash goes off, and this time I don't even flinch. I truly am getting used to my role as princess of Athelia—a role that I never expected I'd come to accept.

A few seconds later, I find myself facing a tall, broad-shouldered man who looks around thirty. Like Augustin, his mustache is impeccably curled and his clothes are crisp and new.

"Princess Katriona." His mouth, which is already rather wide, seems to split his face in half as he grins. His voice is low and sensual, his touch on my hand like a caress, and his gaze remains on my face for such a long moment that I'm rather uncomfortable. "Have we met earlier? Your lovely face seems familiar."

"I…don't think so." He is looking so closely at me that I wonder if I have something on my face.

"Pardon me, but I don't believe I've ever seen you before."

"In that case, let me introduce myself. I am His Majesty's one and only brother, Jérôme Victoire Emmanuel, Count di Corsica." He kisses the back of my hand, and I have an urge to wipe my hand against my gown. "But call me Jérôme, please."

"Jérôme," Augustin says, apparently detecting my discomfort. "I haven't yet introduced you to Lord Sunderland, who has expressed a wish to meet you."

I'm glad when Jérôme is led away. While he hasn't done anything that oversteps the bounds of propriety, I don't understand why he'd be this drawn to me, especially with a stunning beauty like Simone present. What did he mean when he asked if we've met before? Maybe he was at one of the social events when I had my Season, but since I was only the overlooked Bradshaw sister, I didn't have a chance to be introduced to him. Anyway, I just hope that I won't have to interact with the emperor's brother for the rest of the State Visit.

26

The State Visit passes in a flurry of excitement. Every event, from the military review, the Investiture, to the dinner parties, has been an eye-opening experience that I could never have participated in the modern world. Still, I'll be glad when it's over. Both Edward and I sleep for only a few hours these days. Maybe that accounts for why I often felt easily tired, especially in crowds.

The king and queen perform the major roles for most of the time. During the Investiture, for example, the king ties a blue ribbon on Augustin's leg and declares him a Knight of the Highest Order. All I have to do is stand like a statue for a few hours, and try to look rapt and interested. Edward later tells me that he is also tempted to fidget and shout. For all his well-trained discipline, inside he is just like me, concealing a dislike for fussy rituals.

However, there is one occasion that Edward and I have to take the reins. Simone has expressed a desire to visit Fauxe, the most high-end pleasure garden in Athelia. A pleasure garden (I was later to remember I first heard of the term from Mr. Wellesley) is a venue for public entertainment. In the past, the king and queen have sometimes accompanied foreign guests to Fauxe Gardens, like local hosts showing the tourists around.

"Leon and I are wearied from the events running all day long, and would like to rest fully for tomorrow night's ball," the queen tells me. "The gardens will be more fun for you young people."

Naturally we have to change again after dinner. After Mabel and Amelie fuss over my hair and gown and shoes, I enter the sitting room, where Edward is already lounging on the sofa, reading a letter. I don't like keeping him waiting, but then he doesn't have to lace himself into a corset.

"Change it."

"Change what?"

"Your dress." His gaze drops to my collarbone— I'm wearing an off-shoulder gown that reveals my shoulders, but barely any cleavage. "That brother of the emperor is going to be there, and I would not like his eyes on your bare skin."

"Jérôme?" Since that uneasy introduction to the emperor's brother, I've been wary of him, but so far he hasn't done anything improper save for a few curious stares in my direction.

"Haven't you seen how he was gazing at you?" Edward advances a step toward me. He is frowning, and I feel like teasing his mouth into a grin. "He is well known to be sexually promiscuous among the Moryn elite, and I've yet to hear of a Moryn elite who has less than a dozen mistresses or paramours."

"I don't really like how he looks at me either," I confess. "But look at it objectively. There are many women at court who are single and prettier than me, so why would he want to flirt with me? Maybe he's speculating how I came to be princess of Athelia. You know so many people, nobles and commoners included, have wondered why you chose me at the ball."

"I doubt he would have the temerity to make a move on you, but nevertheless, remember that the Moryns are less inhibited when it comes to interacting with the opposite sex. Do not allow him to take advantage and then make excuses for him."

I raise my hand, shaped into a fist. "Don't you worry, Edward. I can defend myself if the need comes for it. He'll never expect that a princess knows how to throw a punch."

He stares at me, the corner of his lip twitching. Feeling self-conscious, I lower my fist, but he moves closer and cups my cheek, his gaze filled with affection.

"If only I had a mirror," he murmurs. "You have no idea how adorable you looked when you talked like that with your fist raised."

My heart starts to flutter and I lean into his touch, wishing that we didn't have to go out. I would much rather stay here with my royal husband.

The clock strikes at that moment. A few seconds later, Amelie enters the sitting room and Edward drops his arm with unfeigned reluctance.

"The Moryns are waiting," she says, her face expressionless as usual. "Due to the number of security guards accompanying you, it is expected that the journey to the gardens will be longer than normally required."

Edward gestures at my gown. "Bring the princess a wrap or scarf. She should not be out walking in the night without some protection."

A quizzical look passes in Amelie's eyes, but it's gone in an instant. "Certainly, Your Highness."

***

Simone and Jérôme are waiting at the foot of the grand staircase near the entrance of the palace. Both of them are dressed exquisitely in the finest silk and velvet, and adorned with glittering jewelry. Simone, in particular, seems to have stepped out of a storybook. In her pale blue gown that must contain a huge crinoline, and a dainty diamond tiara sparkling in her mass of golden hair, she is the quintessential fairytale princess.

"Augustin will not be coming with us to Fauxe Gardens," she says, shaking her long feathery curls. As an unmarried lady, she can have the luxury of

224

having her hair down. "He ate too much lobster at dinner and is currently suffering from a stomachache. Serves him right."

"Hence he sent me in his place." Jérôme makes a grandiloquent bow and offers me his arm. "However, I am confident that you will find me every bit as charming as my brother. May I escort you to the carriage, Princess Katriona?"

I hesitate, but it's unlikely that I can refuse. Augustin would have escorted me if he were present.

"Where's Henry?" Edward says, looking around. "He is supposed to join us."

"I'm afraid he won't be able to make an appearance either," Jérôme says. "He seems to be greatly taken with Francis and wishes to spend more time with him."

I blink. Has Henry suddenly fallen for a man from Moryn?

"Oh, stop teasing her, Jérôme," Simone admonishes in the tone of a bossy older sister, though it's clear she's at least ten years younger than him. "Francis is Augustin's personal doctor. Duke Henry has been asking him about his work since he arrived."

"That may be expected," Edward says. "Dr. Durant is renowned for the introduction of intravenous therapy. Henry has always idolized him."

"But they could have come along as well," Simone says, frowning. "Isn't it common for people to stroll in the gardens and chat?"

"It is not ideal for serious conversation. Music entertainment—whether it may be vocal or instrumental—is always readily available, and there are firework displays during summer nights."

Simone looks excited. "Oh, how positively lovely! I must ask Augustin to build a similar one in Moryn when we go home."

***

Fauxe Gardens is indeed magnificent. At night, you can't see the vibrant colors of the flowerbeds, but there's a magical atmosphere when the walks are illuminated by hundreds of glass lamps swinging gently in the breeze. A golden pavilion is set up in the very middle of the venue, and an orchestra is playing. The spectators gathered around seem to be appreciative of the music—no dancing, however.

"Why aren't they dancing?" Simone asks curiously. "I would dearly enjoy a waltz or quadrille in the open air."

"It depends on the orchestra," Edward explains. As we meander in the gardens, he has taken care to walk behind Jérôme and me—supposedly so he can keep an eye on us. Even when Simone sometimes exclaims at some display and hurries ahead, he doesn't budge. "However, it is my understanding that dancing is discouraged in Fauxe, for the insufficient lighting means that it is likely to facilitate inappropriate contact with the partner. Moreover, the long, dewy grass may cause a nuisance for a lady's dress, especially if the material is particularly fine."

"It is because we are in a fancy establishment, dear sister," Jérôme drawls. "Now, Rayon Gardens is an entirely different matter."

Edward pauses in his step. "You have been to Rayon?"

Jérôme shrugs in a nonchalant manner. I wonder what it would take to unsettle him. As the emperor's brother, he can have anything he wants without the stress and responsibilities that go along with the privileges he is bestowed. "Twice, in fact. I find the lively steps of the bourgeois dances very much to my liking. And the women less prudish."

Simone smacks his arm. "*Remember* what Augustin told you, you oaf. The customs are different here."

Edward had said that Moryns are less fussy with the old-fashioned Athelian rules. Just the action of Simone slapping her future brother-in-law is enough to signify that.

Fireworks start exploding in the sky, a perfect diversion at the moment. As everyone points at the sky and gasps in wonder, the tension between Edward and Jérôme is temporarily on hold.

"Your husband seems uncommonly protective," Jérôme says lightly. "It is not as if I could impregnate a lady from a mere glance, my dear Princess Katriona."

I cough. In Athelia, I doubt any man could say the word 'impregnate' in front of me, unless it's a doctor. "I'm afraid your reputation precedes you, Your Grace."

227

He looks at me closely, and there's the same intense expression that appeared when he arrived at the palace.

"Have you never visited Moryn before?"

I think hard, but I'm positive that I have never set foot in his country. Taking a journey to a foreign country would have left a deep impression in my mind, yet I can't remember anything. Edward never mentioned anything about me visiting Moryn either.

"I don't think so." Then, remembering I have to be diplomatic, I add, "But I'd love to visit one day. Edward has been telling me how beautiful the city is, especially the palace."

"When I was driving in the capital about a month ago, I thought there was a young woman in the streets who looked rather similar to you." Jérôme stares at me for a moment, then shakes his head. "It was a fleeting glance, however, so I could be mistaken."

So, he wasn't leering at me, but rather that I resemble some other girl he saw in Moryn. It's not a big deal, I guess. I came to inhabit Katriona Bradshaw's body because we look alike, so it won't surprise me if there's another girl who also shares similar features. If I were a rare beauty like Bianca . . . well, that would be another story.

And from what I could observe of the Moryns, their features are not much different from the Athenians. Maybe a little shorter, may be a little plumper, and their fashion sense seems to be more extravagant, but I can't observe much difference between the Moryns and the Athelians.

I just hope that Jérôme isn't making things up to excuse his conduct.

27

On the last day of events, Amelie pauses before lacing me into the corset.

"Would you like to go to the bathroom, Your Highness?"

"Why are you asking me as if I'm not going to see a bathroom again?"

"Because you won't get to change clothes for at least six to seven hours," Mabel pipes up, bringing in my shoes. They're beautiful—sheer, sparkling satin the color of rose petals. "There's the concert and the ball, and you can't relieve yourself while wearing this dress."

I touch the whalebone corset and the crinoline that's supposed to go under my skirt. They are stiff, hard, and unbendable, like a cage.

"She is correct," Amelie says, inspecting the laces on the corset. "Don't drink anything or eat anything, not until the end of the ball, which is likely to be past midnight."

"Are you telling me that I'm supposed to whirl around in all these layers on an empty stomach?"

Mabel looks surprised. "But aren't you used to this by now, Your Highness? *You* had to go through tons of balls during your Season."

When I was still an unmarried, unwanted maid at Lady Bradshaw's, I mostly sat in a corner and watched other men vying for a dance with Bianca. However, as princess, it's unlikely that I'll be left alone. Protocol ensures that I'll at least have Edward, and maybe even the emperor, ask me to dance. Augustin may not be a beloved ruler in his country, but he's flawless when it comes to international etiquette. For example, during the military review, despite the commotion and whirlwind action, he still found the occasion to gallop near our carriage and make some kind of lighthearted comment.

Please, I pray with all my might. *Please let me get through this ball without any mishap.*

***

A powerful electric-like jolt rocks through my head when I enter the ballroom, and for a moment my vision swims. It's the same room where the ball was held in *The Ugly Stepsister*. Memories inundate my mind like a flash flood, and I start to remember all the things that I have done here, from waltzing with Edward to revealing Elle's real identity. It takes all my willpower not to clap my hands on my temples, as there are so many memories attacking my mind that I'm unable to concentrate on dancing.

"Kat?" Edward touches my arm. "Are you feeling all right?"

"I . . ." I lean against his shoulder, not caring if it's inappropriate in public. All I want is for my head to stop hurting from the deluge of memories. "Just let me rest for a moment."

The king is dancing with Simone, which is a difficult task, as Simone's height only comes to his chest. It looks like he is dancing with his teenage daughter. On the other hand, Augustin seems to be faring better with the queen, both of them graceful and agile in their steps.

I glance around the ballroom. Jérôme is dancing with a young debutante called Minnie May—she looks positively thrilled to be his partner, though another middle-aged woman is eyeing them with a wary face that's remarkably similar to Edward's when we went to Fauxe Gardens last night. Most likely that she is Minnie May's mother, and has heard of Jérôme's profligacy.

In a corner, Henry is conversing with a middle-aged man who's wearing spectacles. Several paces away, Lady Petunia stands with her arms crossed, her expression filled with annoyance as she glares at her son.

"That's Sir Durant, who serves as Augustin's imperial physician," Edward says.

"The doctor that Henry idolizes? The duchess doesn't seem to like it."

Edward shrugs. "As I told you, she is disapproving when it comes to Henry's interest in medical studies. Instead of dancing with a potential bride-to-be, he chose to socialize with a physician. It's of little importance to her that said physician is a celebrity in his field."

Personally, I'm glad that Durant is here. Elle was invited to this ball at my insistence, but she couldn't attend due to a sudden letter from the earl's estate. Something about a conflict between the tenant farmers, and as the heiress of the earl's lands, it is her duty to return and resolve the problem. Such a pity. I know that she would have loved to dance with Henry at this ball.

Footsteps approach. The Moryn emperor, looking quite distinguished in his long, dark waistcoat, makes me a low bow.

"Would you favor me with the next dance, my dear Princess Katriona?"

Edward gives me a concerned look, but he doesn't say anything. Unless I'm on the verge of fainting, it's imperative that I accept the emperor's request.

Luckily, the assault of memories in my head has faded into a dull ache. "I would be delighted, Your Majesty." I do my best to look gratified, as if dancing with him is the highest honor a lady could expect.

Augustin takes my hand, and off we go. To tell the truth, I'm really nervous about dancing with the emperor, but all I can do is pray that the orchestra won't play some really fast song that I can't keep up with. I'm also thankful that Edward chose to teach me how to dance in his garden. I don't think I could have survived this ball if I forgot the steps.

I'm in luck again. The song is a slow waltz, which means I can actually talk to him while keeping step to the music.

"Simone told me that Jérôme has been casting sheep-eyes in your direction," Augustin says with an apologetic look. "My deepest apologies if my brother has caused you any discomfort, Princess Katriona. I've already issued him a stern warning to strictly adhere to your customs. What he felt was harmless interaction could be regarded as wanton flirting in Athelia."

To be honest, Jérôme hasn't done anything truly offensive. The most he did was stare at me curiously—which, combined with his reputation and Edward's sensitive nature, made my husband concerned.

"Jérôme didn't behave inappropriately," I assure Augustin. "There were a few times he did stare at me, but he told me it was because I reminded him of another girl in Moryn."

Augustin frowns. "Let's hope that he is being truthful. I admit that I would not be surprised that Jérôme would meet a woman that resembles you, since his female acquaintances are too numerous to keep track of."

"I think it's likely as well." I smile. "Your brother is unlikely to desire the wrath of my husband."

Augustin laughs and twirls me around. He is not classically handsome like Edward, but there is a smooth, suave charm in him that might have attracted Simone, apart from his being emperor.

"Last time I visited Athelia was two years ago," Augustin says easily. "Edward was not yet twenty, but already, people were expecting that he take a bride. His parents even asked me if there was any suitable candidate in Moryn that I might recommend. However, when I talked to him, it seemed he was in no rush to marry. In fact, he seemed to be weary of women. 'They're all the same,' he had told me. But apparently, you convinced him to change his mind."

I blush, unable to think of a reply. I can't very well tell him that I'm not 'the same' because I'm from another world.

As the song draws to an end, Augustin gives me another magnificent bow and kisses my hand. "It has been a pleasure dancing with you, Princess Katriona. I hope that you and your husband will grace us with your presence next year, when Simone and I are to be married."

When Augustin walks away and offers his arm to Lady Constance, the wife of Edward's eldest cousin, I reflect that the Moryn emperor has been nothing but a model of perfect behavior. However, the way he treats us must be very different from the way he treats his people; otherwise there wouldn't be the uprising, or the several people holding 'Down with the Dictator' signs when Augustin arrived.

I dance with a Moryn noble for the next song, which happens to be the same tune that was playing at Edward's ball. I can feel the deluge of memories hammering on the barrier in my brain, threatening to break it down. The barrier already feels like a bullet-ridden wall, swaying, and it will fall any time.

"Are you all right, Your Highness? You look very pale."

I dig my fingernails into my palm. "I'm fine," I say, smiling at my partner. "It must be the stuffiness in this room."

Amelie was right to advise me to go to the bathroom before dressing. I wonder how the other women can stand whirling over the dance floor with a tight corset and an empty stomach.

After I dance with a few other noblemen, I start coughing. It feels like the oxygen in the room has evaporated, and I cannot breathe normally.

"May I have the next dance with you, Princess Katriona?" someone—is it Lord Winston, or is it Fretwell?—is asking me.

"I'm sorry," I say thickly, trying to appear normal. "I . . . I'm a little tired after all the dancing. Please allow me to rest for a while."

Not feeling like being waylaid again, I stumble outside into the gardens. The cool, fragrant air surrounds me, and I inhale deeply. The ballroom is way too hot and stuffy. I take another deep breath, wondering how long it'll take before I can get out of this stifling outfit.

"Katriona?"

A dark shadow falls across my path. Although it's nighttime, the gardens are brightly lit with dozens of lanterns, so I'm able to make out the person who interrupted my solitude. It's Bianca, tall and slender, in an elegant turquoise gown lined with pearls and diamonds. She looks like she could shoot a commercial for Chanel.

"Katriona." Her words are cutting, cold, and there's no trace of politeness on her face. Without others nearby, she doesn't bother to keep up appearances.

I'd love to get away from her, but it looks like she wants to talk to me. I straighten my spine and tell myself I have nothing to fear. I am the princess, and my social ranking is far higher than hers. She won't intimidate me, and I won't be intimidated.

"Yes?"

"It should be me receiving the Moryns," she hisses. "Don't you know how drab you look compared to the emperor's fiancée? I never knew you could be this sneaky. You wanted to be princess and tried to imitate me, but knowing you could never succeed, you turned to shady methods."

I stare at her. "Don't be ridiculous."

"We both know you don't have a chance of attracting a man higher-ranked than an earl, not to mention the prince. You may have tricked Edward into marrying you, but how long do you think your seduction spell will work on him?"

"A seduction spell?" I raise an eyebrow. "God, Bianca, do you honestly believe that I caught

237

Edward's attention because of some stupid spell? Have you even seen him beyond his good looks and social standing, and learned that he isn't the type who is drawn by looks alone? If he were, he would have proposed to you long ago."

Cold fury radiates from Bianca. "How dare you criticize me? You, whom nobody bothered to spare a glance toward?"

I probably shouldn't have taunted her, but her attitude got on my nerves. "So what if I was overlooked? I'm the one who married the prince."

"You despicable . . ." Bianca raises a hand, a murderous gleam in her eyes. I step backward, alarmed and surprised at the possibility that she wants to attack me. Not that I'm afraid. Bianca may be taller, but I doubt any lady lessons in Athelia would include karate.

We stare at each other for a moment. Bianca breathes heavily, but she lowers her hand.

"I'm warning you, Katriona, don't think you can get away with your schemes. One day, I'll make you regret stealing what was mine."

I'm about to retort that she has no claim on Edward, but she's already turned on her heel and stalked away.

Frustrated and furious, I quell the temptation to hurl a stone at her retreating back. I hate her. I don't know how Elle could have tolerated her and Lady Bradshaw. And I'm so glad that I didn't let her get Edward.

Speaking of my husband, there seems to be an uncanny connection between us. Only a few minutes after Bianca left, Edward appears, his brow furrowed.

"Kat? Why did you leave the dance?"

I tell him about feeling stifled and uncomfortable.

"Perhaps you'd better sit down and get some rest." He looks concerned. "I remember when we used to practice dancing, you'd be out of breath quite soon."

I shouldn't be this weak. I'm only twenty-four, and I've been in pretty good shape since I joined the karate club. "I hope that the guests won't miss me."

"They're having a fine time dancing," he says, guiding me to a bench among the hedges. As I walk, something snaps, and the slipper on my right foot comes off.

"Dang." I lift my skirts to look for my slipper, but Edward instantly yanks my hand away.

"What are you doing? You should never expose your feet in public."

I resist the temptation to roll my eyes. There's no one around, I'm wearing black silk stockings, and I didn't raise my skirt anywhere above my knees.

"You didn't mind seeing my bare feet when I met you in the gardens on the day of my presentation."

He has the grace to look guilty. He also overlooked the rules when I fell down the stairs in Henry's house and landed in his arms. If he truly cared about propriety, he wouldn't have prevented me from trying to get up.

"My slipper seems to have fallen off."

Alarmed, he kneels down before me. "Let me have a look."

He examines the slipper with disapproval in his face. "I am no expert in women's fashion, but this type of shoe is not fit for dancing. The sole is too thin, and the straps are too flimsy to keep the soles attached. I can tie the straps back, but they are likely to break off again when you dance. Speak to Amelie and tell her not to order any more shoes like these."

I glance at him cradling my ankle, intent on tying the straps into place, and the strongest memory I've ever had hits me with the force of a charging T-rex. I know that he has done this before. He was bent over my foot, his hands gentle, treating my foot as though it were the most exquisite crystal goblet they serve at dinner.

It feels like something goes *pop* in my head, and I shut my eyes for a second, massaging my temples. When the pain gradually abates, I open my eyes and feel like a new person, like I have done meditation in some remote mountain and emerged with a completely different mindset. This gesture of Edward's is the last straw that broke the camel's back. The barrier that prevented me from accessing my memories is completely toppled. Every single thing I've done in Athelia, every moment I've spent with Edward, flips through my mind like a slideshow that never ends.

Tears start to course down my cheeks. Oh, God, how horribly did I treat Edward! Edward, who thought I'd be lost to him forever, and is now desperately trying to keep me at his side. I had known the reasons he wanted me to stay. I had felt sorry for him, but now, with every detail of our past crystal-clear in my head . . . it is now that I can truly put myself in his shoes and fully realize how my initial rejection and hesitation must have hurt him.

"Edward," I gasp.

He looks up at me, puzzled. "Was the binding too tight?"

"No . . . oh, Edward, I'm so, so sorry."

I fling my arms around his neck and bury my face in his shoulder.

"Kat?" he says rather awkwardly. "Will you tell me what happened?"

I shake my head, still unable to stop the tears. Tightening my arms around his waist, I wish I could turn back time and save him these weeks of pain.

"Is there anything I can do?"

Again, I shake my head. His gentleness, under normal circumstances, may be soothing, but now, it only makes me sob harder.

"I . . ." I hiccup. "I'm sorry, Edward. I'm so, so sorry . . ."

He seems to understand, even though I didn't tell him anything about my memory returning. He strokes my back and whispers gentle endearments in my ear while I struggle to tamp down my emotions and stop crying.

I take a deep breath, intending to tell Edward that I've recovered all my memories, but there's a tightness in my chest and I feel like I can't breathe. Then everything goes black and I slump against him.

28

When I open my eyes, I'm lying in bed, and Edward is staring at me with a worried look in his eyes. When I let out a noise of frustration, he immediately sits up and comes to my side.

"Kat! Finally you are awake."

Another man approaches me from the other side. It's Dr. Jensen.

"Your Highness." He bows slightly. "Due to the unfortunate fall, I would ask that you allow me to examine you."

He performs a checkup on me, taking my pulse and asking me questions, but when it's over, he draws his eyebrows and tells me he cannot find fault with my body.

"Perhaps your gown was too tight and you spent too much time dancing with so many people around," Dr. Jensen finally says.

Edward looks alarmed. "I'll order the maids to re-adjust her clothes right away."

Dr. Jensen nods, but he doesn't budge from his chair. He stares at me as though I am a mystery he cannot fathom.

"My apologies for the sudden request, but I wanted this opportunity since we're all frightfully busy," Dr. Jensen says. "It has been nearly three months since the wedding. Have you not shown any signs of pregnancy?"

I think my jaw hit my collarbone. Okay, so that is kind of extreme, but geez, Dr. Jensen sure doesn't beat around the bush.

"Most women conceive within a few weeks after marriage."

That soon? From what I remember in health class, three months is more like it. Maybe the bodies of Athelian women are more fertile.

"Have you been sleeping badly? Are you under any stress? This could make it less easy to conceive."

Yes to those questions. Oh yeah, and the fact that Edward and I never had sex.

"Dr. Jensen," Edward says, and he lays a comforting hand on my shoulder. "We appreciate your concern, but currently, it is unnecessary. Should we actually need to consult you, we shall not hesitate to make an appointment."

Dr. Jensen adjusts his spectacles and stares at my face. "Perhaps I am overly hasty. However, I have been perplexed about the princess's health condition since the wedding day."

Edward's hand tightens on my shoulder.

"You fainted in the wedding ceremony, despite sufficient food and water and a gown that is tailor-made to your figure. Second, you suffered a pain attack in the head and suffered from memory loss. Third, you fainted at the dance. Now, three months since your marriage, you are not yet pregnant." Dr. Jensen frowns, looking genuinely concerned, but how can I tell him the real reason? That the fainting and pains were caused by goblins, and I'm not pregnant because the prince and I aren't sleeping together?

"Frankly speaking, I've been wondering if I may introduce a foreign specialist, especially since the Moryn emperor's physician is here. They do have a more advanced history in the field of medicine—"

"That is for my wife to decide." Edward squeezes my shoulder. "Do you wish to see another doctor, Kat?"

I touch his hand on my shoulder, feeling the warmth of his skin. "Thank you, Dr. Jensen. But currently, I feel fine. I'm sure my conditions are only temporary. I promise you, however, that I'll seek your help if I need advice."

Dr. Jensen lets out a sigh. He turns and jams his bowler hat onto his head.

"Very well, Your Highness. I apologize if my questions have caused you concern. I hope there is no need for the occasion for medical advice, but if there is, you know where to find me."

***

245

Later that night, I toss and turn in bed, unable to sleep, despite the lavender-smelling sheets and soft, cuddly pillows. Now and then, I cough, feeling a tightness in my chest, but I don't have a headache. Dr. Jensen didn't find anything wrong with me. I hope that it's just a weird aftermath of the exhausting State Visit.

I've got all my memories back. I've spent loads of time with the prince. It's time to make a decision.

When I first arrived in Athelia, I was absolutely determined to go home the first chance I get. Usually, when I make a goal, I'll stick to it no matter what. This is one of the very rare occasions that I've changed my mind.

I roll over on the bed and burrow my head in the pillow. All the time I've spent with Edward, plus the retrieval of all my memories, have tipped the scales dramatically. Even if I can go home, I know I won't be able to forget Edward. I can't imagine going out with Jason while knowing that in another world, there's someone who loves me but can never find me.

Turning over, I lie on my back and look up at the canopy. Since I can't think about anything but the prince, I may as well indulge myself. Calling up my now-complete memory, images of Edward flash over the canopy like a screensaver. I can see Edward bringing me flowers from his garden, Edward handing me a new book that he knew I'd appreciate, Edward twirling me in a dance, Edward leaning close with desire in his eyes . . . I put a hand on my cheek. It might be my imagination, but my skin seems warmer than usual. If I hop out of bed and look into the mirror, I'm pretty sure that I'll see a big red tomato looking back at me.

I love him. Compounded with my seventeen-year-old memories, my love for him is stronger, more powerful than ever. He is the ultimate Prince Charming that any girl could ask for. No matter the difficulties I have experienced in Athelia, I'm staying. Mom and Paige will understand, and as for Jason? I hate to say this, but two years with Jason simply can't measure up to three months with Edward.

Tell him. Tell him you love him and want to be with him forever. In fact, why don't you tell him now?

A tingle of pleasure and excitement runs through my mind when I think of entering Edward's bedroom in my nightgown. I'm going to make up for all these nights that he had to sleep alone.

I throw the blankets aside and sit up. Time to go to my husband.

Pop.

A yellow mist forms in the air, and an ugly goblin hovers above my bed, his ears brushing the canopy.

"Krev! Why did you have to appear when I was least expecting you?"

He blows out his cheeks, looking relieved. "You're not sleeping with Eddie? Good. It's better that you not form an attachment to him again."

"What are you talking about? Oh. You're here to help me go home."

If Krev had appeared when I was still in Enrilth, I would be only too thankful to get back. But now, I'm reluctant—unwilling—to go.

To my surprise, the goblin shakes his head. "We still don't have enough magic to transport your body from this realm. I'm only here because I need to check on you."

"What is that supposed to mean?"

"Has anything particularly strange occurred to you since you entered Athelia?"

"Apart from meeting you?"

Apparently that's the wrong thing to say, for he bristles. "I was referring to your physical health."

"Well, I do have a tendency to get dizzy or even faint, thanks to the corsets I have to wear in this place."

"Is that the worst? Good." Is that a relieved expression on Krev's face? "Did you recover your memory?"

I nod. "Yes. Wait . . . how did you know I lost my memory?"

He frowns. "I guess that since you're living in the palace, it's impossible that the spell put on you wouldn't crumble . . ."

"Spell? Are you saying that I lost my memory because of some spell?"

Krev has the grace to look guilty. "Never mind, girlie. What's done is done. Listen, we are working to gather enough magic to send you back to your own world. You can count on that. The next time I come for you, I expect I will be able to send you home."

I sit up. "Krev, actually, I don't think I—"

"However, you must remember one important thing. It is vital that you remember this, or there can be dire consequences."

I begin to feel uneasy. I mean, Krev looks like the type who loves to play tricks on others. He doesn't seem to have a serious outlook on life. It's weird that he should be issuing a serious warning to me.

"I'm listening."

Krev flies closer, and his large eyes seem to bore into my face. "Do not fall in love with Eddie."

If Edward were still courting me, and the queen warned me I couldn't marry him, I'd have expected to hear this kind of warning. But to have it uttered by Krev, who looks nothing like an interfering mother-in-law—I stare at him in total shock.

"What did you just say?"

Krev flies closer, his ugly goblin face disturbingly close. There is this menacing look on his face, a look that jars with his usual mischievous self. If he threatens me, I will do exactly what he asks.

"Keep. Away. From. Eddie. You can't marry him."

"I'm already married to him."

"Whatever you want to call it. The point is that you don't belong in Athelia. You must leave."

"Excuse me? You forced me to return to Athelia, and now you are telling me that I shouldn't stay?"

"It was a huge mistake." Krev looks frustrated. He looks down, and I notice that his legs have disappeared. "Darn it, the magic is fading quicker than I thought. I don't know how much longer I can hold out, so I'd better make this quick. Give me your arm, girlie." When I blink at him in astonishment, he snaps, "Now! Before I disappear!"

I stick out my hand, and he suddenly clamps his hand onto my skin. Something like electricity seems to flow from his hand, and I let out a gasp of pain. Before I can yell at him, he removes his hand and hovers above my head. "That's the best we can do for now. But there's nothing we can do about Eddie, so remember what I said—stay away from him."

"But why?"

Krev says something, but it comes out muffled and unclear. By now, his head is already fading, like a mist thinning out. A second later, he vanishes completely, leaving me staring in the dark.

It has to be a dream. A really bad dream.

I tell myself that Krev didn't pop up after weeks of absence, and he didn't issue a ridiculous warning about keeping away from Edward. But when I enter the bathroom, needing some water to rinse my face, I discover there is a strange mark on my arm, right at the spot where he pressed his hand on my arm. It's a bright red X with a red circle around it, like a bizarre symbol. I am one hundred percent sure that this mark wasn't there last night. I take a cloth and wash my arm with soapy water, trying to see if I can rub it off, but nothing happens. No matter how hard I scrub, the mark remains, a rather sinister-looking presence, especially when reflected in the mirror.

I throw the cloth into the basin and press my forehead against the looking glass. Krev's warning seems to reverberate in the air. Just when I made the decision to stay in Athelia, he has to show up and tell me that Edward and I aren't meant to be.

What did he mean when he told me it was a *huge mistake*? Seven years ago, he had no qualms about my being trapped in Athelia forever. Why is he telling me that I must leave? Why now?

Should I take Krev's warning seriously? Why does he have to be so infuriating? He reminds me of Hercule Poirot, the detective in Agatha Christie's novels. Poirot rarely lets anyone learn a clue, and he prefers to wait to reveal everything in the end.

Have the goblins changed? They seem a lot less powerful, less confident. Another scene comes to my mind—Krev once visited when Edward and I were staying at his eldest cousin's house. He had told me that I had messed up Athelia's history. Normally, the old Katriona would have come back, but since I've returned when I'm not supposed to, I guess the goblins are determined that I not make waves again.

What should I do?

29

It's late in the morning when I wake up. Perhaps because I fainted last night, Amelie doesn't rouse me as she usually does, like an alarm clock. Instead, when I ring the silver bell next to my bed, she comes in and brings me a breakfast tray. Just as well, because my mind is still reeling from Krev's visit last night. I don't feel like facing Edward or his parents now.

"Kat." Edward enters my bedroom, concern written over his face. "How are you feeling now?"

I take a sip of hot milk mixed with honey. "I'm fine. Really." Strangely, this morning I didn't cough even once. It seems that after a fitful sleep, my strength is rejuvenated. Good, because I sure don't want Dr. Jensen visiting again and questioning my childless state.

His eyes soften as he looks at me dressed in my nightgown, my long hair loosely curling down my front. "I'd stay with you, but Father wants me to accompany him. Augustin and Simone will be returning to Moryn today. Their carriages are already waiting in the courtyard."

"Please tell them that I'm sorry that I can't see them off," I say. "And tell them that it's been delightful showing them around, and I hope that they have found the visit a pleasant one."

"Will do." Edward smiles. It's one of the rare occasions that he picks up my phrases. "I already told Augustin that we'll be delighted to attend his wedding next year, and he seems quite pleased. Simone said that she's looking forward to dressing you in Moryn fashion."

I don't miss the implication of his words. In a way, he is making me stay in his world, at least until next year, unless I'm callous enough to have him break his word to the emperor.

"All right."

He smiles and rises from the chair near my bed. But before exiting my bedroom, he pauses. "Kat . . . about last night, in the gardens . . ."

Instantly, I know what he's referring to. He knows that I've recovered all of my memories.

Were it not for Krev, I could have told him I love him. I could have gone to his bedroom last night.

Brisk footsteps head to my room, and Amelie pokes her head through the door. "Your Highness, beg pardon, but His Majesty is waiting outside. The emperor and his fiancée are about to set off."

A lump forms in my throat as Edward leaves my bedroom. With all of my memories intact, it cuts deeply that I can't tell Edward that I love him.

I need to get out. Not to escape, of course, but just for today. I consider going to Poppy's, but she must be super busy with the twins. Elle is currently not at the capital, and if she were, she'd also likely be busy with her family, her multiple foundations, and other charity work.

Eventually, I decide to pay a visit to The Bookworm. While I can't tell Mr. Wellesley the truth, talking to him usually removes some stress. I could also see if the newest release to that Gothic mystery romance series is out. It's your typical commercial genre stuff, and I could pick out a million flaws, but geez, the series is addictive.

Before leaving, I make sure to ring for Amelie and tell her where I'm going. I also leave a note in Edward's bedroom, just in case, and place a glass paperweight over the note. I sneak a glance at his bed—it's huge, with a dark velvet bedspread, and two fat pillows. With a pang, I wonder when I can share his bed.

Traffic is perpetually congested downtown, so I tell Bertram to park the carriage on a side street off the main road and head to The Bookworm on foot.

"Violets, lady? Sweet violets, just for a penny a bunch!"

A young girl, dressed in a ragged shawl and a tattered dress, carries a basket filled with purple sprays. What's more, her face looks familiar.

"Molly?"

"You know Molly, lady?" the girl says, her eyes wide. "How could Molly know a fine lady like yer?"

On a closer look, I realize that the girl isn't Molly, but the resemblance is striking. If she could clean up, wash her face thoroughly and put on decent clothes, she could be quite pretty with her small face and delicate features.

She's still looking at me with incredulity. Given the number of people in this country and that there's no Internet, it's possible that many people have never seen my picture in the paper or stood in the crowd when I was in that carriage ride during the wedding day.

"Did Molly never mention my name? I'm Kat. Katriona Bradshaw."

She gasps and tries to curtsy, but I stop her. My motto is to do away with formalities whenever possible.

"You're the princess! Oh Lord, I never realized it! Forgive me, I didn't know who you are!"

"That's okay, don't worry about it." I study her face. I know I have seen her before, and if she's related to Molly, then . . .

Click.

"Nell," I say quietly. "You're Nell." The girl who got pregnant in her early teens and had her picture in the paper. Now that I've seen her in person, she looks even younger than I remembered.

"How d'ya know me? Oh! Molly must have told ya." She gestures to another small figure who is haggling with a well-dressed couple. The gentleman finally purchases a bunch for the lady, and Molly heads in our direction. She does a double-take when she sees me.

"What're ya doin' here?"

I jerk a finger toward The Bookworm. "Your father made you and your sister sell flowers in the streets after he took you out of school?"

She shrugs. "Couldn't afford to go anymore. I know the headmistress sponsored us and all, but we've got a livin' ter make, ya know." She looks pointedly at Nell. "There's three of us, now, and we need ter survive this winter."

I have a suspicion who the third member is, judging from the uncomfortable expression on Nell's face. I don't see any sign of an infant, though. Never mind. Mr. Wellesley probably knows.

"I'll buy the whole lot," I say. "How much is it?"

A hopeful look springs into Nell's eyes, but Molly catches her arm and shakes her head.

"Don't pay for the entire basket, Princess," she says. "The other girls won't like it. They'll make hell for us if you show favor."

It is then that I notice several other girls clustered at a nearby building. They also look poor and dirty, but there is a sullen, almost savage, look in their faces. It seems as though, if were we not in a crowded street, they would have jumped on me and ripped off everything I'm wearing of value, from my pearl hairnet to the beaded slippers on my feet. Apparently, not all poor girls are helpless waifs.

"Three bunches," I say, lifting my chin. "Three bunches of the biggest, choicest violets you have."

"That'll be three pennies."

"Thank you." I haven't had much opportunity to deal with Athenian currency, but Edward made sure I could recognize the difference between a penny, a shilling, and a crown. When Molly passes me the flowers, I slip three coins plus an extra shilling into her palm.

"Don't let them see," I whisper.

Without a backward glance, I head to The Bookworm. I'll have to give Mr. Wellesley some of the violets, because I sure can't carry them all back to the palace with me. And the number one thing I don't lack in my rooms is flowers.

The shop is the same as I remembered—crooked sign, piles of books, and a magazine stand near the entrance. An old man wearing glasses and a large green apron is arranging books near the magazine stand. On a small table, there's a pile of hardbacks titled, *The Woman in Red,* in a Halloween-style font. The book must be a bestseller to deserve its own space.

"Mr. Wellesley!" I call to him, smiling. He has always been kind to me, though his teasing can be annoying sometimes.

"My favorite lassie!" Mr. Wellesley greets me with a broad grin. "Or should I say . . . our new princess? You haven't been down to see us for a while. I thought you might be expecting a new addition to the family."

"Just busy with official princess stuff." Like I could mention my memory loss. I look for Billy, but then I realize that he's at school now. He doesn't need to work for Mr. Wellesley anymore.

"I met Molly and her sister, Nell, outside. They're selling flowers."

Instantly, the sly grin disappears from his face. "I supposed you would run into them sooner or later."

"Nell has a baby, doesn't she? And so they are experiencing more hardships than before."

Mr. Wellesley nods. "And that is only part of the story. Did you know that Molly dropped out of that girls' school you established, not just because she needs to earn more to keep her sister's baby fed and clothed, but also because McVean slashed their wages into half?"

"He did *what*? Just because there is less output due to the reduced hours?"

Andrew McVean. That horrible, ruthless man who cares for nothing but profit. His immense wealth is built on blood. I had been trying so hard to let the child workers receive better treatment by passing the Eight-Hour Act, and here he goes and makes things worse. Perhaps his action isn't surprising, but my anger rises all the same.

"It is not simply because of the reduced output. Along with the new law, Edward established additional measures. The owners have to pay for health insurance and shoulder part of the expense for appointing inspectors. You know, there have to be inspectors to make sure the factory owners are abiding by the new law. What McVean did was certainly unethical, but there is no law that forbids him to do so."

"You don't even have a minimum wage in this country?"

Mr. Wellesley raises an eyebrow, and I realize how weird my question sounds. I'm talking as if I am not a citizen of this country.

I cough and change the subject. "Isn't there anything we can do to help the children?"

"Much has already been accomplished in the past year. Remember, lass, that change is always gradual in a country like ours. Unless our government is more similar to the Moryn empire . . . but I'd take the parliament over the emperor any day. Meanwhile, I'll keep an eye on Molly and her sister, and if they are tired, they can drop by for a cup of water." Mr. Wellesley pats my hand. "Don't worry, lassie. Give it some time. More changes will be implemented, eventually."

30

I pace in my room—a habit recently acquired from Edward. The sunset is breathtakingly gorgeous, painting the sky red and gold and orange, a view easily appreciated with the huge windows taking up the entire side of the room.

Sooner or later, Liam's voice echoes in my head, *they will all be dropping out.*

I put my hands to my head. McVean slashed Molly's wages, and she is back to working all day. The streets might not be life-threatening compared to the factory, but still, it's no place for a child. I don't want Molly becoming like those other flower-girls with savage expressions. She isn't much better off than before.

And it's all my fault.

Sinking onto the window seat, I try to calm down and think rationally. Would I have acted differently if

I had known Molly would end up selling flowers in the streets? When I remember poor Jimmy with his blood-soaked bandages, I still can't bring myself to regret what I did. But maybe I could have figured out a better way, made some preventative measures that wouldn't have led to McVean cutting wages.

The door to our suite creaks, and footsteps, steady and firm, sound on the polished marble floor. Edward must have returned from Parliament. Good. I need someone to listen to me, to discuss with me, to advise me what I should do. There's no one better than my husband.

Pushing my bangs out of my eyes, I head toward the sitting room. He isn't there, but there's a sound coming from the direction of his bedroom. Without thinking, I stride toward his bedroom, finding the door only half-closed. And then I halt.

Edward has just taken his shirt off. He pauses when he sees me, the white linen material dangling on his arm.

Gah . . . my face is burning up. We're married, but I've never seen him half-naked before, given that we have separate bedrooms and he's always waiting in the sitting room before we go down to breakfast. It lasts only a second, but my glimpse is long enough to take in the muscled, toned body of his. For a moment, I'm tempted to run my hands over his broad golden chest.

"I . . . sorry!" I turn my back on him, feeling my entire head in flames. It's ridiculous, honestly, me blushing at a guy's naked chest? I'm no longer a teenager, and here I'm behaving like a girl in middle school. *Admit it, Kat. Your attraction to him isn't purely because of his character. It doesn't hurt that he's drop-dead gorgeous.*

He chuckles, heightening my embarrassment. A warm hand turns me to face him, and I look up. Edward stands before me, thankfully with his shirt on.

"Never did I expect you'd be so eager to see me." He runs a finger down my cheek. "When will you stop blushing when confronted with my torso? I thought your world taught you to behave with less modesty. Although I have to say, you look adorable."

He's flirting again, but right now, I'm not in the mood.

"I need your help," I blurt. In terse words, I relate to him how I met Molly and her sister near The Bookworm.

"I thought that when I set out to change the law, I was doing the right thing. I thought I was helping the children." I bite my lip and look down on the floor. "But now we're back to the beginning. Nothing has really changed."

"Do not say so." Edward steers me to a chair and gestures that I sit in an armchair near the fireplace. His bedroom is larger than mine, but it contains less furniture. There is only one wardrobe, and the dresser is smaller and less cluttered. The pillows are neatly laid, the blankets wrinkle-free, the canopy held back by velvet ropes—it almost appears as if no one has slept in that bed. The austere condition of the bed reflects the austere sex life of its occupant. I curl my toes and, for a wild moment, I let my mind wander to the idea of taking Edward's hand and leading him to bed.

Edward drops into another chair across from me. "Through your interview, you have made the public aware of the inhumane suffering of child workers. Before I met you, I believed that change must be gradual, and drastic action cannot produce satisfactory results. But your efforts have taught me that some risks are worth taking."

I force my mind return to the present. "I could have done better. I didn't foresee the possibilities of the factory owners adapting to their advantage."

"Kat, while you may believe that you did not successfully alleviate the children's suffering, remember that the Eight-Hour Act was never meant to be an end, but only a step toward our final goal— to completely eliminate child labor."

"Of course." Yet, when I remember how Molly had reacted when her father forced her to go back to work, my confidence wavers. "I still believe that it's the right thing to have the children educated instead of sending them into the streets. Or to the factory. But what can I do if Molly herself doesn't want to come back? She seems to take pride in the fact that she's helping her family's finances. And since her sister's baby needs to be fed . . . Edward, if I were in her place, I don't think I'd choose any other option."

"There *are* other options, though. She could make much more as a shop clerk or tradesman's assistant, if she were willing to complete her education, but my guess is that her family is unlikely to excuse her for several years." Edward sighs and rubs his forehead. "To be honest, I did foresee that families in the lowest rung—like Molly's—will not benefit from the Eight-Hour Act, simply because their financial situations are too dire. But I do not regret advocating for lesser hours, nor our subsequent act of limiting the children's work hours to daytime only."

I wonder how many families like Molly's are out there. Given the number of children I've seen at McVean's factory, we still have a long way to go.

"Recently, Father and I have been discussing a new act," Edward says slowly. "Since there is no shortage of supply, employers like McVean can set the wages however they like. Therefore, we have been contemplating setting a minimum hourly rate for laborers."

"A minimum wage." Another memory comes to my mind. "Wait, that was *my* idea. When I moved into the palace after the ball, I mentioned it to you once, when one of the cooks left for a better-paying job at a top restaurant."

He nods slowly, a smile forming on his face. "And I told you that establishing a minimum wage would not be without problems, for the employer can simply choose to lay off more workers, resulting in a group of people who have no income instead of little."

"But we have passed the law for an eight-hour work day," I say. "McVean can't employ fewer people working fewer hours."

"Adults do not benefit from the Eight-Hour Act."

I privately thank the stars that I'm a princess in this country, or I'd be doomed. Even if I were a man, who enjoys more privileges in Athelia, it must suck when there isn't a limit on work hours or a minimum of pay.

"So, your father is convinced that Athelia could try establishing a minimum wage?"

"It would do no harm to try. But getting Parliament to pass the Act is another matter. The impact would be far greater than limiting child labor."

It doesn't seem an ideal solution, but then, so far, I can't think of anything better. I don't know what Molly's father's job is, but if he is paid a higher wage, he might be less inclined to make her earn a living.

"Okay." I smile at him, feeling my heart brimming with affection. At that moment, I realize one of the reasons I fell in love with him. Edward has always been supportive of my ideas. He may tease me, but he never regards what I care for as trivial.

I rise on tiptoe, intending to kiss his cheek like the time before we went to Poppy's house, but this time Edward is prepared.

Swiftly, he turns, and my gasp of surprise is swallowed by his lips firmly pressed on mine. His arm curls around my waist, drawing me close to his body. Whether it is from memory or not, I react straight away. I wind my arms around his neck and kiss him back, all other thoughts temporarily banished at the moment.

And then Krev's ugly squashed face barges into my mind. *Don't fall in love with him, girlie!*

265

I pull back abruptly. It was a mistake—I should have inched away slowly. From the look on his face, I sense that he's both confused and hurt.

"Kat," Edward says quietly. "I know that your mind is on the children now, but don't tell me that my . . . my advances are unwelcome. There is a world of difference when you look at me now. Before, you looked upon me with suspicion, reservation, and even hostility. You'd blush, but it wasn't genuine affection. But now, you've changed." Gently, he brushes a strand of hair from my face. "I can tell that you want me. Not as much as I want you, but you cannot deny the attraction exists."

Again, Krev appears in my mind, his expression menacing. I wonder if this is some goblin magic, or if he left such a deep impression on me that I'd think of him every time I'm close to disregarding his warning.

"Is it your suitor?" He never refers to Jason by name. "Can you still not forget him?"

The truth be told, I haven't thought of Jason that much since I regained my memories. But still, even if I've fallen for Edward, I can't completely forget my boyfriend in America. We've been together for two years. Everything I've done with him, such as squabbling over the flavor of popcorn in movies, outings at the park, and cozy nights with home-cooked dinners . . . a pang of guilt stabs me. I didn't want it to turn out this way, but it *has* happened. I've left him for another man.

"He is still on your mind," Edward says, disappointment evident on his face.

True, but if it weren't for Krev, I would have confessed that I love him. I debate about telling him that the goblin visited, then decide against it. I need to know from Krev why I can't fall in love with Edward. I need him to stop messing with my mind, especially when Edward tries to kiss me.

"Just give me a bit more time." I might as well use Jason as an excuse. "Jason and I were together for two years. I can't get over him so soon. And you know I'm not the impetuous teen that I was when I first met you. I'll never see my family and friends again if I stay with you. When I say yes, I want to be absolutely sure."

Silence stretches between us for such a long time that I have to speak again. "Edward?"

He exhales. "I'm done with you."

If he'd told me this after the ball, I might have believed him. But telling me he didn't want anything else to do with me right after he kissed me with passion and desire . . . I find it difficult to follow his train of thought.

"Can you say that again?"

A long finger touches the underside of my chin, tilting my face to meet his.

"I'm done with getting to know you," Edward says, his voice husky. His finger is uncommonly warm, sending sparkles down my neck and body. "You told me that we should be re-acquainted. I believe that the months we've spent together since have been sufficient for that purpose."

267

He leans in, so close that his breath warms my ear. "From now on, I am going to seduce you."

31

I enter the sitting room the next morning with a conflicted mix of trepidation and anticipation, Edward's 'threat' of seduction echoing in my head. I simply couldn't kiss Edward with the goblin's shrill voice intruding my mind. It felt like Krev was physically present in the room, hovering over my shoulder, watching me like a hawk. It felt like Krev had cast some stupid curse on me, like the memory spell.

I set my jaw. If I could break through the barrier that withheld my memories of Athelia, then I can also conquer this ridiculous ban, though deep in the recesses of my mind, there's an anxiety that keeps me from being wholly optimistic. *Why doesn't Krev want me to stay in Athelia?*

I touch my left shoulder. The mark Krev gave me is still there, hidden by the long sleeves of my silken petticoats and satin gown. I should be grateful that it's early autumn, or I'd have a lot to explain to Amelie and Mabel about the sinister-looking red circle etched on my skin, like the brand of the devil.

Edward is lounging on the sofa as usual, his long legs crossed casually in front of him. He lowers his paper when I approach him, and a smile, slow and gradual yet effective all the same, spreads over his face.

"Shall we go down to breakfast?"

He stands up and offers his arm. Something strikes me as unusual about him—I squint and discover that his cravat, usually neatly tied around his neck, is crooked.

"Wait." I reach out and try to right the cravat, but somehow, I can't get it positioned correctly.

"I'm afraid that we'll have to loosen and re-tie it," Edward says, sounding amused. "Will you do it for me, Kat?"

Knowing how he keeps himself immaculately groomed, I could bet my annual allowance that he left his cravat askew on purpose. But also, knowing how much he loves me, I'm not at all bothered with this contrivance. Following his instructions, I learn how to wrap the long end over the short end, create a double fold, and finally tuck the fabric into his charcoal gray waistcoat. In the beginning, I was only focusing on how the Athelian cravat compares to a modern necktie, but when I'm almost done, I become aware of his gaze on my face, hot and filled with desire. My cheeks heat up—the act of tying his cravat seems so intimate, even more than the dancing lessons. Any lady could dance with him at a ball, but only a wife can have the privilege of fixing his cravat.

"There." I smooth the front of his waistcoat, my fingers trembling slightly as I sense the heat radiating from his body. "All done."

"All done," he repeats, his voice a deep baritone.

"Breakfast," I say. "We should go down to breakfast."

"In a moment."

Edward's hands slide slowly from my hips, tracing the sides of my body until they rest on my shoulders. A thrill runs down my spine. I meet his eyes, which are glowing like the fire in the grate. Without thinking, I tilt my head, my heart pounding with anticipation. Forget that stupid goblin. I'm not going to care—

"Girlie!" Krev's voice pierces through my head. *"Stay away from him!"*

"Ow!" I break away from Edward and look around wildly, but there's no sign of Krev. How is it that I can still hear him?

"Kat?" Edward looks alarmed. "What happened? You suddenly went as pale as a sheet of paper, as though the world were coming to an end."

"I just felt a bit dizzy," I lie. "Maybe I'm not fully recovered from that day I fainted at the ball. I'm all right now, honestly."

A servant knocks on the door, asking if we're ready to go down to breakfast. Edward releases me, but not before making me promise that I'll see Dr. Jensen if my symptoms become worse.

271

As we head down to the dining room, I decide that I have to go out again. I can't be around Edward when Krev's magic is still strong, especially when Edward is eager to take our relationship to the next level.

After finishing my daily round of letters and scanning through today's paper, I call my maids.

"Amelie, I'm going to visit Poppy Montgomery. Have the kitchens prepare a suitable basket and ask Bertram to prepare my carriage. Mabel, I need to change into a dress of dark color, and of a material that's easy to wash. Just in case."

***

The parlor maid looks doubtful when she opens the door, and she cautions me that her mistress is putting the 'little tyrants' to bed. I hesitate, wondering if I had better hand her the basket of baked goods and go to The Bookworm instead, when Poppy's voice floats from the second floor.

"Is that Kat at the door? Let her in! I want to see her."

And so I trudge up the stairs, full of anticipation. Poppy's hair is frazzled and her dress wrinkled, but her smile is bright and infectious.

"Kat, dear, what took you so long? You promised you'd come visit me soon."

"I'm sorry." I resist the urge to pinch Little Katriona's cheeks. "Our schedule was full from day to night when the Moryn emperor came to visit, and . . ."

One of the twins starts bawling.

"Sebastian, you were supposed to fall asleep after I fed you!" Poppy groans and rushes to the crib while clutching her twin daughter in her right arm.

As if infected by her brother's wails, Little Katriona starts to scream like she's going to have a career in opera in the future. Looks like we won't be able to have a normal conversation unless the babies fall asleep.

"Mercy me, she is hungry again!" Poppy exclaims, flinging a smock over her dress. "I swear, with so many times I have to feed her during the day, she's going to resemble a balloon."

"Is there anything I can do?"

"Can you help me put Sebastian to sleep? I've been trying so hard to have them wake up and go to sleep on the same routine, but they haven't been adapting as well as I hoped. Seems that little Katriona is determined to feed on her own without her brother. She's awfully stubborn." Poppy looks up and gives me a mischievous wink. "Maybe it has something to do with her namesake."

"Oh, I'm sure it has." I have to smile as well. "So how do you usually put a baby to sleep?"

"Try to give him a simple massage. Rub his back, his feet, and his tummy. Sebastian really likes it. Oh, and sing while you're doing it. The softer and slower the tune, the better."

I freeze for a moment. I thought I had learned enough of what I needed to survive in Athelia, but I have yet to remember an entire song. There were times when Lady Bradshaw had me practice on the piano, but I was so incompetent that I can barely remember anything now.

But Poppy is already lifting little Katriona out of the crib and spreading a towel and pillow on her lap. Sebastian looks up at me expectantly with large, limpid eyes, as though he understands what his mother just said. Maybe if she is fully occupied, she won't notice what I'm singing.

"All right, little fellow," I say under my breath. "You are going to have the honor of hearing a tune that no one else in this world has ever heard."

I hum the common lullaby that Mom used to sing to Paige when she was still a baby. While I sing, I reach out and gently massage Sebastian's tummy in small circles. I know this lullaby by heart, since my parents' relationship had drastically gotten worse since Paige's birth. Dad had thought he would be able to go off to focus on his dental degree, but then a new baby had to arrive. So many times, I had witnessed Mom wiping her tears as she tried to sing Paige to sleep.

"Kat? Why are you crying?"

I realize that a big, fat tear had dropped on my arm, wetting my embroidered sleeve. "Oh, nothing. I just thought of something in the past."

Poppy cradles little Katriona in her arms, the latter as quiet as a mouse now. "That tune you were humming . . . was it from your world?"

Wow, Poppy can be super perceptive sometimes. And then I'm reminded that she is the only person in Athelia, apart from Edward, who knows that I am from another world.

"Yes."

Poppy gets me a handkerchief. "There. Suppose we put the twins to sleep and go downstairs. They sleep more soundly if we leave them alone."

It doesn't take long to see both babies breathing quietly, eyes closed, sleeping side by side. It's difficult to imagine what a racket they must make when awake. Poppy takes off her smock, gathers the dirty towels, and beckons to me. "Let's go," she whispers.

In the kitchen, we discover that the cook has returned with a fresh batch of scones from the market. Poppy tells the cook to boil some tea and leads me to the sitting room.

"Take one." Poppy pushes the plate of scones to me. "No, take two. As many as you want. Those scones won't taste as good if they go cold."

I do as she says. The buttery smell is heavenly, matching the tangy taste of dried cranberries sprinkled on the tops.

"I suppose you must miss your family," Poppy says, a sympathetic look in her eyes. "When I got pregnant with Sebastian and little Katriona, I did miss my mother so, especially when Jonathan was working long hours. It must be even more difficult for you, Kat. Is there no way that you can see them again?"

Krev's warning pops into my head, menacing and intimidating. In the past, when I was still Lady Bradshaw's second daughter, I always thought of the goblin as a fun-loving prankster, annoying but never threatening. But I still feel a shudder when I remember how he loomed before me, with those huge yellow eyes unblinking, telling me that I can't fall in love with Edward.

Too late.

"Poppy," I say hesitantly. "Hypothetically, if someone were to tell you that you can't marry Mr. Davenport, and that you must return to your family and stay there and never see him again, what would you do?"

Poppy looks alarmed. "Kat, what are you talking about?"

"Pretend I never told you this." I take a sip of tea. To tell the truth, it's too bitter for my taste, but I revel in it anyway. "Suppose the goblin shows up and tells me that I don't belong in Athelia and I must leave Edward. What should I do?"

Poppy's eyes go so round that she looks like a comedian. "You can't leave His Highness! Why, you've been married for a year!"

"Six months," I correct her. "Anyway, the length doesn't matter. What would you do if you were in my situation?"

"I'd stay," she says stoutly. "I'd tell that goblin to disappear."

I have to smile. "But what if the goblin is right?"

"I'd stay."

She sounds so . . . Poppy-like.

"Now, don't you get any ideas," Poppy says. "His Highness loves you. I've seen how he looks at you. You are not going to desert him. If you do, I'll . . . I'll . . ." She pauses, apparently unable to come up with a threat for her best friend who is also a princess. "Just forget about returning to your own world. You have a new family here."

I nod. I do so want to reciprocate Edward's affection. Next time Krev screams in my head, I'm going to do my best to ignore it. Maybe, if I try hard enough, his annoying voice will go away. Just as I managed to break through the memory barrier.

Someone knocks on the door.

"I'll get it," I say, seeing dark circles under Poppy's eyes. As a mother of newborns, it's impossible that she can sleep well.

Elle stands on the doorstep, her cheeks rosy red from the chilly autumn air and a large wicker basket hanging from her arm. Her dress and cloak are plain—you can't tell that she's an earl's daughter, but she's beautiful anyway. She gives me a radiant smile and takes my hands.

"I'm so glad to see you, Kat."

"And I you," I say, marveling at how Athelian speech patterns have influenced my way of speaking.

"Is that Elle at the door?" Poppy's voice floats from the kitchen.

"Yes, dear cousin." Elle comes in and sets her basket on the table. "I just got back from my father's estate up north. Here, I brought some blueberries from our garden. The housekeeper insists that blueberries are good for new mothers. How are Sebastian and little Katriona? They're sleeping? Then I must come back another time when they're awake. Nothing pleases me more than playing with my niece and nephew."

Poppy jumps up and gives Elle a hug. It's lovely, seeing that my best friend and Cinderella are cousins. I'm already so lucky to have Edward, and even luckier to have these girls as my friends.

"How did you deal with the dispute with the tenants?" I ask. "I mean, since you're not used to the role of a mistress, were they willing to listen to you?"

Elle smiles. "As long as you take the effort to see things from each person's perspective, it is not difficult to persuade them to come to a compromise. I suppose it also helps that I do not issue commands, but rather offer suggestions, so they are less likely to be affronted."

"Good for you," I say, impressed. I knew there's more to Elle than her usual shyness.

"How are things between you and Henry?" Poppy asks. "Has the duchess finally relented? Honestly, I don't understand why she's so stubborn. It's not as if Henry is marrying beneath his station."

"Maybe you can consider running off to Ruby Red," I say, with a wink at Poppy. "I won't mind being a witness at the altar again."

Elle looks down and tugs on her skirt. "Actually, Henry has more important things to worry about."

Both Poppy and I make indignant noises.

"Dr. Durant invited Henry to do research with him for a year."

I let out an unladylike whoop. "Awesome. It's what Henry always wanted." I know that as a general rule, gentlemen don't work. Imagine having a duke asking you if he could take your pulse or prescribe you pills. People are unlikely to take him seriously. However, doing research with the renowned Moryn doctor is another story.

"Who's Dr. Durant?" Poppy asks. I explain, adding that I had seen Henry spending more time conversing with the Moryn physician than dancing at the ball.

"But of course, her ladyship is unwilling to let Henry go. Thomas, Henry's butler, tells me that the grand duke has been in poor health lately. Her ladyship wishes that Henry cease his medical career and inherit the family business."

"Family business?" I say. "What kind of family business is it that Henry has to take over?" It's not as if he were a blacksmith or a shoemaker.

"There is the grand duke's property—for example, Somerset Hall—to take care of. He has to oversee the living conditions of his tenants, make sure that the taxes are collected, and he needs a mistress to supervise the servants in the manor."

"Can't someone else take over instead? Doesn't Henry have any brothers or sisters who could do that for him?"

Elle shakes her head. "He is an only child, like His Highness. He has a few cousins, but they are too young to be seriously considered, not to mention that Henry is the perfect candidate."

"How does Henry feel about this?" Poppy asks.

"He doesn't want to inherit," Elle says quietly. "Being a doctor is all he ever wanted. When Mamsie had cholera, he worked so hard to relieve her pain and oversee her recovery. I could tell he takes pride in his work. But the duchess told him that she had indulged him for far too long."

That totally sucks. I haven't personally experienced it myself, but I've known a few people in college who pursued a career that they didn't really want but were doing it to fulfill their parents' ambitions.

"The duchess should have considered Henry's feelings on this matter," I finally say. "Suppose he inherits the property and everything. He isn't going to do a good job because his heart isn't in it." And if the duchess forces him to marry a girl who would be a perfect duchess, but someone Henry doesn't love, he will be even more unhappy.

Elle twists her fingers on her dress. She always does that when she's agitated. "I don't know what to do, Kat. I can't ask him to give up his duty to his family, nor can I become the ideal wife that the duchess has in mind."

A tear leaks from her eye. Poppy quickly gets her a handkerchief, and I pat Elle on the back, wishing there were something I could do.

"She'll come around," I finally say. "You two deserve a happy ending."

But my voice sounds hollow, flat. Perhaps it's because I can't figure out a way to help Henry and Elle. Or maybe because I'm also frustrated at my relationship with Edward. There's a reason why happily-ever-after is never easy to achieve.

32

I spend almost every day at the palace library and at Edward's office, trying to find any fact, any experiment, any data that would be useful for our argument for the Minimum Wage Act. I would have also helped with the Food and Drugs Act, but there are too many terms that I'm unfamiliar with, so I decide to leave it to Henry. Since I cannot search electronically, I do my best with index cards, and in several days I've managed to accumulate an entire notebook.

One morning, when I'm done with letter-writing, I sit down at the desk and pore over my notes.

"According to the survey done by the University a year ago," I read, "for every year a schoolboy spends in school, he will practically gain five to ten percent of his future salary. This, of course, is a general finding. It should also be noted that the maximum is reached when the student graduates from university."

"Interesting." Edward's voice, husky and deep, is alarmingly close. He leans over my shoulder, peering at my notebook. The warm breath he exhales warms my cheek and his hair brushes against my ear. Yet, he appears to take no notice of me, his attention fixed on my admittedly cramped, messy handwriting.

"When did you come in?" I try to sound annoyed, but my voice comes out breathless. Dang. I hate it when he uses his proximity to distract me.

"You were too focused on your work to notice my appearance," he says, running a finger down a sentence.

"Don't you have to work in the morning?"

"You forgot the tea break," he says, sounding amused. He still hasn't moved from his position behind me. Were it not for the chair, he could have embraced me.

I am going to seduce you, his voice echoes in my mind. I should evade him before Krev returns, yet I don't feel like pulling away. I don't feel like moving.

"How many days do we have?"

"Next Tuesday will be the last day of Parliament." Edward finally gets up, and I wish he hadn't. I admit I enjoyed the nearness of his body, and the thrill from his deep voice was sending dangerous signals to my brain.

He glances at the bookshelves, which are almost filled to the brim. "You know, Kat, if you want anything, you need only to ask. You are as much mistress of this household as I am master."

My heart feels full, touched by his kindness and generosity. "I will. Thank you."

I don't know what happened to me—maybe I wanted to feel his body close to mine again—but I rise from my chair and lean against his chest. He sighs very gently, a slow, contented exhale, then his arms go around me, clasping my waist like a belt. His lips graze my neck, sending sparks running down my spine. Together, we look down at the gardens below. My mind is a blank slate, wiped clean of any thought but the desire to be wrapped in his embrace.

"Stay." He doesn't say it loudly, but the word is distinct. "Don't leave me here alone."

Say yes, my brain screams. *You know that even if you get a chance to go home, you can't forget him.*

I bite my lip, but my mind is made up. Screw the goblins. I'm going to tell him . . .

Don't fall in love with him, girlie!

"Shut. Up," I mutter. Krev's voice isn't as loud as the first time, but it's still bothersome. God, when will he leave me alone?

Edward's body tenses. "What did you say?"

Alarmed, I realize that I just said my words out loud. "Sorry, I didn't mean that. I was . . ."

Girlie!

I grit my teeth. At least Krev's voice is weaker now. It'll die away eventually. It has to.

"I . . . I have scheduled a visit to the school today," I say lamely, forcing myself to slip away from his arms. I shut my notebook and hand it to him. "They are holding a meeting to discuss the decreasing number of students. Here, take my notes. I know my handwriting sucks, but it isn't incomprehensible."

I head to the door, not daring to look at his face. Because if I do, I'm certain I'll beat myself up for causing him pain.

***

Princess College seems quieter than usual when I enter the gates and ascend the steps leading to the entrance.

I'm early, since I had to tear myself away from Edward. Classes are in session, so I can't go and see Rosie right now. I consider talking to Miss Cavendish about Molly and the working-class girls. If anything, I can use a cup of hot cocoa. The wind has been relentless since I stepped off my carriage.

"Katriona." Liam approaches me, a stack of papers under his arm. "How generous of you to continue supporting the school, considering its precarious state."

I do my best to keep my irritation bottled inside. "Good afternoon, Liam. Are you finished with your class today?"

He shakes his head. "My class was done yesterday. Today, I'm here to inform the headmistress of my desire to resign." He indicates the papers he's carrying. "All I need is to hand in the graded papers of my last class and my resignation letter."

"You're dropping out as well?"

"I've been offered another job by a lord. To put it bluntly, this other job provides better pay and more prominence than teaching schoolgirls. Not to mention that I fail to foresee a viable future for the girls."

"That's what you think."

He flashes a cold smile that doesn't reach his eyes. "Indeed, Your Highness, I wish no ill will. I am merely speaking in practical terms. Even if you can prevent the school from shutting down, there are only a handful of students left, and even then there's little you can do for them. The University won't recognize their diploma, nor let the girl students take part in the entrance exams."

"We'll work on that later," I say. "Giving the girls a primary and secondary school education is only the first step. At least it's an improvement. Think of the limited resources they had had, whether it may be an incompetent governess or no instruction at all. I don't believe in deriding girls for their inferior intellect when you haven't even given them a fair chance in the first place."

Liam claps his hands, and the sound echoes in the hallway. "Bravo, Your Highness. Your argument is sound and your intentions most commendable. However, I'm afraid that the majority cannot understand what you endeavor, whether it may be a noble woman like Lady Willoughby or an impoverished laborer like Mr. Ripley."

I fold my arms. "So?"

"You will find that what you've been doing all along, such as writing those essays in the paper and trying to educate girls, are eventually a waste of time and effort. A woman of your position is much better off staying in the palace and producing the next heir to the throne. Life doesn't have to be that difficult."

Oh no. Not that again. I straighten my spine and look at him with as much intimidation as I can muster. "I can't."

He tips his head to one side, apparently surprised by my response. As if he thought that I would be convinced by his cynical speech. "What?"

"Because I care. Even if it's only a few students, even if the public thinks I'm wasting my time, I still believe that I am doing the right thing. And even if I fail in this endeavor, I will re-evaluate and try to improve on the second try. But what I can't do is sit still and do what's traditionally expected of me."

He stares at me, his mouth slightly open.

"Well then." I spread my hands. "If you don't mind, I have a meeting to attend."

I sweep past him and continue on my way to the conference room. When I pass the headmistress's office, voices float from behind the door. The walls here definitely could be more sound-proof, I muse. I can hear every word—wait, is that Bianca speaking?

" . . .have learned that this place is in deep financial trouble. Students are dropping out at an alarming rate. Therefore, I have come to propose to you: I can take it off your hands."

"I beg your pardon," Miss Cavendish is saying, her tone quiet but unable to mask her astonishment. "You wish to become a patron, Lady Pembroke?"

I grip the sides of my head. *Impossible. I'd sooner see Edward filing for divorce.*

Bianca gives a tinkling laugh, which sounds like a xylophone made of glass. "Certainly not, my dear Miss Cavendish. I merely wish to purchase the property."

"Buy . . . the college?"

"But of course." Bianca uses her patronizing tone, as if Miss Cavendish were a child. "The property is centrally located, yet the area it covers is uncommonly large. The playgrounds shall convert very nicely into a tennis court, a garden, and a carriage house plus stables. Where am I to find a place that is ideal in both location and dimensions?"

There is no response from Miss Cavendish, at least not any that I can detect. Oh no, I hope that she isn't considering Bianca's offer.

"Surely you cannot be hesitating." A sound of paper rustling. "Name your sum. As I am the mistress of Pembroke Place and the sister-in-law of Prince Edward, you may freely write whatever you wish."

The bell rings.

"I'm afraid I cannot give you a definite answer today, Lady Pembroke," Miss Cavendish finally says. "I must talk it over with the school committee."

A pause—I imagine Bianca looking incredulous. She must have expected that Miss Cavendish would jump at her offer. From Bianca's perspective, it must be a win-win situation.

A moment later, the door opens. Tall and regal, Bianca steps out, her expression stone-cold.

"The school is not for sale," I say.

"*You.*" Her eyes narrow, and her lip curls in disdain as she takes in my admittedly simple dove gray gown, without a single ruffle or piece of lace. I seldom bother to dress up when I go to Princess College. "How lovely it is to run into you."

I lift my chin. "Lovely indeed."

"How long do you think you can keep this school open? There are only a few pupils left, using a large building established in a central location in the capital. What a colossal waste."

"It's not a waste. We are offering young girls a different opportunity in life."

She stares at me for a long moment. "Since when did you get such peculiar notions in your head? When we were children, you complained of your lessons all the time."

My heart hammers in my chest. I must be a huge departure from what the real Katriona was like, and since I'm no longer living with the Bradshaws, there's less of a necessity to pretend to be Katriona Bradshaw. "Thank you for your concern, Bianca, but as the head patron of Princess College, it is my duty to see that the girls are brought back. I won't hear of anything about selling the school. Now, if you don't have anything further to say, allow me to bid you good day."

I step aside and notice that Liam is standing at the end of the corridor, his expression unreadable. A few girls are also poking their heads from classrooms. I smile reassuringly at them, hoping they don't notice that my shoulders are trembling.

Bianca's eyes are flashing, her nostrils flared. When she speaks, her voice has an edge of a jagged saw. "This isn't the end of it, Katriona. One day you will regret turning me down."

It sounds so comical that I swallow a laugh. As if I would ever feel remorse for refusing her offer. "I look forward to the day," I say sarcastically. "Goodbye, Bianca."

Most of the school board is assembled when the meeting starts. There's the headmistress, her assistant, several members of the aristocracy, a few skilled tradesmen who have their daughters enrolled, a couple of teachers, Elle, and me.

After the teachers report the current progress of the girls, Miss Cavendish stands up. She's a dignified lady in her fifties, and also a great friend with the queen.

"Ladies and gentlemen," she says. "I have no doubt that you are aware that recently, the dropout rate at our school has increased alarmingly. Up to yesterday, we have twenty-four students, down from the one hundred girls we originally had. Hence, we need to figure out a solution to retain these girls and also to attract more pupils."

I pinch my lips together. I knew a lot of students had left school, but I didn't know there were so many.

No wonder Bianca felt that she was being magnanimous when she'd offered to buy the school.

"If we cannot come up with a solution, the school will have to shut down," a teacher says miserably. I glare at her. If the teacher herself is in low spirits, then it will undoubtedly affect the students as well.

"I can set up a scholarship from my foundation," Elle says. "I've been researching what other boys' schools have practiced, and I learned that they offer medals and prizes for attendance and grades. Perhaps if we adopt a similar scheme, the girls will be more inclined to come to school."

"We should also alter the curriculum," an aristocrat says. "There should be more lessons on music and painting, as well as etiquette and deportment. This school should live up to its name. With the enrollment of more upper-class girls, there'll be less concern for financial security."

"No," I say firmly. "This school isn't meant to be a substitute for lady lessons, nor is it limited to students from particular backgrounds. I refuse to change the classes to accommodate them."

The aristocrat pulls on his beard. "Ideal, but impractical. I am not denouncing the poor, but they are affecting the performance of my child, who complains that she cannot concentrate in class with the unwashed stench in the air."

I'm stung by his description, but instead I press my lips together. When Molly's father came to remove her from school, I did note the dismal state of Molly's appearance.

"And the clothes they wear! They can't help wearing rags, and you should have heard some of the girls making fun of them," another woman says. I think she's one of the teachers. "And the filthy state of their hair—why, I have to spend ten minutes before class with a fine-tooth comb to get rid of the lice. Frankly speaking, I don't want to discourage the poor things, but their conditions are not appropriate for school."

"Is there nothing that can be done to improve the situation of the working-class girls?" the headmistress asks.

"I can set up something like a food and clothing fund," I say, remembering that I received a huge sum from the municipality as a wedding gift, and so far I haven't spent even a penny of it. "I'll draw funds from my own allowance and also ask for donations. We'll provide uniforms for the girls, as well as free breakfasts in the mornings."

"I object," the aristocrat growls. "It is the responsibility of the parents to provide for their children. If they find you're giving out free food and clothes, then they'll relax their duties."

To my alarm, most other members of the school board are nodding.

"But what if the parents are too poor to provide for them?" I say. "You make it sound like it's improvidence that is at fault, not the possibility that the poorest simply cannot afford the basic necessities."

"I've been to some of the poor quarters," a man says. "You'd be surprised at how many of them are drinking—men and women—and some of them even feed their babies drugs."

"But in the end, it's still the children that suffer," Elle says, her voice not loud but firm. She is less brash, less impulsive compared to me, and when she speaks up, I find that people are more inclined to listen to her. "Should the children suffer because their parents are neglectful?"

In the end, we agree to Elle's scholarship, as well as maintaining the original curriculum, though my idea of setting aside funds for the poor is on hold. All working-class girls have dropped out now, so unless we enroll more of them, the charity idea is currently useless. Again, I remember Molly crying for buyers in the streets, her voice hoarse and her hands chapped, and I wish I could figure out a better solution.

After the meeting, Elle invites me to her foundation to see about the scholarship, but I have to decline. I had promised to take tea with the queen. Ever since my quarrel with Edward, the queen has made it a point for us to have tea every month, making sure that my life at the palace is well.

Elle hurries off, and I continue to the gates. Bianca's incensed face, her beauty marred by her anger, flashes through my head. Even if I donate all of my annual allowance to maintaining the school, it's going to be useless if all the students are gone.

At the same moment, Lady Gregory emerges from a classroom, along with two girls carrying baskets, who curtsy when they see me. My God, there really is a drastic dip in the attendance. Last time I saw Lady Gregory, the classroom was full.

"Good afternoon, Katriona." Her eyes are twinkling. "Child, are you all right? You look rather pale."

I'm about to answer that I'm fine, but since she is also teaching at Princess College, I might as well let her know our difficulties. So, I brief her on the meeting, adding that I really don't want the school to shut down.

Lady Gregory looks thoughtful. "My great-nephew is enrolled in Heron—it's one of the top secondary schools in the capital. He used to whine about the lessons, but he also mentioned that his favorite activities were the games and school trips."

"Are you suggesting that we could organize some kind of extracurricular activity for the girls?"

"Obviously a football match will not work. But if you could take them to a park or a museum, it might encourage them to stay in school. I am not sure about getting more students, but surely it'll help to retain the few students we have left."

I'm reminded of my original idea to have Edward teach a class. Suddenly, a brilliant idea hits me.

"Thank you, Lady Gregory." Making sure we're alone in the corridor, I add, "By the way, has Meg visited lately?"

"She just dropped by last week." Lady Gregory smiles warmly. "She was excited to learn that you married the prince, especially when she had assisted you going to the ball. Would you like to meet her next time she comes by and regale her with some anecdotes of your royal life?"

"Of course," I say, surprised but pleased. I also wonder if Meg has improved in her spells, but a teacher happens to pass by, so I say goodbye to Lady Gregory. I have a plan to carry out.

33

I race to Edward's office and end up coughing and wheezing when I arrive. Geez, my stamina has really worsened since I came to Athelia.

"Easy there." Edward gets me a glass of water and pats me on the back. "I'm glad that you are so eager to see me, but honestly, there is no need to run. You might trip on those long skirts and twist your ankle."

I cough and take a deep breath, willing myself to calm down. "Edward, I just had a wonderful idea! Let's organize a field trip for the girls. We can bring them to the greenhouses and the menagerie. You can introduce them to all kinds of plants and flowers, and I'll ask the gamekeeper to show them the animals. Oh, and we should get Elle and Henry to come out with us. It will be just the excuse to get them together."

To my disappointment, he doesn't share my enthusiasm. He looks kind of skeptical, in fact.

"Henry and Elle should sort out their problems on their own. We shouldn't interfere."

"But we aren't just interfering. It's also an excellent opportunity to take the girls out and boost their spirits."

"Surely there is no need for me to go."

I wag my finger at him. "Don't underestimate your charisma, Your Highness. What better incentive to draw the girls to school than having the prince of Athelia substitute as a teacher for a day? Besides, don't you want to have a date—I mean, spend some quality time with me?" I bat my eyelashes and attempt a saucy wink.

Edward doesn't fall for my pitiful attempt at flirting. "It's not as if we are alone—"

I shut him up with my lips. Using what moderate experience I have, I wrap my arms around his neck and deepen the kiss. Amazingly, there is no sound from Krev this time. I'll take it that I have again conquered the goblin's enchantment. Excellent.

When I pull away, there's a slightly dazed expression on his face, like he can't believe what I just did.

"May I request the pleasure of your company for an outing, Your Royal Highness?"

"Huh? Right, but . . ."

Grinning, I sweep him a graceful (for my standards) curtsy. "Now that's settled, I'll find George and have him add the event to your schedule. I'll also hop over to the kitchens and ask them to prepare food baskets. I'll pay for the expense out of my own pocket so the lord chamberlain won't complain."

"Kat . . ." he growls, perhaps irritated that I got him to agree by seducing him. Score one, Kat. My first step toward becoming a femme fatale.

I hurry away before he can change his mind. Maybe I shouldn't have kissed him, but it's so rare that I initiate any intimacy that I'm sure he wouldn't mind. Anyway, it should be fun. With this outing, the girls will have an informative lesson and be enticed to continue learning at school, and Henry and Elle will get to spend some time together. Really, with so many objectives, at least one of them will succeed.

**

"What is the name of this queer-looking thing, Your Highness?"

"It's a tulip bulb," Edward says. He is wearing his princely mask of utter politeness and zero emotion— is this the same man who whispered in my ear that he wanted to seduce me? Really, I could award him an Oscar.

"Uncle Ed doesn't seem to be enjoying himself," Rosie whispers.

I glance at my husband. Edward does seem to be in a resigned mood as he patiently explains the various colors a tulip can have. I probably shouldn't have dragged him to this outing, but I didn't expect that he'd be this reluctant.

Seems like only the schoolgirls are having fun. Half of them surround Edward, all wearing identical expressions of starry-eyed adulation. The other half are gathered around Henry, pestering him with questions about being a duke and a doctor at the same time, and if it's possible he'll come back to teach. The difference is that Henry is more affable. There's a benevolent smile on his face as he explains how he must undergo more training at the university. Edward, however, looks like a cubicle worker prepared to commute on Monday morning.

It doesn't help that Parliament rejected the Minimum Wage Act (though they did pass the Food and Drugs Act). Edward had used my notes and did his best to convince the members otherwise, but it was no use. In fact, I have a suspicion that some Members of Parliament oppose to Edward's ideas simply because they know I am the instigator.

"He'll be all right," I whisper back. "Was he also like this when he used to visit you, Rosie?"

Rosie considers a moment. "Uncle Ed is always nice to us. But I think he wants us gone."

"He doesn't want you gone. He isn't used to the role of a teacher," I say, though I know that I'm not entirely being truthful. Edward doesn't like being surrounded by chattering, giggling schoolgirls, even if they are vastly different from the ladies who had been scheming to claim the coveted honor of princess. "By the way, how are you getting along at school now?"

Rosie gives me an account of how lonely she feels and how empty the building is. The second and third floor used to be filled with students, but now only a few classrooms are occupied.

"Why did the others leave, Aunt Kat? They seemed to be having fun."

"It's complicated," I say, squeezing her hand. "But I promise you I'm doing my best to get them back."

"Do you know when that will be?"

I pause. "I really don't know, sweetheart. What we're trying to do now is not to lose anyone else." The last thing I want is to have all students dropping out of Princess College, leaving the place an empty shell. It took Elle months to locate a suitable place and convince the seller to let us purchase the building. I imagine Bianca moving in, populating the rooms with maids and footmen, replacing the books and desks and blackboards with her fine gowns and jewelry, and I curl my fingers into a fist.

A rumble from my stomach reminds me it's time for lunch. Because I went to Princess College today to fetch the students, I didn't join the king and queen for lunch. I only had a piece of buttered toast and a cup of coffee, which is more like the breakfasts I had in Portland.

The students are still gathered around Edward as he introduces them to some new species. Elle and Henry stand a little way off. It seems that they want to talk to each other but aren't daring to. I remember what Elle told me about the duchess needing Henry to inherit the dukedom. Maybe it's not the right thing to do . . . but I walk up to them anyway.

"Elle. Henry. Would you two mind going to the kitchen and bringing back the food baskets for us? I've already instructed the kitchens to prepare lunch for us. Edward and I will set up the tables in the greenhouse over there."

Elle glances at Henry, a hopeful look in her eyes. After a moment's hesitation, he offers his hand. "Let's go."

They head toward the kitchens, hand in hand. "Good luck," I whisper. I hope that my little manipulation will work.

Another rumble from my stomach prompts me to take further action. I clap my hands twice to get the students' attention.

"Girls," I call. "It's time for lunch. Henry and Elle have gone to fetch the food for us."

At the sound of 'food,' the girls perk up with expectant grins. Looks like I'm not the only one who's hungry.

"I've reserved one of the greenhouses, as it's too chilly outside for a picnic. Come on, girls. Let's set up the tables for lunch."

The girls whoop and come over to me. I lead them to an adjoining greenhouse, an extra space that I've managed to convince Galen to let us use. A pile of red-checkered tablecloths, neatly folded, lies in one corner, on top of a stack of stools. I take the pile and start distributing the tablecloths, directing the girls—those who are tall enough—to help me spread out the cloths over the table.

"But Your Highness," a girl says. "Why can't we get the servants to prepare the tables for us?"

"Because they have their own jobs to do," I say, pulling out the stools. "They already had to do extra work because of our outing today. Besides, you wouldn't like to feel helpless without servants, would you?"

The girl stares at me for a moment before shaking her head. "I guess not," she says slowly. I think she isn't unwilling to set the tables, but rather she never thought anything about servants doing extra work.

"Edward?" I crook a finger at my husband. "Can you help me separate these stools?"

A collective gasp comes from the girls. I'm probably the only person they have ever seen who dares to order the prince to do stuff. Well, not exactly 'ordering,' but Edward always seems more like the person to have others serve him, not the other way around.

Edward doesn't say anything. He simply strides toward me and takes the stools.

"Thanks." I smile at him and put my hand on his arm. "You're the best."

His mouth curves up slightly. "Another of your world's phrases?"

Oops. I give him a guilty grin before going over to Rosie, who's struggling with another girl with an overly large tablecloth.

Together, we fix up our lunch in the greenhouse. I made the right decision in having the girls pitch in, as everyone seems to be having fun, though whenever

Edward lends a hand, the girls near him giggle and blush. No surprise there.

Just when we're carrying several glazed pots of pink and purple cineraria, beautifully arranged with asparagus fern, to the tables, Elle and Henry arrive. The aroma of meat pies, apple-and-cinnamon cake, and hot chocolate permeates the air.

"All right, girls, don't push or fight. There's plenty for all," I say. "Elle, can you hand out the forks and knives . . . oh, there's the napkins. Right, let's all sit down and tuck in."

Lunch turns out to be a greater success than I expected. Not only do the girls enjoy the meal, but it seems that Henry and Elle have also grown a bit closer. When Lizzie, an adorable four-year-old who's also the youngest pupil in school, complains that she doesn't want any salad, both Henry and Elle admonish her.

"No, you *have* to eat your greens, or not a spoonful of jam shall you get," Elle says.

"But I don't like the taste of spinach," Lizzie whines.

Henry hands her a salad fork. "Spinach is good for you. You do want to grow up strong and healthy, don't you?"

"Listen to the doctor," Elle says, smiling. "There, we can sprinkle a bit of cheese on top. Try it, Lizzie. You might find the taste better than you expected."

Lizzie reluctantly takes a tiny bite. Both Elle and Henry watch her chew, and when the child concedes that the spinach isn't 'that bad,' the two of them share a knowing smile.

In the afternoon, we move on to the menagerie for lessons on animal behavior. The gamekeeper is more cheerful than Edward. All the children's attention is on him as he demonstrates how a parrot may imitate human speech. I have the instinct that despite his muscular build, the gamekeeper is a softie at heart like Bertram.

As I watch the girls having fun teaching the parrot various phrases, I notice Edward standing a little way from the crowd, arms crossed over his chest. I let go of Rosie's hand and go over to him.

"I thought you'd have left," I say in a low voice. Now that we're no longer in the greenhouse, Edward doesn't need to be here. I can manage the rest with Elle and Henry.

He shrugs. "Parliament has closed for the time being, so my workload has lessened considerably. I would rather spend the afternoon with you."

"Even if we're not alone?"

He pretends to look offended. "You told me once that I have a possessive streak. I am not *that* possessive as to want you alone with me all the time."

A hand tugs on my gown. I look down and find Lizzie looking up at me with wide, plaintive eyes.

"Is there something wrong, Lizzie?"

"I can't see the birdies. Can I get a stool from the greenhouse?"

"Oh, honey, that's too dangerous for you."

Edward suddenly plucks the little girl up and sets her on his shoulders. "Better?"

"Ooh, yes." Lizzie grins and wiggles her body so she can sit more comfortably. "Much better. Oh look, the birdie is so colorful!"

"Wait." I waggle my forefinger at her. "You forgot the magic word."

"Thank you, Your Highness."

I glance at them. Lizzie is obviously delighted. Edward, on the other hand, doesn't seem to enjoy having the little girl swing her legs and play with his hair, but he wears a mask of patience. My heart swells—he could have refused this outing. He could have gone back in the afternoon, and yet because of me, he is willing to tolerate a thankless task. It also occurs to me, as Lizzie paws on Edward's hair, that he would also make a good father.

When we move to the next stop in the menagerie, Edward lets Lizzie slide to the ground. This time, the little girl is astute enough to thank him again before trotting off to join the others.

"Thank you." I sidle up to Edward and slip my hand into his. "For giving the children a memorable lesson."

"It is difficult for me to reject any request from you, as long as it is reasonable. And I have learned much as well, so it is not only you who is gratified."

I look up at him, my heart in my eyes, and for a moment we stand there gazing at each other, like no further words are needed to communicate our feelings for each other.

"Uncle Ed?" Rosie's voice becomes louder. "Aunt Kat? It's time to see the butterfly house."

I break eye contact from Edward, but I don't let go of his hand. That moment we just shared was short—not more than a few minutes probably—but it was so entrancing and magical that any hesitation I have of staying in Athelia has vanished. Edward has bound me to him, both legally and figuratively. I can't imagine the rest of my life without him.

34

After Elle and I see the girls safely conveyed out of the palace, I return to the suite, humming a tune that no one in Athelia would have heard. I had sung a few pop songs for Edward when we were alone, but although he tried to look interested, I could tell that our modern pop is too bizarre for his liking. I feel a bit sad, knowing that I won't be able to listen to songs on my phone anymore. Here, I need an orchestra that only plays classical music.

I discover Edward fast asleep in the study. For some weird reason, he reminds me of *Sleeping Beauty*, albeit a male version. It certainly is a breathtaking picture—him lying on the low sofa near the window seat, and the curtains drawn back, revealing the panorama of magnificent fall foliage in the gardens outside.

He must be exhausted from all the parliamentary sessions. A gust of wind blows in one window that's propped open, causing goosebumps on my arm.

I tiptoe to my bedroom and grab a fine cashmere blanket, planning to drape it over Edward. Even though he has a great physique, it's still possible that he could catch a cold. Just when I'm tucking the material under his chin, he stirs and opens one eye.

"Kat?"

In an instant, he wraps an arm around my shoulders, dragging my body down to his, like a typical romance scene in a shojo manga. I land on his chest, and my head bangs under his chin. Another gust of wind enters the windows, making a stack of papers on the desk flutter. Luckily, there's a paper weight, or those papers would have scattered on the floor by now.

"Edward, the wind is coming in. I should close that window."

His other arm settles over my back in an ironlike grip. Combined with the heat from his body and the blanket underneath, I admit it is warm enough.

"I dreamed of you rising in the air," he murmurs, and there's pain in his voice. "All I could think of was pulling you back. However, you floated away, and no matter how I tried, I couldn't get you."

"It was only a dream."

"But it could happen."

"It won't." The words are out of my mouth before I realize I mean it.

His arms tighten around me. "Truly?"

There's no sound from Krev, not even a teeny whimper. *Good.* I can say and do whatever I want without his annoying influence.

I swallow and take a deep breath. In my mind, I silently apologize to my mother, my sister, and Jason. I really, really don't want to give them up, but if forced to make a choice . . .

"Even if Krev shows up, I'll tell him that I want to stay in Athelia. I'm not going back to my own world."

He suddenly flips me over so I'm lying beneath him. Edward's gaze bores into my face, as though he wants to make sure I'm being sincere. That my facial expression matches my tone.

"Say that again."

I raise my hand and caress his cheek. "I love you, Edward. I promise you that as long as I live, I will never leave your side."

A choked sound escapes him. The next second, he covers my mouth completely. He kisses me, fiercely and hungrily, as though I am the only meal after days of starving. He kisses me over and over again, as though each kiss will anchor me more firmly in Athelia. He kisses me so deeply that I can barely breathe, yet I don't want him to stop.

And for the first time since I was transported to Athelia, joy—unadulterated, encompassing, addictive—washes over me, filling my mind, running in my veins, making my whole being vibrant and alive. I wrap my arms around Edward's back and pull him even closer to me, not caring that my gown is riding up to my knees, my petticoats exposed and my shoes kicked to the floor. Oh, how lovely it is to be able to reciprocate. I won't have to feel guilty whenever he flirts or tries to be intimate.

"Ahh!"

Someone shrieks, followed by a crash. Poor Mabel stands in the doorway, her hands on her mouth, her eyes as round as the moon. On the floor lie scattered pieces from a broken teapot and cups. "Oh," she squeaks. "I'm so . . . so sorry . . ."

I roll off the sofa, tugging my neckline back into place. Geez. This is what comes from months of pent-up energy. But I love it. I love how Edward, so stiff and formal in front of most people, can be so ardent in his desire for me.

"Don't worry about it, Mabel." I squat on the floor and help her gather up the pieces. "It's not your fault. I'll pay for a new tea set."

It takes little time for us to clear away the mess. When Mabel has gathered all the broken pieces in her apron, Edward speaks. "You need not bring a new pot."

Mabel looks both anxious and scared. "As...as you wish, Your Highness. Forgive me—I didn't mean to walk in on you."

"Never mind. However, I need you to inform my parents that the princess and I will not be joining them for supper tonight."

The maid bobs a curtsy. "Of course, Your Highness. I'm so sorry that I—"

"Next time, remember to knock. Even if the door is left open."

When she leaves, I press my hand on his arm. "Edward, you could have used a gentler tone. The poor girl looked terrified, like you were going to fire her."

He frowns. "I wouldn't fire her for simply smashing the teapot."

"I meant that you could smile a little, act friendlier, put her more at ease. You look intimidating when you don't smile." I try to imitate his poker face expression. "Now do you see what I mean?"

Edward doesn't seem affected. "I see no reason to act in a familiar manner unless it is a person I am intimate with." I am about to argue that intimacy isn't the same as friendliness when he leans toward me and brushes his lips over my forehead. "Such as you, dearest wife o' mine. No words are adequate enough to convey how glad I am that you have decided to stay. This merits a celebration."

"Are you planning to ask the kitchens to prepare a private meal?" I ask, since he told Mabel that we won't be dining with his parents tonight.

"I have an even better idea. In your world, a couple would often celebrate a special occasion by going to a restaurant."

"You're taking me out to dinner at a *restaurant?*" It's such a novelty that I can't keep the amazement from my tone. I haven't even been to a restaurant in Athelia, though I've seen a few near The Bookworm.

Our gastronomic delights are limited to the palace or a noble's house.

"You make it sound like I'm taking you to a battlefield."

"No, seriously, it's just . . . I've been here for six months, and I've yet to see you go to a restaurant. Won't we be recognized?"

He opens a drawer and takes out a pair of spectacles. "You'd be surprised at the level of anonymity I can maintain when I used to visit families with Henry. There are hundreds of thousands of people in the capital. I rarely show myself in public, and even in an event like our wedding, most people were too far away to see our faces clearly."

I place the spectacles on his face and giggle. It does add a touch of intellect to his features. He looks more serious than usual, which is saying something.

He raises his eyebrows. "Have I become more alluring? Or are my features less pleasing to your eye?"

I kiss his nose, eliciting a smile from him. "You're perfect either way. But I still find you easily recognizable."

"Were we attending a party for aristocrats, I would most certainly be recognized, but going to a small restaurant downtown? I highly doubt it. Even if an aristocrat craves for food from an ordinary restaurant, he would send a servant to bring the food in a brown paper bag, instead of waiting in queue himself."

I imagine Bianca or Claire queuing outside the restaurant, and I put the image out of my head. He's right. I can't imagine an aristocrat mingling with commoners downtown. For example, I'd never catch Bianca hovering near The Bookworm. She always keeps her shopping to High Street.

After Amelie dresses me in a simple but elegant gown that makes me appear more middle-class than aristocratic, I find Edward in the sitting room, similarly attired. Heck, it's the same suit he wore when I met him for the first time, when he accompanied Henry to Dr. Jensen's house.

"Where are we going?"

"A place renowned for its spicy food."

Since I arrived in Athelia, I never lacked for material comfort, but sometimes I wish that the kitchens would serve something cooked in spices rather than the usual butter and cream. Growing up with Mom, I'm used to having my meat seasoned with chili peppers and my salad liberally sprinkled with cilantro. Here, in the Athelian kitchens, the most common dish is chicken sautéed in white wine and butter sauce. Sometimes, I wonder if the word 'spice' exists in their vocabulary, as I've yet to come across a really spicy dish. Edward once suggested that I ask the kitchens to prepare a different dish for me, but I'd rather not demand special treatment.

"Is that all right with you, Kat?" Edward says, frowning. "I thought you missed spicy food."

"Oh no, I'd love to try it. I was just wondering if it's all right with *you*. Have you ever had a spicy dish in your life?"

He smiles gently. "My tastebuds are of little consequence. Since you have promised to stay, it is natural that I would want you to miss as little of your own world as possible. I cannot replace your family, but I would like to make sure that your life here is not lacking in other areas."

My heart is overflowing with love for him. God, what have I done to deserve such a wonderful husband?

When we get into our carriage, I draw up the curtains and climb into his lap. I lay my head against his chest and thread my fingers through his. At first he stiffens, perhaps surprised that I would take the initiative, but then his arms close around me and he fits his chin in the crook of my neck. We stay there in a comforting embrace, no words spoken between us. But I know that he and I share the same mind. I am here for good, and nothing shall separate us.

35

When Edward opens the door of the restaurant and ushers me inside, the aroma of spices gives me an excellent first impression. Cumin, coriander, cilantro, cinnamon, cloves—along with a lot of other spices I can't name but smell great—are here in plentiful supply.

"Oh my God." I close my eyes for a moment and inhale deeply. "It smells like heaven in here."

When I open my eyes, I find Edward watching me, his expression both amused and tender. "Kat, I cannot tell the difference between you and a puppy that senses a juicy bone nearby."

"Hey." I pretend to look offended. "That is *not* a compliment a man gives to a lady."

"For a lady as remarkable as you, I would say the comparison is apt."

"That's why you need me to edit your drafts, if that's the best comparison you can come up with."

"A mouse, then." His eyes twinkle. "When you sniffed the air, you resembled a mouse twitching its nose."

His analogy is so atrocious that I have no idea whether to laugh, cry, or karate punch him on his chest. Lucky for him, Edward is saved from public humiliation when the waitress comes bustling over to us.

"Table for two?" Her eyes practically sparkle as she gazes at Edward.

"Yes." Edward instantly switches to poker-face-mode. "We would appreciate a table out of the way."

"Of course!" she chirps, showing a dimpled smile. "Come along this way, sir."

The restaurant is small, cozy, and crowded. It reminds me of a cute little Thai place near Jason's college campus. Lively folk music blares from a trio strumming on instruments that look like banjos. As Edward says, without expensive clothes and jewelry, we mingle easily in the crowd, although when we are led to our table, quite a few women are stealing glances at Edward. Even with the glasses, he's hot in a nerdy way—like a young professor. Combined with a distinct noble air, from the way he helped me off the carriage to the cultured accent he uses when talking to the waitress, I can't help feeling privileged to be out on a date with him.

We're shown to a tiny booth in a corner. It's so small that it can't seat more than two. When I sit down, the chair creaks and the table wobbles a little. The napkins are rough, and the red-checkered tablecloth is old and worn, but I don't mind. The less-than-perfect conditions of the restaurant make me more at ease than the fancy dinners at some of the aristocrats' places. I don't have to worry about the various eating utensils or keeping modern me at bay when conversing with those lords and ladies.

"What would you like to have?" the waitress asks, pulling a lead pencil from her apron pocket. She directs her full attention on Edward (no surprise there), who merely indicates his chin at me.

"Whatever she wants."

My cheeks heat up, and I know it has nothing to do with the coal stove burning in the back of the room. I glance at the menu, which is written in chalk on a blackboard. In Athelia, the closest thing I had gotten to reading a menu was at this dinner party, in which the hostess took the trouble of having each course written up in an elaborately folded card, though it's useless for me—the names of the food sound more like French than English.

Here, the food is a kind of Indian/Mexican comfort food with some non-spicy options for customers like Edward. After a moment's consideration, I order a hearty chicken soup flavored with spicy peppers, potatoes fried in cumin and sprinkled with lemon juice, chickpeas dipped in a spicy tomato sauce, boiled white rice, and a watercress-and-bacon sandwich for Edward.

After the waitress leaves, I take the jug on the table and pour two glasses of water. It feels a bit strange; at those aristocrats' houses, I'm used to fluttering my fingers at a liveried servant and asking if I could have my glass filled. Then I notice Edward staring at the condiment holder, which contains a row of petite glass jars and wooden spoons. They're quaint, really, and much better than the ugly plastic containers I usually get in chain diners.

"There is no price tag," he says gravely, examining a jar of dark red sauce.

"It's provided gratis. You use whatever amount you prefer on your food."

He uncorks the jar and gazes at the contents, his expression so serious that I have to stifle a grin.

"Edward," I say, unable to hide the amusement in my voice. "You look like the condiment is going to bite your nose. Can't you tell what it is?"

He sniffs obligingly, and the next second he sneezes. I guess the spicy fumes were too much for his delicate olfactory senses. I can't hold it any longer. I collapse against the back of my chair, dissolving in a fit of giggles.

"Oh my God. I wish I could snap your picture, Edward. That expression you had was *priceless*."

He sends me a peeved look, but I mollify him by leaning across the table and giving him a quick peck on the lips. We're so far back in the corner and I was so quick that I doubt anyone noticed. Edward is surprised but pleased, and that's all that matters.

"We should do this more often," he remarks, replacing the cork on the bottle. I wonder which he is referring to—going to a restaurant or my lightning-fast kiss. "Since Parliament is now closed, we have more leisure time."

I frown when he mentions Parliament. The Minimum Wage Act is rejected, which means I still need to figure out an alternative if I want to help Molly, but I haven't had time since I was busy organizing the palace outing. Tomorrow, I think. Tonight I want to celebrate my first restaurant date with Edward.

"How come there is a restaurant like this in Athelia? And how did you learn of a restaurant like this?"

Edward folds his napkin onto his lap. "Recently, there has been an uptick in the number of immigrants. Many of them have chosen to open restaurants here. As for how I received the information—I heard it from Bertram. He was trying to find a restaurant that might impress Amelie, so he asked around and drew up a list. However, Amelie is less tolerant of spicy food, so in the end he chose another one."

I smile, imagining Bertram asking Amelie on a date. "I hope he is progressing with Amelie. She is always so serious, but it seems that she is still reluctant to enter a relationship."

"Bertram had asked me for advice." Edward gives me a pointed look. "Like him, I was unable to win the affections of my lady for a long time. However, there is little that I can offer him, since your case is very different from Amelie's." He pauses, his expression hesitant. "When did you fall in love with me? You were so concerned about getting back to your own world that I do not recall any obvious emotion until I confessed my feelings to you."

I blush. To tell the truth, I can't remember when I first fell in love with him either. "It's . . . it's a gradual process," I say lamely. "By the time I realized that I'm in love with you, I was in too deep." And also dreadfully miserable, because at that time I still wanted to go home to my family.

Our orders arrive—big, hearty portions, freshly cooked and prepared, served in plain tableware that need no rules for their usage. I ladle a bowl of spicy chicken soup, and the multitude of flavors seems to explode in my mouth. It's almost as if the chef knew my preferences. God, how long has it been since I had a taste of something like home?

"This is *so* good." I let out a moan, and Edward glances up abruptly.

"What's wrong?"

"Nothing," he quickly says. "Can I try some of that soup?"

Having witnessed his reaction to the condiment, I warn him to take a small helping, but still he ends up coughing into his napkin and I have to ask for some yogurt to dilute the heat.

"This is a better cure than water." I scoop up the yogurt in a large wooden spoon and hold it out to him. "Trust me."

He does what I say, and soon he stops coughing. "Now I know why you're from another world. Your tastebuds are formed of steel."

I have to laugh. "It's just an acquired taste, Edward. If you grew up eating spicy food like me, you'll be accustomed to it too. Shall we ask for some more food? You can't be satisfied with that sandwich alone. When we get back to the palace, I'll ask Amelie to send up a food tray."

"Don't worry about me," he says, draining a glass of wine. He looks up at me with half-lidded eyes. "I can think of other ways to compensate a hungry stomach."

The heat in his eyes suggests that he wants to take our relationship to the next level. I blush hotly, but I can't deny that I want him as well.

There's still some champagne left in the bottle. Edward fills up our glasses and indicates that I take a toast with him.

"To our future," he says, our glasses clinking gently. "To the rest of our lives—together."

"Together," I echo.

After the meal, we make our way slowly back to the carriage. Since it is downtown, Bertram had to park the carriage a long distance from the restaurant. As we walk together, hand in hand, enjoying this freedom to be together without the scrutiny of servants and guards, a girl's scream reaches our ears above the noise of the people around us.

"Let me go!"

Near a building, there is a young girl struggling with a man who is trying to grab her arm.

It's Molly.

"Behave yourself, girl. You should have been home long ago."

"You're not my . . ." The man slaps her face so hard that she stumbles, and her hand goes to her cheek. Tears spill from her eyes.

I feel like my blood is boiling as I stalk over to them. "What are you doing, trying to abduct this girl? Explain, or I'll call the police."

The man gives me a toothless grin. "I'm taking my daughter home, lady. She has always been a disobedient child. It ain't acceptable to have her running around the town at this hour."

Molly catches my sleeve and shakes her head. "He . . . not . . ." Her speech comes out garbled, which must be the result from that hard slap the man gave her. To my horror, her right cheek is completely swollen.

I move in front of Molly, blocking her from the man. "You say that she's your daughter?"

"Told you already," the man says with a sullen face. "Hand her back to me, you interfering wench."

"Excuse me," Edward says sternly, but I place a restraining hand on his arm. What's more important now is to protect Molly.

"Do you even know her last name? Do you know how many siblings she has?" I fire off the questions. "As a matter of fact, *I* have seen her father, and you look nothing like him." I tap my cheek. "Her father has a scar right here."

322

The man goes pale. By this time, a small crowd has surrounded us, and dozens of eager eyes are surveying us curiously.

Before the man can run off, my body reacts faster than I expected. I take a step toward him, grab his arm, and punch him in a perfect demonstration of the crane fist. Perhaps taken by surprise, the man goes down like a sandbag. A few people nearby gasp and gape at us.

"Ooh!"

"Did she really do that?"

"Did he faint away?"

I stare at my fist, also in shock. Before I can figure out how to follow up my attack, Edward steps in front of me, shielding me and Molly from the man.

"Get back."

While I'm sure that Edward can handle that crook, I don't want him getting into a fight either. Looking around, I spot Bertram's hulk-like figure near our carriage. Never before have I been so grateful that he's such a large man. If he were of normal height, I might not be able to locate him in the crowd.

"Bertram!" I shout, waving my hands wildly. "Over here!"

Once the guard arrives, I gesture at Edward, who has twisted the man's arm behind his back and pinned him to the ground.

"Take this piece of scum to the police," I say. "Ask them to check and see if he has a record of abducting innocent girls."

Bertram gives me a salute. Like the way he did to Mr. Tolliver, he easily picks up the man and slings him over his shoulder.

I turn to Molly, who is crying hard by now. Edward has given her his handkerchief, but her shoulders are still shaking.

"Let's take her to the nearest doctor," I say. "She has to get her cheek treated."

36

It is not easy to find a doctor at night, but through Henry, Edward had made the acquaintance of several reputable doctors, and soon Molly is treated in the hands of a competent young man who graduated top in his class a few years ago. He applies a poultice to her cheek which he remarks lightly is usually meant for professional boxers. When Molly is more inclined to speak, I ask her how she came to be struggling with the man downtown.

"He came up to me in the afternoon, Princess," she says in a small voice. "He wanted me to deliver a bouquet to his sweetheart before the theatre started. Told me he wanted it to be a surprise. But when I got there, he started yellin' that I was a naughty girl and had no business running around in the streets, and I must go home with him."

Edward's face darkens. "I believe I've read of a similar event in the papers, but the abductor escaped before others could catch him."

I glance at Molly, who is sitting on a stool with a downcast expression. Her arm is pale and spindly as she holds the poultice. If we didn't happen to be in the same area, or if I had never seen Molly's father, that horrible man might have succeeded in dragging her off. Considering what had happened to her sister . . . I shiver involuntarily. That black-and-white image of Nell with a swelling belly still haunts me occasionally.

"It'll be all right," Edward says. "Bertram has taken that man to the police, and they will deal with him. He won't bother you again."

Still, I feel awful when we return to the palace. Our first date—a wonderful, magical dinner—is spoiled. Completely.

***

A few days later, Bertram brings us good news.

"That man tryin' ter abduct the young girl has been prosecuted," he announces. "The police are now tryin' ter round up the whole gang. Nasty business those men are in—they kidnap innocent girls and ship 'em to brothels in Moryn. The most common method is ter get the girl drugged and ruined, then sell her off."

Edward's face hardens. I suspect mine is the same.

"Lucky you were close by, Princess Kat, or that man could've dragged the girl away. You saved her." Bertram looks up at me with admiration. "How did yer knock him out? You ain't tiny, but I didn't expect you'd have the strength ter do it."

"I taught her a few moves," Edward says, managing to keep a straight face. "You know how she often places herself in danger, so I had to teach her a bit of self-defense."

Bertram nods. No doubt he's reminded of that day when Mr. Tolliver tried to attack me with a bottle, and if Bertram hadn't happened to be nearby, I could have been seriously injured.

"The police ought to award you a medal of courage, Princess Kat," he remarks and gives me a low bow.

I jump up, embarrassed. "Oh, come on, it was only a punch on the nose."

Edward catches my elbow. "Kat, there's no need to be modest about it. It's the first time in our history that a princess has helped crack a case in human trafficking."

I part my lips into an obligatory grin, but while I'm relieved that Molly is safe, the problem about the children still remains. I doubt Molly's father will let her off the hook. She is probably back in the streets, trying to earn enough to support her sister and the baby. And there's nothing I can do about it.

After Bertram leaves, Edward makes me sit down at the window seat. Outside, the garden is a glorious spectacle of orange and gold, but I'm in no mood to appreciate it.

"I know that you are still anxious about the children," he says quietly. "Would that I were able to promise you an immediate solution. But Kat, you have already made progress, even if the current situation isn't satisfactory. It will only get better."

"I know, but still." I sigh and lean against him. "I understand that it's going to take a long time, but oh, I can't help seeing red when that man slapped Molly. If he could be that violent in public, then what might have happened to her if he'd succeeded? If you hadn't suggested that we go to that restaurant, she might be lost forever."

He strokes my hair. "Think no more of that night, love. She's safe now, and we are going to figure out the next step to protect her and the others from harm."

"But how?" I sit up and stare at him. "I can't forbid Mr. Ripley from making his daughter hawk in the street. I can't foresee any way to prohibit child labor when the parents are the ones who encourage their children to work. The Minimum Wage Act is rejected. And even if it were passed, I don't think Mr. Ripley would change his mind and allow Molly to stop working."

"What about the people in your world? Surely the wealth cannot be equally distributed, and you must have some impoverished families over there. Did their children not have to work? Did their children attend school?"

328

"Everyone has to go to school because they're required to . . ." I grab his hand, excitement pumping through my veins. "Oh Edward, it's so simple! All we have to do is establish a law that states education must be mandatory for all children! If they *have* to go to school, then they can't go to work."

He stares at me as though I have just spoken Spanish to him. Speaking of Spanish, it's such a long time since I've used it. I still miss home, no matter how much in love I am with Edward.

"Such a notion is without precedent," he admits. "It does seem the most likely method to do away with child labor, but I can already foresee that the difficulty will be much greater."

"We've got to try anyway. You told me that Athelia is slow in making progress, but we can't just sit here and do nothing. Let's submit a bill to Parliament, like you did with child labor."

"Parliament will not open until early next spring."

"Isn't there any other way we can convince the...the Ministry of Education, for instance, to consider compulsory education?"

Edward gazes at the view outside, his brow creased. "A few years ago, I had an idea to transform an old cemetery into a public park. Father taught me the proper way to implement my plan. I was to submit a proposal to the municipality, detailing the purpose, the preparations, and the expected results. We can do the same with this."

"Okay." Back when I was working in the publishing industry, before I lost my job, I had assisted in planning for a new column for the magazine. There wasn't much I was assigned to do, being a novice, but anyway, I have an idea of how a proposal works. "Sign me up."

***

A few days later, I receive a message from Lady Gregory. Meg would be visiting this afternoon, and if I don't have anything planned, I'm welcome to drop by.

I quickly pen a reply, answering in the affirmative. I've spent all morning sorting the background material for the proposal for compulsory education, and I appreciate the chance to go out and let my brain relax for a while. I had borrowed books from the palace library, and Edward even got me a pass to use the archives in the University. My desk became so cluttered that I'm considering asking for a larger one, so I can better manage the books and articles I've accumulated.

As the carriage rattles on the street, I rub my hands on my gown, praying that I won't run into the Mansfields. In *The Ugly Stepsister*, I had caused a scene by throwing wine on a ruthless, avaricious factory owner, right in the middle of Lord Mansfield's party. I doubt Mansfield has any friendly feelings toward me.

We stop outside a huge mansion. The doorman yawns widely as he asks for my card. I stare at him, not expecting that I had to bring a card. Nor did I expect the doorman would be sleepy when it's early afternoon.

"I am Princess Katriona." I gesture toward the carriage, which looks fancy enough, since it's from the palace. I hold out my hand, and my wedding ring flashes, the diamonds glittering under the sun. "My . . . sister is married to your master's nephew."

"Please wait outside, lady."

A moment later, the doorman returns and apologizes for not recognizing me. "Her ladyship is pleased to receive you. If you'd follow me, Your Highness?"

The house is pretty quiet. There's no one in the parlor or sitting room, not even a servant cleaning up.

"Isn't your master home?"

"He's gone for the weekend, Your Highness. On a hunting trip in the country."

I'm reminded of that house party thrown by Philip and Constance, right before Edward and I were engaged. As I've grown accustomed to Athelian culture, I've learned that the hunting party is a common pastime among aristocrats during autumn. With Parliament closed, the Season over, and few things to occupy the time, shooting for grouse and stag in the moorlands has become popular. It's also an excellent way for the men to demonstrate their athletic spirits.

It may also be why Lady Gregory specifically chose this weekend for her half-fae, half-human daughter to visit. The servants seem to have their own vacation as well, judging from the lax attitude of the doorman and the lack of servants present in such a large house.

Lady Gregory is knitting a bright yellow sock when I enter her room. She looks up and smiles, gesturing that I take a seat.

"Hello, dearie. Sit down and have some tea. Meg should appear shortly."

"How do you communicate?"

She points to a handheld mirror on the dresser. I remember that when Meg agreed to help me get Elle to the ball, she traveled through the mirror as well. I hope that she won't get stuck this time.

We chat for some time. Lady Gregory asks how the outing went, and I tell her that it was a success.

"It's mostly because of Edward and Henry—you should have seen how the girls looked during the lessons."

"Ah, to be young and filled with romantic feelings." Lady Gregory catches the ball of yarn, which is in danger of rolling off the table. "You should organize another one."

"Maybe we can try something different next time," I say, crossing my legs. "Is there a skating rink in the capital? It's going to be winter soon, and the girls might enjoy an excursion. They'll need the exercise too. Some parents think it's necessary to keep their daughters indoors."

She looks puzzled, and I realize that I've blundered. I shouldn't be asking her about a skating rink when I'm more likely to know the answer than her.

To cover up, I change the subject and pretend to admire one of her crocheted bags hanging on another table placed under a window.

"It's really beautiful," I say, fingering the intricate patterns and the perfect combination of colors. "If I weren't so busy, I'd take up crocheting as well. I have a pair of godchildren . . ."

Lady Gregory slumps across the table, and her knitting needles clatter on the floor.

"Oh, my God." I hurry to her side and check her pulse. She's alive, but her face has gone deathly pale. "Lady Gregory? Can you hear me?"

She doesn't budge. Her eyes remain closed, her mouth slightly open.

Alarmed, I rush out of the room, calling for help.

To my annoyance, the servants—that consist of the doorman and one maid—are slow to emerge.

"Call the doctor! Lady Gregory has fainted away."

They stare at me in disbelief. The doorman is still rubbing sleep from his eyes, and the maid even looks tipsy. God, what's up with this place? Once the master is absent, the servants act like it's Christmas.

I decide to run for a doctor myself. I dash outside and yell for Bertram, who immediately drives for a doctor. I've never been more thankful that Edward used to accompany Henry with his visits, as it turns out that Bertram is super quick in finding a doctor.

The doctor checks Lady Gregory, who is still unconscious, her arm hanging limply to a side. For a moment, I'm scared stiff she is dead, but after the doctor applies a tube to her mouth—I suspect it has to do with pumping air into her lungs—he tells us to transport her to a hospital immediately.

"What's wrong with her?" I ask.

"Heart attack," he says succinctly. "It's a good thing you called for me right away, or she could be dead. We need to start additional treatments to restore her blood flow. Can your servant carry her to the carriage?"

"No problem." I get to my feet and call Bertram.

When Bertram carries Lady Gregory from her room, I glance at the handheld mirror, which is glowing on the bed. For a second, I wonder if I should bring the mirror, but I soon decide against it. It'll be a disaster if Meg appears in a hospital room. It'll be the doctor's turn to have a heart attack.

It doesn't take long before we arrive at the hospital. When Lady Gregory finally recovers consciousness, I breathe a sigh of relief, then send a message to Mansfield House, informing them that Lady Gregory is all right, but the doctor thought it best that she remain at the hospital for the night.

"I cannot thank you enough, dearie." Lady Gregory grasps my hand when I have to go. "At my age, there's little I crave in life, but I'd consider it a tragedy if I couldn't see my daughter before I die."

"I'm glad I came to see you," I say, and I mean it. Even if the servants at Mansfield House were vigilant, it's unlikely that they would discover Lady Gregory until it was too late. "Take care. I'll come back to see you sometime."

37

Back at the palace, I trudge up the stairs to the suite, feeling tired. I should continue preparing for the proposal, but to be honest, it's hard to keep my attention focused on the dry, tedious texts. After struggling for a while, I pick up *The Woman in Red* instead. It proves to be such an intriguing page-turner that I barely register the knock on my door.

"Kat."

Edward walks toward me, a curious light gleaming in his eyes. I was feeling drowsy, but any thought of dropping off to sleep is banished when I discover what he is carrying.

"Is that . . . *cake*?"

He smiles and sets a plate on the table. The piece of cake looks positively sinful, with luscious chocolate curls heaped on top with several dark cherries. "Happy birthday," he says in a low voice.

My heart leaps. Katriona's birthday falls some time in spring, but as Katherine Wilson, my birthday is today. "You remembered?"

"Last year, you told me when your birthday was, as well as what you usually do to celebrate it." Edward pulls out a candle from his pocket, along with a box of matches. "You mentioned that there were candles shaped to resemble numbers in your world, but I'm afraid I was unable to procure one. I hope this will be acceptable."

Wordlessly, I watch him jab the candle on the cake and strike a match. The flame flickers, illuminating the side of his face. He could be plain, ugly, or even scarred . . . whatever he looks like, he will always be number one in my heart.

"Make a wish, Kat." He smiles at me.

I kneel beside him, clasp my hands, and shut my eyes. *Please,* I say in my mind. *Please let me stay with him forever.*

Blowing out the candle, I settle back on my haunches.

"Can I ask what you wished for?"

I giggle and prod his arm lightly. "I think you can guess what it is."

He puts his hand on my shoulder. "Does it concern me?"

"Of course." I take the silver fork that lies next the cake and cut the cake into half. "Did you order the kitchen chef to make this especially for me?"

"I told them I had suddenly developed a sweet tooth. It is an unusual request, but fortunately they were accommodating."

I giggle. "I'd love to see the pastry chef's face."

Forking a delectable piece with a dollop of chocolate cream, I put it in my mouth. Oh, my God. I could present the chef a medal—the cake is that good. An explosion of rich decadence, sweet and addictive, goes straight through my mouth, sparking my senses. I can't help it. I let out a moan.

Beside me, Edward inhales sharply. I realize that what I'm doing is fanning the flames, but at this moment I no longer have any reservations.

I scrape a generous piece of cake and hold it out to him. "Have some birthday cake, Edward."

He blinks, as though he didn't hear me.

"Huh?"

"Open your mouth."

Edward obliges. I feed him the cake, watching him munch in a mechanical manner. He'd probably stand on his hands if I told him to. It looks like the rational part of his brain took a holiday.

"Delicious, isn't it?"

"Very," he says hoarsely and swallows.

There's a smudge of chocolate cream on the corner of his mouth. I dab it away, and that's when he snaps.

The fork clatters on the floor. Edward gathers my face in his hands and kisses me. He tastes of dark chocolate—sweet, decadent, and utterly addictive. I

337

kiss him back, wanting nothing but the feel of his lips on mine.

"Ow!"

Edward lets me go, his expression contrite. Somehow, we've ended up on the floor, my back flat against the carpet and hairpins sticking into my scalp.

"Sorry." He helps me sit up. "Did I hurt you?"

"Terribly. My tender skin cannot withstand the pricks from these tiny hairpins."

"Then allow me to assist you with their removal."

He starts pulling the pins from my hair, slowly yet deliberately. Heat rises in my cheeks. Amelie and Mabel have done this countless times, but Edward's actions are entirely different—I am acutely aware of his fingers moving over my hair and brushing against the rim of my ear, the nape of my neck, the curve of my cheek. It almost feels like he is removing my clothes. Unrestrained by the pins and hairnets, my hair springs free in thick, wavy ringlets, falling over my back and curling on my shoulders.

"I believe this is the last one." Edward sets the hairpin on the table. I look up at him and smile. His eyes darken and he moistens his lips. He's like a traveler who finally discovered an oasis after hours of trekking in a desert.

He tips my head and crushes his lips over mine, and this time there's nothing gentle about his kiss. He devours my mouth with a fierce, all-consuming intensity, like he's been waiting a lifetime for this kiss. As he closes the space between us, my head bumps against the bed post, which is made of solid black walnut and intricately carved.

"Ow!"

I rub the back of my head. First the pins, then the bed post. "Why are we sitting on the floor when there's a bed nearby?"

His eyes crinkle with amusement. "Indeed."

A gasp escapes me when he suddenly lifts me up in a powerful swoop. A second later, I'm lying on the bed, my hair spread over the sheets, my breath coming out in short bursts.

A shadow blots out the violet canopy over my head. Edward leans over me, his fingers undoing the buttons on my collar.

"You'll have to help me," he says. "I have no experience unlacing a corset."

I smile and kiss him. "With pleasure."

He loosens my heavy gown, and I lift my arms so he can peel it away from my body. Due to the cool autumn weather, I'm wearing a fine cotton chemise, a flannel petticoat, a silken petticoat, and a long-sleeved camisole, but still, he gazes at me like a starved man who is presented with a five-course gourmet meal.

"I love you, Kat," he rasps, running his hands over my body. "I never wanted anyone as much as I want you."

My heart contracts. I ache so much for him, not just physically, but also for the pain I've caused him. Come to think of it, I didn't reciprocate his affection for at least half of the time that I've known him, and when I did, our time spent together was blighted by the knowledge that I'd eventually have to return to my own world.

"You have me," I tell him, arching into his touch. "Heart, body, soul."

His breath catches in his throat. No more words are said between us—our actions replace what words were meant to convey. The bed creaks as we fall on each other, kissing and touching like there's no tomorrow. Like we're the only beings in the universe.

When we are finally joined together as one, I feel complete. This is where I want to be. I no longer want to go home, back to the modern world. Edward is my home.

38

I wake up, and for a second, my breath hitches. I'm stark naked in bed, and as my gaze strays over the floor, there is a heap of clothes including garments that aren't mine. There's the heavy gown I was wearing earlier, the laces torn out by impatient, hasty fingers. And when I turn to the other side, I'm greeted by the shocking—I mean *mouthwatering*—appearance of the prince of Athelia, his face as perfect as a chiseled sculpture. My husband. My love.

Memories of the previous night return, and a mix of embarrassment and exhilaration sweeps over me. It has been the wildest, sweetest experience ever. I don't think we got to sleep until well past midnight.

Edward opens his eyes. A smile breaks over his face, lighting his countenance like a rising sun. "Good morning, love."

I yawn, and then, remembering something else, I can't help giggling.

"What is it?" He kisses me. "Is my hair sticking in all directions?"

"No, I just remembered that day when I told your mother that you kept me up until late night." I make a face at him. "Last night, I didn't know whether you're a prince or a caveman."

His grin broadens. "Do you remember that day when you set up your own space in my office because you thought I was too tired from our nightly talks and needed assistance with my work?"

"Of course I do. And you told me the conversations had nothing to do with your not getting enough sleep."

"Because I wasn't able to fall asleep, whether we stayed up or not. The more time I spent with you, the stronger my desire grew for you. Every night, when we had to retire to our own bedrooms, I had to restrain myself from the urge to seize you. When I lay alone and stared at the canopy above, I couldn't think of anything else except having you in my bed. I yearned for a moment like this—waking up with you by my side. I wanted you so much, but I couldn't take you to bed."

I prop up on my elbow and lean over him, tracing his nose and lips. "I know. But I just can't . . . I can't sleep with you unless I'm in love with you."

"I knew that I should appreciate your integrity, but I wished that you could have fallen in love sooner." He snakes an arm around me, pressing me close against his chest. "So, when the goblin comes, you will tell him you're not going with him?" There is a note of hesitancy in his tone, like he still doesn't fully trust that I won't change my mind.

"Of course." I raise my head to give him a stern, reproving glare. "You're stuck with me, Edward. I don't even care if you eventually get tired of me."

"Never." His voice is raspy, hoarse. "That will never happen."

"There is just one thing I need to do before I commit myself to you. I want to go back to my family to say goodbye." Seeing the hesitation in his eyes, I quickly add, "Just once! I promise that I'll only take the time to say farewell to my family and friends, and I'll come back."

He exhales. "Do you think the goblin could let me come with you? I would like to meet your family."

My heart leaps at the possibility. "I would like my family to meet you as well. Mom would like you, I'm sure of it. You could do that courtly bow of yours and kiss her hand, and she'll definitely be charmed. But don't do that to Paige. She'll laugh, and besides, her boyfriend might bite your head off."

"There was a time I resented your family," he says. "If it weren't for them, you would have agreed to marry me. But later, I made myself see sense. Even if you accepted my proposal, according to the spell, you have achieved the happy ending and had to go back anyway. And if it weren't for your mother and sister, you wouldn't have become the woman I've come to love. I should thank your mother for bringing you into existence. I could even thank the goblin for transporting you here."

343

"Oh Edward." I laugh. "I know I'm special to you, but seriously, stop putting me on a pedestal. You're making me sound like some unearthly phenomenon, like a goddess."

He kisses me, slowly and deeply, until I'm panting for breath. "Never underestimate how precious you are to me. Where am I to find a woman with such an extraordinary mind and character?"

Oh my. Looks like last night wasn't enough for him. A moan escapes me as he kisses a fiery trail downward, but suddenly he goes still.

"What is this?

"Huh?"

He traces the mark on my shoulder. "What happened to your shoulder? This doesn't look like a bug bite."

"Um . . ." Though I don't want to cause him worry, I owe him my honesty. "Krev gave it to me."

"Why did he do it?" Alarm is evident in his voice. "Does it hurt when I touch you like this?"

"No, I don't feel any pain." I relate to him that Krev showed up, but I omit the part of the goblin telling me to stay away from Edward. "It seems that the goblin world isn't the same as before. Before we married, Krev never seemed to have any trouble when he came by to visit."

"I don't like this," he says darkly. "The goblin told you that you had to go home and gave you this mark. Maybe the next time the goblin comes, magic will trigger the mark and you'll be sent away to your world."

"Well, if that's the case, then he'd better give you a mark as well, because you're coming with me," I say. "And we'll both come back to Athelia."

But deep down inside, I feel that it isn't going to be that simple. From my experience with the goblins, rarely does Krev ever grant what I want. Anyway, we'll make it work. Nothing will make me leave Edward.

Little did I know how wrong I was.

***

The following days pass in a period of hazy bliss. As if to make up for the nights that he had to sleep alone, Edward refuses to go to bed until I join him. I wonder what the king and queen would say if they knew their son, who usually looks so serious in public, could be so passionate in private. His desire burns fiercely and intensely from the restraint of several months and the need to ensure that I'm not going anywhere. I had to sew the buttons back onto my nightgown one morning. I could have asked the maids to do it, but I'd rather not endure Mabel's smirking.

Anyway, apart from admonishing Edward about the nightgown, I don't mind—it's sweet that I can reciprocate his affection. Sometimes, it feels like his passion isn't merely to satiate his hunger, but that the act could bind me more securely to him, to this world. If I get pregnant, it'll be very unlikely that I'll want to return home. Even when I've promised him I won't leave him, there are times that he still gets anxious that I might change my mind if Krev shows up. But if we have a child, I'll have a greater incentive to stay.

Not all the time is spent in his arms, however. I have to comb through the books and articles I've found on education, jot down copious notes, work out advantageous points, and eventually organize everything together into a coherent draft.

One evening, I finally have the proposal done. I have Edward sit with me on the window seat and go through the steps toward achieving compulsory education.

"First, there must be funding allocated to establish enough schools," Edward reads from the paper. "Actually, I could append a suggestion. When we were planning for model housing to demolish city slums, it was intended that a number of parks would be arranged with the new housing. I suggest that for every three parks, there should be an elementary school to go with it."

I give him a thumbs-up. "Sounds good to me."

"Second, parents have to send their children to school, or they will face sanctions. In the case of the working-class, the parents are usually the ones who most oppose letting their children attend school."

"We have to persuade them that in the long run, it'll be better for the children to be educated," I say. "Think of all the opportunities a child can have if he can read and write."

"Three, set the minimum age that children are allowed to leave school."

"I suppose eighteen is asking too much?"

346

Edward smiles wryly. "I'd say twelve would be the ideal age. Father replaced my tutors when I turned twelve. From what I've heard of the boys' schools in the city, students are usually twelve or thirteen when they begin secondary school."

I nod. I still don't like the idea of a twelve-year-old in the factories—Paige was still impossibly cute when she was twelve—but it's Athelia. Making education mandatory is already something akin to a miracle.

"Let us submit the plan to the Minister of Education tomorrow. I don't expect we will have any remote chance of success right away, but we can plant the idea in their heads."

"*Drill* the idea into their heads," I say emphatically. "In advertising, consumers usually have to see a product seven times before they're convinced to buy it."

Edward looks amused. "Never can I estimate the breadth and variety of knowledge in your head."

I grin at him. "That's why you married me."

***

The very next day, Edward asks George to schedule an appointment with Lord Dudley, the Minister of Education. I wonder why the government officials have a title. Even Edward's own secretary is called Sir George.

"Your Highness," Lord Dudley says, giving me a dubious glance when he enters Edward's office. I had refused to remove my desk, even though gossip had informed me that some courtiers disapprove strongly of me working at Edward's side. "To what honor do I have that you wish to see me?"

"Have a seat." Edward gestures to a chair directly opposite him. "George, bring us some tea."

Lord Dudley sits down, but the bemused look in his eyes still remains. Tea means a discussion, not simply a command or question. Back when I was going on calls with Bianca, I could tell whether it was going to be a short or long call, judging by whether the lady asked us to remove our hats or called for tea.

"We apologize for this sudden appointment," I say, which earns another suspicious look from Lord Dudley, who glances quickly at Edward, as if I'm supposed to be invisible or deaf. "You see, Edward and I have this plan."

I swear, a frightened look passes his face. You'd think I were announcing a plan to take over Athelia and crown myself as empress.

Edward slides a sheaf of papers toward Lord Dudley. The latter takes it, and his jaw drops when he glances at the very first page.

"Are you suggesting, Your Highness, that ALL CHILDREN before the age of twelve must attend school?"

I really don't see what he has to be so astonished about, but then I remind myself for the umpteenth time that this is Athelia.

"I understand that this is going to be a monstrous project, and it might even take years for it to be realized," Edward says, steepling his fingers together. "However, we believe that the benefits will be worth it in the long run."

I cannot help but grin when he says *we*. If there wasn't a space between our desks, I would have reached out and taken his hand.

Lord Dudley, however, still looks dazed, as though he hasn't recovered from a strong blow. "But . . . I really don't think that this is feasible, Your Highness. Are you saying that this applies to *all* children of Athelia? Most parents won't be able to spare their children! And think of the amount of funding required! You are taking a radical leap here."

"I am well aware," Edward says in his aristocratic tone, which I can't help but appreciate for now, "of the difficulties you outlined. Hence, we chose to submit a plan on paper. If you would kindly take the time to go through the plan, instead of skimming through the first page, we would be glad to hear what can be improved."

Lord Dudley starts reading like an obedient child. I raise an eyebrow at Edward, my feelings mixed. Even if he has no executive power in Athelia, it appears that being a prince still commands a great deal of respect and deference from his subjects.

Edward only winks.

I finish my second cup of tea when Lord Dudley raises his head. "Your Highness," he says, still looking at Edward only. "I . . . I fear that I cannot advance an opinion at this moment. I would beg that you allow me to show this project to my colleagues and discuss it with them."

Edward and I look at each other. I guess it is too much to ask for the Minister of Education to agree at this point. Indeed, were I in his place, I would also prefer to have a discussion with several people rather than accepting it right away. Still, with the reluctance he shows, I think it is more of an unwillingness to reject us right away rather than seriously considering the possibility of the project.

"Certainly, Dudley," Edward says. "This is no simple task. Take all the time you need. We anticipate a favorable answer."

When Lord Dudley leaves, I sink in my chair. "Do you think it's possible that the Ministry of Education will approve the project?"

Edward takes a book from the shelf and lays it on his desk. "They will, eventually. I read through your proposal this morning, when you were still dealing with your letters in our suite, and the more I think about it, the more I'm convinced of the necessity of compulsory education. Whatever job our citizens take, all will benefit from literacy, math, and basic knowledge."

He comes to my side and lays his hand over mine, his back facing the entrance. Although we're spending every night together, Edward still snatches the chance for a covert caress or whispered endearment during the day. "If it weren't for you, Kat, this idea wouldn't have occurred to me." His fingers stroke the back of my hand. "Having you by my side is the best thing that ever happened to me."

I smile up at him. "That was my line."

Someone coughs in the doorway. Startled, I pull my hand back and Edward turns around. Uh-oh. We were so focused on each other that neither of us heard the approaching footsteps. I can't entirely blame those courtiers for criticizing my working in Edward's office.

It's Lord Mansfield. His black wool hat is askew, and he is breathing heavily, both hands pressed on his knees. He must have sprinted on his way here.

Edward calmly pours him a glass of water. Lord Mansfield takes a swig, but soon he sets the glass on a table.

"Thank you, Your Highness. I…uh…actually, I was informed that Princess Katriona is here."

I stand up, surprised. "You wanted to speak to me?"

He adjusts the cuffs of his sleeves, as though they were chafing his wrists. There's anxiety written in his face. "Several days ago, when I was on a hunting trip up north, Aunt Margaret invited you to tea. She had a sudden heart attack, and you brought her to the hospital. The staff contacted me when I returned."

I nod. "Is she all right now?"

Lord Mansfield wipes his forehead, which is dotted with sweat. "She has disappeared."

"No! Seriously? She never returned home?"

"Never. Her conditions were stabilized, and the doctor was all prepared to write me a note and ask to

351

have her sent home, but when he went to check on her, her bed was empty. They conducted a search in the entire hospital—they even looked for footprints under the windows—but there was no trace of her."

"Maybe—" I start, then shut my mouth. Can it be that Meg came for her mother? But why would she take Lady Gregory away, when the old lady is content to remain in Athelia? "How long has it been since she disappeared?"

"Two days." Lord Mansfield swallows. "I've asked her friends in her crochet group, but no one has any idea. Then I remembered the staff had mentioned that you were the one who brought her to the hospital, so I decided to come and ask if you might have any idea."

I wonder if I should mention Meg, but I decide not to risk it. Athelians don't believe in fairies and magic. It's more likely that Lord Mansfield doesn't know about Lady Gregory's fairy husband and half-fae daughter; otherwise she wouldn't have needed me to give that silver lily to Lysander.

"I'm sorry, but I really don't know." I give him an apologetic shrug. On the other hand, if Lady Gregory's disappearance has nothing to do with the fairies, then it is indeed cause for concern. "Have you notified the police?"

"Not yet. You're the last person I thought of, and since you don't know where Aunt Margaret might be, I'll head over to the Metropolitan Police Headquarters now." Lord Mansfield picks up his hat, then makes me a bow. "I haven't yet had a chance to thank you, Princess Katriona, for saving my aunt's life."

I incline my head in a perfect angle that would make the king and queen proud. "You're very welcome, Lord Mansfield. I'm glad that I was there that day; Lady Gregory is my friend. Please send a message to me if you receive any word of her whereabouts."

"I certainly shall." He bows slightly at Edward and says, "Apologies for interrupting you at work, Your Highness."

Once Lord Mansfield has left the office, Edward and I look at each other. I had told him all about Lady Gregory. Though he has never met her, Edward always shows concern because if it weren't for her and Meg, I couldn't have made it to the ball.

"What do you make of this?" Edward says in a low voice.

I bite the inside of my cheek. "My guess is that Meg came that day when Lady Gregory had a heart attack, failed to see her mother, and later found her at the hospital. But I'm only guessing here. I just hope that she is safe."

39

A few days later, there's still no word of Lady Gregory. I pay a visit to Mansfield House; her room looks exactly the same as when I left it, until I realize the handheld mirror is missing. Maybe Lysander finally persuaded Lady Gregory to go back to him and spend the remaining time of her life in the fae realm. Maybe the heart attack changed her mind. Hopefully I'll hear from her soon.

Back at the palace, I arrive at Edward's office later than usual. I almost crash into Lord Dudley, who happens to be emerging from Edward's office.

"Sorry, Your Highness. Didn't see you coming this way." He raises his hat and bows. "I . . . His Highness will inform you of my visit."

And he rushes out, as though he couldn't bear my presence any longer. Maybe the air that comes from my nostrils is poisoning him.

I shrug and enter Edward's office. "Did he come to tell you of his decision? Don't tell me that he accepted our plan. It is easier to believe that Andrew McVean suddenly decided to donate all of his income to charity."

"His decision is not surprising," Edward says, pulling out my chair. I once mentioned to him that I can do it by myself, but he tells me that he is doing it because he welcomes my company, not because he's adhering to some old-fashioned gentleman code in Athelia. "He told me that the ministry would support the plan once Parliament approves."

"So, this is it, then." I sigh. "We'll have to go through the same process as we did for the Eight-Hour Act."

"There is still a long time until Parliament re-opens," Edward says in a soothing tone. "You can do research in the library, and with experience from last time, we can use a similar sentiment to appeal to the public."

I nod. It's likely to be a long journey, but I'm going to do my best to improve the welfare of my subjects. I refuse to be a conventional princess whose only purpose in life is to bear heirs.

After helping him proofread a draft for a trade agreement, I return to the suite, feeling like taking a nice long nap on the sofa near the window seat. No sooner have I snuggled on the sofa with a couple of cushions, when Mabel comes bouncing into the study, exclaiming that I have a party invitation.

"It's from Lady Maynard! She's getting engaged to the Marquess of Sunderland! She sent an invitation for her engagement party."

Lady Maynard? I take the card and turn it over on my palm. *You are cordially invited to the Engagement Event of Mr. David Waterford, the Marquess of Sunderland, and Miss Lillie Maynard, younger sister of the Duchess of Northport.*

An angelic face framed by strawberry blonde hair enters my mind. So, it's Lillie, the younger sister of Constance, who married Edward's cousin. Lillie had a crush on Edward. She tried to get his attention before we were officially engaged, but naturally she didn't succeed.

I shudder. Thankfully, I didn't let her marry Edward. What if I returned and found it was Lillie at the wedding altar?

"Do you know anything about Sunderland?" I say. Mabel lives for gossip.

"Oh, he has two townhouses and a country manor and an old castle in the north! I've heard he keeps more than a thousand servants, and . . ."

"Is he a nice guy? I mean, what is his reputation?"

Mabel puckers her forehead. "If he has any illegitimate children, he is being very discreet."

God, I really need to adjust to the Athelian mind. On the other hand, it seems that if a man is stupendously rich, then it's expected that he would have children out of wedlock. Really, Edward is a rare species.

"He must have some good qualities. Lady Maynard doesn't seem the type to settle for an ordinary man," Mabel says confidently. "Anyway, you'll meet him soon at the engagement. Now, would you like to see the surprise Amelie and I got for you?"

Somehow, her excited voice doesn't make me excited as well.

"Come, Princess," Mabel urges. "Come and see the surprise we got."

I follow her to my bedroom, wondering if it's some new flower from Edward's garden, but I don't see anything unusual in the room.

"Over there!" Mabel points. "The tailors have designed a new gown for you!"

"Another one?" I stifle a groan. "I told them I have more than enough."

"Oh, but I'm sure that you would like this! Weren't you complaining about corsets that are too tight? Well, Moryn's latest fashion trend is this tea gown—it has built-in padding so you needn't wear a corset!"

I glance at the bed, where said tea gown is spread out on the sheets. It is the color of heliotropes, trimmed with satin ribbons, with a fancy bow at the neckline and a skirt long enough to trail on the ground. It looks similar to any fancy gown, but when I pick it up, I notice that the chest area is padded like a bra top, but the material is much thicker.

"Aren't you going to that engagement party for Lady Maynard? This will be just the thing! You won't have to worry about your corset squeezing your ribs when you dance, and His Highness won't have to worry if you get dizzy and faint! Although it has become quite fashionable to faint, especially when there's a crowd . . ."

I roll my eyes. Still, I'm a bit skeptical about this tea gown. "Are you sure it's all right? Are you sure I don't need to wear a corset under this . . ." My voice trails off.

Edward is leaning in the entrance of the doorway, arms crossed in front of his chest. I swear, there is a predatory glint in his eyes as he looks at me. Like he's undressing me in his mind.

"Did you hear our conversation?"

"Every word."

"You shouldn't eavesdrop, you know."

"I wasn't. I was here the entire time. You simply didn't notice me."

Sometimes, His Royal Highness, Edward, can be the most obnoxious person I have ever met.

"However." Edward uncrosses his arms and takes a step toward me. "Don't wear this gown to Lillie's engagement."

He's using his bossy prince tone—ever since our first real quarrel, he has seldom used it. "Why not? It should be more comfortable when dancing. And there's padding. It's not like the gown is some flimsy nightwear."

"Do you know how the tea gown received its name? It is because the Moryn aristocracy found afternoon teas the most convenient time of the day to conduct extra-marital affairs. If you wear this gown, others may have the wrong idea."

"Um, Your Highness?" Mabel says tentatively. "We don't have much time left. If you prefer a different gown—"

"I want to try it on," I say, ignoring the noise of disapproval from my husband.

Moments later, I enter the sitting room in my tea gown. Mabel wasn't kidding when she said that the gown would be much more comfortable to wear compared to the corset. In fact, due to the heavy padding, it's even more comfortable than a bra.

Edward's eyes widen and he swallows, but when he speaks, his voice remains harsh. "Don't wear it."

"I beg your pardon?" I am fully covered from neck to toe.

"Don't wear it to the engagement party."

"Why not? It's a lot more comfortable than the corset."

He mutters under his breath, but thanks to his proximity, I hear him fine. "No man should see you in that gown, other than I."

I could have smacked my head on the wall. "Geez, do you know I've worn far less than this in college? I could show my arms and my thighs. And how many times do I have to tell you that I'm not your property?"

"Stop using this excuse that you are from another world. You are in Athelia now."

Edward finally relents, as I tell him that I get to decide what I wear, but there is still a strained silence in the carriage ride to Lillie's party.

"Come on, Edward," I say in a coaxing tone. "Don't you remember when I was Katriona Bradshaw and no one noticed me? Only Bianca got all the attention."

He looks out the window. "I cannot be glad about the fact that you revealed so much skin to other men. I'm sure that suitor of yours has seen your arms bare."

Jason saw me naked, but of course, I don't say that. In an effort to pacify and comfort him, I clamber onto his lap, making him look at me.

"Listen up, Your Highness." I take his face in both of my hands. "There's no point dwelling in the past. It's just a bit of skin. So what if there were other guys who saw my arms and legs? I am married to *you*." And I kiss him right on the lips.

To my surprise, he doesn't respond. It's like I kissed a statue.

"Edward?"

"Another," he orders in his bossy, princely tone.

I shrug and kiss him again.

"Another."

I have a notion to poke his ribs, but I comply. This time he reciprocates, setting his hands on my shoulders, his lips chasing mine. It's not until the coachman hollers that Edward releases me.

Pulling my collar back into place, I wonder what the public would say if they knew the stately Prince Edward can be so immature at times.

***

Lillie's husband, the Marquess of Sunderland, greets us with warmth and kindness. He is average-looking—standing next to Lillie's flowerlike features, he pales in comparison. Now if it were Edward and Lillie, that would be a different picture.

Lillie is arrayed in a sapphire-blue gown lined with diamonds, which makes her look more sophisticated than her real age. She gives us a bright, wide smile which seems a tad strained.

"Congratulations," I say. "I hope you'll be very happy."

"Thank you, Katriona," she says, clasping my hand. "I'm glad that you were able to come." She pauses, as though she has something to say but is holding back. I really hope it doesn't have anything to do with Edward.

"Princess Katriona," a lady gushes, sidling over to us, her expression filled with curiosity. "Forgive me for this brazen question, but is it true that you punched a man in the street?"

Lillie gasps. So do the other ladies surrounding us. I realize the story of me punching Molly's abductor has gotten out.

"Is it true that you prevented a detestable thug from abducting an innocent child by detaining him by force?"

"How were you able to land a blow on him?"

"I suppose that he wasn't expecting a lady could use her fist," I say, wishing that they wouldn't gaze at me like I'm a weird species.

"How did you learn how to attack a man?"

Without thinking, I open my fan, even though it isn't really necessary. It's warm in the room, thanks to the fire and the number of guests, but it's snowing outside. "Well, I . . ."

"Excuse me." Edward loops his arm around my waist, an intimate gesture that makes the ladies gasp again, though for a different reason this time. "I'm afraid it's necessary to remind the princess to get some refreshments. She has barely eaten anything since lunch, and I certainly don't want her fainting again."

As a matter of fact, I had consumed a hearty afternoon tea, but I'm glad for an excuse to get away from the women. After a while, Philip and Constance, along with the parents of the Marquess of Sunderland, appear and ask us to move to the corners so that Lillie and her betrothed may open the ball.

At first, Edward dances with me alone. I wonder if it's because the men are afraid I might punch some of them as I did to Molly's abductor. Which is absurd.

Edward doesn't seem to mind, however. He really meant it when he said he doesn't want other gentlemen to discover I'm wearing a tea gown, even though he's being ridiculous. As if any man would want a dalliance with me, when most of the women present are prettier than me. Not to mention that Edward is certain to eviscerate any man who dares to leer at me.

During the break, I pause for some water. The past two songs were fast tracks, and I need to regain my breath. When I reach for a glass of water, it seems that my lungs are suddenly robbed of air, and I choke. Geez, I really should exercise more.

"Are you all right, Katriona?" A courteous, cold tone.

I whirl around and find myself facing Bianca. "Good evening."

"Enjoying yourself?"

I dab my mouth with my handkerchief and nod. "Perfectly, thank you."

"I assure you, I have no design on your precious school anymore. My husband has found another location for our new house." Bianca adjusts her necklace. "In fact, why don't you come to our house tomorrow morning? There is a young girl who is extremely eager to meet you."

I wonder how any acquaintance of Bianca's would want to meet me, given my notoriety. "She wishes to attend Princess College?"

There's a flash of emotion in Bianca's eyes, but she shrugs. "Something like that, but you'll have to convince her first and introduce her to the school. I couldn't have her meet you in an event like this."

I am not sure if Bianca is sincere. She doesn't seem to care whether the girl wants to enroll in our school. Maybe the girl heard of our palace outing and got interested? We did have a few more girls sign up after the outing.

Anyway, as the co-founder of Princess College, if a student is interested in the school, who am I to refuse? Even if she may be Bianca's relative.

"Kat." Edward approaches us, and there's a worried look in his eyes before he turns to Bianca. "Lady Pembroke."

She curtsies and looks up at him through her eyelashes. "Your Highness."

Edward nods. "If you have finished your conversation, I would like to ask Kat to come and sit with me. She looks rather pale."

I jump at the chance of getting away from Bianca. "Sorry, Bianca, but I *am* feeling a bit weary, to be honest."

When Edward leads me away, his hand on the small of my back, I can sense Bianca's eyes on us. I glance at her and flinch at the anger in her glare. She looks like she wants to take up the nearest decanter of brandy and hit me over the head with it.

40

I shiver when I open my eyes in the morning. Although the drapes around the bed are still drawn, it's not warm enough. It has started snowing, and no matter how big a fire Amelie kindles before we go to sleep, it's bound to die out in the morning. If only we had electric heaters in here—I tell myself to stop this nostalgia for modern appliances. When I made the decision to stay in Athelia, I was prepared to accept its state of technology as well. It's something that I have no control of. Anyway, Edward is worth all the trouble.

I wonder what time it is. Lillie's engagement party lasted well past midnight, and it was early morning when we got home. I wonder how we're going to manage when Parliament reopens. Luckily, it's the weekend today.

"Kat?" Edward stirs. He wraps an arm around my waist and nuzzles the curve of my collarbone, his warm breath tickling my skin. I could stay in this position and never want to get up. "What time is it?"

I stretch my arm through the opening in the drapes and grab my pocket watch, which is usually set on the nightstand. My fingers close around the metal chain, and I bring the clock face to my eyes. "Holy crap," I gasp. "It's nearly nine."

Edward yawns. "Send in a breakfast tray."

When I attempt to get up, his arms tighten around me. "What's the hurry, love? You don't have anything scheduled this morning."

"Actually, I do. Last night at Lillie's party, Bianca asked me to meet her at her new house."

There is a moment of silence. "So that was what you were talking about last night. But why would she volunteer an appointment with you?"

"I don't quite get it either," I say honestly. "But she wanted to introduce a pupil to me. Maybe it could be some truce."

"Then let me accompany you to her house." Edward sits up and looks for his dressing gown. With his hair tousled and stubble on his chin, he still looks gorgeous.

"I appreciate the offer, but I doubt that's a good idea." I hop out of bed and attempt to rekindle the fire. "Every time she sees you with me, she looks furious. Don't worry about me, Edward. I'm not going into a shady alley to negotiate with some drug lord. And now, I am the notorious princess who punched a man in the street and sent him reeling. Bianca won't dare to do anything to me."

"Very well." Edward draws me to him and kisses me deeply. "Go, but remember to be back for lunch."

"Of course." I smile at him. "Trust me, I would much rather spend my time in your company than hers."

***

Bianca's residence is a perfect representation of her character. There is an elegant yet frosty atmosphere as I step inside the house. Marble pillars, glass-topped tables, stone fireplace. It lacks a touch of wood to give the home a cozy feel. The colors are mostly blue and silver, colors that match her ice queen persona.

"Good morning." The mistress of the house greets me with a smile that doesn't reach her eyes. "Do step in before the wind brings the snow inside the parlor."

Two servants take my coat, my muffler, and my hat. I thank them courteously, as I do with any servant in the palace, and they look at me with a brief moment of surprise. I doubt Bianca has ever bothered to thank them.

"You have a beautiful house," I say, making an effort to be friendly. "And very well furnished."

"It is nothing compared to *your* quarters," Bianca says coldly. "The size of this house isn't any larger than the greenhouse in the palace."

She definitely still holds a grudge toward me. Then why did she invite me here to introduce me to a prospective student? It has to be pressure from an elder relative. She'd never be this benevolent to encourage more pupils for my sake.

Or does she have something more sinister in mind? But as much as she hates me, surely Bianca doesn't have the nerve to harm the princess of Athelia. Lady Bradshaw was ostracized since I made it known that she tried to have Elle drowned. Besides, I'm sure Edward would expel Bianca from Athelia if she tried to do anything to me.

We pass through the sitting room, which is decorated in the same blue-and-silver theme of the other rooms. I pause, but Bianca doesn't stop. "What are you looking at, Katriona?"

"Nothing. I just thought, since this is the sitting room . . ."

She gives a tinkling laugh, a laugh that contains derision. "And I thought you had grown used to being a princess! Did you not know that there can be more than one sitting room in a house? Did you not know that I usually receive close acquaintances in my drawing room upstairs? Come along."

I shrug and follow her upstairs, though there's an uneasy feeling in my stomach. A housemaid, who's dusting the landing on top of the stairs, stares at me when I pass. Like I'm a freak.

By now, I have a feeling that Bianca didn't invite me here to introduce a new pupil. I swallow and wish that we could get this over quickly so I can return to the palace. Even though there is nothing to be afraid of, and it's not the first time that I have gone to pay calls alone, I don't like this house. It has the same unwelcoming atmosphere as the hostility Bianca holds toward me.

Bianca leads me not to the second floor, but curiously, the third floor. Strange. I desperately try to recall the typical layout of a wealthy family's townhouse—the third floor is usually reserved for the members of the family. Well, I *am* supposed to be family, but still, it's weird that she would bring me to this area.

"Is your husband home?" I ask.

"Gone out to the casino," Bianca says dismissively. She doesn't seem to care much for her husband, even though Lord Mansfield's nephew is considered a catch. "He can't hunt or shoot during winter, so the casino is his favorite place. It is dreadfully difficult to occupy oneself when it's snowing outside."

She leads me to a small room, the door locked. I clench my fists and brace myself. If she dares to do anything to me, I won't hesitate to punch her. Bertram is outside, and if I am gone for too long, he will definitely come in and inquire for me.

Inside is a room that is sparsely furnished. There is a bed in a corner, a few chairs, and a compact fireplace. Then, as my gaze wanders around the room, a girl who is sitting on the bed rises and comes forward.

This must be the person that Bianca wishes me to meet.

I gasp and squeeze my eyes shut, but when I open them, the girl is still there. For a moment, I am frozen like the icicles hanging from the roof. The girl looks exactly like me. Red hair, gray eyes, freckles splashed over her face.

Katriona Bradshaw. The real sister of Bianca, the real younger daughter of the Bradshaws.

The other girl is apparently shocked as well, for she takes a step back and grabs one of the posts of the bed. "It cannot be . . ." she whispers, her face chalk-white.

"Mercy me," someone else utters. I whirl around and find myself facing Lady Bradshaw. I haven't seen her since a year ago, when I accidentally ran into her and Bianca moving out of their old house. She looks much thinner than when I last saw her, and older as well. I guess country life didn't suit her. "Who are you? Which one of you is my daughter?"

My first thought is to bolt out of the room, but I am paralyzed with shock. How could Katriona Bradshaw suddenly turn up? Am I not supposed to be inhabiting her body? Where was she all this time? Did something go wrong with the goblins' spell?

All I can think of is, *This is bad. Really bad. Bianca's revenge on me has started off with a bang.*

"Witch," Bianca hisses, pointing a long, accusing finger at me. "You have been masquerading as my sister. You used some despicable charm to get the prince. You should be burned at the stake."

"No." I fall backward and cower against the wall. "I didn't do anything. There must be some mistake here."

Bianca steps closer, her eyes glowing with fury. "Then tell me this: what is our mother's middle name?"

I lick my lips. No idea. I rack my brain frantically, but I don't think I've ever heard it during the year I was in Lady Bradshaw's house.

"Coraline," the other girl says. "Aileen Coraline Hamilton."

"What is the name of the first governess we had when we were ten?"

Governess? I didn't even know we had governesses. When I was still at Lady Bradshaw's house, there was only this music and dancing master called Pierre.

"Miss Dawson," the other girl says in a monotonous voice. "I never liked her."

There is no point in continuing this interrogation.

Bianca turns toward me, eyes blazing, and crosses her arms. "Explain yourself, witch."

***

The king and queen are already in the dining room when we arrive. Both of them look surprised when I enter with Bianca and Lady Bradshaw accompanying me.

"Katriona?" The queen raises a quizzical eyebrow. "Did you want to invite your mother and sister for lunch?"

"She is not who you think she is," Bianca says coldly. "In fact, I doubt her name is Katriona at all."

The king and queen look at each other, and then at Bianca, as though she's lost her mind. Like in a drama onstage, Bianca steps aside, revealing the real Katriona.

I feel like throwing up or running away. If only I could think of a better way to handle this. But try as I might, nothing comes to mind. Even if I had prevented Bianca from coming to the palace today, she could find other ways to expose me. Katriona Bradshaw's presence at Bianca's house must have already attracted gossip. The best that I can hope for is that Edward might figure out a miracle to save me. He'll stand by me. That's for certain.

"My goodness." The queen puts a hand to her mouth. The king rubs his eyes, looks at us, then rubs his eyes again.

We do look similar, Katriona and I. When we were in the carriage on our way to the palace, I had taken a good look at her. Her face isn't as round as mine, and she has more freckles over her face, but it's no problem passing us off as twins.

And then an alarming realization enters my mind—*she looks more like me when I was seventeen.* The reality of the situation starts to sink in. I have not entered Katriona's body like I did last time. I am here in my twenty-four-year-old self, while she . . . where was she when I was sent to Athelia this second time?

It was a huge mistake, Krev's voice echoes in my head. He must be referring to Katriona Bradshaw. No wonder the goblin didn't seem to mind when I was in Athelia for the first time, because I was *in Katriona's body*. But now, looking at my doppelgänger standing quietly behind Bianca, hands folded and eyes downcast, it registers in my mind that this is indeed a huge, thorny issue.

It's impossible that I can prove that I am Katriona Bradshaw. But if I'm not Katriona, what is to become of me? Even if I tell them the truth, the king and queen won't believe me. They'll think I'm crazy. My palms grow moist as my anxiety heightens. I hunch my back and hold my elbows tightly, trying to make myself seem inconspicuous. How am I going to get out of this situation unscathed?

"We need to move to a private room," the king says finally. "This is a problem that deserves our full attention."

We are led through a corridor until we reach the king's receiving chamber. On our way, servants halt and stare at us in disbelief. Oh no. Now everyone knows or is going to know that I am not Katriona Bradshaw. I'm a fraud.

When we enter the receiving chamber, footsteps pound outside, and Edward appears. His hair is mussed up, his chest heaving, and when he sees me and Katriona, he looks as though someone has struck him on the head.

373

"Kat," he starts. "Why are you . . . what happened?"

"That," the king says, "is what we need to find out now."

I head to the throne—four seats are set for us, but Bianca grabs my arm. "You do not deserve to sit on the throne, witch."

"Remove your hand, Lady Pembroke." Edward's tone is freezing. "Whatever you wish to say, she is still the princess."

The king sends us a disapproving look, but he does not comment when Edward pulls me along. The king, queen, Edward and I sit on the thrones, while Bianca, Lady Bradshaw, and Katriona occupy the seats below. I close my eyes for a second and pray. There must be a way out of this. There must.

"Bianca Bradshaw," the queen says slowly. "Are you saying that the woman sitting beside you is your real sister, while the woman my son married is not?"

Bianca lifts her chin. "We were deceived. I don't know what kind of magic she has been using, but somehow she took advantage of my sister's identity, called herself Katriona Bradshaw, and tried to gain favor with you."

"There is no magic in this country," the king says sharply. A bit too vehemently, like the mention of magic offends his ears. "What proof do you have that the woman with you is your real sister?"

Bianca repeats our conversation at our house, describing in detail how I failed to answer all those basic questions. "I would guess that this woman" —

she points at me— "is some despicable commoner, and upon discovering that she resembles my sister, she hatched this plot. She abducted my sister, sneaked into our house, and used every opportunity behind our backs to seduce Prince Edward."

"Kat never tried to seduce me," Edward says sharply. "If anything, *I* had to persuade her to marry me."

He deals her an intense glare, and Bianca flinches.

"Pardon me, Your Majesties," Lady Bradshaw says, speaking for the first time. Compared to Bianca, she looks nervous. Possibly because she had been convicted of her crime committed toward Elle. "But this is not uncommon. If you had read the latest gothic novel, *The Woman in Red*, you will find a similar occurrence in the plot—two women who look alike are exchanged."

My heart jumps. I've read the novel she has been talking about. Two women who look similar enough to be passed off as twins, one rich and one poor, are exchanged so that the poor woman could inherit the rich one's fortune. The narrative is chilling and horrifying, and it fascinated the public (including me), and according to Mr. Wellesley, it has sold thousands of copies.

"Let us not bring fiction into this," the king says contemptuously. "How could Kat manage to remove Katriona Bradshaw? Were there any accomplices? And if she has been masquerading as Katriona Bradshaw, then where was Katriona Bradshaw this whole time?"

Bianca colors. "It seems to have occurred after the wedding, Your Majesty. My sister was unconscious, and when she woke up, she found herself in a small Moryn village."

I feel as if cold water was splashed over me. *Jérôme told me that he saw a girl who looked like me in Moryn. It had to be Katriona Bradshaw.* And to think I dismissed his comment, never imagining that she'd come back and stir up all this trouble.

The real Katriona speaks. "Forgive me, Your Majesty, but I truly don't know what happened to me. When I woke up in the village, I was wearing a wedding dress and I had this." She holds up a glittering ring. Next to me, Edward catches his breath. It is our wedding ring, the ring I lost when I arrived in Athelia.

What have the goblins done? I open my mouth, but no sound comes out. Instead, I sink further into my chair, wishing that this were a nightmare and I'd wake up soon.

"What is that?" the king and queen say at the same time.

Katriona starts to tremble. "Apparently, it seems that I have been kidnapped from my wedding to . . . Edward." My husband's jaw tightens. Apart from his family and close friends, no one calls him by his first name.

"Bring the ring to me," the king commands. "Kat, your ring, please."

I hold my breath as he compares the ring to the one I am wearing. They look exactly the same.

"That day when you returned from your honeymoon," the king says slowly, turning to Edward. "You told me that you had to go to the jewelers because Katriona had lost her ring."

Edward nods slowly. "It doesn't matter, Father. I don't know how this woman acquired the wedding dress and ring, but Kat is the one I wanted to marry. Not her."

"She deceived you!" Bianca screams. "Ask her who she is! Ask her why she took the name of Katriona Bradshaw! She shouldn't even be on that throne."

"Calm down, Lady Pembroke," the queen says coolly. Bianca looks down and apologizes in a low voice, but the wrath remains in her eyes.

My hands feel cold, numb. I should speak, but what can I say? I have no idea how Katriona Bradshaw got transported to Moryn.

"Well," the king addresses me. "What do you have to say?"

Edward grasps my hand so tightly, I think my bones might break. "I . . . I'm sorry," I say. It is no use trying to prove that I am Katriona. "But I swear, I didn't mean to do you any harm."

"I don't care who she is, nor where she came from," Edward says fiercely. "She is the woman I love and the only woman I desire for my wife."

"Edward." The king's voice is stern. "This is not a moment for a passionate outburst. If this lady had knowingly taken the identity of Katriona Bradshaw and sent her away to a foreign country, it is a crime that cannot be overlooked. Even if she is considered royal."

"Exactly!" Bianca exclaims. "This woman, whoever she is, may look innocent, but inside, she harbors a mind more poisonous than a viper. She has stripped everything from my family, condemned my mother to the country, kidnapped my sister, and forced her to live, helpless and alone, in a foreign country. If my sister didn't have a will of steel and persisted until she found a chance to journey back to our country, she might have died in Moryn. I demand you seize this heartless person and make her pay for the crimes she committed."

There is a moment of silence. "What should we do?" the queen says quietly.

The king lands a fist on the arm of his chair. "I need some time to figure out how to deal with this. For now, bring Kat . . . these two women . . . to separate rooms and keep them there. If necessary, I will let the High Court decide what is to be done to them."

Edward stands up, his face agitated. "Father! You cannot order my wife to be locked up."

"This is a very serious matter," the king says gravely. "I promise you, if Kat is not found guilty, I will personally issue a pardon. For now, the most important thing is to discover the truth."

"What is to become of me?" The question slips from my lips before I know what I'm saying.

Edward squeezes my hand so hard that tears spring into my eyes. "Nothing will happen to you, love. I will find a way to fix this. You are my wife, and I intend to keep you with me. Whatever it takes."

The exact words he said to me during our first quarrel. I smile at him, trying not to let him see how worried I am. Bianca is bent on revenge—she won't stop until I am punished. I have to come up with a plausible story. Otherwise, I am doomed.

41

Before I am escorted back to my room, I glimpse Bianca sending me a look as sharp as a knife. If I were a piece of meat, she would have cloven me in half. I try to catch a glimpse of Katriona as well, but her back is turned toward me. Multiple questions race through my head. What is she thinking? She must hate me for stealing her identity and telling everyone that I am her. Is she going to take advantage of my fortune? My hands shake. No. Never. Even if I am denounced a liar, a cheat, or even a witch, I will never give Edward up. Not after all the trouble it took me to get here.

Both Amelie and Mabel are dusting the furniture when I return. One of the palace guards—not Bertram—has been assigned to stand outside my door in case I suddenly escape. I could laugh. Where could I escape to? I have no family, no relatives in

Athelia. I do have Elle and Poppy, but it's unlikely they are able to shield me.

I wonder what Poppy would say. After all, she is the only one, apart from Edward, who knows I am not from Athelia. Still, I don't know what she might think of me if she believes that I had taken Katriona Bradshaw's identity through some nefarious scheme.

Think, I command myself. I have to think of an explanation to convince the king and queen, and maybe even the people of Athelia, that I am a victim as well. But no matter what excuse I come up with, there's no denying the real Katriona Bradshaw's existence, and I had been using her identity. She is also a victim of this mess. If I defend myself and call her a liar, I'll be inflicting further harm on a girl who hasn't done anything wrong. But if Katriona Bradshaw obeys Bianca and convicts me of fraud and abduction, I'm dead meat for sure.

I drop into my window seat and gaze outside. The palace gardens are a snowy paradise, and there are even a few children pelting snowballs at each other. I shiver slightly, despite a roaring fire lit inside, and grab a satin wrap hanging on the back of my chair. Is there a book of Athelian law in here? What kind of punishment will I get for deceiving the royal family? From what I have known about Athelian society from the papers, one could be sentenced to hard labor for just stealing a loaf of bread. Granted, it's less likely for aristocrats to be punished, but they could decide that I'm not noble. I'm just ordinary Katherine Wilson.

"Princess?" Mabel pokes her head through the door. "Lady Elle has come to see you."

"Of course," I say. "Show her in."

"Certainly, Princess. By the way, why is there a guard outside the door? Not that I'm complaining. He's so good-looking!"

Another time I would have laughed and encouraged her to go for the guy, but I can barely crack a smile when that guard is here to watch over me.

Light footsteps tread on the carpet and Elle bursts in. She looks lovely, with her rosy cheeks and golden hair. Any other time, I would have been glad to receive her. But now, with my head still hurting from the story I need to come up with to defend myself, I don't feel like seeing anyone.

"Hello, Elle." I manage a fake smile.

Her eyes are sparkling, and she comes forward and takes my hands. "You won't believe the news, Kat."

"You ran away to Ruby Red with Henry and got married?"

Elle gasps. "Oh, no! Of course, I wouldn't dare to do that. His parents would never forgive me. However." She looks like she is going to explode from happiness. "We are engaged."

This temporarily knocks the thorny issue of Katriona Bradshaw from my mind. "Oh, my goodness," I exclaim. "How did you manage to persuade her? She has been against your marrying

Henry for ages. What could possibly make her change her mind?"

Elle smiles and casts herself on the low sofa. "It's a shock for me too. Sometimes I still feel that this is all a dream, and one day I'll wake up and discover that Henry is engaged to another girl."

"So how did it happen?"

"Do you remember that Dr. Durant had invited Henry to Moryn? I know he really wants to go, but when I went to see him, I found that he was gone. Thomas told me that the duchess made Henry return to Somerset Hall with her. I was able to spare some time from the orphanage and school, so I decided I had to do something. With the train, it is so much easier to get to the country." Elle folds her hands together. "I bought a ticket and went down to Somerset alone."

"Oh, my God." The things that she is willing to risk for love. "Have you ever taken the train before?"

"Never. You should have seen me at the platform; I didn't know which direction to go." Elle smiles softly. "I wasn't thinking of persuading the duchess to approve our marriage. You see, I wanted to see for myself if Henry was willing to give up the chance of going to Moryn and instead inherit Somerset. I dressed as a commoner and tried talking to the gardener, the housekeeper, and the servants. I learned that Henry was indeed unhappy coming back and being forced to inherit the estate. I know him, Kat. I know that all he has ever wanted was to be a doctor. I didn't want to let the duchess force him to give up what he loved."

"So . . . what did you do?" I still don't get how Elle managed to change the duchess's mind.

Elle takes a deep breath. "I changed into the clothes of a lady. I hired a carriage and drove up to the estate and handed in my card. The duchess had no choice but to receive me. I told her that I am willing to give up Henry, but on one condition—only if he is allowed to go to Moryn and later pursue his career in medicine."

I cannot freaking believe it. "That's incredible. Did you really mean it? Did Henry hear you say that?"

"It doesn't matter what I think," Elle says. "I was determined. If I cannot marry Henry, I won't settle for anyone else. I love him, but because I love him, I want to see him happy and doing what he loves. If that means I need to sacrifice myself, I am prepared to do it."

I feel like saying that Henry wouldn't be happy either if he cannot marry her, but considering that the outcome is a success, I keep my thoughts to myself. "And the duchess relented?"

"She was furious. She told me I had no right to decide what her son does. I told her that all I wanted was for Henry to be happy. And then our conversation reached the grand duke, who was still convalescing. He told the duchess to show me in, and he asked me if I truly meant what I promised." Elle takes a sip of water and continues. "I told him how I valued Henry's happiness above my own. I also told him that even if I could marry Henry, if I were to become the mistress of this house, I would rather not marry him at all. Because of who both of us are, we would never be able to become conventional rulers of this district."

She paces for a few seconds and turns to me. "Henry happened to return at that moment, and his father told him about our conversation. Henry stated that he would have no one but me. They had a huge row, but the grand duke took our side, and eventually the duchess relented. A distant cousin is going to inherit the estate. Henry asked for my hand, and we are unofficially engaged. Once he finishes his year with Dr. Durant, he's going to come back to Athelia and we will be married."

Unbelievable. After all this time, they are finally together. Oh, how I wish I could have been at the estate to witness Elle confronting the duchess. And I'm glad that the grand duke is more open-minded compared to the duchess. Then I remember Sir Montgomery. Maybe the grand duke has something in common with Sir Montgomery, who eventually gave in to his daughter's choice.

"Congratulations!" On an impulse, I get up and hug her. "I'm so glad for you both."

Elle laughs. "When I was a servant, I only dared to hope that my mother and my brothers could be safe and healthy. I only prayed that I could support them. I never dreamed that I could marry the man of my dreams. I must have been born when lady luck smiled upon me."

Speaking of luck, I am brought back to reality. I will certainly need some luck when it comes to dealing with the real Katriona.

"By the way," Elle says. "There's a man stationed outside your door. Did you meet any trouble or threats that you require a bodyguard?"

I think of the Bradshaws. "Something has happened," I finally say. "But it's really complicated. I don't know how I can explain it."

"Princess!" Mabel pops her head through the door. "Sorry to interrupt, but His Highness insisted on coming in."

Edward strides into the room. When he sees me, relief breaks over his face. Despite Elle's presence, he strides up to me and embraces me fiercely.

"I'll come back some other time," Elle says, smiling. "Please relay the happy news for me."

Edward gives her a nod, but it's clear from his expression that he wants to be alone with me. When I look at him closely, I notice that he looks exhausted, like someone made him sit through a five-hour-long meeting.

"I'm sorry," I say without thinking. "Trust me, I have no idea how it happened. I never knew that Katriona Bradshaw existed. I thought I came back into her body, but it turned out that she was still living somewhere."

He grabs my arm, pulling me into his lap. "I had a lengthy conversation with my parents. They asked if I knew I was married to a commoner. I told them that I didn't care whether you were a lady or a servant. All I want is you."

"Did the Bradshaws leave?"

"Katriona Bradshaw is assigned to a room downstairs and a guard stationed at her door. Father also suggested that you be relocated, but I told him that anyone who tries to remove you from our suite has to get past me first." He presses his forehead on mine, and I cling to him, as if the next second the guards will burst in and take me away. "I promise you I am not going to let you go. Even if it means that I have to abdicate, I will not give you up. Never."

He captures my lips in a deep, lingering kiss. It lasts so long that I have to push him away because I can't breathe. I cough, reaching for a glass of water, my head dizzy. "Sorry," Edward says a bit sheepishly. "When it comes to you, it sometimes seems that all the discipline I have is sorely tested."

I don't answer. My mind is blank, and there's a strange feeling that something isn't quite right with me.

We don't hear from the Bradshaws for a few days. Amazingly, there hasn't been much news about Katriona looking like me. And that's when disaster strikes.

Three days later, I receive an urgent letter when I'm having breakfast in the suite. It is from the High Court, summoning me. Bianca has accused me of fraud.

I am to appear at court.

42

Bianca has charged me by filing a writ of identity theft. It feels like the world is crumbling around me—my identity as princess is going to be ruthlessly torn away from me, and I have no right to stay in the palace any more. My hands are cold and clammy, and I feel like throwing up when I imagine going to court.

Edward had gone white when he read the letter. "If I had the power," he says quietly, though his tone carries a determination of iron, "I would banish Bianca Bradshaw to the mountains up north, never to return."

"Well," I say, trying to cheer him up. Even though I am scared stiff myself, for Edward's sake I've got to act calm and unaffected. Like Amelie. "Since I have to appear in court, I might as well figure out the best way to deal with it. Am I allowed to have a lawyer represent me?"

Edward rubs his chin, his eyes thoughtful. "Let me check. Frankly speaking, I am not well acquainted with such legal matters. The last time a royal member of the family had to appear in court was hundreds of years ago."

"So it's done already? Too bad." I try to look disappointed. "I thought I was setting a precedent."

He doesn't smile, though. "You *are* a precedent, love. In so many ways."

It turns out that yes, I am allowed to have a lawyer, and even though it's literally unheard of for a princess to be accused of a crime, the law still exists anyway. I am to appear in High Court, a privilege of the peers and royals. In Athelia, the commoners and the aristocracy are tried in different courts, which means that the latter is rarely convicted, but in my case, I'm not so sure.

"Do you suppose Mr. Davenport could take my case? There are other lawyers who are more well-known than he is, but I can't tell them the truth."

"We must ask him," Edward says. "But I believe that as a friend and loyal subject, he will not refuse."

***

We have no problem asking Mr. Davenport to defend me. To my surprise, Poppy accompanies Mr. Davenport when we schedule a meeting at my study. She rushes to me and takes my hands, concern written all over her round face. Gratitude fills my heart—she looks exhausted, most likely from taking care of the twins, but she still came to see me. "Kat! How dreadful it is to have this happen to you!"

"How are you able to get away from Sebastian and Little Katriona?"

"They're fine. My parents and in-laws have arrived, and I'm positive the four of them will take excellent care of the twins." Poppy spreads out a newspaper on the table. "Oh my God, Kat. You'll probably need special transportation to get to court, because there certainly is going to be a crowd."

I had already read the paper in the morning, but the headlines still make me cringe. '*Who is Princess Katriona?*' '*Lady Pembroke Accuses the Princess of Identity Theft.*' '*Stranger Than Fiction: a Royal Scandal of* The Woman in Red.'

Edward shows Mr. Davenport to my desk, while Poppy huddles with me on the window seat. The door to our suite is locked, and Edward orders that no one, not even Amelie or Mabel, may enter.

Mr. Davenport pulls out a yellow pad and a fountain pen, along with a few thick leather-bound books on marriage law and royals. "Let's not waste any time. Katriona, pardon me for asking you this, but you *are* Katriona Bradshaw?"

I meet Poppy's eyes, glance at Edward, and take a deep breath. "I'm sorry."

Mr. Davenport's eyebrows shoot toward his forehead. "Are you telling me that you are guilty of the charge?"

Poppy hangs her head. "I'm sorry as well, Jonathan. I promised you that there will be no secrets between us, but you see, I couldn't tell you about something like this."

Edward folds his arms. "Just tell us the best approach to take."

Mr. Davenport clears his throat. "In that case, we need to consider if there are any mitigating circumstances. For example, if Katriona—"

"Katherine," I say. "My real name is Katherine Wilson."

Mr. Davenport blinks. "Katherine, then. How did this happen to you? Why did you choose to masquerade as Katriona Bradshaw?" He glances at Edward. "Your Highness, did you know about this recently?"

"I have known it for more than a year."

Mr. Davenport looks astonished. "Your Highness, this is…unheard of."

Edward looks at me, and his gaze is mixed with love and pain. "There were certain special circumstances, which are too complicated to explain. I beg you, Jonathan, to find a way that will pardon Kat and make her suffer as little as possible. If it helps, shift the blame onto me. As an accomplice, I cannot escape censure either."

"No," I say immediately. "Don't let the people lose their trust in you, Edward. You're not going to be punished for my sake."

"It's mostly my fault. I knew you weren't Katriona Bradshaw, but I insisted on marrying you. I should have foreseen the possibility that you would be discovered."

"How could you have predicted this? Edward, you are *not* going to tell the court that you knew my identity all along."

Mr. Davenport looks toward Poppy, apparently unsure what to do.

"What happens after Kat gets her identity back?" Poppy asks. "The entire nation still thinks that the princess is called Katriona Bradshaw. All the neighboring countries also have you as Katriona Bradshaw in their records. It's going to take a lot of effort to change and replace that with your real name."

"It would take even more than that," Mr. Davenport says grimly. "I'm assuming that Katherine signed the name of Katriona Bradshaw on the wedding register. It is criminal to use someone's name, especially in such an important event. Moreover, this would mean that His Highness is lawfully wedded to the other girl, the real Katriona Bradshaw."

Poppy gasps. "But that's ridiculous! If we all wrote our names wrong, that would be a complete chaos."

"I also agree it is a faulty law. In Moryn, such a mistake would only render the marriage null and void," Mr. Davenport says, regret in his tone. "Originally, it was meant to ensure that the married couple would not regard the ceremony as a farce. But since more than one witness is required during the signing, it is almost impossible that the bride or groom will write the wrong name."

Edward's palm lands on the table with a resounding thud. "I will not accept that woman as my wife. No one except Kat."

"Unfortunately, if Katherine has to admit that she isn't Katriona Bradshaw, apart from the punishment that she will receive, she will lose her status as princess. Katherine, are you a commoner?"

I nod, feeling like sinking into the ground. "Is that a problem?"

"Unfortunately, the law of Athelia prohibits it. Unless the prince is willing to consent to a morganatic marriage?"

"What's a morganatic marriage?"

"A situation that is normally considered undesirable, but not unheard of. Your children will not be able to ascend the throne. You will only be known as the spouse, and you will not assume the title of princess."

Is that all? But even if I don't mind, what will Edward think?

"If that is the only way available, then so be it," Edward says, as if he read my anxious look. "I suppose I do not need to remind you that I would do anything not to lose Kat."

Poppy, who is clutching her handkerchief, sends me a brief glance. I think she means that it's touching to see Edward so determined to stay with me.

"In that case," Mr. Davenport says slowly, "you will have to file a divorce case. After you divorce Katriona Bradshaw, it is only then that you are free to marry Katherine."

"I'll do it."

"You do not understand how difficult it is. While divorce cases are becoming more and more common these days, they often take six months to two years. And pardon me for saying this, but it's unlikely that Katriona Bradshaw will be willing to grant you a divorce."

Edward looks thunderstruck. Obviously, he never contemplated divorce and is unfamiliar with the rules concerning it. I jump up and reach for his hand, trying to calm him down. His grip is hot, almost painful, conveying that he is deeply shaken.

"She'll have to," he says flatly.

"It might not come down to that," I say, alarmed at how agitated he is.

"The grounds of divorce require that the wife must have done something to wrong you," Mr. Davenport continues. "Unless Katriona Bradshaw has committed adultery or a similar crime, it is unlikely you will be granted a divorce. Even if you are the prince. Now, are you certain that you wish to proceed with the idea of acknowledging that she isn't Katriona Bradshaw?"

43

My hands are trembling when I am conducted to High Court. Much to my relief, there is an underground tunnel that runs from the palace to the court, which Edward explains has been in existence since three hundred years ago, when the king himself was tried for treason. Athelia had gone to war with Moryn, and the king was considering surrendering to the colonial empire in secret. They couldn't get him to High Court because of the angry mob of people pelting him with rotten tomatoes and eggs. And so the tunnel was built, though it is unlikely for a member of the royal family to be accused again.

"You will be all right," Edward says, placing his hands on my shoulders. "I won't let anyone take you away from me. Whatever sentence is meted out—if there is one—I'll have Father issue a pardon to you."

He kisses me right on the lips, completely ignoring that Mr. Davenport is only several paces away. It's my fault. The queen once told the king that since he married me, Edward had become less inhibited, but she thought it was a good thing. He needed to relax more.

"I know." I smile at him and kiss him back. "Let's hope that this case will be over soon."

Edward directs his attention toward Mr. Davenport and holds out his hand. "Jonathan, I trust that you will do your best to defend her. I am asking you, not as a prince, not as a command, but simply as a husband who doesn't want to be separated from his wife."

Mr. Davenport gives him a firm handshake. "Understood. As a husband, I would do anything to keep my wife at my side."

I don't know how many people have come to watch the trial, but I can feel their presence even before I enter the courtroom. The air seems thinner. It seems that there is less oxygen left in the courtroom, making it difficult to breathe freely.

I wonder what the people are thinking. Are they disappointed, angry? Do they believe Bianca's accusation? I wonder what's going on in Katriona Bradshaw's mind. If she is anything like Bianca, she is unlikely to give up this chance to be princess. I clench my hands and take a deep breath. No matter what it takes, I am not going to surrender. I will not let anything, anyone, come between Edward and me again.

When I enter the courtroom, a hush falls over the audience. No matter what the outcome is, I bet that they will boast to their future grandchildren that they had once seen the princess summoned to court, an event that possibly won't occur for another three hundred years.

Bianca, Lady Bradshaw, and Katriona are already sitting on the bench, accompanied by their lawyer—Mr. Jones, I think, from what Mr. Davenport had found out. The three of them instantly look at me when I am guided to my bench, my head held high, and their gazes give me shivers, just like the icy wind on my face before I went down to the tunnel. I tuck my hands in my ermine muff and will myself to stay calm. I must put my trust in Mr. Davenport and pray that it won't come to Edward having to file for divorce.

The magistrate asks us to step forward. We go over the usual procedure, swearing that anything we say in court is the absolute truth. My heart beats quicker when it's time to begin the interrogation. I look back, just once, and see Edward, who is sitting with Elle and Henry. I wonder what Elle is thinking. Would she believe that I am Katriona Bradshaw? More than once, she had thought that I had lost my memory.

The magistrate summons Bianca and Mr. Jones.

"Lady Pembroke," Mr. Davenport says. "It is my understanding that you have accused my client of the crime of identity theft, passing herself as your sister."

Bianca raises her chin and inclines her head ever so slightly, as though *she* were princess. "That is correct."

"And when would you say that this identity theft occurred?"

"I had my suspicions," Bianca says, sending me a look filled with venom. "When I accompanied my husband's niece to her court presentation last year, this woman failed to recognize me. She asked me who I am."

Mr. Davenport raises his eyebrows. "And about this lady whom you call your sister now, when did she show up? When did you become certain that the identity theft had taken place?"

"When my sister showed up at my house, several days ago, shivering in a threadbare gown, asking to see me. She had traveled all the way from Moryn, where she was stranded."

"Stranded?" Mr. Davenport says, an incredulous lilt in his tone. "This lady you call Katriona Bradshaw, who is your sister, was stranded in Moryn?"

"Precisely. She arrived there last June, wearing a wedding dress and a wedding ring."

What happened at the wedding ceremony comes to my mind. When I first arrived in Athelia, I was in my Victoria's Secret babydoll slip. Edward had to buy a new wedding ring for me. Somehow, possibly through the goblin's magic, Katriona Bradshaw must have been transported to Moryn in my wedding dress and still wearing my ring. That accounts for why I lost my ring and had to have it replaced.

The magistrate compares my ring with Katriona's. Needless to say, they match perfectly.

"The rings are identical," he announces.

Gasps come from the onlookers.

"*Two* wedding rings?"

"How come there are identical rings?"

"How did she procure it?"

"If that is the case," Mr. Davenport says, "is it safe to say that the identity theft occurred last June? That somehow Katriona Bradshaw was kidnapped and sent to Moryn, and this lady became princess?"

"It must be!" Bianca's voice rises to a shrill tone. "She fainted during the wedding! It must be at that time that this woman came in and stole my sister away!"

Instantly, the crowd starts talking and making a commotion.

"Witch!" someone yells. He might as well have hit me over the head.

"Who is she?"

"Why did she kidnap Katriona Bradshaw?"

I bite my lip until I taste blood. Bianca must be enjoying this. She has found a way to knock me off my pedestal as princess when I believed that it couldn't be achieved.

The magistrate has to bang his gavel on the table a few times, ordering the crowd to control themselves, or he will close the court to outsiders. That shuts them up pretty quickly.

Mr. Davenport, however, remains calm as he fixes his gaze on Bianca. "Are you implying that my client had the ability to smuggle Katriona Bradshaw out of St. James Cathedral, with all the security guards outside, and enter the church without anyone's notice?"

A thrill runs through me. When he phrases it that way, it does make Bianca seem ridiculous.

"I object," Mr. Jones says. "The manner in which the identity theft took place is irrelevant for now. What's important is that the lady my client accuses is not Katriona Bradshaw. My client had personally questioned the princess and confirmed that she couldn't even remember her mother's middle name, nor certain events that occurred to her as a child."

"Objection, Your Honor." Mr. Davenport stands up. "We only have Lady Pembroke's word that my client isn't Katriona Bradshaw. But why did they never raise objection until now? Could it possibly be that Lady Pembroke holds a grudge toward her own sister?"

Bianca looks as if she is ready to jump out of her box and claw Mr. Davenport's face. "Why you . . ."

The magistrate has to call for Bianca to restrain herself.

"Your Honor," Mr. Davenport says. "I would like to bring in a witness who could assist with the motive behind Lady Pembroke's desire to accuse my client of identity theft."

Bianca instantly looks around, her face contorted in a nasty snarl. For that moment, she looks repulsive—nothing like the stunning beauty that everyone expected would be queen.

A tall, lanky young man walks slowly down the aisle. It's Liam.

My jaw drops. Why did Mr. Davenport summon him? Did he suddenly think about it, or did Liam go to him voluntarily? I'll have to ask him later.

"Mr. Liam Charingford," Mr. Davenport says. "Tell us what you overheard on November 11th, when you were still a teacher at Princess College."

"Certainly," Liam says, staring straight ahead. "I was on my way to the headmistress's office, when I heard Lady Pembroke speaking in angry tones toward Princess Katriona. She wanted to buy the school, and Princess Katriona refused. When Princess Katriona walked off, Lady Pembroke muttered that she would regret refusing her."

A murmur runs through the crowd. It is not enough to rouse them into a noisy crowd though. Bianca stares at Liam, her eyes as hard as stones. I'm stupefied—Liam, who always treated me with contempt and even hostility, is defending me.

Bianca looks like she could kill Liam.

"We only have Mr. Charingford's word for it," Mr. Jones speaks up.

Liam's lip curls slightly. "As a matter of fact, I was not the only one who heard the conversation between Lady Pembroke and Princess Katriona. Several schoolgirls were also nearby. If necessary, they can also be summoned."

"Is it true, Lady Pembroke?" Mr. Davenport asks. "Is it true that you have been harboring jealousy toward your sister ever since she married the prince?"

"Objection, Your Honor!" Mr. Jones says. "This is hardly relevant to the issue at hand."

"On the contrary," Mr. Davenport says. "It seems that Lady Pembroke, when she decided to take revenge on her own sister, found a woman who looked very similar to Katriona Bradshaw, and then accused the princess of identity theft."

This time, Bianca loses composure completely. "How dare you!" she screams. "How dare you excuse me of doing such a despicable thing!"

The crowd starts to hiss and boo at her. Looks like Mr. Davenport has the upper hand. And I didn't even have to claim that I am Katriona Bradshaw. Well done, Mr. Davenport. Even though it is a lie . . .

I glance toward the real Katriona Bradshaw. She meets my eyes, and I'm struck by the hardness in her gaze. While she looks nothing like Bianca, she also has the ability to glare with the intensity of a knife.

Yet, while I feel nothing but anger at Bianca, I can understand why Katriona hates me so. She didn't ask to be transported to Moryn. Imagine how she must have tried to survive, and how she had to explain to the Moryn people when she arrived in the wedding dress. It took her several months before she succeeded in returning to Athelia.

Mr. Jones is calling me. I stand up, and it seems that the whole crowd is waiting with bated breath as I walk up to the box. And . . . I don't know what happens, maybe it's because I have been sitting for such a long time, or maybe that there are too many people in the courtroom, but suddenly my vision goes black, the familiar dizzy feeling returns to my head, and I collapse.

44

I wake up in pain. My shoulder—the part where Krev left his mark—is burning. I sit up, toss the blanket off, and totter to the bathroom. The size of the room and the relatively spartan layout tell me that I was lying on Edward's bed before I woke up.

Grimacing, I try to remember what happened before I lost consciousness. I was in the courtroom, Bianca was furious, and I had a pretty good chance at convincing everyone else that she was out to get me. But somehow, I got dizzy again. Coldness surrounds me when I get out of bed, and I realize that I am wearing only my petticoats and a shift. I must have been carried from the court back to the palace and undressed.

I groan. Something is wrong with me. My shoulder feels like it's on fire. I rush to the bathroom and turn on the taps, grab a towel, and dab at my shoulder. In the mirror, I can see that the bright red mark has faded, and it looks more like pink instead of red.

The cold dampness of the towel does nothing to ease my pain. I should see the doctor, but I'm afraid of what Dr. Jensen might say. It looks abnormal, sinister, like only a witch could bear such a thing. And considering my precarious situation, I can't afford any more suspicion.

The familiar popping noise occurs. The next second, Krev hovers above my head in the mirror's reflection, arms crossed and wings flapping.

"Finally." I would have wrung his neck if my shoulder wasn't in pain. "I've been waiting for you all this time. What did you do to my shoulder? It hurts like hell."

Krev makes something like a blue fire appear on his palm, and he presses on my shoulder. Instantly, a cool, soothing power like water seeps through my skin.

"Ah, that's much better." I pull my shift back over my shoulder. "Krev, I know what you said last time, but I'm not going back to my own world. I'm staying here."

"Not going back!" The goblin splutters. "Girlie, you have no choice. You must leave. Weren't you desperate to be home?"

"This is my home." I turn around so I'm facing him, rather than looking at his reflection. "I'm sorry that I didn't listen to you, but considering the circumstances, it can't be helped. I love Edward, so much that it hurts if I'm not with him. I'll go back, but only temporarily. Edward wants to meet my family. I'll say farewell, and then we'll come back. Please tell me you have enough magic to do that."

Krev shakes his head slowly.

"Are you saying there isn't enough magic to transport both of us? Then is there enough magic to just get me back?" Then, seeing that his expression doesn't change, I say, "Are you telling me that you can't even get me back?"

Krev lets out a noisy sigh. "You're getting this all wrong, girlie. It is not a question of taking you back to your own world. The problem is that you cannot stay in Athelia. Didn't I tell you last time?"

"You disappeared before I could ask you for an explanation. Why? Why not? Is it because of Katriona Bradshaw? I promise you that I'm not going to regret it. I'm absolutely sure that I want to be with Edward."

"Even if it costs you your life?"

I stare at him, dumbfounded. I have never seen Krev look so serious before. It almost seems that he has become a completely different person—goblin, I mean. "What are you talking about?" Then an alarming thought strikes me. "Does it have something to do with the mark you gave me? What does it have to do with my life?"

Krev pauses. "I suppose I can't blame you for being ignorant, as there wasn't enough time to explain it to you. Now listen carefully. The thing is, girlie, your human body *cannot survive in Athelia.* The air that exists here is of a different composition. It's very different from the stuff you call oxygen in your world. You are only able to stay alive because of a spell."

I think my jaw must have dropped on the floor. It takes a moment before I'm able to speak. "But when I was in Athelia the first time, you never told me anything about the oxygen not being the same. You didn't seem to care if I was trapped in the book forever."

"Because the first time you ripped up the book and were transported into Athelia, it was your soul taking possession of Katriona Bradshaw's body. But the second time around, since he couldn't force you to rip the book again, Borg used an illegal spell to snatch you while you were in your own body. He banished Katriona Bradshaw to Moryn by force."

"Who's Borg?"

"The king's no-good brother who always wanted the throne. He made a deal with Barthelius's daughter, who's sympathetic to you and Edward, and promised he'd send you back to Athelia if she would steal Barthelius's ring for him. The ring contained enough magic that would allow him to challenge the king. But there was a loophole in the deal—he never promised how long you could stay in Athelia. So, he put a spell on you that would allow your body to have a limited supply of oxygen. Once it is used up, you will die."

My hand goes to the mark on my shoulder. "Is this the spell? Are you telling me that the last time you came, you were giving me a supply of oxygen so I could survive longer in Athelia?"

"Correct. Doing this spell requires us to travel to your world to gather the oxygen, compress it, and use an enchanted container to preserve it for you. But the elements used to produce the container have been destroyed by the war, so we can no longer perform the spell for you. Besides, it's also extremely risky. You've been lucky so far, but if there was a tiny flaw in the spell, you could lose all the oxygen and die. Anyway, considering the amount I gave you last time…" He ticks off his fingers. "I would say you have only a few days to live."

"No way." My feet slip on the floor, and I grab onto the sink to prevent myself from falling. "This can't be true. Tell me it's a big joke and I'll even forgive you."

Krev sighs heavily and sits cross-legged on one of the taps. "Since you came to Athelia, have you not experienced bouts of dizziness? Especially when you engage in strenuous exercise or when there is a crowd in an enclosed space?"

Realization sinks in. True, I was easily out of breath when I practiced dancing, even though I was perfectly healthy and fit. I fainted at the ball held for the Moryn emperor, and also at the courtroom. "Why would I experience dizziness under those circumstances?"

"Because when you are exercising or when there are too many people in the same room, your body requires more oxygen than usual, and the spell couldn't keep up a steady supply. Hence, you felt dizzy or even fainted because the spell failed to deliver enough oxygen in time. When your body no longer required that much, you would return to consciousness."

I wish I were in a dream. A nightmare. I wish I could pretend that Krev didn't show up, didn't tell me this. Because as much as I don't want to believe it, there is no reason for Krev to lie to me. And his explanation has offered a good reason why I could easily faint or run out of breath, despite being perfectly healthy.

"Did you say I only have a few days to live?"

"If I don't take you back in three days, you will use up all the oxygen in the spell. Without the oxygen, you won't survive."

"So my only options are either I die in Athelia or you send me back to Portland?"

Krev sighs again. "Frankly speaking, after all this time, I don't want to see you dead. I would rather send you back to your own world. I'm sorry about Eddie, but you know he was prepared to let you go the first time."

"But he didn't deserve this!" I can no longer control my emotions. My voice rises into a shriek, and I don't bother to wipe away the tears running down my face. "He already had to suffer the first time, and now that we're finally together, he has to deal with this as well?" I can't believe that I have to leave Edward again—all because my body can't adapt to Athelia. No matter what choice I make, we will only have a few days together. It's too cruel.

Krev flies a bit closer and lays a tiny hand on my cheek. There's nothing but sympathy on his squashed face. "Make a choice, girlie. I will be back at midnight in three days."

Then he vanishes in a puff of smoke.

***

I am not sure how long I've been in the bathroom, slumped against the wall, sitting with my arms draped limply on my sides. Add a bottle of pills, and you could take me for a person contemplating suicide. I've never felt this depressed. My life wasn't completely smooth-sailing, especially when Dad deserted us, but whatever difficulties I experienced were nothing compared to this.

I have to leave Edward. Again.

I didn't even hear Edward coming in until his voice, filled with concern, reaches me. "Kat! Why are you sitting on the floor?"

I look at him, but I can't move. There are so many things I want to say, but all the words seem stuck in my throat. I don't know how I'm going to tell him. But somehow, even though I can't lift a limb, tears flow down my cheeks again.

"You've been crying." Gently, he wipes away my tears with his thumb. "Kat, are you devastated by what happened today at court? Bianca won't succeed. She might be planning to bring more witnesses and try to prove that you are not her sister, but Mr.

Davenport will find a way to block her efforts. Don't you worry, love. It's not the end of the world."

"What if I say it is?" I don't sound like myself. My voice is cracking.

"What are you talking about?" Edward hooks his arms under my body and sweeps me up from the floor. "I brought some food with me. I thought you would need it after fainting away at court. It must have been an awful trial for you. Also, we really must cure your tendency to faint. Come and work in the garden with me. Your constitution needs to be strengthened."

He sets me on the edge of his bed. The aroma of hot, savory chicken soup reaches my nostrils. Edward presses a spoon into my hand. "Get some nourishment inside your body," he urges. "Then lie down, and you'll feel better. Don't think about the trial. We can discuss it tomorrow morning."

I don't feel like eating anything, but if I am to break the news to him, I might as well get more strength. I do my best to choke down some of the soup, wondering how I am going to explain my eventual doom.

"That's enough. I'm better now." I put the spoon back on the tray. I really don't want to disclose the inevitable, but what's the use of putting it off? As princess, I can't stay silent and disappear three days later. I must tell Edward the truth, and discuss whatever necessary arrangements that have to be made. "Edward, I need to talk to you."

Puzzled, he takes my hands and kisses my forehead. "What are you worried about? Honestly, even if Bianca convinces and proves to everyone that you are not her sister, I am willing to face it. I will file for divorce, no matter what it does to my reputation, and I will marry you again. Everything will be properly done, so no one can question the legality of our marriage. I'll abdicate if necessary. I'll . . ."

I put a finger on his lips. "Edward," I say in a small voice. "Krev finally showed up."

He goes still. His hands fall on my waist, holding me in place, as though I might suddenly levitate and disappear. "He came to take you back and you refused him?"

"Yes, but it's much worse than that." In a broken voice, my shoulders shaking, I tell him what Krev had told me. I struggle to stay calm, but in the end I can't help it any longer. I start crying again, and I fling my arms around him, sobbing into his chest.

Edward seems to have turned into a marble statue. When I finish, he pushes back slightly and looks into my face. "Nonsense," he says flatly.

"I want to believe it's nonsense too. But what has Krev to gain from lying to me?" I tug down the sleeve of my petticoat, baring my shoulder. The mark is pink, and unless my eyes are deceiving me, it's a shade lighter now. "This is the reason I was able to stay alive. This is the reason I keep getting dizzy whenever there is a crowd or when I'm out of breath. It's because I'm not from your world and I cannot survive."

His fingers press into my skin as he grips my waist so hard that I'm sure he leaves marks on my skin. Not that it matters now. "There must be a way out of this," he says fiercely. "You simply cannot leave me again."

"The only way for me to stay is for me to become an Athelian," I say. "And that's not going to happen unless the goblin can make me enter another person's body. But I can't, Edward. You know it's impossible. Even if the goblins can do it, I can't take another person's body."

"Summon the goblin," he suddenly says. "We'll talk to him—discuss with him—anything. We've got to figure out an alternative to save you."

"In three days? Then perhaps we can start digging my grave, because if I don't leave with Krev, then I will die in Athelia."

"No." He crushes me to him. "I thought that when the other girl showed up, I had prepared myself for anything, but this…this is beyond what I could imagine."

"The trial doesn't mean anything anymore," I whisper. "It's pointless, even if I prove that I am Katriona Bradshaw, because I'm going to die."

His embrace is so tight that my vision goes black again. A moment later, water splashes onto my face and I open my eyes. If we need any proof of my eventual demise, then perhaps this is it. If I can faint just because he was holding me too tightly, then what Krev says is likely true.

Edward brushes the hair from my face, using a handkerchief to dab away the wetness from my face. I'm pained to see the redness in his eyes—he must have been crying as well. "I'm sorry, Kat."

It's the goblins who should apologize. After everything that we have been through, we still can't be together. But what's the use of blaming them? If it weren't for Barthelius's spell, I would have never met Edward twice. Would I prefer it that way—living a normal life and settling down with Jason, and never knowing Athelia existed?

No. Never.

Three days. I've got to make the remaining three days the longest ever. Fortunately, we have had the experience of preparing for a permanent farewell.

45

It takes a tremendous amount of effort not to break down and weep as I stack the letters in neat piles on my writing desk. Usually I face my daily letter-writing with the mindset of a cubicle worker—it's a job that has to be done, whether I like it or not. However, today it's with a heavy heart that I survey my desk. I don't plan on composing any letter today—save for the one I'm going to write for Edward. It's one of the last things I can do — pour all the love I have toward my husband on paper.

When I look back at our rocky relationship, it's incredible that he never gave up on me, no matter how determined I was to leave Athelia or that he had plenty of chances to marry another girl. He could have suffered far less if he chose someone else, but he didn't. The best I can do, on the verge of leaving, is to let him know how much I treasure his affection, and that this time I won't have my memories be erased. I want to remember him forever. It will be painful, of course, but I'd rather have the pain than ignorance.

Snow is falling outside—the flakes come down with the speed of heavy rain, coating the ground in a thick white layer. This is one of the few instances that I'm thankful for bad weather. Edward had gone to High Court the first thing after breakfast, to request that my court trial be re-scheduled due to a terrible cold. I sure don't want myself returning to the trial and fainting again.

I smooth a piece of blank paper on the desk and take up my pen. But the words won't come. It feels like once I've written this farewell letter, my departure will be irrevocable.

While dallying, I notice the morning papers lying on the upper left-hand corner of the desk. Since I decided to move in Edward's office, I asked Amelie to deliver an extra copy of the papers for me in the mornings. If I were to assist him, I'd better be informed of current events. There are three different papers from three agencies, each with its own political preference.

Unjust Slanders On The Princess's Identity—from a paper that favors the royal family.

Princess Katriona and Lady Pembroke Appear in Court is the title of a paper aimed at those apathetic to royals and aristocracy. There's a lengthy article that describes the entirety of my trial, including the details of what occurred after I fainted. Edward had leaped from his bench and carried me out of the room, while Bertram warded off a swarm of reporters who wanted to know the prince's opinion on this messy affair.

Princess Katriona: A Royal Fraud? reads the one that enjoys long popularity for satirizing and lampooning the royals, or simply anyone who's a celebrity. There's even a cartoon showing Bianca in an unflattering caricature, towering over me like a monster. Maybe the person who did the illustrations was at court that day. He (in Athelia it's most likely to be male) captured Bianca's twisted fury in perfect strokes of genius. I wonder if Bianca would dare to claim defamation of her movie-star looks—it's one of the very rare instances that she appears unattractive.

What will the papers say when I leave the palace? I suppose the question mark in the last headline would be replaced by a period. I was never Katriona Bradshaw in the beginning. Perhaps this is my punishment for meddling with Story World.

If only Krev's appearance yesterday was a hallucination. Maybe I was so stressed out from the appearance of Katriona Bradshaw that my imagination has taken a wild, dramatic turn.

"It's a lie," I say aloud. "It must be a nightmare."

As though my words were meant to be refuted, a violent spasm seizes my chest and I start coughing so hard that I have to grab the edge of the desk. Letters tumble onto the ground, but I can barely stand up, not to mention pick them up.

"Princess!" Mabel hurries into the study, her round face filled with alarm. "Oh dear, when did you catch such a bad cold? I'll get the doctor for you right away."

I grab her arm and shake my head, while trying to contain my coughing. A moment later, which seems like a century, the itchiness in my throat gradually subsides and I am able to drink some water.

"It must be that horrible trial," Mabel says with a vehemence that isn't like her normal cheery self. "You've been worrying too much about that nasty woman who's pretending to be you, and the weather turned bad when you were most vulnerable."

"That's… most likely."

"Put this on." Mabel brings me a heavy cloak lined with ermine. "You've got to stay warm and get well soon. How dare Lady Pembroke accuse you of fraud! I was *completely* flabbergasted when I heard the story. Honestly, how did she find someone who looks so similar to you? Do you think it's possible that you could be twins?" She presses a hand on her chest. "Maybe that other girl was a sickly baby, but later survived when everyone presumed she was dead?"

I pull the cloak around my shoulders and am rewarded with instant warmth. "Thanks, Mabel. And no, I don't think she is a long-lost twin sister."

"Oh well." Mabel shrugs. "Guess what—I found out the name of the guard outside! His name is Percival. Doesn't it sound romantic?" She ducks her head, suddenly shy. "Do you, uh, do you think you can teach me a few tricks?"

418

"Teach you?"

"Well, you know, you attracted His Highness, and he's so hard to please. So I wondered if you had, uh, some tips. Men never take me seriously." She sounds so doleful that I have to smile, even when my own situation is down in the dumps.

"Be yourself." I don't dare to speak too loud, in case of another fit of coughing. "No tricks, honestly. It happens that Edward likes me the way I am. He likes that I'm different from most of the women of his acquaintance."

She tilts her head, then her eyes widen. "Your... Your Highness!"

Edward has entered the study. He looks older than his age, and there's a depressing aura surrounding him like a dark cloud.

"The magistrate has agreed to a re-schedule of the trial." He looks straight at me, as though Mabel isn't in the room.

"Great," I say, managing a fake smile.

"And... I hate to disturb you, but my parents have requested an attendance."

Finally. Ever since the trial, I'm surprised that my in-laws did not summon me for a private conversation. Or maybe Edward had already told them all they wanted to know. But now the inevitable has arrived.

I smooth my hair and straighten my skirts before I leave, but it turns out that the king and queen are already in the sitting room. I don't know if it's because of my 'cold,' or they can't wait to see me.

The queen gives me a small smile, but the king sits with his arms folded. Clearly, they are here to talk to me about the problem of Katriona Bradshaw.

"Leave us." The king snaps his fingers. Mabel drops a curtsy and scuttles out of the room. If there is anyone more intimidating than Edward, it has to be the king. His Majesty is said to be liberal-minded and conscientious, but I could tell he still has an authoritarian side. Edward prefers to argue in a roundabout manner whenever he gets into a disagreement with his father.

"Kat, dear," the queen says, looking at me intently. "How are you feeling now?"

"The events that concern you recently have been enough to pen a sensational novel." King Leon fixes a hard gaze on me. His gaze can be just as intense as Edward's, but completely lacking in warmth. "First, we have a girl who looks exactly like you and claims to be the real daughter of Lady Bradshaw. And now Edward tells us that you have contracted an illness that cannot be cured, and you plan to leave the palace in three days."

I open my mouth, but no sound comes out. All I can do is nod.

"Why didn't you send for the palace physician?"

"Kat knows she cannot recover." Edward holds my hand tightly. "It is quite certain."

"Why didn't you tell us until now?"

Edward gives an explanation about the disease being of a dormant kind that didn't manifest its deadliness until recently. He also cites Dr. Jensen, and that it's possible my barrenness is related to this disease. His calm, rational attitude makes my incredible situation sound convincing, and while the king and queen still look skeptical, they no longer stare at me like I'm a witch.

"This is dire." The king looks grim. "We cannot afford a scandal. The whole country is abuzz with the news of you and your doppelgänger. And how are we to explain to the people when they learn that you're leaving the palace and my son will be left a widower?"

I don't know what to say. And honestly, even if I tell them about the goblins, what can the king and queen do? I have to leave Athelia.

"Kat, is it absolutely necessary that you must go?"

"Yes." I repress the urge to burst out crying. "I'm sorry."

"In that case," the king says slowly, "when you leave, Katriona Bradshaw should move into the palace. She will take your place."

The queen and I gasp. Katriona Bradshaw—as Edward's wife and princess of Athelia? I do want Edward to find happiness after I'm gone, but is it necessary to find someone who looks like me?

Edward stands up, his expression livid. "That's the most ridiculous thing I've ever heard of."

The king remains unperturbed. "Frankly speaking, it is too much trouble explaining to the press. If your illness is fatal, then the best thing to do is pretend that you're alive. Let Katriona Bradshaw pose as you, and you can pretend to be the girl Bianca Bradshaw brought. We can inform the public that after the court

421

trial, you realized the errors of the accusation and decided to disappear."

I had thought that King Leon was a good father-in-law, and to be fair he has treated me with respect and courtesy, but when it comes to a situation like this, he chooses reputation over family. Anxious to preserve the royal image, the king is willing to manipulate matters and disregard his son's feelings. He had warned me that I shouldn't quarrel with Edward in public. No wonder he could make this callous suggestion.

"I will not accept that woman." Edward's tone is hard and flinty. "Kat cannot be carelessly replaced as though she were a cut of beef."

"Sit down."

He remains on his feet.

"Edward, *sit down.*"

I tug on his sleeve, and Edward reluctantly seats himself next to me.

"Remember that your privilege as the crown prince comes with a price. It is our duty to uphold moral values and set a model for our nation."

Edward looks up, and I feel like my heart is shattering into a million pieces. He looks like a kid whose only toy is taken away. "I've done my best to adhere to your inculcations since I was a child. I promised that I would conduct myself with utmost propriety and never become a profligate like my grandfather. I never asked you for anything, except for the occasional leisure to tend to my garden, and the freedom to choose a wife I love. And now you deprive me of that freedom when Kat is gone."

"*Leon*," the queen says in a warning tone. "Enough of this. Can't you see that he's devastated by Kat's illness?"

The king still looks stern, but when he speaks, his tone has softened considerably. "I understand that you are attached to Kat and unwilling to take another. As a matter of fact, I am not displeased of your refusal. I would not have you lack heart and emotion, like an automaton. However, I would ask that you pull yourself together after Kat leaves. Currently our nation is in an uproar of Katriona Bradshaw's appearance. Reporters at our gates have been demanding for interviews. And Katriona's name on the register alone is enough reason to bind her to you."

Mr. Davenport had said the same thing. Legally, Katriona Bradshaw should be princess. Even if I could stay, Edward has to divorce her first before marrying me.

"And do not forget that Kat fainted in the trial. Some already perceive it as an admission of guilt. If she disappears now, people will be even more inclined to believe she stole the rightful identity of Katriona Bradshaw. Surely you don't want Kat's name in the mud when she's gone?"

Edward doesn't answer. I don't care about what propriety dictates; I take his arm and stare at the king and queen, silently begging them to leave. The queen takes the cue and tugs on the king's sleeve. He looks at me for a long moment, and then stands up.

"Are you absolutely certain that nothing can be done for you?"

This time I can't hold it in any longer. I nod, and a tear slides down my cheek.

When the door closes behind them, I bury my face into Edward's chest and hold him tight. He is uncommonly indifferent, which shows how much affected he is by the king's orders. Normally he'd caress my hair, stroke my back, or simply carry me to bed.

"Please don't feel guilty about what your father said," I whisper. "I understand how difficult your position is."

"I wish I weren't a prince," he says bitterly. "I wish that you were an Athelian, or I lived in your world. After everything we have been through, I can't bear losing you, much less forcing myself to pretend Katriona Bradshaw is you."

What I feel like doing at the moment is to break down and sob into his chest. But seeing him so broken-hearted, I resolve to be strong. I have to think of something to make us feel better.

"Look at it this way," I say softly. "I wasn't supposed to come back a second time. But I did, and we had eight months together. Well, maybe there were only a few months that we truly lived as a married couple, but if the goblins didn't send me back, we'd only have my seventeen-year-old memories."

I take his face in my hands. He stares into my eyes, drinking me in, like I am the only person who can make him feel alive.

"This second time, we've grown even closer." I smile, though another tear trickles down my cheek. "Compared to the first time I was transported to Athelia, we have had more chances being together. We got to live together as husband and wife."

He nods, but the pain remains in his eyes.

"Take me to bed." I take his hand and kiss his fingertips. "No matter whether I die or go back to my own world, I want to remember you. I am definitely not going to get my memories erased this time."

46

Amelie and Mabel are surprised when they find me sitting at my desk, engaged in letter-writing.

"But it's the weekend!" Mabel says, as if I should do nothing but laze around. "You don't have to work through the letters until tomorrow."

I move my arm to block the paper on the desk, because I don't want them to see what I'm actually writing. "It's all right. Since I don't have anything to do, I might as well get some work done. That way, I'll have less to work on tomorrow."

When they are gone, I let out a sigh of relief. Only Edward knows what I am actually doing. I am writing letters to my friends, to be read after I leave Athelia. Actually, I had written similar letters last year before the wedding, but they were never posted since

I returned to Athelia. This time, I will be gone for good. Unless some miracle happens . . .

I try very hard not to break down and cry as I write to Poppy how much I value her friendship and how I wish that I could see my godchildren grow up. "Give them my love, and let them know that on the other side of the universe, there is someone always thinking about them."

For Elle, I send her the best wishes for her marriage with Henry. Finally, they have reached the happy ending that is long overdue. Still, I'm sad that I won't get to see her in a veil and wedding dress. She was absolutely stunning in that fairy-made gown in the ball.

I thank Henry for his help with my social reforms and also for bringing Edward and me together. I hope that he and Elle will be very happy. I wish him a safe trip, and also warn him that he had better not cheat on Elle with some Moryn girl, or I will get the duchess to summon him back to Somerset.

When I seal up the last letter, which is for Mr. Wellesley, I find a ribbon, bundle the letters together and lock them in a drawer. I will leave the key for Edward so that he can give those letters to my friends after I'm gone.

A fit of coughing seizes me and I try my best to keep it under control. The last thing I want is the maids insisting on bringing a doctor for me, and risk exposing the mark on my shoulder. Then I would really be guilty of witchcraft.

After managing to stop the coughing with a mug of warm water, I rise and approach the windows, taking in the winter wonderland outside. Icicles glisten on the trees, the ground looks like a giant piece of marshmallow, and the wind stirs a flurry of flakes in the air, glittering under the sunlight. If only my body wasn't getting weaker, I would have ventured into the gardens. While Edward still holds hope that Krev was kidding, deep down inside I can feel my life ebbing out of my body bit by bit.

At least I've been forewarned. It would be a real tragedy if Krev didn't show up and I ran out of oxygen in the middle of the court trial.

"Princess?" Mabel knocks on the door. "Your visitor has arrived."

"Very well. I will be out in a moment."

I tuck the key of the drawer in my pocket before going into the sitting room. There, sitting on the sofa, is Katriona Bradshaw, while Bianca stands beside her, arms crossed and eyes flashing.

I frown. I had only asked for Katriona Bradshaw "Thank you for accepting my invitation," I say, addressing Katriona. "If you don't mind, can I have a private conversation with you? I have another room inside."

"What are you planning to say to her?" Bianca says, eying me as if I have a knife under my sleeve. "I can't allow her to speak to you if I don't know what you are planning to do."

"You may stay here while we talk in the other room. I promise you that I have no intention of doing anything." I hand her an envelope. "In fact, if you read this, you will know that I mean no harm."

Bianca snatches the envelope from my hands and reads the paper it contains. Her eyes get bigger and bigger, and she looks up at me, incredulous. "You are withdrawing from the case? You are willing to admit that you are not my sister?"

"Yes."

Bianca looks as if she has swallowed a whole apple. "If you were going to admit the truth, then why didn't you do it in the beginning? Why waste the time going to court? What are you playing at?"

Because of the goblins. My head goes dizzy for a second, and I try not to let it show. I must keep a clear mind when talking to Katriona Bradshaw.

"If you don't believe me, go ask my husband." I savor the words 'my husband' as I say them. No matter how Bianca strives, she will never be able to refer to Edward as her spouse. "He is already conveying my decision to the king and queen. Now, if you will excuse us." I gesture to my study. "Miss Katriona, if you please."

Katriona darts an anxious look at Bianca, who shrugs and tells her she'll be waiting in the sitting room. Slowly, Katriona rises and follows me into the study. In a way, I could see why Bianca didn't suspect me when I was first transported to Athelia. Katriona looks like someone who is used to being bullied and ignored. However, unlike Elle, who remains sweet and kind-hearted, something in Katriona's aura lacks benevolence.

429

I close the door and ask her to take a seat. She does, her gaze shifting cautiously around the room, and I sit across from her. I am thinking of how to begin this conversation when Katriona opens her mouth.

"Why?"

"Can you be a bit more specific?" I say. "I'm sure there are many things that you are wondering about."

She raises her head and stares at me. "Why did you withdraw? You were succeeding in making the court believe you were the victim."

I shrug. "Aren't you happy I did it?"

"I wouldn't know what goes on in a witch's mind."

I laugh. "I can see that Bianca has planted some strange ideas in your head. Believe me or not, I'm a victim just like you. I can't tell you how you ended up in Moryn, and I can't tell you why we happen to look alike. But I *can* tell you that I became princess because Edward fell in love with my character. I didn't resort to spells or charms—which I'm sure Bianca is convinced that I dabble in—because I'm not a witch. I can't do any magic."

Katriona continues to stare at me, as if trying to discern any witchlike characteristics in me. For a country that doesn't believe in magic, the citizens are surprisingly superstitious.

"Why did you choose me?" she finally says. "I've never seen you before. Is it because we look so alike that you chose to kidnap me and have me brought to Moryn?"

430

"I would like to know the answers as well. But for now, in exchange for my volunteering to step down and admit that you are Katriona Bradshaw, I would ask you for something."

"What can I do? You're better off asking Bianca."

"Great, but number one, she hates me. Number two, only you can help me with this." I lean forward and will myself not to choke or cough. My supply of oxygen is vanishing quickly. "When it is made known that you are indeed Katriona Bradshaw, I will not be able to stay in the palace. I know you must have suffered through some hard times in Moryn, but those hard days are over. You will be princess, and even if Edward decides to file for divorce, you will still have a handsome allowance."

I tell her about compulsory education, and also about Princess College. "Please don't undo the work I have accomplished so far. And please don't hate Edward if he doesn't treat you well."

A curious gleam shines in her eyes, and she leans forward. "Are you telling me that I can take your place and be princess of this country?"

I feel bad for Edward. The more I talk to her, the more I dislike Katriona. If only she were more like Elle, he might have resigned himself to the marriage. Katriona may not be stunning or intimidating, as Bianca is, but there are characteristics that the Bradshaw sisters share in common—such as an obsession with becoming royal.

"Yes. After all, it's your name in the wedding register. You are wedded to him. In two days, I will leave the palace. If Edward asks for a divorce, please try to understand."

"Because he wants you back?"

I shake my head. "I don't think that will happen. But Katriona, please consider what I say. If you can help Edward improve the lives of the citizens of Athelia, that will be wonderful. But even if you can't, please continue to support the school. I am not the wicked, scheming, evil person that Bianca tries to paint me to be. Trust me, I didn't mean to impersonate you. All I ask is that you be receptive to whatever Edward asks of you. Including a divorce."

She tilts her head. "All right." But it's not hard to read the craftiness in her eyes. I'd bet my entire wardrobe that she won't agree to a divorce. She's going to take advantage of this sudden turn of fortune.

In my mind, I apologize to Edward. I can only hope that Mr. Davenport, or some other lawyer well-versed in marriage laws, will be able to obtain a divorce for him as soon as possible. I don't want to give Edward up, but since it has to happen, I want him to eventually find love, no matter how long it takes for him to get over me. I want him to meet a nice girl who genuinely cares for him, regardless of his royal status, a girl who can soften his gaze and make his eyes twinkle with amusement. I very much doubt Katriona fits these criteria.

47

On the last day, we have no doubt that what Krev says is true. The mark on my shoulder has faded into an almost indistinguishable shade of pink. If I didn't know it was there, I wouldn't have noticed unless I looked really hard in the mirror. And my health has deteriorated dramatically. I'm having trouble breathing, and I cough every five minutes as I move around. So, I try to avoid walking as much as possible. Fortunately, I had already asked Elle and Poppy and Henry around to visit me, under the pretense that I'm worried about the trial. They comfort me and tell me that no matter what happens, Edward will stand by me. I don't dare to tell them the truth of my health, of course. It's too much of a hassle to explain everything.

"Here's a mug of hot water and lemon and honey for your throat, Your Highness," Mabel says, setting a tray on the table.

Amelie enters my bedroom, carrying a pile of glossy pink and green satin. "I unearthed an extra handmade quilt from the storage closet. It's the warmest one we have."

"Thank you. Oh, by the way, Amelie? I know you don't want to get married, but you're still so young, and there are good men out there. Trust me."

Amelie blinks her pretty brown eyes. Seldom have I lectured her on men. "Yes, Your Highness."

"It's the other way for you, Mabel. Spend some time getting to know that handsome palace guard you've been ogling, and if his character is as wonderful as his looks, then you can consider a serious relationship with him."

I smile at them, then turn away abruptly so they can't see the tears threatening to slide down my face. I've grown very fond of my maids, and I'm sorry that I can't live to see what will become of them.

***

By the afternoon, I just sit in the study and gaze out of the windows. I am swathed in blankets, leaning against the back of the window seat. Edward doesn't leave my side. He does most of the talking, since I tend to cough as I attempt conversation.

My last day in Athelia. I feel like crying, but strangely, there are no tears. It's as if all the tears I

434

have were used up on the day that Krev told me I was going to die. I clutch Edward's hand and wish that I could imprint this image of him in my mind permanently.

"I don't want to go home," I say suddenly. "I want to stay with you. I want to stay!" My voice turns into a cough, and Edward gets me some water.

"When I said I would do anything to keep you in Athelia, I thought that once I had your heart, everything would be all right. But now, I see how powerless I am. I can only stand here and cannot do anything to save you." He looks away before I can make sure there's a tear glistening in his eye.

"Just hold me, Edward."

He draws his arms around me, and I lay my head against his chest. Because I have a problem breathing, he doesn't dare to embrace me tightly. Nor does he kiss me on the lips, for fear that I might be short of breath. Only butterfly kisses on my face and neck, but never my lips. I feel so bad—I'm reminded of the last day we said goodbye to each other before the wedding day. This time, it feels even more tragic, not just because of my emaciated body, but also because we have grown closer to each other in body and spirit.

"Say you love me." Edward's voice sounds broken. "Say that you will never forget me."

I lift my head and kiss his jaw. "I love you, Edward. Even if I go back to my own world, I will never, ever, forget you." I pull back so I can look at him in the eye. "You have spoiled me for life. I expect that I will remain single always, because no one in my world will ever measure up to you."

"I could foresee the same for myself." He adjusts his position so I can snuggle more comfortably in his arms. "After you . . . go, I am going to tell my parents that I will abdicate. Henry can have the throne. I will not be pressurized into taking a wife and begetting an heir."

My hand goes to my stomach, which is flat and smooth. Edward and I slept together for some time, but I never showed any sign of pregnancy. Maybe I can never get pregnant unless I am an Athelian. "You can't do that. You are your parents' only son."

"They will understand," he says quietly. "And I will not bring some hapless maid into a loveless marriage."

"You shouldn't think like that," I mumble. "But I'm glad you do."

***

When night falls, a snowstorm sets in like an ill omen. I am coughing so frequently that I don't even bother to speak. Edward has to bring me paper and a pen for communication. By this time, though, neither of us feels inclined to speak anyway. Most of the time, I just lean against him, my head tucked snugly under his chin, his arms around my body. Now and then, he gets up to pour me some water, but for most of the time, we remain in a comfortable embrace.

'Do you know what was the first thing I thought when I met you at Elle's house?' Edward writes.

'An idiot who couldn't keep her mouth shut?'

'A bold and brave girl, as charming as she is compassionate.'

I grin and take the pen from him. 'Do you know what's the first thing *I* thought when I met you?'

'An arrogant man who could do nothing when encountering sickness and poverty?'

'A man with devastating good looks who could never be interested in me.'

His response is to kiss the corner of my jaw. "How could I not?" he murmurs in my ear. "Even though, in the beginning, you made it clear you weren't interested in me, I couldn't help wanting to see you, talk to you, and make you be aware of my existence."

We end up playing a game of tic-tac-toe, surprisingly. But at this moment, there really is nothing more that can be said or done. In my heart, I pray for some miracle that one day we can still be reunited.

The familiar popping sound. Krev appears in midair, above the fireplace. Edward jerks his head back, his eyes wide.

"Can you see him?"

Krev puts his hands on his hips. "I have chosen to show myself to make things easier."

Edward gently sets me aside and goes over to face Krev. "Is there absolutely no way that she can survive in Athelia?"

Krev holds out his hands, palms up. "How will a fish and a bird live together?"

I cough at the same time, a cough so violent that bloodstains appear on my sleeve. Edward rushes to my side, his face ashen. "You must go," he says tonelessly, but his face looks as if life has drained out of it. "You must get well. Get well, and don't ever forget me."

The book. Somehow, it has appeared and hovers in the air. There's something strange about it—the title on the cover is different. I make out the words, *Twice Upon a Time*. Krev starts to chant some indecipherable words, and the book begins to spin. I should go to the goblin, but my feet refuse to budge. I don't want to leave Edward. I turn and throw myself in his arms. I kiss him, and tears run down my face.

"Rather . . . die," I croak. "Don't . . . wanna . . . leave . . ."

"Kat." Edward clamps his hands on my shoulders. "You cannot die. I would rather see you alive in another world than unable to survive in Athelia. Go."

And he carries me, bridal style, toward Krev. I try to struggle—I try to move away from the book, but Edward keeps a firm grip on my body.

"That's right, girlie," Krev is saying. "Just a little bit farther . . . come along, you only have a few minutes left!"

"I love you," Edward whispers in my ear. "I will always love you, Kat."

I open my mouth, but no sound comes out. Nevertheless, I make my mouth form the words, "I love you too."

The next second, the yellow-green glow from the book engulfs me. Edward's face flashes before me for a moment. I want to reach out to him, but everything turns black.

Farewell, my love.

48

The goblin king surveyed his court with a heavy heart. Littered with broken rocks and debris, some of them smeared with blood, the once-magnificent royal dwelling was now a pathetic sight. Here the final battle with Borg took place—a long, drawn-out fight that claimed dozens of lives. He could still hear the sounds of magic sizzling as the two sides clashed and fought, the shrieks and screams of goblins when hit by powerful spells, and the ear-splitting explosions when entire pillars were split into half.

Finally it was all over…no, it wasn't. Borg may be defeated, but there was a long list of things they had to do.

Barthelius raised his hand. The emerald green ring on his finger glittered and flashed. When Borg had received the ring from Pippi, he had stirred up a rebellion by using the magic contained within the ring—magic that was accumulated from several generations. Empowered by the ancient magic, Borg was able to challenge Barthelius and threaten him to step down. It took months of fighting, hundreds of casualties on both sides, until Barthelius finally prevailed.

But the damage was already done. Never in his life had Barthelius felt so helpless, so deprived of magic. If he were at the height of his powers—like when he created Athelia a hundred years ago—he could have sent Katherine Wilson back to her family. She wouldn't have stayed long enough to break through the memory spell Morag put on her, and fallen hopelessly in love with Prince Edward—again. According to Krev, Kat had been close to a mental breakdown when she learned that her body wasn't equipped to survive in Athelia.

But he was well past middle age for a goblin, and his powers had dwindled to a fraction of his peak. Like something they call an Olympic athlete in the human world—in his prime he could win a gold medal, but there was no way he could sprint or turn somersaults at his age now.

There was a popping sound; a female goblin appeared by his side, her wings flapping. Bruises and cuts marred her slender arms, and a white bandage was wrapped around her ankle.

"Just saw the remaining members of Borg's gang expelled from the realm," she said. "I've also ordered Grex and Zanok to strengthen the border lines and ensure none of the rebels have the power to enter our realm again."

"Very good." Barthelius didn't turn around or look at her. His expression remained pensive as he stared at a pillar lying on the ground. "When Borg and I were mere weaklings, he used to jump out behind this pillar and laugh at me if I squealed in surprise. He used to call me the midget of the family, and he was always there to cheer me up when Father got mad at me. We were *pals*." He gestured at the cracked stone floor. "Since Father chose me as the successor, our relationship has been fractured like this, until the point of no return." He sank down on the floor, cross-legged and head bowed.

Morag put a hand on his shoulder. "Borg brought this onto himself. If he didn't use live creatures as sacrifices in order to gain greater powers, your father might have chosen him to inherit the ring. Didn't you tell me that Borg was actually stronger than you when your father made the decision that you be the future king?"

"Theoretically he was more powerful, but Father said my powers were still latent, and when fully developed, no goblin could compete with me. Even when I did become the most powerful goblin in the realm, Borg still harbored a grudge. It was a terrible blow to his pride that he was passed over as the eldest son."

Morag nodded and sat down beside him. Blood sacrifices may be a shortcut, but it was not how a king—or simply a normal goblin—would perform magic. Borg could never be allowed to lead, considering his blatant disregard for goblin rights.

Barthelius patted his wife's hand, careful to avoid a rather nasty bruise. "Were it not for you, dear, we could have been defeated. I've long passed the peak of my powers, and without the ring, I'm no match for my brother. If you didn't attack him with that lightning spell, he might have made us prisoners—or worse."

"If he didn't try to harm Pippi I couldn't have channeled my inner magic." Morag shivered and leaned against her husband's shoulder. She still had chills when she thought of the possibility of Pippi being injured. "So what do you plan to do now?"

"Rebuild our kingdom, of course."

"You know what I'm referring to."

Barthelius sighed. "You're talking about the human girl."

When they found out that Borg had forced Kat out of her own world and pushed her into Athelia, Barthelius was thunderstruck. Getting a human into Athelia was vastly different from letting a human soul enter an Athelian's body. If there was any tiny flaw in the spell that provided a finite amount of oxygen, she could have been dead within minutes. But since they were at war, the best he could do was to preserve just enough magic to send Krev to Athelia, and make sure Kat lived long enough until they could send her back. Pippi would be devastated, of course, but what could they do? It was like making a human survive on Mars, the only outer space planet he could remember. A lifetime beyond Earth was impossible.

Pop. A squashed-faced goblin with pointed ears and bulbous eyes appeared in the air.

"Well?" Barthelius said. "Have you taken Katherine Wilson back to her own world?"

"How's her condition?" Morag asked.

"She's weak, but she's home." Krev flew to the ground and sat down. He exhaled and relaxed his limbs. "Her family will take good care of her."

"The poor girl," Morag said, remembering the one time she visited Athelia to administer a memory spell on Kat. She would have done it this time, if only she wasn't completely exhausted after the war. "She has suffered so much. Falling in love with the prince for a second time, and now going back to her own world...she's going to be depressed."

"At least she is alive," Barthelius said. He crossed his arms, and a determined look came over his face. "Something has to be done. We must not allow this disaster to happen again."

***

The goblin king and queen went to find their baby daughter, who was staying in an earthen-mound dwelling hidden under a thick cluster of trees and bushes. Normally they didn't use this dwelling except in a case of emergency. Muscular goblin guards stood at the entrance, carrying heavy clubs and maces.

"Afternoon, Your Majesty." The leader bowed. "The princess is inside, taking her nap. She might wake any time soon."

Barthelius nodded. "You may reduce the number of guards, now that the queen and I are here."

Pippi was lying on a soft bed formed of moss, her curly hair a bright contrast to the dark green moss. Not long after Barthelius and Morag entered, she stirred and opened her eyes. "Daddy? You're back?"

Barthelius flew over to her. "Do you now realize the enormity of what you did?"

Pippi started to cry. "I… I'm so sorry, Daddy."

"Husband," Morag chided. "If it's anyone's fault, it should be Borg's. How was Pippi to know?"

"She may be excused because of her age, but she has to be taught a lesson. Look at the consequences. Dozens have died, many more injured, and Katherine Wilson nearly lost her life. If I didn't manage to send Krev back and give her that mark, she could have run out of oxygen and had brain death in minutes."

Pippi jumped up. "Where's Kat now?"

"I had Krev send her back to her own world. She isn't from Athelia; she cannot survive living without oxygen."

Pippi burst into tears again.

Barthelius remembered there was this human story in which a serpent convinced a woman to eat forbidden fruit. In a way, Borg reminded him of that serpent. "I know this isn't entirely your fault," he said gently, "but nevertheless, Borg would never have been able to create so much trouble if you didn't help him in the first place. You have to do penance and make up for your mistakes."

"No!" Morag rushed over and hugged her child. "Don't you lay a finger on her. She knows that she committed a grave error."

"She *stole* the ring. How many times have we told her that stealing is deplorable?" Barthelius narrowed his eyes. "Pippi, you could have asked me or your mother first. You didn't have to listen to Borg and steal that ring for him. You must be taught a lesson."

Pippi wiped her eyes. She was still sniffling, but she had calmed down. "What must I do?"

"We still have a few books lying around in the human world. Morag, you shall take Pippi, find all the remaining books, and destroy them. We cannot allow any human to have the chance to rip any book and be transported to Athelia again."

"But not all cases are like Kat's," Morag protested. "Don't you remember the last time it worked for that other human?"

"The risks aren't worth it. It was my fault also for creating the books in the first place and placing the curse on the books. Now I have to pay for what I did. I will create a detector, and Morag, you must teach Pippi how to become invisible." Barthelius squatted and placed his hands on his daughter's shoulders. "Sweetie, if you don't want something like Kat's story happening again, then you must help me make all those books disappear."

Pippi gazed at him, her eyes wide. "But Daddy... will Kat never be able to see Edward again?"

Morag patted her daughter's head. "Darling, we've been through this so many times already."

Barthelius stood up. He gazed at the mustard-yellow sky—the color of the sky in the goblin realm was quite different to the human world's. "Destroying the books won't be enough. After the books are gone, all the portals to the human world must be removed and the tunnels blown up. No human shall ever be able to travel to Athelia again."

AFTERWORD

Thank you! I hope you enjoyed *Twice Upon A Time*. Kat and Edward's story will be continued in *Ever After*, which will be released in 2017.

To be the first to know exactly when Ever After will be published, sign up here: http://www.ayaling.com/newsletter.html

What you'll get for joining the club:

1. Receive an exclusive short story told from Edward's point of view, plus extra/deleted scenes. I may add new material from time to time once I get the ideas.

2. Be the first to know when I have a new release.

3. Be the first to know when I give away free stuff, call for advanced readers, run a poll, or other fun activities.

For more information about future releases and current books, connect with me at my website:

http://www.ayaling.com

~Aya~

BOOKS BY AYA

THE UNFINISHED FAIRY TALES
The Ugly Stepsister (Book 1)
Princess of Athelia (companion novella)
Twice Upon a Time (Book 2)
Ever After (Book 3, coming in 2017)

THE PRINCESS SERIES
Princesses Don't Get Fat
Princesses Don't Fight in Skirts
Princesses Don't Become Engineers

GIRL WITH FLYING WEAPONS
Girl with Flying Weapons

ABOUT THE AUTHOR

Aya is from Taiwan, where she struggles daily to contain her obsession with mouthwatering and unhealthy foods. Often she will devour a good book instead. Her favourite books include martial arts romances, fairy tale retellings, high fantasy, cozy mysteries, and manga.

~www.ayaling.com ~

CPSIA information can be obtained
at www.ICGtesting.com
Printed in the USA
LVHW041831050619
620218LV00002B/118/P